Battle Cruiser

by
B. V. Larson

Books by B. V. Larson:

UNDYING MERCENARIES
Steel World
Dust World
Tech World
Machine World
Death World

STAR FORCE SERIES
Swarm
Extinction
Rebellion
Conquest
Battle Station
Empire
Annihilation
Storm Assault
The Dead Sun
Outcast
Exile
Gauntlet

OTHER SF BOOKS
Starfire
Element-X

Visit BVLarson.com for more information.

Copyright © 2015 by the author.

This book is a work of fiction. Names, characters, places and incidents are either products of the author's imagination or used fictitiously. Any resemblance to actual events, locales or persons, living or dead, is entirely coincidental. All rights reserved. No part of this publication can be reproduced or transmitted in any form or by any means, without permission in writing from the author.

ISBN-13: 978-1515076223
ISBN-10: 1515076229
BISAC: Fiction / Science Fiction / Military

Earth. Fortunately, their long experience had turned them into wizards when it came to repairing the ship's systems. All of *Cutlass'* components had been patched a thousand times.

Earth's navy as a whole had been the victim of endless slashed budgets and deferred maintenance plans. *Cutlass* was just one more boat at the end of a very long line of hungry vessels.

Despite her problems, I'd fallen instantly in love with the ship when she'd become my first command six years ago.

"Well?" I asked Rumbold about a minute later. "What's the word from *Altair*?"

"They haven't managed to identify the contact—but they say it's probably a piece of junk from the rocks, sir. Maybe even a chunk of ice from out-system."

I eyed Rumbold for a moment. He was a stout man with burly arms, a hard circular face and eyes that always looked like he needed more sleep. His nose had the shape of a potato and there was more fat on his belly than regulations allowed, but I liked him nonetheless.

He'd been a guardsman for a century, maybe longer. I'd never asked his exact age. It was considered rude to question a man concerning how long he'd extended his lifespan with cheap treatments. He still managed to perform his duties—that was good enough for the Guard and good enough for me.

My gaze returned to my cracked screen. We had several foggy triangles of ballistic glass that passed for windows, but looking for a spacecraft visually with bare eyes was pointless unless you were trying to dock with it.

"They've got no positive ID, but *Altair's* sensor operators presume it's a piece of junk?" I asked. "I don't understand their reasoning."

The Chief shrugged in a noncommittal response. That wasn't the norm for him. He was technically the second in command of my tiny crew and he was never slow to offer an opinion. He was usually excitable by nature.

Looking back at my scopes, I thought I could see a flare of radiation from the distant target.

"What's that, then?" I demanded.

Rumbold shrugged again. "Could be a pocket of gas. The contact registers as quite cold. Must have come from out-system. Maybe the venting is a melting effect."

"I don't think it's natural," I said.

Rumbold looked at me for a moment, narrowing his eyes. "*Altair's* sensors are much better than ours, sir. They've reported there's nothing to be alarmed about."

I nodded thoughtfully. "Have you plotted that intercept course?" I asked.

"I have, sir."

"Send it to my screen."

He did so with a flick of his thumb. I tapped on it and brought up the details.

"We've only got a small window," I said. "I'm going to pursue this one, Rumbold. It's been a slow patrol."

"They almost always are, sir," he replied, giving me a wheezing laugh.

I touched the course file he'd sent me and slid the icon to the engines. The ship did the rest automatically.

Straps snaked out of our seats to grip our bodies. The pinnace slewed around, and the amount of thrust applied was surprising.

The Solar System was difficult to patrol. There was too much void between the relatively small spots of mass called planets that we all held so dear. There was so much nothingness, in fact, that the task of policing any star system was damned near impossible.

Undaunted, the aging ships of Earth's Star Guard were still vigilant, and as one of the younger officers in the service, I was determined to do what could be done.

"A query is incoming from *Altair*, sir," Rumbold said a few short minutes later.

"I see that, Rumbold," I said, ignoring the request as it blinked on my screen.

The other crewmen aboard weren't on the bridge proper, but as the ship was built with only two long decks, they weren't far away. They couldn't help but overhear us. They exchanged concerned glances, but none of them commented.

His words made me recheck my target's trajectory. I saw he was right; the new course had it heading directly for Earth. A small angular variation in spaceflight often became magnified when the effects of gravity played in. Singh disconnected at last, leaving me in peace.

"The target is on a curve now, Rumbold," I said.

"I see that, Skipper. What now?"

"Speed up. Full thrust."

Rumbold hesitated. His tongue darted out, then vanished again. "Full thrust, sir? This ship—sir, *Cutlass'* rated specs are more than she can handle in reality."

"I'm well aware. Full thrust, Rumbold."

He tapped in the change, and our running lights turned amber and began to spin. The crew who'd left their seats when we'd reached cruising velocity now scrambled back to their chairs and urged the straps to cinch up tightly. Moments later, we were pressed back into our seats. The Gs mounted quickly and speech became difficult.

"Captain," Rumbold grunted out, "I recommend we ease off now."

"Surely we can survive a few extra gravities of thrust, Chief."

"It's not that," he said, straining to reach out and flick a report from his screen to mine. "Take a look at this."

I stared at the report from the AI and cursed. "Overheating? We've only been at full burn for ninety seconds."

"We're overdue for a rebuild, sir. The seals—they won't take this for long. They'll burn clean through."

I knew what that meant, at least in theory. Our engines were essentially contained fusion reactions: explosions that were bottled up within a field generated by the explosion itself. If any part of that delicate balance was thrown out of synch, the entire vessel would transform from matter into energy within a fraction of a second. During that singular moment, *Cutlass* would outdo the brilliance of old Sol herself.

"Dial back, ease down."

His fingers were on the controls before I completed the order. The roaring sound droned downward in pitch, and my crew began to breathe evenly again.

"What's our range to the target?" I demanded.

"Less than ten thousand kilometers—we can't catch him before he hits the atmosphere—and sir, he's braking hard now. It's a ship, by damn, just as you suspected."

"He's going to get away," I said between clenched teeth.

An acrid smell filled my lungs, and I quickly closed my visor, trying not to cough. Damn it, there were more systems failing on *Cutlass* than her engines.

Working numbers and curving projections on my screen, I came up with an option.

"Hail the target," I ordered. "Order them to heave-to."

"Did that, sir…no response."

"Repeat the signal in a loop. Leave the channel open for any response."

"Done…nothing."

A growling sound stirred in my throat. They were running from us.

No one fled from a Guard ship without good cause. They had to know we'd spotted them, and we'd be watching them closely. How could they expect to get away with whatever they were up to?

I could only surmise they were smugglers, probably from the farthest rocks of the belt, where men were often lawless. Perhaps they had ground transportation waiting for them down on Earth—I just didn't know, but I didn't want this ship to slip away from me now.

"Open the forward gun port," I ordered.

Rumbold's bloodshot gaze swept to meet mine. "Sir—that's not what we were ordered to do."

"The target is taking active evasive action. The situation has therefore changed. According to regs, in this scenario I'm within my rights to force the target to submit to search and seizure."

"But sir, in this universe there are regulations, and then there's pissing on your commander's shoes…if you know what I mean."

"Open the gun port or I'll do it myself."

Rumbold did as he was ordered.

I glanced at him sharply, but I ignored the insult. Rude people who were angry with guardsmen often called us "peacocks" as we were considered ineffectual show-offs.

Without a word, I tapped out a citation and touched his computer with mine. The ticket was instantly transferred and logged.

"What's that for?" Edvar demanded.

"Read it. Resisting search, refusal to obey an officer pursuant, etc. I had to fire across your bow to get you to stop running. That's a crime."

"You dick!" he raged at me. "My customers are big! They won't like this."

I dared hope he would throw a punch—but sadly, he knew better. Instead, he filled the air with invective as Rumbold and I retreated from his ship. When we were safely through the airlock and gone, he fired up his engines and dove down toward Earth. I could see his anger in every course correction.

"You haven't lost your touch, sir," Rumbold remarked.

"He was hiding something. No one runs from the Guard for the hell of it."

"Yeah, probably…but then again, maybe he's just a man with a vile personality. There are many who become spacers because no one can stand to have them around."

Returning to my station, I found the com light blinking again.

"Message incoming from *Altair*, sir," Rumbold said. "Looks like the boss pulled up behind us while we were inspecting that ship. He's not in the best mood, I'd imagine."

Sighing, I answered the call. Captain Singh's lips were pulled back to show his teeth. The effect was unpleasant.

"Mission accomplished, sir," I said.

"What mission? You weren't given orders—"

"My orders are clear, sir. See the rules of engagement signed March 22nd—signed by you, Captain. They stipulate what to do in the case of a fugitive with possibly dangerous cargo heading for—"

"What fugitive? He had nothing! I've seen your automatic logs. That was abuse, Guardsman. Pure and simple."

"What's our range to the target?" I demanded.

"Less than ten thousand kilometers—we can't catch him before he hits the atmosphere—and sir, he's braking hard now. It's a ship, by damn, just as you suspected."

"He's going to get away," I said between clenched teeth.

An acrid smell filled my lungs, and I quickly closed my visor, trying not to cough. Damn it, there were more systems failing on *Cutlass* than her engines.

Working numbers and curving projections on my screen, I came up with an option.

"Hail the target," I ordered. "Order them to heave-to."

"Did that, sir...no response."

"Repeat the signal in a loop. Leave the channel open for any response."

"Done...nothing."

A growling sound stirred in my throat. They were running from us.

No one fled from a Guard ship without good cause. They had to know we'd spotted them, and we'd be watching them closely. How could they expect to get away with whatever they were up to?

I could only surmise they were smugglers, probably from the farthest rocks of the belt, where men were often lawless. Perhaps they had ground transportation waiting for them down on Earth—I just didn't know, but I didn't want this ship to slip away from me now.

"Open the forward gun port," I ordered.

Rumbold's bloodshot gaze swept to meet mine. "Sir—that's not what we were ordered to do."

"The target is taking active evasive action. The situation has therefore changed. According to regs, in this scenario I'm within my rights to force the target to submit to search and seizure."

"But sir, in this universe there are regulations, and then there's pissing on your commander's shoes...if you know what I mean."

"Open the gun port or I'll do it myself."

Rumbold did as he was ordered.

I suspected it must be hard on a man of his years to take orders from someone who might be as much as a century younger. But he did it, just the same. I valued his service more in that moment than I ever had, and if this ended well I vowed to reward him if I could.

"Firing solution completed," he said. "We're locked on target."

"Retarget the cannon. Fire two kilometers off his bow."

Rumbold did as I asked with a sigh of relief. I was surprised he'd thought I was mad enough to direct lethal fire at a ship without authorization. I wondered, too, if he'd have done it if I'd given the order—it was my belief that he would have.

"Ready," he said.

"Fire on my mark…mark!"

Rumbold fired the forward cannon, and it sent a spray of invisible radiation toward the target.

Cutlass' primary armament was a single, particle-beam weapon. A pulse of neutrons were released, an optional function of the same continuous reaction in the ship's core that drove the engines. The pencil-thin beam wasn't quite as accurate as a laser might have been, but it was more deadly at this range.

We waited several seconds while our threat was perceived. I was gratified when the channel opened at last and an irate man with an odd accent appeared on my cracked screen. He sounded as though he might have been European.

"Are you crazy?" he demanded. "Fuck you, you goat!"

The man's face was red and veins stood out on his neck.

"This is Captain William Sparhawk of the Guard," I said calmly. "You're hereby ordered to heave-to or suffer the consequences."

"William Sparhawk," the man said slowly, as if memorizing my name. "This will be the end of you."

I made a show of lifting my arm above the camera pickup on my board. I allowed my hand to hover out of view. "Obey me, or I will be the end of you right now."

The screen went dark. The operating system automatically returned to projecting our course visually.

Still expecting some kind of response, I said nothing until Rumbold spun the ship around and began braking hard to slow us down.

"What are you doing?" I demanded.

"The smuggler is slowing down, sir. We have to brake now, or we'll plunge right into Earth ourselves."

I blinked at the controls. Rumbold was right.

I dared to grin. The smuggler had believed my bluff. He was slowing down, and he was going to allow us to board.

While the two ships matched speeds, I had time to wonder about my threat. Had it been a bluff? Would I have fired upon the smuggler's ship?

It was the first time I'd been in such a situation, and I felt untested. I'd searched dozens of small vessels, some innocent and others packed with contraband, but I'd never shot one down before.

Technically, I'd be within my rights to do it—but that's not always how these things worked out. There would have been an investigation afterward, and if some prosecutor could argue successfully that the smuggler had been performing an innocent emergency landing due to a systems failure, I'd have been in trouble. I might not have been court-martialed, but my career would have been at an end.

So, I asked myself as we slid through space and prepared to search the floating vessel in low orbit—would I have done it?

Yes, I admitted to myself, I might have fired in an attempt to disable her engines. That could have resulted in the destruction of the spacecraft.

Why fire? Because I was a Sparhawk. My House had been famous for producing stern leaders with harsh tempers for centuries.

-2-

Most people think of space as being infinite, and I suppose that in the abstract, it is. But when one is hunched inside a cramped ship with engines that strain and shudder whenever thrust is applied, space seems finite indeed.

Searching the smuggler's ship was one of the tightest squeezes I'd ever endured. There were pockets where a man could stand if he hunched, but they were few and far between. Every centimeter of space was crammed with goods.

Despite the crowding, the smuggler's ship appeared to be well-maintained. Every system was operating with perfect efficiency. It did nothing for my mood to see the relative wealth of the other side.

The worst part was I couldn't find anything on the contraband list aboard her. I wanted to cite the pilot for smuggling—but I couldn't.

He stood with his arms crossed as Rumbold and I inspected his vessel, worming our way over packages from the forward cockpit to the frozen confines of the aft hold. It was in the depths of the hold where I finally found something interesting.

"What are these?" I asked, holding up a silver tube with a screw-cap and a temperature readout on the side.

"That's an embryonic storage unit," he said. "That's someone's child, unaltered."

I stared at the tube in surprise.

"Why would you be carrying something medical?" I asked.

He snorted. The pilot's name was Edvar-something, and he hadn't been the most gracious smuggler I'd ever met.

"That's how they do it out in the rocks," he said. "You can't conceive normally. There aren't a lot of eligible mates running around for most spacers. Some get the urge, and they buy a premade like these."

I opened a large carton. There were dozens of them—silver tubes with rounded ends and readouts on the side.

"Frozen..." I said thoughtfully. "I'll have to open one to check your story."

The man looked at me balefully. "That will ruin my stock. These aren't cheap and many of them are special orders."

"All the same, I can't simply take your word for it."

"Can't you just check my manifest?" he demanded. "They're all listed and cataloged."

I shook my head. "Such things can be easily doctored."

Edvar groaned and shook his head. "Do it in the hold, then. Just open one, and do it where it's cold enough to keep the contents from melting. Open it delicately, all right? And reseal it as if it were your own kid you were exposing to space."

Eyeing him, I frowned. I didn't like the idea of endangering someone's future child—but it couldn't be helped. The man had no company listed—no one he was working with. There wasn't anyone I could call and ask for confirmation. He was an independent operator, something that was rare on Earth but common on the fringe of the system.

"All right," I said. Taking the tube into the hold while Rumbold kept his eye on the man, I carefully unscrewed the top.

I don't know what I expected to find inside. A vial of white powder, perhaps. Or maybe instant death as a bomb went off in my face.

But I discovered nothing so dramatic. The tube was a tiny, monitored environment. The embryo inside floated in a tube of frozen yellow liquid.

I photographed it, ran a quick scan, then carefully sealed it again. When I returned to the cab, the smuggler leered at me.

"Did you snort it all?" he asked. "Most inspectors leave some for me. Good stuff, isn't it, peacock-man?"

I glanced at him sharply, but I ignored the insult. Rude people who were angry with guardsmen often called us "peacocks" as we were considered ineffectual show-offs.

Without a word, I tapped out a citation and touched his computer with mine. The ticket was instantly transferred and logged.

"What's that for?" Edvar demanded.

"Read it. Resisting search, refusal to obey an officer pursuant, etc. I had to fire across your bow to get you to stop running. That's a crime."

"You dick!" he raged at me. "My customers are big! They won't like this."

I dared hope he would throw a punch—but sadly, he knew better. Instead, he filled the air with invective as Rumbold and I retreated from his ship. When we were safely through the airlock and gone, he fired up his engines and dove down toward Earth. I could see his anger in every course correction.

"You haven't lost your touch, sir," Rumbold remarked.

"He was hiding something. No one runs from the Guard for the hell of it."

"Yeah, probably…but then again, maybe he's just a man with a vile personality. There are many who become spacers because no one can stand to have them around."

Returning to my station, I found the com light blinking again.

"Message incoming from *Altair*, sir," Rumbold said. "Looks like the boss pulled up behind us while we were inspecting that ship. He's not in the best mood, I'd imagine."

Sighing, I answered the call. Captain Singh's lips were pulled back to show his teeth. The effect was unpleasant.

"Mission accomplished, sir," I said.

"What mission? You weren't given orders—"

"My orders are clear, sir. See the rules of engagement signed March 22nd—signed by you, Captain. They stipulate what to do in the case of a fugitive with possibly dangerous cargo heading for—"

"What fugitive? He had nothing! I've seen your automatic logs. That was abuse, Guardsman. Pure and simple."

I frowned. Singh wasn't always a reasonable man, but he generally came down on the side of the law. What had Edvar said about having powerful friends? I'd expected perhaps to hear from an irritating space-rights lawyer, maybe even one who would manage to drag me into an auto-court to make a deposition. But this...

"Sorry if I was overzealous, sir," I said. "It was my belief that the man was a smuggler. I'm still not sure that he wasn't hiding something. Searching a spaceship properly takes a full ground crew of yard-dogs."

"Oh, are you going to request that next?" Singh demanded.

I hesitated, but then I nodded slowly. "That might be a good idea."

Singh threw up his hands and waved them at me as if I was a misbehaving animal. "Forget I said that. We're returning to the station. There's something else I need to talk to you about."

"What's that, sir?" I asked, happy to change the topic.

"Your presence has been formally requested on Earth. You're going down to the capital tonight. Put on your service dress, and make sure you shave first."

I didn't know what to say for a few moments. "Is this in regard to the incident with the smuggler?"

"He wasn't a smuggler. You just confirmed that fact."

"I reported that I couldn't find anything with a cursory inspection."

"Never mind. No, this isn't about your obsession with small-time criminals. I've been 'asked' by CENTCOM to deliver you to Capital City."

"Ah," I said, understanding at last.

A major part of my mistreatment among the guardsmen came from the fact I was a member of a prominent family. My father was a Public Servant, one of several hundred such individuals on Earth. Together, they ran what passed for our government. As my father hadn't approved of my joining the Guard, we hadn't spoken in years. He was a stern man when things didn't go his way.

But that reality had never sunk in with most of the guardsmen I knew. They hated me for being from House Sparhawk. Everything I did was second-guessed and assumed to be motivated by arrogance. If I was promoted, it was because of my family name. If I failed in some task, it was because I was incompetent. It was assumed without question I'd only gotten to my station through cheating and favoritism in the first place.

There was no winning with those who harbored these attitudes, so I didn't bother. Fortunately a few men, like Rumbold, judged me as one more man in the Guard rather than as an heir to a fortune.

"What's the occasion, sir?" I asked Singh.

He made a flippant gesture. "Who knows? Maybe they'll give you command of my ship. Or maybe it's a royal wedding of some kind. Or maybe your father is going to give another of his long speeches on the net tonight, and he can't bear to be apart from you during the ceremony."

That last part made me smile. "My father might be giving a speech, it's true," I said. "But if he's requested my presence, it isn't because he's dying to see me."

Singh leaned forward, peering at me for a moment. "I get it. You disappointed him, didn't you? You rebelled by joining the Guard, the last ditch holdout for romantics and oldsters who don't want to quit working."

"That's an unfair assessment of my motivations," I said, "but it's a good analysis of my father's opinion."

"He heads the Equality Party," Singh said, "the short-sighted geniuses who move to slash our budgets every single year. Yes, I can see how joining the Guard offended him. You offend everyone, Sparhawk."

"That's not my goal, Captain."

"I've got a new goal for you, then," he said, a sly grin spreading over his face. "I'm sending you down with a full squad as a color guard."

"I'm not sure if that's the best—"

"I don't care, Sparhawk. Your old man can reach out and stick a pin in an admiral, forcing him to make a special request regarding you, but he can't control every detail of your visit, any more than I can control how you run that tiny ship of yours."

"But, sir…"

"Get cleaned up and dock at the station in three hours. Dismissed."

The screen faded then flickered as it returned to the normal status display. I glanced over at Rumbold, who was pretending he hadn't been listening..

"My father isn't going to like this. I don't think he's ever seen me in my uniform."

"We'd better get our dress-blues on then!" he said. "I'll open the locker."

"We?" I asked. "Who said you were going?"

"Did you hear the captain? He said you're going down with a full color guard. As your second in command, I must attend."

I eyed him doubtfully.

"I'd love to see a high-society gathering, Skipper," he said.

"All right," I said with a sigh. I flopped back in my creaking command chair the moment he went below decks.

This was looking worse all the time. I couldn't imagine a more conspicuous character than Rumbold who might attend one of my father's gatherings. Loyal he might be—but beautiful and well-mannered he was not.

-3-

The trip down from orbit to Capital City was relatively uneventful. I arrived at the grand ballroom of the Equality Party headquarters with a squadron of guardsmen and left them all outside, except for Rumbold.

Our presence as guardsmen in formal dress was met with an almost disdainful response from political cronies in the ballroom. I had to remind myself they were annoyed by my uniform, rather than my face.

Fortunately, few of those present seemed to recognize me. I supposed it was my dress-blues that served to hide my identity. Political people tended to look right through men in uniform as if they weren't there unless they were of very high rank.

Despite the uniform, I found it surprising more people didn't recognize me. I reminded myself it'd been several years since I'd attended a state function such as this one, and I'd probably matured in my appearance.

Making no effort to introduce myself to anyone, I moved through the crowds with relative anonymity.

My parents had asked that I attend, but upon learning I would be arriving with a squadron of guardsmen and serving as part of a security detail, their attitude had shifted abruptly. They were no longer responding to my implant messages—they had apologetic staffers do it for them instead.

The staffers repeatedly made polite responses to my requests for information, saying how busy everyone was. They gave me no further details as to the nature of the event nor anything personal from my parents. As the child of a politician, I was able to translate their meaning: my parents didn't want my presence to overshadow the event. They didn't want to go off-message with the press.

The bottom line was that politics came first. Whatever policy announcement, newly declared House alliance or proposed cure-all legislation they were cooking up was more important to them than visiting with their errant son.

I felt only mild resentment as I came to this conclusion. I wasn't surprised or dismayed. I was used to this sort of thing. My parents were political animals. They were a team focused like twin lasers upon their goals. They would get around to hugging me later—or not. I really didn't care which way it went.

That said, this was exactly the sort of situation that had driven me to join the Guard in the first place. Life in the public eye meant too much sacrifice for my comfort.

Once I'd swept the grounds for security threats—of which there were none that I could detect—I headed for the open bar and took a seat with a nervous Rumbold at my side.

After two narco-beers, I found my mood had been elevated. I entertained myself by watching the steady drumbeat of arriving guests in their fanciful costumes. The most attention-seeking people always came in late.

A lovely young lady who hailed from House Astra riveted my wandering eyes. Her entrance was carefully choreographed to be as impactful upon the audience as possible.

This particular lady had achieved her aims with dramatic ease and confidence. She kept my attention effortlessly. It was as if she was born to the part—and it was likely that she had been.

She stepped down the short marble staircase from the portal onto a crimson ribbon that ran through the crowd. Her careful gait would have suited a member of a wedding march. She kept her eyes front, never allowing herself to focus for more than a split-second upon any single member of her staring audience.

Her hair was woven into a complex pattern and adorned with silver points of light. Her earrings were golden spheres, like twin suns amidst the star-scape glitter of her hair. These spheres gave off brilliant gleams now and then, one of which dazzled my eye. I suspected the earrings were enhanced with tiny lasers, as the effect was beyond that which a natural reflection could create.

Her dress, by comparison, was a muted affair. There were no fountains of artificial plasma, splayed holographic feathers or mirrored finishes. It was an intelligent garment of course, but the fabric was a simple, pleasant-looking, sea-foam green. The dress sought to enhance her curves, but it only revealed her skin in modest allotments. As she took each precise step, the dress shifted as per its programming to give the audience tantalizing flashes of the sculpted flesh beneath.

It was her face, however, that attracted my fixed attention. It was so perfectly shaped with jutting cheekbones and unblinking sapphire eyes...

My loutish companion leaned close to me and interrupted my fascination. He whispered with whisky-tainted breath into my right ear.

"Not bad, is she, sir?" Rumbold asked.

"What's her name?" I responded without shifting my gaze from the woman's entrancing form.

"You must have noticed the sunburst crest of House Astra. I'm surprised you don't know the rest of her story. Her lineage is impressive!"

I glanced at Rumbold briefly. "I don't care about her lineage," I told him. "I want to know her name."

"Chloe, sir," he said, flashing me a gray-toothed grin. "Her name is Chloe Astra."

My eyes returned to the lady and followed her until she vanished into the morphing crowd.

Another arrival was announced at the entrance. It was a paired couple this time. They were clad in the stalwart midnight black of Grantholm—but I ignored them. I kept looking for the woman in sea-foam green, and I managed to catch glimpses of her lithe shape now and then.

"Chloe of Astra," I said, rolling the name off my tongue. I swilled down the last of my whiskey and continued to stare.

Rumbold chuckled roughly. "Making plans for tonight? I wish you Godspeed in your quest. You'll need it!"

I tossed him a glance. "Why's that?"

"Tonight is her blossoming. She's fresh from the House and has never been in public before as an adult."

My mouth opened, then closed again in disappointment.

"Ah," I said, "a pity she's so young."

"Some would say otherwise, but I understand your thinking. You're a traditional gentleman of the old school. Don't think that's not appreciated by men like myself!"

I nodded vaguely and addressed my beverage. The drug-laced alcohol tingled on my tongue and burned my throat, but it had done little to affect my mental capacities. I'd set my blood-toxin monitors at their highest filtration levels. It wouldn't do to have a guardsman seen drunk at a public event while on duty.

The formal arrivals ended, and the party went into full swing. It was a subdued event by the standards of the general populace. There were very few loud, boisterous attendees. This was an affair of state, a party at which those attending were more worried about their appearance than any real social contact. Being here, being seen in attendance of an important engagement, that's what mattered to most of them.

Rumbold and I got up and walked slowly around the crowd, making ourselves visible and simultaneously observing the guests. We were the only two guardsmen inside the building. The rest were posted at the entrances and exits, or on the roof in the cold. Our mission, as I saw it, was to be visible but discreet. Anyone thinking of making a protest to any of the government officials present would thus be dissuaded from overt action.

"William?" asked a female as we passed the Grantholm group. "William Sparhawk, is that you?"

I paused, feeling a twinge of discomfort. I'd been recognized. I'd hoped to avoid embarrassment—but pretending not to hear the woman wouldn't help matters now.

Turning, I forced a smile and bowed as a handsome woman approached. She was a lady who allowed her age to show more than most. She had gray hair, a careworn face, and sharp, intelligent eyes. She wore a flowing dress that was as black as space.

"Well, if this isn't a surprise!" she said. "I'd heard you'd joined the Guard, but I'd never expected to see you—well, never mind. It's good to see you, William."

"You as well, Lady Grantholm," I said.

"You do look dashing," she said, running her eyes over my person. "All gold braids and epaulets. Are those weapons real? The pistol and the saber both?"

"Certainly madam. How else might I serve my duties?"

She appeared mildly concerned. In modern times, each House maintained personal security forces. Confronting an actual military man who she was personally acquainted with, even circumstantially, was a novelty to her.

We no longer had a separate navy or army on Earth; there remained only Star Guard. My organization served both functions as best we could.

"Well, in any regard," Lady Grantholm said, "give my congratulations to your father on his reaffirmation as the party leader."

"Yes, of course."

"He'll be here tonight, you know," she said, eyeing me closely.

I attempted to contain any form of reaction, but perhaps my cheek jumped, or my eye twitched. Whatever it was, it was an unavoidable reflex which she observed and misinterpreted.

"You claim you didn't know?" she gasped.

"Not at all, milady."

"Hmm," she said. She stepped closer and lowered her voice. Politely, I leaned forward to catch her words.

"You didn't set this up, did you?" she asked. "Dressing up as a guardsman to embarrass him?"

I frowned. "No madam. I'd never do such a thing. Moreover, I fail to see how either of us would be embarrassed by an honorable meeting tonight—be it a surprise or not."

She stiffened and withdrew. She clasped her hands in front of her body.

"Of course not," she said, generating a false smile.

As her entire demeanor indicated she didn't believe me, it was all I could do to not snap a retort back her.

Sensing my mood, Lady Grantholm excused herself quickly. She scuttled away to a group of her cronies. There, I pretended not to notice as she whispered and waved vaguely in my direction. I could feel their curious, scandal-seeking gazes, but I never returned them.

"Can it be true, sir?" Rumbold asked as we continued to walk the crowd. "I've heard from several people the Guard isn't welcome at the Equality Party. I knew your father's followers aren't made up of our most ardent supporters, but they invited you all the same. Couldn't they forgive and forget this one night?

"Singh's joke wouldn't be as keen-edged if they did, would it, Rumbold?" I asked with a bitter note I couldn't hide. "Remember, we're not here as guests. We're like the hired security you see at the doorways. Someone among my father's staffers screwed up, I bet. They'd hoped for good political optics, but now they're horrified to see me working the floor."

"But that's your job!"

"Indeed it is, and we should get back to it."

We continued to perform a slow patrol, but I was now in a sour mood. All I could think about was my father. We hadn't spoken for a long time, not since I'd been promoted to Lieutenant Commander.

To my father, my commission was a vast embarrassment. He was a high official, a Servant of the people, and I was his sole declared heir. I'd been fully registered, and he was legally committed to the relationship. If he died, I'd take his place at the head of a powerful political party. The trouble was his party saw every credit spent on the military as a credit wasted.

I could see Father's point of view, of course. I'd been expected to serve as his aide. A good son would operate quietly in his father's shadow over the several decades until such a time as chance or retirement removed his elder from office.

Instead of following this expected path, I'd signed on with the Guard. To make matters worse, father's political affiliates didn't even *like* the Guard, much less respect a guardsman. Never had a general session gone by without one of them proposing a further slashing of our budget or the disbanding of Earth's last military organization entirely.

For most people, Star Guard was known as the "Old Guard." The name wasn't entirely inaccurate, as the service consisted largely of people of great age. Since the organization was forced to provide low wages, few young people of quality bothered to volunteer, despite the opportunities for rapid advancement. Young vibrant people rarely joined our ranks.

Many of those who did continue to serve did so out of loyalty and sheer stubbornness. Like Rumbold, they were a fossilized group from one or even two centuries past. They were steeped in tradition and fixed in their ways. Those that left the Guard often did so feet-first, dead at their posts due to some complication created by their longevity drugs.

But for all that, I loved Star Guard, and I'd joined up despite the protests of my peers and my parents. Had there been a hint of rebellion in the act? Perhaps, but I enjoyed my uniform and my duties. Joining the Guard had been a dream since I was young, but it was a dream that had never been shared by my family.

-4-

A tinkling sound began, announcing the coming of a speech. All around the vast ballroom, others took up the call, tapping on their cocktail glasses.

Quiet fell gently over the group. A man entered the party and stepped forward to a lectern that had been hastily set up on a marble dais. The man was my father.

"Uh oh," Rumbold said at my side.

Instead of echoing his concern, I lifted my chin. It was my impression that there were as many eyes upon me now as there were upon my father.

Lady Grantholm had done her work well, circulating around the chamber and pointing me out to all who would listen.

I stood steadfast and put a hand on the hilt of my saber. I would not cower and hide, no matter what was being said by those around me. My eyes were locked upon my father, as he smiled at everyone and raised his hands to salute us.

He took in a breath, as if he were about to speak—and that's when his eyes met mine. A shock of recognition froze him there.

But he was too much of a professional to be rattled for long. Still smiling, he turned to an aide and whispered a terse message. Then he turned back toward the crowd and began his speech.

My father was nothing if not long-winded. He began with a preamble of gracious thanks to everyone present and to half a dozen who weren't. Before he'd moved on to the meat of his talk, the aide he'd dispatched a minute or two earlier finally reached me.

A hand laid itself over the gold braids on my dark blue sleeve.

"Commander Sparhawk?"

I looked at the man. He was Miles Tannish, a simpering fellow who I thought of as one of my father's most dedicated lapdogs.

"Yes, Miles?" I asked.

"Could you step this way, please?"

Slowly, I shook my head and turned my attention back to scanning the crowd.

"Sorry Miles," I said. "I'm on duty. Surely, whatever it is can wait until after the event has concluded."

Miles tugged at me slightly, hinting physically that I should go with him. My years of hard training had transformed me, however. I wasn't a boy any longer. I was not budged.

Miles made a sound of frustration. "Really, William, your father appreciates your dedication, but—"

"Does he?" I asked in disbelief.

"Yes, of course he does. But he'd rather have you attend to his security from another post. Surely, you could trade positions with one of the guardsmen outside, or—"

"No, Miles. That's not happening. Good evening."

"Very well," he said, withdrawing his hand reluctantly. He slid away into the crowd and vanished.

"I wanted to remove that hand myself," Rumbold said quietly. "With my saber, if need be."

"Now, now, Rumbold," I said, maintaining a mild expression through force of will. "That's not our mission here."

My father moved on, announcing formally that he had been reaffirmed as the head of the party by unanimous vote. I wasn't fooled by this. Like everyone present, I knew the Servants gathered in private and wrangled until it was clear one person had the votes to win. After that, they all pretended to have supported the victor from the start of the process. The party thus always appeared to be united.

As the speech continued, I became increasingly annoyed with the situation. The tensions between my chosen profession and my father's wishes had never been resolved. I'd hoped that the time spent apart had healed wounds. It now appeared nothing had changed.

My father and I were much alike. Neither one of us took well to insults and slights. We could be bad-tempered, a thing we generally hid from others, but which came out in moments of stress.

This was one such moment. I felt I couldn't just stand in the shadows while others whispered and plotted to remove me from the chamber. I had as much right to listen to my father's words as any of these political hacks.

"Rumbold," I said, "let's move closer to the speaker."

His mouth hung open. His bulging, bloodshot eyes, a sure sign of longevity-treatment overdoses, flapped wide.

"Are you sure that's a good idea, sir? There are camera spheres everywhere."

He was right. A half dozen drones, none of them more than two centimeters in diameter, floated around my father, capturing him from many angles at once.

I smiled tightly. "That just means he plans on making an important announcement. I wish to hear it clearly."

"Ahem, sir..."

But Rumbold was already talking to the cape on my back. I marched smartly through the crowd, which melted at my official approach.

If my father saw me coming toward him, he never let on. He just kept talking as if everything was going exactly as he'd planned. His speech moved on from the mundane, and he now shifted to speaking eloquently about the future. He discussed the challenges that lay ahead. He lamented past failures and promised that future policy changes would be of critical import to the people.

I soon managed to wend my way through the thickening crowd at the foot of the marble steps. Rumbold reluctantly joined me, looking out of place and uncomfortable. Seeking to strike a confident pose, I placed one boot on the polished bottom step of the dais and threw back my cape to reveal my saber.

The crowd looked from my father to me and back again. The audience whispered among themselves in confusion and mild alarm. Word of my unexpected appearance had spread everywhere among the hundreds present.

This suited me just fine. I was no longer in the mood for hiding in shadows. I watched as my father pressed doggedly onward, chewing through his speech without glancing at me more than once or twice.

Truthfully, I was impressed. I doubted I could have maintain such a determined performance if the roles had been reversed. My urge to embarrass him faded as my admiration for him grew—he was, after all, my father.

I almost withdrew when he came to the crux of his message. I thought about retreating, certainly, and I would have done so if I could think of a way to withdraw gracefully—but I couldn't. I'd walked up here, bold as brass, and presented myself to the crowd. I couldn't very well retreat now.

Instead of slinking away, I decided to play a different part. When my father paused for a polite round of applause, I clapped my gloved hands together harder than anyone present. I grinned broadly, rather than giving him a wintery smile.

It was at the point of this transition in my demeanor that I noticed another individual in the crowd near at hand. A flash of unmistakable sea-foam green captured my eye. Even more riveting were the rhythmic flashes of bare flesh the dress revealed as the girl approached.

She was Lady Chloe of House Astra. Up close, her beauty was even more dramatic than it had appeared at a distance. I was mesmerized. She walked with such perfect steps. Each pace was exact, and she appeared to glide forward through the crowd in my direction.

Staring, I watched as she passed me by and mounted the steps. Where was she going?

My father had reached the climax of his speech at that moment. Most were hanging on his words by this time, but I barely heard them.

"...and so it is with certainty of purpose that I will acquiesce to the call," he said. "My duties are clear and immutable. I will accept the greatest of possible sacrifices, and enter my name humbly in the running for the high office of President. I want to thank you all personally for your relentless support!"

The crowd began cheering then. Up until that point they'd applauded, but none had actually lowered themselves to the act of uttering a cry. Emotion finally overwhelmed them—as did their instincts. They were political animals, and they knew their fates were now tied to their leader. If he failed now that he'd announced his official intentions, they failed as well.

Throughout this surprising twist of events, I have to admit, I was still paying more than half my attention to the woman who'd mounted the steps. She'd all but brushed by me in the process. She was a captivating creature, but somehow, I felt a certain *otherness* about her when she was close at hand. She was distracted at the very least. Could she be drugged, or worse...?

It wasn't until she reached the top of the dais where my father was standing with hands raised over his head that it dawned on me Lady Astra wasn't going to stop. Father was too busy accepting the cheers of his party members to notice.

Almost without thinking, I mounted the steps, taking two strides after the woman in green.

"Lady Astra," I called, "there will be time for personal congratulations after—"

That was as far as I got. The words died in my throat as she reached for my father, who was at last gazing at her in puzzlement.

Two blades—that's the only way I could describe them—emerged from her hands. They were gray polymer, from the look of them.

Those lithe, lovely hands had split apart, peeling away with a wet slap of blood and flesh. It was as if the bones of her hands had fused and transformed into stained gray blades, cutting their way out of the thin meat covering her slight body.

Shocked, my father took a half-step back, but the thing that Lady Astra had transformed into advanced with wicked speed.

It thrust its gory twin weapons at his midsection. Each blade came to a triangular point, and the two moved with unerring aim.

For my own part, I knew my father was dead. He was to be butchered in front of my eyes. That was a foregone conclusion. Revenge already simmered in my mind.

Cursing myself for reacting so slowly, my hands flew to my sides. I drew my pistol and my saber.

Regulations hampered me. My gun came up, but it would not fire. The power pack inside was charged and ready to release a bolt, but the safety system wasn't so easily activated. One of the many precautions my government had seen fit to install included an elaborate safety system in my sidearm. Ostensibly, this "smart" system was to prevent accidents or to stop someone from stealing my weapon and discharging it without authorization. When first drawn, the pistol had to recognize the operator and confirm my identity through remote transponders.

That process should only have taken a fraction of a second—but it wasn't working. I fumbled with the override, but I realized I didn't have a second to spare.

I dropped the pistol and charged up the steps with only my saber. The blade was likewise neutered, as it could not be powered without an elaborate safety procedure—that said the edge was still razor-sharp steel.

Off to my sides, I saw other security people swarming in. They'd been kept outside, naturally, as the mere sight of them had been deemed inappropriate by the party. None of them could possibly get through the backpedaling crowd and beat me to the assassin, not even Rumbold who stood cursing at his pistol at the bottom of the steps.

The woman's twin triangular blades stabbed into my father again. They withdrew and thrust repeatedly like pistons with hammering force. My father went down, howling in pain. But he was still alive, still writhing.

The woman in the sea-foam gown stalked him. She crouched like an animal and moved with unnatural bird-like jerks and twists.

Her gray blades stopped plunging into Father's abdomen. Retargeting, they lifted upward, aiming now for his face.

She never managed to stab out his eyes or cut his throat, if that was her plan, because I managed to ram my saber into her back first. She stiffened and straightened her spine. She whirled and almost took my saber out of my hands.

Two bloody points came up into a defensive pose as she faced me. Shocked, I retreated a step, and I made a cut at her head. She blocked with one blade, and then thrust with the other. I dodged away, but felt the point catch and draw a line, cutting apart my shirt over my ribs.

The look on her face was inhuman. There was no emotion in those lovely eyes.

Touching the clasp of my cloak, I activated my personal shielding. Not all guardsmen had such devices as they were so expensive even the officers couldn't afford them.

The cape flickered into life, surrounding me with a glimmering band of force. The creature that was battling me struck twice more, but shed only sparks rather than blood.

Lifting my saber high, I brought it down with both hands wrapped around the hilt. I attempted to hack away her arms. When the blow landed, it stung my hands but didn't cut all the way through her upraised blocking limb. I'd damaged it enough to make it hang limp, but that was all.

A wild slash caught the flat of my sword and sent it clattering away from my numbed fingers. She advanced, slashing.

Then a pistol sizzled behind me. A bolt caught her in the chest and spun her around. She heaved herself up—but two more bolts put her back down. She didn't attempt to stand again.

"Thanks, Rumbold," I said, panting and staring at the creature that had all but slain me. "I see you managed to get the safety off."

Rumbold puffed and stared with me.

"I should never have turned it on," he said, flashing me a look of relief. "Let's see to your father."

Together, we pressed through the security and medical people who had begun to arrive. My father was breathing in hitches and gasps.

"Father," I said. "You live?"

"I do, William," he said. "No Sparhawk can be taken down so easily."

Looking at him quizzically, I was at a loss. Those blades...

He saw my hesitancy, and he realized I thought he must be badly wounded and in shock. His eyes caught mine, and he lifted the edge of his shirt. There I saw a thin suit of body armor. The stab wounds had imprinted the fabric but hadn't penetrated.

"Ah," I said in sudden understanding.

"She cut my arms and broke my ribs," he said, "but she didn't kill me. What of you, William?"

I showed him the slash in my clothing. "I'll be fine," I said.

My father struggled to stand. He slapped away the hands that sought to keep him down.

Everyone present sought to make him stay on his back, waiting for the medical people, but I thought he'd earned the right to do as he pleased. Reaching to clasp his hand, I hauled him to his feet.

We caught one another's eye as he stood, unsteady and swaying. There was a moment, a look in his eye. It was a look I hadn't seen for a decade or more. A closeness was there between us—perhaps even a touch of gratitude.

Then, just as quickly as it had come, that spark died. My father was again cold, distant, professional. The lines in his face hardened, and he gave me a slight nod of thanks. It was the sort of nod a man might award to an attentive waiter who has replaced a dropped fork without being asked.

In response, my demeanor shifted almost as swiftly as his. I straightened and turned my face into an expressionless mask. We'd transitioned from the informal back to the formal again, just like that.

There were no hugs. No hardy congratulations. Nothing like there might have been in my youth.

I felt a pang. In that frozen moment, I'd dared to hope. It was a hope I hadn't realized I'd retained through all the long years to this very day.

In that fraction of a second, I'd believed my father had let go of his misgivings concerning my chosen profession. I had hoped that he'd come to accept my choices in life and forgiven the embarrassment I'd caused him by becoming a mere guardsman.

Part of me understood his anguish, naturally. I was more than just a son to him. I was his heir. A man was only allowed a single legal heir: one individual that had been carefully designed with selected genetic traits. I'd been built, rather than bred, using gene-splicing enzymes and a thousand other medical procedures.

Thus William Sparhawk Senior and Junior shared more than names. My DNA was a seventy percent match to his—the legal limit. I was, for the most part, a copy of him. I'd been genetically designed to contain the best of his body and mind. I was meant to be perfect in every way, meant to be a copy of my father but somewhat better.

Instead, I'd turned out to be a discouraging failure. An incalculable disappointment. Possibly, I was the only blunder in his existence that he'd not yet corrected.

"We must get you to the hospital," I said.

He shook his head. He was no longer looking at me. He was looking and thinking of the cameras, the optics. "No. She broke every rib on my right side—but no. I'm going to take the lectern again."

"Sir, this is madness," said a voice at his elbow.

One step below us stood Miles Tannish. His hands were clasped together before him as if he was pleading for his life.

Tannish dared to reach toward my tottering father, but I pressed him back, putting my hand on *his* wrist this time. Rumbold followed my lead. We pushed back the aides and arriving medical people so my father could face the cameras.

"He's earned the right to finish his damned speech if he wants to, Miles," I said.

Stubbornly, my father did finish a shortened version of his speech. I was too busy watching the crowd for further assassins to listen to the details. If nothing else, I found myself taking my job much more seriously than I had previously.

Occasionally Father coughed, but he always stood tall. There were bloodstains on his shirt, and his jacket was torn—but he continued speaking.

The ballroom was all but empty by this time, of course, as the guests had fled the chamber. But the cameras were still on him.

I understood perfectly. He wasn't speaking to the assembled party members in their fine suits and gowns, he was talking to the people at home who were watching on the net. It was for their benefit he had to appear strong and undaunted.

Although several agents pressed close and looked at me curiously, I continued serving as Father's guard until the end. At last, he finished his presentation and stepped away from the lectern under his own power. The tiny floating spheres stopped transmitting and flew away.

I sighed in relief, glad it was over.

-5-

After he'd finished his speech, Father moved painfully down the gray marble steps. An agent hustled up to help with a hand on his elbow. I thought of taking my father's other arm—but a sour glance from him stopped me. I let him go, not wanting to shame him further.

When he'd been placed upon a gurney and whisked to the hospital aboard an air car, I was accosted again by Miles Tannish.

"Would you like to accompany the Servant?" he asked.

I considered the offer. It might provide an opportunity to rekindle with my father. I could see the value in that, but I had other thoughts preoccupying my mind.

Shaking my head, I gestured toward the lectern and the twisted corpse that lay nearby. "I want to know more about her, first."

Miles raised his eyebrows in surprise, but then nodded quickly and left. His pursed lips indicated he thought my interests were odd—but I didn't care what he thought.

More men from various security details were arriving every minute, descending upon the ballroom. A bevy of agents cordoned off the area, and my guardsmen looked uncertain. Was this a planetary issue, thus under the jurisdiction of the Guard, or should we let the private forces handle it?

From the bottom of the steps, Rumbold called up to me. "Sir? Have a care—we don't want to disturb the scene. Experts will be arriving soon. Your father's party employs several detectives. You and I are guardsmen, not sleuths."

"Point taken, Rumbold. But I'm not attempting to perform nanoscopic forensics. I merely wish to examine the creature that attacked my father."

With a rumbling laugh, Rumbold shook his head. "I would have thought you'd done enough of that already this evening."

I could have taken offense, but I chose not to. Rumbold was a good man, if an indelicate one.

The scene at the top of the steps was a mess. The corpse of the girl I'd stared at with such fascination was splayed in death on the floor. She'd been burned and disfigured by Rumbold's power bolt.

The odd behavior she'd displayed and the unnatural pose of her body made me doubt she was human at all. Walking around her fallen form in a circle, I saw twisted black hair, charred flesh and those strange break-away limbs. Discarded fingers lay in a randomly scattered pattern, some of them sitting in the midst of dark blood-puddles on the marble.

Rumbold could not contain his own curiosity for long. He mounted the steps, grunting up behind me, and peered over my shoulder.

"Such a shame. A pretty girl—if she was one."

"Look at the exposed left eye," I said. "It's artificial, I think."

"How can you tell, sir? They grow these androids so perfectly now. It's a wonder more men don't wed them!"

"See there?" I asked. "The whites of her eyes are dry. No moisture at all. Even the most perfectly attractive woman in the world has tears and maybe a red squiggle or two in her eyes when you look up close."

"Are you sure? There are mini-projectors to shroud every imperfection."

My hand reached out to her power pack, a small box everyone wore at the waist these days. I shut it off, but we observed little change in her appearance.

"It's off," I said. "It's reality we're observing, not a fiction of light and shadow."

"Huh," Rumbold grunted. "If she's artificial, why'd they put a power-pack on her at all?"

"Realism, perhaps? At the very least, something had to power the movement of the dress and those earrings that shone like lasers."

"Yes, right…"

Straightening up, I inhaled deeply. "She's an android. A robot clothed in flesh and dressed up like a guest."

"I see by your face that relieves you," Rumbold said.

I noticed he was studying me, rather than the corpse.

"Aren't you glad to know you didn't shoot a real woman tonight?" I asked.

"If she'd been a human assassin, killing her would have been no less satisfactory to me."

"I suppose," I agreed, but I was still glad the creature on the floor was a simulation. I didn't want to know in my heart I'd thrust my saber into a young woman's back—even if she was a killer.

I stepped away from the scene, and Rumbold hurried after me.

"Excuse me, sir," he called as I headed for the stairs to the roof.

"What is it now?"

"You aren't thinking of leaving, are you? Captain Singh will be here shortly, and he'll expect a full report from everyone."

"All the more reason to move quickly."

When I reached the roof I climbed into a waiting air car. The car was owned by my family and had been left behind for my use. Rumbold stood outside the canopy. His face was long, and he reminded me of a pet who was uncertain of its loyalties. I could tell he wanted to climb in at my side, but he felt he might be punished for it.

"Rumbold," I shouted over the rising whine of the turbines. "Stay here, man. Make a report in my stead to Captain Singh. Tell him I was called away to my father's side at the hospital."

"Yes, sir," he said promptly. "Will do! Best of luck."

With a nod, I left him there on the roof. The car lifted on autopilot and glided toward the destination I'd punched in.

Such was the speed of cross-town air travel that it took longer to lift off and land than it did to fly over the intervening kilometers.

My family's security people met me at the entrance and gave me a hard look. Their suspicion quickly melted away when I was recognized. They appeared surprised to see me.

"Is my father all right?" I asked the nearest of the plainclothes agents.

"He's alive, sir," she said noncommittally. "We're here to make sure he stays that way."

I thought of pointing out that their security at the ballroom had been lacking, but I didn't. No one had expected the assassination attempt. Kidnappings and the like *did* occur from time to time, but an outright attempt to kill a sitting Public Servant? That hadn't been seen for decades. Possibly, I hadn't even been born the last time it had happened.

Brushing past the agents, I headed inside. After a battery of formal identification procedures, I was at last escorted to Father's private suite.

"William?" asked my father in surprise. "I wasn't expecting you. Don't you have duties to attend to?"

"Yes father—that's what I'm doing right now. The Guard was responsible for security at your speech, and it would appear to me that we failed you."

"Nonsense. You killed the assassin in the end. How can I help you?"

"I need your assistance. I wish to investigate House Astra."

"Do you think that would be wise? Won't it be a little obvious if I send a family member under the guise of being a guardsman?"

"I *am* a guardsman."

"Hmm, yes... I suppose you could be mistaken for a neutral party. But if I understand the situation, your Captain hasn't officially assigned the investigation of the attack to you?"

"He hasn't. That's why I need your help to gain access to the Astra estate."

Father frowned. "I see... You've never asked me for a favor of this nature before."

"I've never witnessed the attempted assassination of a Servant before."

"You're requesting that I use my personal influence to get you assigned to this investigation—is that correct?"

"Yes."

Thinking it over, Father finally nodded. "All right. It could be a good use of bargaining power. House Astra must be embarrassed to have been connected with this unfortunate affair. I'll make the arrangements. Go now—your visit will be expected by the time you arrive."

"Thank you, Father," I said, and I turned to go.

Part of my busy mind wondered why I hadn't inquired into the details of my father's health. Wasn't I concerned for his well-being? I took solace in the fact he'd looked better than when I'd last seen him. His face was no longer white and drawn. It was pink and hale again, flush with an infusion of fresh artificial blood and surgical nanites.

I asked that a guard be posted outside his room. Then, giving Father a nod, I left him there in his sick bed and made my way back into the general ward. It was there that my mother accosted me.

She was a Grantholm by birth. Twenty years my father's junior, she was still quite old. My father was in his second century of life—but she wasn't far behind him. Neither of them looked a day over forty, however, due to the miracles of longevity treatments that worked to weed out aging cells and encourage only the best to flourish.

"How are you, Mother?" I asked as she laid her hand upon the back of mine.

"You were hurt," she said. It was not a question, but a state of fact. "I saw it, when the mad bitch stabbed you."

"She only cut my clothing. And she was an android, mother. A simulacrum. A robot clothed in flesh."

"You're right of course. She only resembled a member of that House. Astra is our rival, but they would never do this to us."

I frowned at her in confusion. I wasn't quite sure what she was thinking. Was she angry with Astra or defending them? I suspected she was conflicted.

"Never mind, William," she said. "Why are you here? What are you trying to accomplish?"

"I wanted to check on Father, naturally."

She hesitated for a fraction of a second too long before responding.

"Naturally…" she said at last.

"What's more, I've been assigned to investigate the attack," I said.

"What?" she asked in alarm. "You? There are plenty of guardsmen and private agents who—"

"But none of them were personally involved."

"I see," she said. Her hand withdrew from mine, and she looked troubled.

I found this annoying as I didn't believe myself to be incompetent. "I'm proceeding to House Astra immediately. I'll question their members."

Her eyes widened. "Tonight? You can't do that. It's too soon."

"Too soon? On the contrary. Any evidence might be gone by the time I get there if I delay."

"House Astra isn't our enemy, William. They're not in our party, but we have long history of cooperation. The office of a Public Servant must be respected and—"

"Mother, if you don't have anything specific to aid me in my investigation, I'm afraid I must go."

"All right," she said, "but I insist that you take a companion."

"Agreed," I said. "I was thinking of dragooning Rumbold for that job, but I left him behind at the scene of the crime."

"Who's Rumbold?" she asked in puzzlement. "Never mind. I'm talking about one of our most competent agents: Miles Tannish. I insist you take him with you."

Wincing visibly, my face revealed my pain at her suggestion.

"What's wrong with Tannish?" she demanded.

"He's a sycophant of the lowest order."

Her face took on a stern expression. "He's an expert in delicate matters, and he understands House Astra's eccentricities of protocol."

"But this isn't a matter of pomp and circumstance! Father has been attacked—apparently by a member of their House. They should be anxious to clear their names."

She shook her head bemusedly. "You demonstrate your ignorance of the situation with every word. They're probably highly embarrassed, but that only means they'll want nothing more than to forget about the incident entirely."

"I will not allow that."

"Your attitude confirms my worst fears."

"Don't you want to know the truth?" I demanded.

"Of course I do," she said in a softer tone, "but this must be done delicately. You have doggedness, son, and wit, but you lack the appropriate sense of decorum. Take Miles with you. He'll guide you and soften your demeanor. House Astra has already suffered a blow to their honor tonight, and we can't afford—"

"Surely you're not serious," I interrupted. "It is *our* House that has suffered. They should be more than willing to consult with me, if only due to their apparent guilt. Let them *prove* they're innocent."

She sighed and tapped her neck just behind her ear. She stopped walking with me and her gaze became unfixed. I knew she was making a call, and that the interior of her retina was now displaying data.

After taking two steps farther, I spun on my heel and looked back. "Mother, who are you contacting?"

"I'm going to change your father's mind. There's no point in sending you—I can't believe he approved of the idea in the first place. Possibly, it's due to the drugs in his system."

Reversing my march, I returned to her side. My expression had transformed into one of irritation. "Please disconnect. I'll take Tannish, if I must."

"Yes dear?" she said, talking to no one I could see. "How are you holding up? Sleeping…? Of course, forgive me. I'll check on you again in the morning. I'll see that there are no further interruptions."

She tapped behind her ear again. Her eyes returned to my face and refocused there. She allowed herself a tiny smile of victory.

"Tannish will be waiting upstairs to fly you to House Astra," she said. "Please, William, listen to him. I know you're angry, but you must control any rudeness you may have picked up in the Guard. There's an election coming soon, and we must have the support of every House if we're to have a chance."

Her thinking was thus revealed to me. She was more interested in the election of my father to the office of President than she was in discovering who had attacked him. It would seem odd to an outsider, but I understood. My parents were ambitious to a fault.

Heaving a sigh, I assured her I would do as she asked. I gave her a peck on the cheek, which she returned. Then I left her side quickly, before she could insist on any more conditions.

Miles was indeed waiting for me on the roof. It had begun to rain in the city; the dark clouds overhead drizzled onto my upturned face.

The turbines of the air car whined, slowly gaining in pitch as I approached the passenger side. I climbed in and shook myself off. The hydrophobic surfaces of the upholstery shed the rainwater, sending every droplet quickly to a drain in the bottom of the cabin.

"I'm so glad you found time to visit your father in his hour of need, William," Miles said. "House Sparhawk is blessed to have a man such as yourself representing our—"

"Save the praise for House Astra, Miles," I said. "You're coming along to massage their egos, not mine."

Tannish fell silent as the airship lifted off.

I glanced at him, and I quickly determined that he was annoyed.

"Why does everyone think offending the House Astra is worth ignoring a violent attack?" I asked him.

He set the autopilot and leaned back in his seat, glancing at me. "Is that a serious question?"

"I rarely ask any other kind."

"House Sparhawk has considerable political influence, William. Your father is a popular man. But he isn't all-powerful. He needs funding."

"Ah," I said, "and House Astra is one of the richest Houses in the Ministry."

"Exactly. Now, I'm supposed to coach you on civility. How long has it been since you've visited another of the Great Houses? As an official representative of House Sparhawk, I mean?"

Shrugging my shoulders, I avoided his gaze. "I don't recall the specifics. As a child, I'm sure I—"

"That's what I thought," he said, heaving a sigh. "Let's go over the basics. It's critical that you maintain certain realities in your mind at all times during the visit. First of all, we'll be in their home, not ours. We must conduct ourselves with decorum and respect."

My eyes rolled of their own accord. "I'm a guardsman, Miles. I can't conduct an investigation without impressing them with my authority."

"You may find that they're more forthcoming if they like you—or if they at least feel you're a welcome guest from an allied House."

"Friendship and alliance—these things are not my goals. I seek cooperation and truthfulness."

My statement did not seem to deter Miles. He continued to lecture me as we flew out of the city and across several districts toward the north. When the lights below were few and far between, we came upon a constellation of light nestled in a forest on a mountaintop.

Intrigued despite my mood, I watched as we glided down into the estate grounds. The service road resembled a thread of light winding up the mountain to the bejeweled crown of brilliant stars that was the estate itself.

"It's much larger than our estate," I said.

"As I said, they have the wealth, if not the most charismatic leader."

Mesmerized, I watched as we landed in a fairytale scene. The estate was walled, with six tiers of boulders laser-cut into a perfect jigsaw puzzle pattern.

"Bricks were too ordinary for them as well, I see," I remarked.

"Each of those stones was quarried from living rock on a distant colony," he said.

I glanced at him in surprise. "A colony? This castle is that old?"

"Yes, it dates back to before the Cataclysm, as does House Astra. There are many wonders here. You would do well to—"

"Wait," I said in concern, "we're passing the landing zone."

"Naturally. We invited ourselves, not the other way around. Accordingly, we'll be using the tradesman's entrance at the rear of the House."

Glaring at him, I couldn't believe what he was saying. He landed with a thump in a poorly-lit back alley behind the main structure. He popped open the canopy and climbed out. I didn't follow him.

"Miles," I said, "you will immediately take me back to the front entrance."

He poked his head back into the cab and looked at me.

"Unthinkable," he said. "This is exactly the sort of thing that made your mother insist on my guidance. We're not invited guests here, William. We represent the interests of House Sparhawk, yes, but—"

"I'm not walking in that door."

Miles shook his head and sighed. He steepled his fingers and took on a pained expression as he readied himself to explain the harsh realities of the situation to me once again.

Two butlers in livery had caught sight of us by this time and were hastening out to help us from the air car. Miles turned and greeted them effusively.

That was the last straw for me. I'd suffered a great deal tonight, and it was getting late. I wasn't in the mood for another moment of decorum and pretended humility.

Laying my hands on the controls, I flipped it into manual control mode. The stick slid neatly and automatically over to my side of the cab, and I pulled back on it.

Miles was left on the landing pad wearing a stunned expression. Matching him on either side were the two butlers, holding their felt caps to their heads and gaping up at me.

-6-

After a minute-long flight, I bumped down in front of the mansion on the very edge of the landing pad. Admittedly, it had been a few years since I'd flown an air car without a program to follow.

I popped open the canopy and climbed out. This time, the service people moved with much greater speed. They rushed toward my side. One of them carried a fire extinguisher.

"Sir?" asked the one with the extinguisher. "Has your vehicle malfunctioned?"

"No," I said. "Please care for it. I'll be needing it on my return journey."

That said, I walked toward the house. Their eyes followed me in astonishment. Their mouths opened, but no words escaped until after I'd passed by. At that point, they whispered intensely amongst themselves.

Taking the oddly cut stone steps in single strides, despite the fact the steps were placed too widely apart for such treatment, I reached the towering front door.

At first, when faced by a door that had to be six meters tall and equally as wide, I was at a loss as how to enter. Then I saw the smaller door cut into the larger. I reached for a knocker made of what appeared to be dulled silver—but I suspected it was platinum or perhaps titanium.

Before my fingers could grasp it, the door creaked open. An elderly gentleman peered at me as if I were a stray dog.

"Can I help you, sir?" he asked.

"Yes, you can let me pass. I'm here to meet with the membership of House Astra. I'm a guardsman who's been charged as an investigator—"

"Ah," interrupted the elderly doorman. "I see. This is a misunderstanding. The appropriate entrance, sir, is around to the back. You'd best return to your vehicle, it's nearly a kilometer-long walk."

Feeling a flush come over me, I struggled to control an outburst.

"I'm William Sparhawk," I said quietly, "of House Sparhawk. Are you refusing to allow me to enter?"

The doorman eyed me uncertainly. "One moment Mr. Sparhawk," he said, and left me standing there.

A full minute passed, then another. During this time, I tried not to peek into the interior of the mansion but found myself drawn to do so. There were startling sights inside; I could see that from where I stood.

Paintings stood as tall as the door at which I'd been abandoned. Steps of polished onyx gleamed under a chandelier of translucent, custom-grown crystal.

Craning my neck a fraction, I caught sight of the doorman. He was talking to an elderly, white-haired lady in a fur robe.

I froze in recognition. The robed figure was none other than Gwen Astra, the head of the House.

Almost without conscious thought, my hand reached out to push open the door another dozen centimeters. A creaking sound resulted, and the two looked in my direction.

Gwen caught herself quickly. She clapped her leathery hands together and beckoned for me enter.

"There you are, young Sparhawk!" she said. "Come inside and warm yourself by my fire."

I was by no means chilled, but I did as she asked. I followed her to a circular arrangement of chairs and sofas in the midst of which was a roaring fire as tall as a man. I glanced upward, but saw no obvious means by which the smoke was being removed from the chamber. Perhaps the fire was an illusion, although it gave off a great deal of flickering light and heat.

"Sit, sit," Gwen insisted, waving me to a settee, which I perched upon uncomfortably. In contrast, she stretched out like a Roman empress.

It was all I could do not to stare at her. She was a member of a select group known as "oldsters." She'd been alive at the cusp of the longevity revolution. From a time before science had perfected the process.

Oldsters were people of great age who were among the first humans to have the wealth and foresight to begin taking the treatments when they were first made available.

The results of those early treatments were quite strange. Oldsters were hale, healthy and even physically powerful at times—but they looked *old*. Their hair hung thin, white and lank as did their sallow skins. The drugs hadn't been able to freeze the aging process until it had taken a dreadful toll.

Seeing an old person wasn't what made a man stare at them, however. Among the poor, plenty of aged persons existed. What was alarming was the horrible vigor these oldsters possessed.

Gwen had feet like those of a pale frog. Her eyes looked too big for their sockets, and her skin appeared stretched over the bones beneath. For all that, she moved with energy. She smiled broadly, and I could see the sharp wit trapped within her ancient skin.

How old was this woman? I could have looked it up, but I hadn't bothered. If I had to guess, I would have said she was past the two century mark. Most of the oldsters were.

"Madam," I began, "I'm sorry to trouble you at this late hour, but I'm afraid a serious crime has been committed tonight."

"Really?" she asked, reaching out and grabbing a bunch of grapes from a nearby table. "You must be talking about that dreadful business at the ballroom. As I understood it, no great harm was done."

As Gwen spoke and I watched, she popped tiny purple fruits, one at a time, into the air. She caught each grape with her mouth, demonstrating alarming dexterity. I was left with the impression she did this often.

"No great harm?" I demanded, forcing my voice to sound even with a conscious effort. "That's hardly the case. I was slightly injured, and my father was nearly killed."

"You have my heartfelt sympathies," she said. "But I'm not quite sure what I can do to help you."

"There are certain questions I'd like to ask, madam."

"Is this, then, a formal affair? You are wearing the uniform of a guardsman, after all."

"Yes, it is," I said. "I've been assigned to investigate the assassination attempt."

"That reminds me," she said, making a fluttering gesture with her fingers. Each of them was tipped with a long, pink nail. "Please do not take offense, but the customary path for a guardsman when entering a Great House for an official visit is through the back entrance. It's a trivial matter, but at House Astra we do prefer that traditions are maintained."

My eyes hardened. I said nothing as I could not trust my words to be civil at that moment. When I felt I could speak in an even tone, I answered her. "As you say, a trivial matter. Now then, can we proceed with the interview? Do you, madam, have any knowledge of—?"

Gwen interrupted me with a loudly stifled yawn.

"I'm sorry, William," she said. "Could I possibly trouble you to return in the morning at a decent hour? I'm an oldster, you must understand, and we're not always in perfect condition. Extended life isn't the panacea that some might have you believe."

"But if you would only—"

"I'm sorry," she said, standing suddenly. "I must excuse myself. My doorman will show you out. Give my best to your parents. I'll send them a gift in the morning, be assured."

Open-mouthed, I stood and stared at her back as she headed for the stairs. She paused at the top and looked down at me from that lofty perch.

"One more thing," she called down to me, "should you decide to return, would you be so good as to use the appropriate entrance next time? It would make things so much easier for everyone."

I was at a loss. The urge to shout, to command her to sit down and answer my questions was almost overwhelming.

But I restrained myself. I was a Sparhawk, and a guardsman. It wouldn't do to throw a fit in House Astra in front of its matriarch. It occurred to me that she might be attempting to elicit just such a response.

"Good night, Gwen of Astra," I said.

She left, and I sighed deeply. The doorman approached, gesturing for me to follow. I frowned as he wasn't leading me to the entrance I'd used not ten minutes before. Instead, he beckoned for me to follow him into a side passage.

"What is it?" I asked him in a husky whisper. "Do you have something to tell me?"

The doorman looked confused. "No sir. I'm merely leading you back to your vehicle."

"But I left it out front."

"Ah, yes, well…it's been moved to a more appropriate location."

Simmering, I allowed the old man to lead me into passages that grew increasingly dim in illumination and less grand of aspect with every step. When we'd found an area with ringing concrete floors and doors so low I was almost forced to stoop to enter them, I passed by the scullery. There, I caught sight of a familiar face.

Her dress wasn't sea-foam green. Nor was her hair filled with sparkling jewels, but she was lovely all the same.

"Lady Chloe of Astra?" I asked.

"The same," she replied.

She turned her eyes toward the elderly doorman, who was gaping at both of us uncertainly.

"You can go, Tobias," she said. "I'll show him the way."

"But Miss…."

"Don't worry, I'm of age now."

He smiled tightly and nodded. After he'd vanished, Chloe offered me her hand. I took it and touched it briefly then let it gently drop.

"To what do I owe this honor?" I asked.

"It's you who honors me, Officer Sparhawk."

For a moment, we looked at one another, full of uncertain formality. In our time, such chance meetings were embarrassing for both parties.

Suddenly, she laughed.

"Such foolishness," she said. "Do you want a drink?"

"I'd love one."

I quickly found that following Lady Astra the Younger was a far more pleasant experience than following the doorman had been. She led me to the kitchens where pots simmered and refrigerators sighed. We helped ourselves to a fine soup and a bottle of the best beer I'd tasted in years.

"Tell me about what happened tonight," she asked me. "Did you really kill me—a copy of me?"

Her eyes were big, and I felt embarrassed to tell her the truth. "It wasn't like you. It didn't speak. It moved with perfectly even steps. It had your face, but that's all."

"How did you kill it? The news wasn't clear."

I shifted on the bench opposite her. Between us was a polished table of fine hardwood and two open bottles.

"I...I thrust my saber into the creature. But I didn't actually kill her. She was shot down by another guardsman."

"Another guardsman? A man under your command?"

"Yes."

Chloe nodded and studied me. I found her gaze discomfiting, and it left me wondering how I'd ever mistaken the false version for a real, living person.

"What are you thinking about?" I asked her.

She laughed. "That's your first question? Don't you want to know if I did it or not? If I built that robot, clothed it in my flesh, then sent it to slay your father?"

"I'm getting to that part," I assured her.

"Ah, make the subject feel at ease first, then elicit information? Is that the procedure they teach guardsmen? But I apologize, I'll tell you what I'm thinking about: here's a man, sitting before me, who had no trouble driving a saber into my back."

"Now hold on," I protested.

"No, no, it's true. Don't bother to deny it. I'm staring because I've never faced a killer before. Especially not *my* killer."

"I understand your concern," I said. "But from my point of view, you're the one I witnessed attack my father. Wouldn't you stop me if the situation were reversed?"

"I suppose," she said uncertainly.

"All right then. Let me ask you a few questions: Did you know anything about this before tonight?"

"You mean the attempted assassination? No, of course not."

"Do you know of anyone from House Astra who might want to take such a drastic action?"

"There aren't that many of us, no more than a dozen. Most don't even visit the mansion if they can help it. Only Mother is truly a political animal. The rest of us have less focused interests."

"Your mother?" I asked, not getting it for a second, then I realized what she must have meant. "You mean Gwen is your mother? I didn't know..."

"Didn't know what? That such an oldster could still produce young? They can, you know. Their organs typically work quite well. It's just some of the external elements that show the years."

"I meant no offense."

"None taken. I'm quite used to it."

She'd revealed a few things about herself I'd not expected her to share with me. I smiled at her, and she looked down shyly. I felt our conversation had taken a different turn. It had become informal, almost flirtatious.

"Perhaps we might meet sometime," I offered. "In a less contentious setting."

She studied her hands. "I'd like that—but I doubt my mother would cooperate."

"I thought you'd come of age."

"Yes..."

Every heir to one of the Great Houses had a key date in their lives, which generally occurred upon their twenty-first birthday. It was an old tradition, but a sound one. After that date, they gained a great deal of autonomy, but could still be disinherited for behavior their parents found abhorrent.

"My date wasn't all that long ago," I said. "It occurred on a Sunday morning in June. That very same day I came downstairs to breakfast and announced to my parents that I intended to join Star Guard."

Her eyes flashed up at me then back to the table between us. I could tell she was not yet comfortable with her role as an independent woman.

"How upset they must have been," she said. "It's a wonder that they didn't disinherit you on the spot."

My face darkened. "Is that what you believe? That I've insulted my family by electing to do an honest day's work?"

"I'm sorry, that's not my opinion. But I know how oldsters think, you see. Did they lecture you on the demeaning nature of a military career?"

"Yes, of course. They reacted exactly as you imagined they might. Disregard my previous outburst. I shouldn't take offense at your accurate description."

"I can tell it's still a sore point for you. I won't bring it up again."

"Back to the assassin, if you will—"

She reached out suddenly and put her hand over mine. I fell instantly silent, and my demeanor softened. For a moment, I believed she'd decided to make a pass at me—but that happy thought faded as I saw she was just leaning to look over my shoulder. Her expression was alarmed, not amorous.

"We've got to get you out of here," she whispered. "My mother's agents must have learned you're still in the house."

We stood and headed for the exit, but we didn't make it. I was impressed by the quality of Chloe's hearing, because the two agents who appeared to block the exit moved with the quiet feet of jungle predators.

They wore midnight blue, from their capes down to their gloves and boots. The powered truncheons in their hands gleamed to match the rage in their eyes.

"You're under arrest, intruder," said the first.

Both had short dark hair, wide shoulders and slits for mouths. The agents had been designed for this job, I could tell. They weren't clones, but they were the equivalent of a special breed of dog. They'd been cultivated for centuries to serve their masters with unquestioned zeal.

Their kind was neither bright, nor thoughtful. But what they lacked in personality they made up for in tenacity, loyalty and vigilance.

"Where is your mistress?" I asked them. "I'll answer to her."

"You've been dismissed," said the first agent. "When it was learned that you'd lingered here, we were released. You will be driven from this place with pain."

The pair stepped into the room, and I automatically placed a gentle hand upon Chloe, urging her away from me. I knew they wouldn't harm her on purpose, but if there were difficulties, I didn't want her to be injured accidentally.

"William, I can stop them," she said. "Agents, there's been a mistake. This is William Sparhawk of—"

"No," I said to her dangerously. "Let them come. I'm a guardsman performing my duties in accordance to Earth's laws and traditions. That must be good enough unless *they* wish to experience pain."

"But William, there's no need—"

"Let me judge the need," I said.

Quite frankly I'd had enough. It was one thing to hinder an investigation and politely delay it, but another thing entirely to send agents to attack a guardsman in the performance of his duty.

Chloe fell silent, but her face was concerned. Her eyes fell upon the sword on my left hip, and the pistol on my right.

"Don't kill them!" she said suddenly.

I would have assured her further, but the pair of agents had been circling to either side of me with unblinking eyes and upraised truncheons. They chose that moment to rush me.

Deciding not to draw either of my weapons, I slipped my hand to the clasp at my throat and activated my cloak. My personal shield, humming with translucent vibrancy, sprang into existence around my person. Looking through it was somewhat like observing the world through a water glass, but I was used to the effect.

The man on my right landed his truncheon first. The weapon crackled with force, and sparks showered down my back. It would have been enough to stun me, or perhaps even drop me to my knees, if it hadn't been for the deflection shield.

I lunged for the second agent, who was only a moment behind the first. I caught his wrist and used his forward motion against him. Spinning around, I thrust his crackling truncheon into the belly of the first man, who had recovered and was coming back for more.

There was a blue-white flash upon contact. The jolt made the victim stiffen, then crumple, vomiting.

The second agent wasn't finished yet, however. He must have fought men in shields before. Perhaps it was part of his training. He snaked his arm around my neck and squeezed.

That sort of attack was effective on a shielded man. A strangling arm didn't trigger the shield's automated defensive behavior because it was slow and organic. A bullet or knife was much easier to identify and repel. Personal shields weren't terribly smart, and they couldn't tell a strangulation attempt from a hug or from the desire to scratch one's own face.

The agent and I strove against one another, grunting and shuffling over the floor.

"William, you've made your point!" Chloe said in concern.

"Almost," I wheezed out, still sucking in a ragged breath now and then. The agent was stronger than I was but less flexible of mind. I thought I had a way to defeat him.

When he had his arm fully around my throat, I leaned forward, forcing him off balance. Then I touched the shield button again. The shield vanished, and his weight shifted as a result.

With a deft twist, I threw him onto the ground and placed my boot on his neck. I still had his wrist with the truncheon in my grasp, but he wouldn't let go of it. He struggled, growling, and I looked at the lady of the house.

"Tell him who I am."

"Eight," she said, "this person is a guest of mine. He's a member of House Sparhawk. He's not to be harmed."

Eight stopped struggling. He lay still, panting and revealing his teeth at me. His twin had managed to climb to his feet again, nearby.

"What are your orders, lady?" Eight asked, coughing.

"Retreat. My guest was just leaving."

I helped him to his feet, but he seemed not to appreciate the gesture. I watched him go with a smile on my face.

When I turned back to Chloe, I realized I'd made an error. She now looked at me as if I were a dangerous stranger.

"I can see now how you must have appeared when you killed my duplicate," she said.

"But, madam..." I said. "I only meant to—"

"I understand your intentions. You wanted to show off. To beat my agents down for daring to do their sworn jobs. They thought they were protecting me."

I rubbed at my throat. "They served you well, I admit."

"I'd like you to leave now, Mr. Sparhawk."

"Guardsman Sparhawk," I said, correcting her. "I wish you good night."

I walked out pridefully, but inside I was kicking myself. Why couldn't I have let them throw me out without thrashing them?

As soon as my mind posed that question, another darker corner of me answered. It was because they'd angered me. Someone had set their beasts upon me, treating me as a man who didn't belong inside House Astra. I wanted to send them a message in return.

I hoped they'd gotten that message—but I doubted it was worth losing favor with Chloe. Whatever the girl was, I was certain she wasn't a murderer. I was already entertaining hopes of seeing her again.

As I climbed into my air car under the baleful eye of Miles Tannish, my mind churned with thoughts. Chief among them was wondering how I could determine who had sent the android to kill my father. Second on the list was how I might manage to get back into Chloe's good graces.

Miles complained steadily as we flew back toward Capital City. He recounted my misdeeds and listed alternate paths I might have taken which would have pleased him more. I didn't listen, but I amused myself by imagining what he would say if he ever learned what I'd done to two of the Astra agents.

-7-

I spent the night at the hospital with the leave of Captain Singh, who'd demanded I return to space by noon.

Altair and her pinnaces, including my own beloved *Cutlass*, were docked at Araminta Station. The station was visible to the naked eye from the city streets. It was a gray and silver disk that hung permanently over the capital.

Riding the sky lift up the umbilical took nearly an hour. It was a commute many were forced to make daily. I was glad I only had to do it now and then.

The umbilical was typical in design. Built with flexible, molecularly-aligned links and force fields, it hung down from space all the way to Earth's surface. At the bottom was a terminal rather like a spaceport, and at the top, which was many kilometers above Earth's troposphere, Araminta Station hung in geosynchronous orbit. There, at the station, most of Star Guard's ships were docked, fueled and repaired.

The umbilical was essentially a thick filament that ran down the center of the structure. Traffic in the form of crescent-shaped platforms glided up and down on either side of the filament.

I rode the sky-lift upward, standing on one of these half-disks. On the other side of the umbilical I often saw other matching platforms zooming downward.

The view was breathtaking as always, but I had no interest in it today. All I could think about were the events of last night, and the lovely face of Chloe Astra.

"This thing is slow," complained Rumbold at my side. "I wish it would go faster."

"We'd all die if it did," I said absently.

"How's that?"

"Friction. The cars are traveling at remarkable speeds, and they generate heat doing so. If the system generated any more heat, the central cable would melt. Have you noticed that we move faster with every kilometer we go upward?"

"No, not really. It seems like we're going slower to me."

"That's an illusion. The Earth is farther away so our speed appears to be dropping when it's actually increasing."

"Huh," he grunted. "If you say so, sir. I suppose it's better than being crammed into one of those bullets they fire up into orbit now and then."

Rumbold was talking about a cargo delivery system that sent containers into orbit at violent velocities.

"The acceleration on those systems would scramble our guts," I pointed out, "but as I was saying, we're actually traveling faster the farther we go up. While we're not in direct sunlight, the umbilical cars go faster still. As we leave the atmosphere the heat is dissipated by the subzero temperatures."

Rumbold fell silent. Together, we stared down at Earth. We could see the curvature of the planet now. He looked at me and frowned as if struck by a sudden thought.

"Did you learn anything useful at House Astra?" he asked.

"Just that Chloe Astra is real and unharmed."

"Do you think she had anything to do with the attempt on your father's life?"

"No, I'm fairly certain she didn't."

"What proof did she offer?"

I glanced over at him, and then looked back down at the clouds. A small thunderstorm shed silver rain out over the Atlantic as we watched.

"She's not the type for subterfuge and assassination. If you'd met her, you'd understand."

He released a rumbling laugh. "She charmed you! The ice prince has been smitten!"

"I don't like that name, Rumbold. I'm just one more officer of the Guard up here. But I admit I've been affected by Lady

Astra's charm. I'm quite certain someone purposefully built a replica of her person and sent it to kill my father—but without her knowledge."

"Who then?"

"She recently came of age. As the newly declared heir to her house, her DNA must be mapped."

"Oh, right. So that in the case of an extreme event, she could be regrown and assume her place at the head of the house..." Rumbold studied me thoughtfully. "I get it. You think that's when they did it. Officials copied her DNA to secure her genetics—and someone stole the file."

"That's my suspicion."

"How will you pursue the matter?"

"It will be difficult," I admitted. "Captain Singh is anxious to go out patrolling again."

Rumbold boggled at me. "That's not so bad! Advancement for a young officer like yourself requires time logged in space."

"Contrary to popular belief, I'm not a desperate rank-climber."

He grunted. "Then you should spend your time convincing your family to vote more funding for the Guard. We can't fly our ships on spit, sir."

I heaved a sigh. "I'm afraid my family is on the wrong side of the fence on that point, Rumbold. They'd be happy to see the last ship in the fleet dismantled and dropped into the sea to make a reef."

"Could that be why someone tried to kill your dad?"

Frowning, I turned back to him. "What?"

"He's on the wrong side of many votes, from the point of view of a spacer. I hate to bring bad news, but I'd say plenty of guardsmen would have liked to see him die last night."

Shaking my head, I returned my gaze to the streaked tubing that flowed by like a waterfall just a few meters away from my face. Above us, the space station was now visible. Closer and closer it loomed, brightening every minute. The station transformed into a glaring white disk as it shifted out of Earth's shadow and into sunlight. In response, the sky-lift's outer casing darkened around us automatically, protecting us from radiation and the blinding glare.

Rumbold's ideas had disturbed me, even though I took pains not to show it. Could my family truly be hated by the rank and file of the Guard? Certainly, my father was well-known as the head of a party of domestic spenders. His policies demanded that tax money be spent on public works first, with the military getting the scraps after. But could that simple truth have driven someone to murder? Worse, could one of my fellow guardsmen be behind the plot?

I felt and heard the sky lift shudder, interrupting my thoughts. We were slowing down as we finally came to a rest at the station. The crowd in our car—there had to be at least a hundred aboard, many with carts of luggage in tow—moved quickly for the exits. The gravity was light, but it provided enough weight on our boots to allow us to walk normally.

Instructions in Standard were blared from every speaker, ordering us off the elevator and into the station proper. The car was on a tight schedule, so we were urged to depart without fanfare.

A two hundred meter escalator took me to customs. As a guardsman, the process was blissfully brief. Emigrants and tourists were given a much more thorough examination.

Joining the general river of people moving to and fro on the station, Rumbold and I were soon ferried by escalators and tubes to our assigned berths. Captain Singh was waiting for us there, and he dismissed Rumbold with a stern glance.

"I'll be off if you don't mind, sirs," Rumbold said. He vanished, doubtlessly planning on raiding a bar somewhere.

My own stomach churned, but I could tell by the look on Singh's face that he had no interest in my personal comfort.

"You requested my immediate presence, sir?" I asked.

"You took your time getting up here, Sparhawk."

"Sorry sir—there were difficulties last night."

"Yes, I heard about that. Who gave you permission to take over the local investigation? We have teams for things like that, you know?"

"I took a personal interest," I answered carefully, "as I was personally involved."

"That's another mystery," Singh said, crossing his arms. "How did you know the assassination was going to play out right then?"

My face froze. I hadn't expected recriminations upon my return.

"Sir, I had no idea the attack was coming."

Singh pulled a computer scroll out of his pocket and thrust it under my nose. I stretched it out and eyed the video it was playing on its thin, glossy surface. I watched myself stand at the bottom of the marble steps. My attention was distracted, that was plain to see. I was watching the android raptly.

I cleared my throat in embarrassment. "I can understand how this might be misinterpreted. But I wasn't expecting the android to do anything rash."

"You're asking me to believe you moved to the base of those steps at the exact moment the assassin attacked by chance? That you were staring at this—*thing* because it was clothed in plastic flesh pressed into a female shape? I don't know which story is worse, Sparhawk."

"May I ask, sir, how you came into possession of this video? Who shot it? Who gave it to you?"

"Does that matter?"

"Yes, it might."

"It was shot by a camera drone. The Grantholm people sent it to me saying it might be useful. I think they're right."

I handed the scroll back to him. "Grantholm. I might have known."

"Isn't your mother a Grantholm?"

"That doesn't mean they consider us to be family."

He eyed me intently for a few moments. "You know what I think, Sparhawk? I think you and your father set this up. I'm not sure why—but it's the only explanation that makes sense."

"I'm not following you, sir," I said, feeling a certain heat around my neck. I fought that sensation down. An outburst of prideful anger wouldn't help me now.

"An assassin in the guise of an Astra female stalked your father. Everyone knows that House Astra is a rival, but they're a rich rival and very much a focus of your father's political machine. The assassin fails, miraculously leaving him unharmed by her attack. Meanwhile you're on hand as the hero to save the day. The whole thing smells like a setup to me."

"Your theories have merit," I said, "but I would point out a critical flaw: my father's party doesn't want any guardsman to look like a hero. That doesn't play into their narrative about budgetary waste."

Singh nodded thoughtfully. "Yes, that's the part I haven't figured out yet. But then, I still haven't figured out why you joined Star Guard in the first place."

"What must I do to prove my true loyalties?"

Singh gave me a predatory smile. "Resign your commission. Take your father's place, urging him into early retirement. Then, with ruthless speed, increase our budget exponentially. At that point, I will happily concede you are a loyal supporter of the Guard."

My lips twisted in disgust. It was one thing for my family to complain about my life choices, but I found it even more disappointing when my fellow guardsmen suggested I should throw away my commission.

"I think I can do more for the Guard on the inside than I can on the outside," I said. "Not everything hinges on a budget, sir."

"I guess we'll have to part ways on that note without finding common ground. A pity—oh, and there's one more thing."

"Yes, Captain?"

"I'm putting you on deep patrol. I think it's best no one sees your face around the station for a time after your recent stunts."

"Stunts? Plural?"

"Yes. First you chased down a harmless merchant accusing him of being a smuggler. He's initiating legal action over that, you know. Then you presided over a very fishy, possibly staged, assassination. You're attracting attention from the admiralty—the kind I don't need."

I wasn't sure what to say. "Did someone draw up charges in either of these cases, sir?"

"Yes, the merchant did. But they were dismissed almost the moment they were filed. Isn't that strange?"

I knew he was insinuating that I'd used my father's influence to defend myself. I had to admit, my father might well have done so reflexively. I wouldn't have been surprised to learn that he'd found out about the charges before I had. When someone accused a Sparhawk of a misdeed, they checked with my father immediately.

"That is strange," I agreed. "A deep patrol, you say? Mars again?"

Smiling still, Singh made a pushing gesture with his hands, suggesting I should think of a place farther out.

"The rocks?" I asked in dismay.

"Now you're catching on. The rock rats out there near Ceres have been requesting a survey be done on various bodies beyond their prospecting zones. They've apparently discovered several high-metal masses near the orbit of Jupiter. They're asking for permission to mine them. As you know, the Guard must inspect all new discoveries before permits are formally drawn up. That's where you come in."

Inwardly, I was appalled, but I kept a straight face.

"*Cutlass* can be refitted and underway within seventy-two hours, sir," I said.

"Step that up. I want you off this station by tomorrow morning. Take supplies with you and perform your maintenance en route. There's one more thing, as this is an exploratory mission, I have to assign you a technical officer. You'll be taking Ensign Yamada with you."

"She'll do find, sir," I said.

Yamada was a good officer and very competent. I had to wonder if she would play the part of a spy for Singh, however, reporting back any mistakes I might make when we returned.

Having no choice, I accepted his orders. Crestfallen, I headed toward *Cutlass'* berth and delivered the news to my crew. Their response was sullen rather than mutinous. They'd been promised shore leave, but they were accustomed to unplanned changes in their missions.

Such was the thankless life of a guardsman.

-8-

Altair's pinnaces went in every direction. We weren't the only ones cast far and wide to look at lifeless rocks—but it seemed to me that our destination was the farthest out.

We traveled past Mars, pressing out to the rocks and beyond, pushing *Cutlass* to her limits. The journey to the outer system took over a month, and we were all worn out by the time we reached the coordinates we'd been given.

The trouble was our ship wasn't built for long voyages. It was small, cramped and lacking in amenities. Just taking enough supplies along was a challenge. We started with a vast supply of food, packed into every nook aboard. The ship had a decent water recycler, and our carbon-scrubbers took care of providing breathable air. The trouble was always food. The pinnace was too small to handle hydroponics. We were forced to load up with traditional foodstuffs, and we had no way reuse solid waste. Even the dining table was buried for more than week on the way out, until we'd managed to eat our way through enough supplies to sit down.

Singh's plan to do our maintenance on the fly was another farce. *Cutlass* was still in bad shape by the time we reached our goal. The yard-dogs had patched her, overhauled her and added new components continuously since her original construction over a century ago—but there was only so much an old ship could take.

Metal fatigue, causing nanoscopic fractures, was a serious problem. The core electronics worked only intermittently. The ship was simply too old and should've been scuttled decades ago.

But she'd been forced to keep flying instead, always in the name of budgetary concerns. Just opening up the hatches that revealed the space between the inner and outer hull was enough to make a man shudder. The region was layered with obsolete components. Old fiber optic cables ran everywhere without purpose. Rather than removing them during upgrades, the yard-dogs had seen fit to sever the existing lines and leave the obsolete equipment in place. Then they'd add new components on top, shoving aside the old ones to squeeze in the new. Doing it that way was faster—and cheaper.

All these realities didn't matter much as long as the ship stayed in Earth's gravity well. She'd been designed for near-orbital work at low speeds, tasks which applied only mild stresses to her frame. Taking her out into the darkest voids of open space was, by comparison, a risky endeavor.

To their credit, my crewmen did their work stoically. They refitted everything they could with an easy familiarity that spoke of decades of experience. They cursed, hammered, and forced sharp edges into worn out sockets—but they got almost every subsystem to operate eventually.

After two months of repairs, slow travel and constant surveillance using the new sensor pods we'd installed on the way out, we finally located the anomaly in space. It turned out not to be as a big of a surprise as we'd thought it might be.

"It's a comet, Skipper," Rumbold said. "It has to be. It's coated in a thick layer of ice, indicating it's from way out in the Oort Cloud."

Data kept coming in, but for me, some of it didn't add up. "I don't know..." I said. "If this comet has grazed the Sun in the past, it shouldn't be so thick with ice, should it?"

"Grazed the Sun?"

"I've projected this rock's orbit. Take a look. Given its trajectory, it must have come close to our star in the past."

Rumbold studied my data. "That does seem odd..." he said. "Most comets that have gotten close to a star are darker. Burned up."

"Right," I said, "on top of that, the shape is unusual. Looks like the head of an axe more than it does a snowball."

"Well, sir, I've seen plenty of oddly shaped rocks. Once, there was this duck-shaped one that—"

"Let's review what we've got," I said, interrupting him. Rumbold's space-stories about mysterious objects were legendary, but I wasn't in the mood this time. "We have metallic readings, indicating a very high density core under a lower density coating of ice. Strange. To me, it looks like a flat chunk of asteroid that's been dusted liberally with frost."

"Yeah, that's about right."

"And that core—the purity ratings are high for any rock," I said, intrigued. I leaned back and crossed my arms. "With this kind of heavy metal content, I think it's clear why the rats are asking for permission to come out here and mine it."

"Excellent work, Captain," Rumbold said with sudden hopefulness in his voice. "Looks like we've done the survey. Should I plot a course back home?"

I laughed. "I'm sure you've got one already set up, Chief, but I don't think we're done yet."

I heard a moan from another of my crewmen, probably Jimmy in engineering. Aboard *Cutlass*, engineering was an area on the main deck in the aft section, so he could hear me if he was listening closely enough. Apparently, he had been. They probably *all* had been.

Cutlass had a crew of nine, including myself. All of my people were experienced hands. Some of them, like Rumbold and Jimmy, were *very* experienced. They were stubborn souls who were as tough as the ship they inhabited. I knew they weren't afraid or surly, but they were worn out. None of them wanted to do much investigating. They would have preferred to stamp "approved" on this rock and turn around promptly, heading home as fast as we could make our rust-bucket fly.

I could understand that, but I wasn't going to shirk my duty for crew comfort. Nodding thoughtfully, I made a fateful decision.

"Let's go in for a closer look," I said.

Long sighs were released. Many of my crewmen had been holding their breath, it would seem. Without a word, Rumbold laid in the course. I approved it with a double-tap, and we powered in carefully toward the target.

We'd been braking during our approach and soon our flight path intersected the object. Instead of running into it, I had the crew ease us closer, stabilizing the craft and matching the target's course and speed.

Once that was done, we edged even closer, nudging our way toward the object and matching its trajectory precisely.

"We'll be right on top of it by tomorrow," Rumbold informed me. "What's the plan?"

"We'll do a full orbital scan, looking for anything special."

"Special?"

I looked at him. Rumbold had a good poker face, but I could tell he thought I was a little crazy this time. He wanted to know what I hoping to learn.

"Regulations state that a survey must include a full up-close scan," I said. "If, that is, the object being surveyed is nonstandard in composition or structure."

"So we're going by the book," Rumbold said. "Nothing unusual there. We always go by the book. Very well, Skipper—if you don't mind, I'll be taking a nap while *Cutlass'* nav system gets us nose to nose."

He leaned back and settled into his chair, sliding his cap down over his eyes. We didn't have separate quarters. Our crash seats were our bunks, although we had two private zones below decks with hammocks and null-G showers to relax in. For the most part, the crew just slept on their seats—Rumbold pretty much lived on his.

I felt an urge to further explain myself. "This isn't just about regulations, Rumbold."

He lifted one corner of his cap to look at me questioningly. I could tell he didn't believe me.

"I'm a stickler for rules, yes," I admitted. "But this rock—it's not normal. There may be plenty of odd things in space, but I want to know more about this one."

"Well sir, we'll satisfy your curiosity in the morning. Now, if you don't mind..."

"Not at all."

Rumbold was soon snoring, while I continued sifting through the constant trickle of sensor data. It was indeed an oddly shaped, frozen rock. It was about a kilometer across and half that in depth. Except for its shape, the Solar System contained literally millions of comparable objects.

I could have let the rock go, but I didn't want to give Captain Singh any excuse to tell me I'd failed to perform my assigned mission. Perhaps I was still stinging after being rebuked by him for chasing down the smuggler back on Earth. Whatever the case, I was determined to do a more thorough job this time.

After a few hours of reviewing data, Rumbold took over and manned the conn while I slept. *Cutlass'* internal lights brightened gently several hours later, simulating a rising sun. All over the ship, my crewmen stretched and yawned. It was another glorious morning in the Guard.

"Any changes overnight?" I asked Rumbold.

It was part of his job to continue reviewing all the data the ship had stored up overnight. If anything serious had been detected, the ship would have awakened us for guidance. But there were always reports and details that the AI deemed less than critical, but which still deserved our attention.

"Fuel levels are one percent lower than expected," Rumbold said. "Could be that the deceleration had a miscalculation, or that our engine chambers are leaking gas again."

"What else?"

"The comet seems stable. During the night, it rotated twice as we approached. There are variations in the surface…hmm."

"What?"

"Probably nothing," he said. "A few chunks of debris have been detected in loose orbit around the rock."

"What kind of debris?"

"Metallic objects—not large, but too big to be dust."

I looked at him. "Something made it out of that ice coating? Could another object have struck it recently, breaking through to the core?"

He shrugged. "Possibly."

"This is an opportunity," I said. "Let's pick up a sample."

"The robot arm is malfunctioning, sir," he pointed out.

"I thought that was on our to-be-fixed list."

"It was, but we had to prioritize."

"Let me guess: Jimmy didn't want to suit up and go out there to do it?"

"Well, sir…"

"Jimmy!" I shouted aft. I didn't bother using the intercom. I knew he could hear me.

"Coming, Skipper!"

Hand over hand, Jimmy propelled himself toward us using the loops and handles placed along the ceiling and the back of each crewman's seat. *Cutlass* was too small for artificial gravity of any kind, so we'd all become quite good at maneuvering in null-G.

Old Jimmy yawned and chewed a breakfast bar as I explained to him that he was going outside personally to gather one of those floating objects for me.

My reasoning wasn't lost on him. He knew the score. He hadn't felt like going on a spacewalk for the last month, so now he was going to make up for that.

Without argument, he headed for the airlock. He sealed his suit with Rumbold's help. A few minutes later he was outside, drifting around the ship on a tether.

Working in space is physically taxing. It's rather like treading water. Your suit resists you, and you have to hold onto things to get leverage. The experience was uncomfortable, too. There were always hot and cold spots inside your suit. Often, your foot might be freezing while the back of your neck was burning. High-priced newly constructed spacesuits rarely had these difficulties, of course, but *Cutlass* wasn't equipped with the best of the line. In fact, we had some of the most outdated suits you could find in the Guard.

Still, Jimmy worked stoically. He climbed out of the airlock dragging a specimen bag, a magnetic hook, and a long probe-stick. Working his way over the ship's outer hull, he saw several of the objects drift by, but he couldn't catch them.

Watching on our screens while we ate a dismal breakfast, Rumbold and I stayed alert. Any man spacewalking was in danger by definition. Quick action on our part could save his life if something went wrong.

While watching, I noted something odd—a flashing object passed by.

"Was that one of the pieces of debris?" I asked over the com-link.

"Yes sir," Jimmy confirmed, "that sure was. I can't catch the fast ones. They're orbiting the comet at a pretty good clip."

Frowning, I tried to zoom in with the cameras, but failed to get a better image. I backed up the recent video cue instead, and I was rewarded with several frames that depicted the object in question.

"Jimmy?" I called out.

"Yes, Skipper?" he grunted back. He was up high on the starboard sensor array, trying to get a good spot to catch one of the objects.

"What do those things look like to you?"

"I don't know. Oblong, about the size of a flashlight, I'd say."

"A flashlight? Are they metallic?"

"Yes, certainly. I thought that's what we were looking for."

I framed through the video, my mind racing. We had a dozen blurry frames, that was all, but that was enough. The object was regular in size and shape, with a bright metallic finish. Whatever it was, it *had* to be artificial.

I froze in my seat, staring at the spinning object captured on my monitor. Then I turned to Rumbold. I could see his bloodshot eyes bulging in my direction.

"It's metal, sir," he said, almost whispering. "An artifact—not high grade ore."

"*Refined* metal. And it's presumably been built into this shape purposefully. What have we found out here?"

"I don't know, sir, but I'm fairly certain your hunch to investigate was a good one. To think that we almost gave some rock rat permission to salvage this find without—"

A siren went off then, startling us both. My screen flashed a red block of print on it. The block had two words stenciled in the center that displayed glaring, blinking words.

James Munoz, the red words repeated, *James Munoz*. Jimmy was dead.

-9-

"All hands, emergency stations!" I shouted. "Rumbold, deploy the arm!"

He glanced at me apologetically. "It's still broken, Skipper."

I muttered curses. "Of course," I said, my heart and brain racing.

This was my first death—my first real emergency. We'd run down a score of threatening smugglers, and we'd faced radiation, misfiring engines and leaking tanks, but this was different. One of my crew had died of unknown causes. This was the moment when *Cutlass'* captain had to step up and perform.

Forcing myself to suck in a breath and think, I read the data on my screen. Jimmy was dead—but that could be a false reading. He might have a severed line, or—

"Jimmy," I said. "Respond."

Nothing came back.

"Rumbold," I said, "keep trying to reach him. I'm suiting up."

His gauntlet reached out to touch my arm.

"Sir," he said, "the captain shouldn't leave the bridge when the boat's in trouble."

"The ship is in immediate danger?" I demanded.

"Well, no sir…not that we know of."

"Munoz has suffered some kind of accident, I'll wager. I'm going to retrieve him quickly, and we'll withdraw as soon I get back into the airlock."

"Sir...I still say you shouldn't go."

Part of me felt I should listen to him. He was my senior, noncom or not. He'd been in space longer than I'd been alive.

"I can't send another man out now," I said in a low voice.

Rumbold shook his head. "I'm not suggesting that. We should burn out of here and proceed with our investigation from a safe distance."

I hesitated for less than a second. "I'm not leaving Jimmy out there. I sent him into space, and I'm bringing him back in, dead or alive."

Moving decisively, I double-checked my helmet and my air tanks, then slid into the airlock. The air began to pump out, but I was impatient. I blew the outer seal, wasting a few cubic meters of precious oxygen.

Riding a gentle puff of air out into space, I caught a loop of steel on the hull and began to hand-over-hand my way down the ship's skin.

As soon as I was outside the ship, drifting in the cold void, I felt the hairs on the back of my neck tickle and stand up. I knew that whatever had nailed Jimmy could just as easily do the same to me.

The methods by which a man can die in space are truly countless. There's no more dangerous environment we've ever tried to inhabit. Radiation, heat, cold, vacuum—every aspect of open space is deadly and uncomfortable.

People often compare flights aboard spacecraft to a voyage over an ocean, but the comparison only goes so far. Men who fall overboard into an earthly sea might survive for days or even weeks.

But there were no such false hopes out here. The void was as unforgiving as it was eternal.

It didn't take me long to find Jimmy. He was drifting, still tethered to the ship near the exhaust ports. Moving along the hull carefully, I kept one of the magnets on my hands, knees or elbows in contact with the ship at all times.

I soon reached him. Grabbing him by the thick cloth of his suit's shoulder, I dragged him back toward the airlock. I didn't take the time to investigate what had happened to him. Every second out here was potentially deadly.

Three grunting heaves took me to the airlock, where the hatch hung open. I dragged him inside and noticed his body was already stiff—his hands seemed to be stuck together, somehow.

Stuffing us both into the tight airlock, I struggled to close it. My breath was labored, but I managed to fold myself into the coffin-like chamber with Jimmy.

"Skipper?" Rumbold called worriedly. "I'm reading high stress levels. Are you okay, sir?"

"I'm fine. As soon as this door cycles open—wait, I think Jimmy's alive!"

"How's that, sir?"

"I'm seeing steam on the inside of his helmet. He's breathing. I can't—"

The airlock hatch swung open then, and I tumbled down into the ship. Rumbold was there, waiting with several others. They had haunted eyes and upraised hands. We were both brought down into the ship with firm care.

In the red light of the cabin we examined Jimmy. He was alive, but he wasn't in good shape.

"Something's taken off his hand!" Rumbold said, marveling. "See here? His right hand is gripping the stump of his left wrist."

Rumbold was right. Jimmy was in a strange state, but I thought I understood what had happened to him—if not why.

"Something severed his left hand at the wrist," I said. "The blood that didn't boil away froze solid."

"I've seen more than my share of accidents in space," Rumbold said, "but this is a weird one."

We worked on Jimmy, who was still breathing shallowly. His suit had done its best to save his life, but he'd lost consciousness. Losing air and blood, he'd grabbed onto the stump. It must have leaked out blood which quickly froze, creating a poor seal.

"He didn't even cry out," I said, marveling.

"He probably didn't have any air in his lungs for it," Rumbold said. "Decompression—he'll have permanent damage, most likely. Poor kid."

Jimmy was twice my age, at least. But among this crew, that wasn't anything unusual.

Rumbold himself, having the most medical training of the crew, performed the task of patching up Jimmy's wound. Then he sealed him into the automated medical pod.

"The stump is clean," he said. "Some fibers from the suit are in there, but not much else."

Working as gently and quickly as we could, we reached into the pod with gloved hands. We didn't have a full robotic survival system, but our single pod was capable of keeping a man alive by supplying carefully measured sustenance and injecting programmed drugs. It couldn't perform surgeries or other complicated medical procedures. It was too basic and out of date for that.

"No sign of the hand, was there?"

"None," I said. I shook my head, staring out through the clear polymer shell. "It's a bit too dark out there to find a missing body part."

"Pity. A regrow will set him back years."

"The Guard will pay for it," I said with a certainty I didn't feel.

Rumbold chuckled and shook his head, but he didn't openly reject my premise.

After a half hour or so, Jimmy woke up. His breathing was ragged and labored. Sweat sheened his face despite the whirring of fans inside the pod.

His eyes sought mine. "I'm not dead," he said, almost in a whisper. He seemed quite surprised.

"No, you're not!" Rumbold laughed, clapping me on the shoulder. "The skipper went nuts and took off after you, dragging you back in here."

Jimmy's mouth was drawn in pain and shock. He was under sedation, but the drug only went so far. The medical computer had recommended we keep him comfortable, but not to lower his blood pressure too much. He'd already gotten a packet of artificial blood, but it had been past its expiration date. We didn't want to push things.

"Skipper—did you see them? The tubes?"

I stared at Jimmy for a second. "Tubes?"

"Flying around—I caught one. That's what killed me, I think."

"You're alive, Jimmy," Rumbold said worriedly. He was thumbing the interface on the medical computer, double-checking everything.

"No," Jimmy said. "I'm not—or at least, that thing out there thought it had killed me. I'm sure of that much."

"You're not making sense, Jimmy," Rumbold said gently. "I'm going to increase your sedative, hold on—"

"Not yet," I said, leaning against the glass. "Jimmy, listen to me. You said you caught one of the objects. Where is it?"

"In my bag. Did you bring it back in?"

I cursed. I hadn't thought to do so. There had been equipment, but I'd left it all. Just dragging Jimmy back into the ship by the harness had been a struggle.

"Disgusting," I said. "If I hadn't been so worried about my own skin, I'd have taken the time to retrieve the bag."

"Skipper," Rumbold said, shaking his head. "You were thinking of safety first. No spacer lasts long without having his priorities straight when he's on the wrong side of his ship's hull. Jimmy's breathing, as are you, and that's the best result we could have hoped for."

I looked up and nodded as my eyes roved over the hull he spoke of.

"Chief, what kind of acceleration did you put us under when we left the object?"

"You could feel it, I'm sure. Less than a G. Nice and steady, so Jimmy wouldn't get thrown around."

My eyes drifted along the ceiling to the airlock and fixated there. Rumbold followed my gaze.

"Oh, no sir! Don't even think about it."

"I'm going out again. Watch the conn for me."

Rumbold complained and cursed under his breath while I suited up and climbed back outside through the lock again. He'd pulled us a good distance away from the object. I could

73

barely see it anymore. Perhaps if the Sun hit the surface just right...

"I've killed the engines," Rumbold said in my ear. "Find anything?"

"No, not yet."

Climbing over the ship from stem to stern, then switching to the far side and doing it again, I'd almost given up when I spotted Jimmy's bag.

There it was, hanging from a parabolic antennae. I smiled, took the bag gently and slung it over my shoulder. Then I crawled my way back into the hatch.

The crew cheered me this time as I entered the main cabin. I could see by their relieved faces they'd thought I might not manage to beat the odds twice.

It made me glad to think these old spacers wanted me alive more than they wanted me dead. When I'd first come aboard there hadn't been a kind eye in the group. My appointment to command tiny *Cutlass* was initially assumed to have been gained through leverage and nepotism. From their point of view, I was a rich snot from the Academy.

The truth was my family would never have helped my career in the Guard, not directly. My father didn't approve of it. He'd *wanted* me to fail. Service in space? For his heir? I was an embarrassment, a public relations disaster.

But my crusty crewmen hadn't understood the attitude of House Sparhawk. They'd assumed my commission had been arranged, rather than earned. I hadn't made a direct effort to enlighten them. If they'd understood how my family really felt about the Guard, they might have disliked me even more.

Despite the cold beginning, I'd managed to win them over and at some point over the years, and we'd bonded. We'd come to trust one another. Men who are forced to live in cramped conditions and depend on each other for a long period of time either go mad and kill one other, or they become brothers. Fortunately, we'd chosen the latter path.

"What'cha got in the bag, Skipper?" Rumbold asked.

As I was curious myself, I unslung the bag and opened it. I stared at the object inside, unable to speak for a moment.

Of all the things I'd expected to find, for some reason, this wasn't among them—although in retrospect perhaps it should have been.

The object was oblong and tube-shaped. When I drew it out into the open, white mist drifted from its cold surface. It was smooth metal, identical to the first such tube I'd seen aboard a smuggler's ship several weeks ago.

"It's one of those *things*, sir!" Rumbold gasped in recognition. "A tube like the ones that smuggler was transporting!"

Nodding slowly, I stared at the object.

How could such an artifact be so far out in space? And in such numbers? The sensors were now tracking hundreds of similar objects in the vicinity. I suspected they were all identical floating tubes.

"A frozen embryo," I said, checking the contents briefly before resealing the container. "There's no doubt of it. But what's an embryo doing out here in deep space, orbiting a comet?"

Rumbold's bloodshot eyes ran over the tube, but he didn't reach for it. He stared warily as if it were a venomous snake rather than an innocuous steel tube.

I, for one, couldn't fault his cautious attitude.

-10-

We withdrew a thousand kilometers from the object and reported our findings to Captain Singh aboard *Altair*. I described the injured crewman, the readings from the comet, and the inexplicable cloud of tubes floating in the area.

Due to the vast distances involved, we had to wait for the better part of an hour to hear his reply. When the signal finally came through, I didn't display it publicly as I suspected it might be bad for morale to do so. Instead, I put on a worn mind-link headset. Utilizing the twin implants inside my skull that stimulated my optic nerves directly, I watched as Singh's recorded message was replayed.

Singh slouched in his captain's chair aboard *Altair* and regarded me with an expression of frank disgust.

"Let me get this straight, Sparhawk," he began. "I sent you out on a routine mission to investigate a rock and approve it for exploitation. Somehow, you've managed to get a crewman seriously injured during the execution of this simple task. Worse, upon discovering evidence of a small cargo of dumped goods, you made an emergency call and further wasted my time and strained the Guard's budget."

He heaved a sigh and shook his head. His attitude was that of a parent speaking to a small child.

I felt a natural urge to shout back at my superior, but I knew it was futile in several ways. For one, my words would take an hour to get to him. And even if he'd been able to hear me immediately, he was unlikely to listen.

"Where do I begin?" he asked rhetorically. "Your lack of experience in these matters is painful. The worst part is this tendency to jump to absurd conclusions rather than assuming the most likely scenario is the correct one until proven otherwise. Let me explain: you've uncovered evidence that some rock rat or another has flown out there and tried to start mining illegally. From your own admissions, they carry these embryonic trade goods. Don't you find the most likely scenario is that the pilot suffered a mishap, and he lost part of his cargo? We can only hope he lost his life as well."

Gritting my teeth, I listened to the rest of his transmission.

"Here are your new orders: immediately approve the site for mining and bring your ship home. We'll have the tube you found analyzed—although it's obviously pointless. *Altair* out."

Glaring and muttering to myself, I removed the mind-link and examined my board. Working with rapid swipes and tapping motions, I accessed the online regulation books. After a few moments of perusal, I found what I was looking for.

For the first time in hours, a smile graced my features.

"What's the good news from *Altair*, Skipper?" Rumbold asked. He'd been watching me carefully throughout the exchange, and I could tell he was concerned about my focused behavior.

I turned to him and flashed him a toothy grin.

"There is indeed good news, Rumbold," I said. "Excellent news, in fact. Did you know the salvage identification bylaws of 2125 stipulate that only the senior officer present at a discovery site can legally determine its status?"

Rumbold's expression became cautious. "I…uh…I'm not sure how that applies to our current situation, sir."

"Use your imagination, man," I responded with enthusiasm. "It means that Singh can't make an inspection determination from Earth orbit. I, without a doubt, am the senior officer present. I'm going to mark this find's status as undetermined. Plot a course for home."

Rumbold did as I asked glumly. He didn't seem to be enjoying my newfound regulatory standing.

It was about three hours later that we began a long, slow burn back toward the inner planets. We watched as our fuel supply dwindled, along with the local presence of Jupiter.

Some six hours after that, another communication came in from *Altair*. It just so happened that I was sleeping at that point. Rumbold tapped me awake.

"Sir?" he hissed, his eyes wide and staring. "Sir, it's Singh again. He sounds upset."

Rolling into a sitting position on my seat and stretching, I activated my mind-link again and played Singh's message directly into my skull. He wasn't happy, just as Rumbold had indicated.

"Lieutenant Commander Sparhawk," he began sternly. "I've been monitoring all transmissions from your quadrant to Guard Command, just in case you decided to send your report in directly. I've yet to receive any updates from your expedition. Your original report has still not been amended. Fix the situation immediately. Singh out."

Chewing over my options, I drank stimulating fluids laced with glucose and caffeine to wake myself up. I realized that I couldn't ignore him completely.

Sprucing up my appearance as much as possible, I addressed the camera in my console formally and spoke to it.

"Captain Singh," I said. "Unfortunately, I'm unable to comply with your wishes. As the senior officer present during the inspection of the object in question, I was not able to classify it as innocuous, nor was I able to determine exactly what it was. Additionally, we've now expended too much of our remaining fuel supply to return to the object for further investigation. My report to Guard Command must, therefore, stand unedited. I thank you for your concern, and I apologize for any misunderstanding."

Nearly two hours passed as the message flew at the speed of light toward Earth. I imagined that a reply would be transcribed and transmitted in return, but I could only wait to hear what it was.

During that time, my tiny ship continued to accelerate. It would take days to reach our full cruising speed. At that point, we'd shut down the engines. We would coast sunward until we came close to Earth weeks from now, where we'd begin braking. When we came close to home, we'd allow ourselves to be caught by the planetary gravity well and slip into a stable orbit.

When the incoming message light blinked again, Rumbold glanced at me. He made no move to open the channel himself.

"Is it my imagination, or are you sweating, Rumbold?" I asked. "Have our air conditioning systems failed again?"

"It does seem a little warm in here to me, sir," he said smoothly. "Perhaps it was that long burn we pulled. The heat shields aren't as good as they were decades back."

I gave him a half-smile. We both knew he was sweating due to the possible content of Captain Singh's reply, but since it would have been rude to point this out directly, I avoided doing so.

Instead, I opened the channel and listened to Singh's response privately.

The captain's face had transformed into a mask of rage. His fingers gripped the arms of his chair like claws.

"All right, Sparhawk," he said. "We've pinged your vessel. According to our estimates, you're correct, you don't have the fuel to go back to the object and return to Earth in a timely manner. However, you could return and stay on station until a relief ship arrives. I'm hereby ordering you to do exactly that. If you do not comply, I'm going to formally request that you be transferred off my command roster. While I can't directly revoke your commission, I can assure you that you'll never see another promotion in the Guard. Make your choice and get back to me. Singh out."

Slumping back in my seat with a sigh, I turned to Rumbold. "Kill our engines and begin to glide, Chief."

He stared at me for a long moment. "But sir...we aren't up to cruising speed yet—"

"Immediately," I ordered.

Rumbold reached out and throttled down the engines. We coasted in silence, and weightlessness quickly resumed.

Rumbold watched meuneasily. "A bad message, sir?"

"Indeed."

"What are your orders, sir?"

"I'm thinking."

He fell quiet. The rest of the crew muttered and watched us curiously. They wanted to know what was going on, but they didn't quite dare to approach and demand answers. That was just as well as my mood had turned grim.

Singh had called my bluff. I was within my rights to disobey his order to amend my report. However, he was within his rights as my commanding officer to punish me for my transgressions. He could post me out here as long as necessary to get me to write a report that pleased him.

I fought to push back my anger and resentment. I'd signed with the Guard, and like it or not, I was subject to the whims of my superiors in situations like this one. As I always did in such moments, I returned to the letter of the law for guidance. Honorable service and the discipline of the Guard, those two pillars always clarified my thinking.

After surveying the pertinent regulations, I could find no loopholes. Singh could order me to stand this post indefinitely. In the meantime, he could freely trash my reputation with the flag officers while I was stuck out here, unable to defend myself in person.

"Rumbold," I said, "what's Jimmy's prognosis?"

"Pretty good, sir," he said. "He's stable, and he'll make a full recovery after they grow a new hand for him back home."

"That's going to have to wait," I said.

"Excuse me?"

"Captain Singh has seen fit to order us back to the object to reevaluate it. He'll send a relief ship eventually as we'll no longer have sufficient fuel to return after complying with his orders."

Alarmed, Rumbold tapped rapidly at his board. He slapped a hand to his face and covered his eyes with it when he'd finished.

"You're right. It would take years to return without relief. We'll be stuck out there."

"An unfortunate circumstance."

Rumbold closed his eyes and bared his long teeth. "I almost wish Jimmy was dying."

I looked at him. "No you don't," I said.

He sighed. "You're right, Skipper. No, I don't...but may I make a suggestion?"

He'd lowered his voice and his eyes were intense.

"Speak."

"Change the report right now and take us home, sir," he said quietly. He was almost pleading.

His statement indicated that he'd listened in on Singh's transmissions. I could have chastised him for this, but I chose not to.

"I can't do that," I said. "There's something going on out here, Rumbold, and I'm not going to paper it over. The object—it's not safe. It's not normal. Didn't you feel it?"

He hesitated. "Yes sir, I guess I did. Very well. Reversing course."

The crew groaned and complained aloud, but in the end, we returned to the strange object that drifted in space toward Earth. Too bad it was moving so slowly.

As we closed again with the anomaly, I wondered about my choices. Was I being pigheaded? My mother would have said I was. But I just couldn't bring myself to alter my report.

I couldn't bring myself to lie. There was something odd going on out there. I hadn't intended to investigate and learn the truth alone—but now, I had no choice.

My tiny ship and sparse crew were going to be stuck out here in the dark with this mysterious object for a long time.

-11-

There was little sense of urgency in my crewmen as we turned around and faced the anomalous mass we'd left behind in space. Instead, there was an air of wariness, almost dread.

We no longer called it a comet—we didn't know what it was, but we knew it wasn't something natural and harmless.

"Take us in slow, Rumbold," I said. "Let's conserve fuel and look for opportunities."

"Opportunities? What kind of opportunities, Skipper? A chance to die mysteriously?"

I glanced at him quizzically. "What are you talking about? The object isn't dangerous."

His eyes all but bugged out of his head as he studied me. "Have you forgotten Jimmy's hand, sir?"

I shrugged. "A freak accident caused by a scrap of debris—probably by one of these tubes whirling along in a fast orbit."

Rumbold shook his head. "The boys in back have run the numbers. It's not possible, sir. The tubes aren't sharp. As blunt at they are, they'd have to be moving at an amazing speed to sever a man's hand."

"A freak meteor, perhaps. A rock the size of a bullet might have struck out of the blue. We're only half an AU from the belt, after all."

"I'd agree, that's the most likely case, but as I examined this mystery I came upon another possibility."

"Explain."

"These orbiting tubes—they're moving too fast. They should be able to escape the minimal tug of an object this size. That's when I discovered this snowball has more gravity than it should have."

His statement made me frown. On the face of it, Rumbold was right. Only dust could be effectively captured by the gravity of a rock this size. In all the events of the day, I hadn't had time to consider the ultimate nature of the object before us.

"Let's see the gravitational readings," I said.

Rumbold had been waiting for that request. He instantly flicked his screen and sent the data to my console. I examined the details with a growing sense of disbelief.

"How's this possible? That object can't exert such a powerful pull. It's like a small moon—I don't believe it. The sensors must be off."

Rumbold shook his head slowly. "That's what I thought at first, too, when I noticed the readings. That thing is pulling as if it's made of collapsed stardust."

Turning back to the raw imagery, I could see the object growing on my screen again. Dark edges. Bright reflective surfaces. My mind raced.

"There are only two possibilities," I said. "Both are alarming. Either that object actually has a collapsed core, and is an escaped chunk of stellar debris, or it has an artificial field around it. In either case, it has a stronger gravitational field than it should."

"Like I said, sir. It's a mystery—and it's dangerous."

After considering my options I spoke again. "Let's approach more slowly this time. Try to analyze the pattern of debris. Track it carefully, map it. We want to get close without damaging the ship."

Several shifts passed as we revolved around the object at a safe distance. We hung back, staying farther out than we'd done before. I didn't want any more strange accidents.

"Rumbold," I said with a yawn some thirty hours later, "you've been with the Guard a long time. How come you never sought promotion into the officer ranks?"

"Ah," he said, smiling at me. "You'd think an old spacer like me would seek it out, wouldn't you? That I'd demand my turn at the tiller. Well sir, let me explain—none of us here want your job."

I eyed him in surprise, uncertain if I was being insulted or enlightened. I suspected it was a little of both.

"Go on," I said in a neutral voice.

"You see, sir, it's like this. A man who's in the officer ranks is eventually forced to retire. There are only so many spots left in the Guard, and every young fellow who graduates from the Academy dreams of a command—like you sir, no offense."

"None taken. Continue."

"Well," he shrugged, "that's about all there is to say. I want to serve in the Guard, so I take the jobs that are least sought after. When the cutbacks come every few years, I've always been passed over and left alone."

I nodded thoughtfully. "That's dedication," I said. "I'm impressed."

"That's part of it, certainly."

Glancing at him again, I frowned. "What's the other part?"

Rumbold shifted uncomfortably. We'd served together for years, but I'd rarely asked him probing questions about his personal choices in life. I guess that's because we'd never been in space so long together before. A week-long mission didn't compare to the one we were on now. Before this was over, we would experience many months of being just a few feet apart.

Rumbold sighed. "I suppose someone ought to tell you our motivations. Why would rattling old men like Jimmy and I choose this life? The truth is we don't have much choice. It's the longevity drugs, sir. Active-duty personnel get them for free. Once we're out of the service, well, we won't be able to afford them."

"Ah," I said in sudden understanding. "I get it. You *can't* leave. If you did, you'd die."

"That's the long and the short of it, Captain. We're old, and we're fragile. Without those drugs…" He shrugged.

"You might not last a year," I said thoughtfully. The whole system seemed monumentally unfair. But longevity was a tricky thing. Long ago, Earth's government had publicly stated they would dole out extended life on the basis of service and merit.

But the truth was that Earth's wealthy citizens could expect to live on without concern for centuries. Average men like Rumbold could never afford the treatments on their own. They had to serve in the Guard to stay alive.

"Rumbold, would you mind another personal question?" I asked.

"Another one? All right, why not?"

"Tell me, how long have you been around? Can you recall how life was on Earth before the Cataclysm?"

"No," he said. "I was alive back then but only as a baby. My parents often spoke of the early days, however. They said it was a golden time. Trade ships came every month from the colonies bringing foods, fabrics and entertainments we can only dream of now. Visitors came as well, some taller than any earthborn man. Others sported strangely colored flesh or wore outlandish costumes. What I would give to have seen them myself in person."

"Yes..." I said thoughtfully. I'd been half-joking when I'd asked him if he'd been alive so long, and his answer had surprised me. The Cataclysm had broken the network of wormholes that connected Earth to her colonies over a hundred and fifty years back.

How old did that make Rumbold? A hundred and sixty? Amazing.

"My age should better explain why I must stay in the Guard," he continued. "When I started taking longevity drugs, they were primitive. Today, the new formulas rewrite a man's DNA. They erase errors at the tail end of the sequence and youthful cells are produced in abundance. But they didn't have that kind of technology when I started."

"Right. What was the old method? Cellular replacement?"

"Yes, exactly. The first drug in wide distribution was called Rejuv. We thought it was a miracle back then, and so it was. But all it did was cull out cells that were produced with errors. It didn't stop the aging process completely. Consequently, my body continued to age for half a dozen decades, albeit slowly. When the rewriting drugs came out, my original programming had faded away. Even the best drugs can't repair and improve my cells, returning youth, because all of those original DNA strands had been edited out. It's as if they lost my disk, and I'm running on a RAM-only copy."

He seemed to find his predicament funny, but I found his references dated in the extreme. Modern computers never used anything like disks or RAM.

He laughed until he had a coughing fit, then laughed some more. I smiled politely, as I often did for the benefit of my most ancient crewmen.

In time, we plotted a course through the debris and eased our way closer to the surface of the snowball. Nearly a week had passed by the time we found ourselves touching down on the surface.

During that time, Singh had occasionally contacted me for updates. He informed me that *Altair* had been ordered to render assistance to *Cutlass* directly because no other ship was in range.

These new orders hadn't improved his mood. He'd meant to punish me with a long sit out in space, but that objective had backfired. Now he'd been ordered to fly out and meet me.

Fortunately for everyone involved, *Altair's* engines were far larger and more efficient than those possessed by my tiny pinnace. They'd reach us within a week's time. We were to investigate cautiously until the destroyer arrived.

Rumbold watched me carefully when I received this news. "You know sir," he said in a conspiratorially low voice, "we could just sit here and wait. We've surveyed half this snowball from a few meters above the surface. No one could claim we haven't done our assigned task."

I shook my head. "No," I said firmly. "I'm going for a walk. I want Weaver and Yamada to join me. You stay at the boards to watch over us."

"There are likely to be crevasses and the like," he protested. "This slushy surface is unstable and dangerous. Let's just send the probe—"

"You know as well as I do our probe is faulty," I said.

Rumbold shrugged. "So? If it falls in the snow and gets sucked to the bottom, who's to know? We'll make our report, showing we did our best, and wait for *Altair*."

On the surface of it, Rumbold's suggestions made sense. His ideas were cautious and almost foolproof. All I had to do was drag my feet a little more, and we'd be cleared of all responsibilities.

But I wasn't interested in shirking my duty. Far from it. I found it annoying, in fact, that others continually suggested I should do so.

"Tell Weaver and Yamada the three of us are exiting this ship," I repeated more forcefully. "We're going for a walk in one hour. Issue them spacesuits with the best integrity among those we have left."

Releasing a heavy sigh, Rumbold stopped arguing and did as I'd ordered. Soon, he had the two spacers I'd requested dressed and prepped for the walk. They were all grumbling, but not loudly enough for me to overhear their specific words. That was acceptable in my book.

When the hour had passed, we climbed out onto the surface of the tiny, ice-crusted world. Yamada was slight and quiet. Weaver was the polar opposite, a loud, broad-shouldered man with opinions he couldn't keep to himself.

I had no idea then that the three of us were about to change the fate of all humanity.

-12-

We were hip-deep in the slushy surface with the first step. The frost covering the rock was like the finest powdered snow imaginable back on Earth. Fortunately, the gravity was only a fraction of what we were used to. If we'd been heavier, we would have sunk in and possibly vanished.

"All right, hook up belts and keep vigilant," I said. "We'll start off tethered to the ship."

"With any luck we'll take that down too, "Weaver complained, "when we find a crevasse that's deep enough."

I'd brought Weaver along as he was one of the most muscular, physically capable people in my crew. He was quite young, compared to the majority, as was Yamada.

Unfortunately, he also had a big mouth. I'd known that, but I'd selected him anyway. I almost turned to reprimand Weaver, but I decided to let his comment pass.

My crew wasn't made up of the easiest going people in the fleet. They'd been assigned to *Cutlass* as a form of neglect at best, a punishment at worst. They had a right to be annoyed.

Ensign Yamada brought up the rear of our three-person team. She was the closest thing we had to a biologist aboard *Cutlass* and the only other officer. She was essentially a medic with training in scientific instrumentation. Unlike most of my crew, her longevity treatments had kicked in early in life and she looked to be less than thirty years of age—although I knew she was older.

She had out a device in her hands that operated as a mobile sensor array. It didn't have much range, but this rock wasn't very large to begin with.

"I'm getting a reading off to our right," she said. "A lower density area of snow."

"Thinner?" demanded Weaver. "How can it be thinner? This is like swimming in cotton candy as it is!"

"General direction and distance, Yamada?" I asked.

"Two o'clock. Less than a hundred meters out, Skipper."

I veered right and headed in the indicated direction. Weaver trudged after me. He was up to his chest at times and almost floundering. He was the heaviest member of the team, and the snow seemed to be hampering his movements the most.

"Can I ask you something, Captain?" he asked.

"Certainly," I replied.

"Why are we heading toward a hole? When we get close, we'll slide right in. You might not have been on small, ice-crusted rocks like this before. You don't want to find the thin spot, let me assure you."

"I understand your concerns, Weaver," I said. "How far now, Ensign?"

"Another fifty meters should do it, sir."

"How large is the affected area?"

She tapped at her instruments for a few seconds before answering. "Looks like it's about ten meters around. Sir, it's a perfect circle."

Frowning, I almost halted. While still aboard *Cutlass*, we'd circled this entire rock multiple times, pinging it from space. But being down on the surface gave the instruments a different perspective. I didn't recall a ten meter wide hole, filled with snow or not, but we might have missed it.

We moved forward another dozen steps then halted. I felt my way along every step now, nudging the snow aside and making certain I had firm footing before putting my full weight on each boot.

"Am I close?" I asked.

"Very."

"I don't see anything."

"Take a look, sir," Yamada said, struggling up next to me.

"Careful," I said, not letting her pass my position.

Weaver came close too, and he forced his helmeted head in between the two of us to see the instrument.

The image was clear. Directly in front of us was a circular area of lower density snow. It was distinct, and it had a regular circumference.

"I don't like it," I said. "Unlimber the torch, Weaver."

We'd brought along a drilling laser. It wasn't much, but it was more than up to the task of removing thin ice.

"Step back, guys," he said. "This will probably vaporize the snow with an explosive release."

I stepped back with Yamada, and the two of us checked the lines that linked our belts to Weaver's belt. We set our feet as he directed the torch toward the snow and lowered his outer visor.

When he powered up the device, our vision was immediately clouded by a gush of vapor. Within seconds, Rumbold was trying to contact me.

"Captain Sparhawk?" he demanded. "Are you all right, sir?"

"We're fine," I said, wiping steam and chunks of ice from my visor. "We've found a low-density area and we're burning off the ice to take a look."

"Is that wise, sir? This surface is unstable. You could—"

Overhearing Rumbold, Weaver had stopped operating his torch.

"I'm well aware of the dangers, Chief," I said. "I thank you for your concern. Continue, Weaver."

He shrugged his big shoulders and went back to work. After he'd worked for several minutes, I ordered him to halt. After a time, our vision cleared.

We stepped up to the lip of a circular hole and stared down into it.

"How can this be here? "Weaver asked.

"It's a mining plug," Yamada said. "A test hole drilled by a tug, probably."

I nodded in sudden understanding. "The miners requested permission to exploit this object, but they apparently ran out of patience."

"Yes. They've already started drilling. But there is a layer of fresh ice over the spot—that indicates they must have drilled this hole quite a while ago."

"Either that, "Weaver suggested, "or they covered up their tracks. Look here!"

He stepped around the rim of the hole, which was several meters deep and perfectly circular in configuration. He plunged his gauntlet down into the snow and tugged, pulling an object up into our view.

"It's a sensor-blot," he said, bringing it to me.

"These are illegal," Yamada said, examining the device.

It looked homemade. It was about the size of a man's fist, and several small dish antennas sprouted from the central metal hub.

"That's why we couldn't see this hole from space, "Weaver said. "They didn't want us to find it."

"I've noted that criminals rarely wish to be discovered," I said, examining the device. Using a tool from my belt, I switched it off and tossed it aside.

I stepped to the very edge of the hole. It had frosted up again almost immediately after Weaver had exposed it. I gazed into the find.

"The interesting question," I said, "is why someone is working so hard to keep this spot a secret. Weaver, keep burning away the snow. I want to see what's at the bottom of this hole."

"On it, Skipper," he said, shouldering forward and going to work.

I noticed both of them had changed in their attitudes. At first, they'd given the impression they were humoring their young commander. Now, they were paying full attention.

Weaver was working with purpose. He was as curious as I was.

Ensign Yamada, however, had become more cautious. She'd retreated a few steps to the limits of her tether and stood there, watching with a frown.

I walked to her side and we were able to see one another despite the geyser-like venting Weaver was sending into space with his torch.

"What's the matter?" I asked her. "You seem worried."

"Aren't you? This is freaky. I don't like this rock, and I don't like the fact there's a hidden hole on the surface of it."

"It's our job to investigate."

"That doesn't mean I have to like it."

I chuckled. "Indeed it doesn't."

"Sparhawk?" called Weaver. "Come see this!"

Moving with careful hops, I joined him at the rim of the hole. The gases thinned and froze again, and I was soon able to see. A dark shape lay in the hole.

"Is that a discarded spacesuit?" I asked.

"Close," laughed Weaver. "The suit's occupied. It's a body. I burned it slightly, sorry. Didn't even see it until after I'd crisscrossed over the legs a few times."

"My God," Yamada said, coming closer and staring in with us. "Who is it?"

"Some rock rat, "Weaver said in disgust. "He screwed up. They usually don't live long, you know. Not more than twenty years on average after leaving Earth. Even the people who are born out here only make it to thirty or so."

"A dead man," I said thoughtfully. "Way out here. Let's get him out of that hole. We need to know how he died."

I sent Weaver down to retrieve the body, which he did with ill grace. He complained for a time, claiming that the body was tethered, but he managed to cut the line and haul it out eventually.

The march back to the ship with the feather-weight body on our shoulders was less jovial than it had been on the way out. The corpse had been burned and disfigured by Weaver's torch. I'd begun to wish I'd brought shovels instead of a laser to the site.

"Skipper?" Yamada said as we approached *Cutlass*. "I'm sorry, but I've been thinking."

"What's wrong?"

"I don't think we should bring the corpse into the ship."

I halted. Weaver stared at us like we were crazy. "We're almost back inside! Don't stop now!"

"What's the problem, Yamada?" I asked.

"It's my job, as the senior science crewmember aboard, to warn you there could be contagion of some kind."

"Oh come on, "Weaver groaned. "You just don't want to do the autopsy. Admit it."

"That's not it," she said, looking from one of us to the next, then back to the dead body we were carrying. "I just can't recommend that we carry this person aboard."

"Are you enacting protocol?" I asked her calmly.

She hesitated, then nodded. "I am."

Weaver groaned aloud and dropped his half of the dead man we were carrying. The corpse fell stiffly into the snowdrifts.

"Very well," I said, my attention fixed solely upon Yamada. "I require a clear statement of your reasoning, and I won't hesitate to countermand it if it seems frivolous."

"Understood, Captain," she said. "Let me explain myself. This rock—it's not normal. I don't understand what's going on out here, but I'm sure this is more than a comet or an asteroid. That's point one."

"Go on."

"Further, we've had two deadly accidents. Jimmy nearly died, and this man was even less lucky. Both incidents have no clear-cut cause. Therefore, as is my responsibility, I can't condone taking this body into the enclosed space of *Cutlass* and possibly exposing the entire crew to whatever killed this individual."

I nodded thoughtfully, going over the regulations in my head. "Proven hazardous environment. Unknown dangers encountered… Yes, I see your point. We'll leave the corpse outside. You can set up a tent on the ice to perform the autopsy."

Yamada stood still for a moment in shock. "Sir?"

"You heard me. Weaver, get a survival unit out here. I'll help you set up camp, Yamada."

Weaver hooted and climbed into the ship's airlock. He returned shortly with several packages. It took more than an hour to set them up, but once we'd done so, I sent Yamada into the tent to figure out what had happened to the corpse we'd found.

I wasn't without sympathy. The look on her face was a mixture of disgust and shock. I doubted she'd participated in an autopsy since her days in training, and then she'd probably not been alone. But I wanted to know what had happened to the man we'd found.

After I learned the truth, I intended to head back to the spot where we'd found him and dig deeper into that hole. All the way to the bottom.

-13-

I wanted to question Yamada about it as soon as she was done with the autopsy, but the woman looked the worse for wear. She came back to the ship and went straight to the showers. She exited after several minutes and moved into the molecular cleansing booth which used ultraviolet light and tickling micro vibrations to tease loose and kill all pathogens.

At last, a little sweaty and breathing hard, she came to the bridge to make her report. Seeing her state of mind, Rumbold eased out of his chair and let her slide into it.

"Human, sir," she said. "A rock rat, as we figured, judging by the elevated radiation levels in his bone marrow. Lots of heavy metals too—he doesn't have any implants, so he must have been taking pills to clear his blood for a long time."

I nodded patiently. All this I'd surmised just by looking at him.

"Cause of death is harder to determine," she went on. "But I think it was blunt force trauma."

Frowning, I tried to envision how this could happen in space on a low-gravity object. "Someone beat him to death? Were there skull fractures? Was his visor intact?"

"That's the thing...his visor's blast shield was rolled shut. Rock rats face a lot of radiation out here, and they often have full metal shielding around their heads. Otherwise, they can get dementia over time."

"Okay, so how did he die of blunt force trauma if he wasn't hit on the head?"

"His helmet was dented, but it held up. The rest of his body was only protected by a relatively thin spacer's suit. He was pummeled to death. It was as if he'd been hit by a thousand rocks—or one hammer hundreds of times. Most of his ribs were broken as were all four of his limbs."

I winced, envisioning such a death. It didn't sound pleasant.

"If he was murdered," I mused, "it sounds like his murderer was enraged and wanted him to suffer. It would have been much easier just to shoot the poor guy."

"Yes—but I don't think it was murder. I think it was something else. You see, all the injuries appear to have come from the direction of the object—from deeper down in the hole."

We made eye contact as I absorbed what she was saying.

"You mean he was down there and something—or someone—fired a massive number of rocks at him?"

"I think so."

"Hard to envision. It might have been a drilling accident."

"Maybe, sir. What are we going to do now?"

Rumbold had maintained his silence up until this point, but I could see by the look on his face he wanted to join into the discussion.

"What is it, Chief?" I asked.

"Let's just wait here. I've got an update from *Altair*. They're only a few million miles out, and they'll be here in the morning. They've already begun braking hard. Singh must be really pushing those engines. There'll be hell to pay when he gets back to Araminta Station and has to explain his reckless use of fuel to the quartermaster!"

He laughed, but the sound turned into a cough and died. I was staring out a porthole. Frost rimed the glass, and the light outside was a bluish-white.

"He's speeding out here," I said with sudden certainty, "to make sure he's on hand if we discover anything unexpected."

"What, sir?" Rumbold asked, bewildered.

"I don't know, but it's the only thing that makes sense," I explained. "Singh doesn't love us, wouldn't you agree?"

"Hardly. He hates us, more like."

"Yes. So why is he hurrying out to help us now? He wanted to leave us out here as punishment. But now he's changed his mind. He probably got around to reading those reports I sent him. I think he figured out that we've found something interesting and he wants in on the find."

Rumbold's eyes bugged at me. "I can tell you've got something in mind, sir. Something I'm not going to like."

"We're going out again, Rumbold. Let's find out why rock rats, smugglers and even our brave Captain Singh are so interested in this discovery."

There was less grumbling than before as we prepared to exit the ship again. I thought the rest of the crew might be growing curious as well.

Yamada was an exception, however. She clearly needed a break. The unexpected autopsy duty had taken its toll on her.

"Yamada," I said, "you're in charge of the ship in our absence. Rumbold, Weaver, follow me."

Rumbold made a gargling sound. There were no intelligible words in his response, so I ignored it.

Within the hour we were back out on the ice again, plowing through the snow. Fortunately, the snow only fell lightly here. About a centimeter a day, as far as I could determine. Following our trail to the site was easy.

Along the way, I had a thought. Radioing Yamada, I asked her opinion on the matter.

"This is another mystery," I said. "There isn't enough precipitation on this rock to dust over the hole we found, not in a thousand years. How did it fill in?"

"Someone must have done it deliberately," she answered back. "Either that, or there was some kind of impact that kicked up the snow and it settled down again since the miner died."

"Yes, those are the only two answers that have occurred to me." I thanked her and disconnected.

Rumbold hung back when we reached the lip of the hole. He stared from a safe distance. With a blade or a gun, the man was a stalwart companion. But he didn't like holes on alien worlds.

I spent several minutes pacing around the location while Weaver kept beaming, melting snow in the hole. It was soon ten meters deep—then fifteen.

Several things occurred to me during the interval while he worked. One was the surprising lack of equipment. This hole was perfectly round and somewhat conical. It sank down into the ground as if laser-cut—which I expected it had been. But, where was the laser that had done the cutting? And for that matter, where was the dead man's ship?

"It seems he was left behind," I said after I explained these discrepancies to my crewmen. "Something big burned this hole then retreated after he was killed."

"Either that, or they dumped him into the hole after beating him to death," Weaver offered. "Have you ever been to a rock rat cantina, Skipper?"

"Can't say that I have."

"They're like stray dogs—worse than that. They pack up to do jobs, but they're as likely to shank any man they don't get along with as share their loot with him."

I had my doubts about his statement, but I didn't argue. The rock rats were mean and almost lawless, but they had their own code of honor. They couldn't have survived in space for so long without it.

After another few minutes, we were down to the bottom of the hole. I examined the steaming walls and the blackened floor. It was rough and pitted.

"That's a different material, "Weaver said of the bottom. "They sealed it."

"What do you mean?"

"I've seen things like this," he said, rappelling down the side some fifteen meters to the bottom. "This is a plug. A mix of polymers meant to seal a ship's hull. They burned their way down this far, and they sealed the bottom. How strange. Do you want me to burn through it, sir?"

I stared down at him. There he was, aiming his laser drill at the dark, dimpled surface at the bottom of the hole.

"No," I said.

"Why not? We came this far. I doubt it's very thick."

"Because," I said calmly, "I think if you burn through that plug, you'll die."

He stared at me uncomprehendingly, but when I tossed down a line, he climbed out quickly enough.

When he'd rejoined me at the top, I explained my thinking.

"This object we're standing on—it isn't a comet," I said.

"Well, I kind of figured that much. It's too dense for that. Must be from out-system…maybe."

"What I mean is," I said, kneeling and rapping my gauntlets on the edge of the hole. The material didn't crumble. It was so uniform, so dense. It reminded me of concrete more than anything else. "What I mean is this entire thing is artificial. It's a construct."

The two men gaped at me as if I'd gone insane.

Rumbold laughed first, uncertainly. "Are you having us on, sir? There's never been a ship this large. It's almost as big as Araminta Station!"

"Almost," I agreed, "I looked it up. Think of it: we're standing on a ship. A ship a kilometer long and nearly half that in thickness. The snow is just frosting on top, coating the external hull."

"If it's a ship," Weaver demanded, "why cover the hull in snow?"

"Maybe they wanted to be invisible. Just one more cold rock in the sky. Or maybe, the ship is dead and collected ice over the years as it drifted. I think that explanation is more likely."

"Hold on, sir!" Rumbold said. "What makes you so sure it's a ship at all?"

I pointed upward. The two men gaped at the stars, but they didn't get it.

"Remember the tubes? Thousands of them. They orbit this ship—but where did they come from?"

"I don't know," Rumbold said.

"Well, I think I do. The rock rats came out here, and they found this gap and they cut their way through the hull. When they managed to break in at last, an explosive decompression occurred. Whatever chamber they cut into was full of those tubes. They came pouring out into space, and then they orbited this gigantic craft."

"What proof do—"

"Remember the body?" I asked. "That man was probably using a laser drill like yours, Weaver, but bigger. He cut into the ship, and the rush of tubes pummeled him to death."

The two men stared at one another, then at me. They stopped talking.

"But a *ship*, sir?" Rumbold said. "How can it be? Earth's never built anything so large. Not even the colony vessels were this size."

"You're right about the old ships," I said. "I looked them up last night. Some were quite large—but never this big."

The two men stared into the dark hold. Frost sifted down the sides of it, and the refrozen liquids formed glassy runnels everywhere.

"What do we do next?" Rumbold asked.

That was the question I was wrestling with. Part of me wanted to burn through that plug to see what the rock rats had sealed up inside this vessel. What had they found in there? What had they wanted to keep from escaping?

But I passed on that idea as soon as it occurred to me. I didn't have the resources to explore a ship this large. I wasn't even sure if Weaver's drill was up to the task of breaking through. I didn't want to start something I couldn't finish.

"I'm going to find out what kind of people brought this ship here to our star system," I said.

"How can we do that?"

I pointed upward again. "These tubes—they contain their young. We'll take a tiny sample and test it. Maybe from several tubes. Then we'll know who sent out this ship—if not their intentions."

With that, we gathered our things and retreated from the edge of the hole. We made our way back to the ship, and I ordered Yamada to carefully open the tube that Jimmy had collected.

Ensign Yamada's face was drawn, and her eyes were red-rimmed, but she nodded and went to work immediately.

-14-

Yamada worked quickly and never took a break. I appreciated her dedication.

"Well," she said a few hours later, "I ran the tests twice, and I'm still confused."

"What's the trouble?"

"The samples...I took a few cells from each of the three tubes. The first sample came from the tube Jimmy captured in space. The crew found two more of them in the vicinity of the ship using metal detectors while you were gone."

"Excellent," I said. "Three samples should be conclusive."

"They are...to a point. The samples are all human embryos, as expected. But that's not all: they appear to be the *same* human embryo."

I stared at her for a moment. "Are you saying these are illegal clones?"

"Yes. One hundred percent matches. The phenotypes, every dichotomous trait—it all matches for all three samples. There's no mistake."

"Hmm. Perhaps that's why they're out here, hidden? Full clones would be destroyed if detected by Earth authorities."

"Right," she said, "but I don't think that's what's going on here. These clones are not from Earth, Captain."

She had my full attention at this point. I could tell Rumbold was listening intently as well, while trying to pretend he wasn't.

"Explain," I said.

"I projected the growth of the clones to adulthood. The program took a while, but the data is conclusive. All of these women, if implanted in a growth chamber, would become large, muscular and obviously built for a different biosphere."

"How are they different?"

"Well, for one, these unborn women are highly resistant to radiation—that has to be engineered in. They're also powerfully built. I'll show you the computer projections."

"Did you say women?"

"Yes sir. All the clones are female."

She tossed a file to my screen, and my computer caught it. I examined the displayed image of an unusually large human female. She was Asiatic in appearance. Her face wasn't unattractive, but her body was built with thicker musculature than normal. I could tell the bones under those heavy limbs were quite solid.

"She looks dense," I said. "Powerful."

"That's probably true. If I had to guess, I'd say these women would weigh fifty percent more than a typical earth female of the same height—and that's without an ounce of fat on them."

It was a lot to digest. I wasn't sure where to begin. Female clones built like weight-lifters? Who would engineer such people much less manufacture thousands of them?

"Good work, Yamada," I said, studying the image. "I want you to capture ten more samples and test them all."

"Is that really—?"

"Yes, I believe it is. When Captain Singh arrives, I want no arguments. We're going to do our homework. No one aboard *Altair* will deride us for our mistakes, because there won't be any. When I tell Singh I've found a ship full of hulking clones, I want to be certain that I am correct."

"I understand. I'm on it, sir."

"Have Weaver help with the collection duty," I suggested. "He'll love it."

She moved off, calling to Weaver. I soon heard a gust of complaints from him. I smiled bemusedly.

Rumbold's red face loomed close. "Sir? Did I hear rightly? *Clones*, sir? From a heavy gravity world?"

"It would seem so."

"How could they make it through? The wormholes have been shut down for so long... They must be Betas. To think that they could really be here..."

"Betas?"

"Oh, that's right. You're probably too young to remember. I doubt they even bother to tell kids about the various colony worlds these days. Just putting real history in a history text might be considered subversive. But you look them up. Betas settled on a world that was twice the size of Earth. The gravity was supposed to be crushing, but they reengineered themselves to take the load. These clones—I bet they come from Beta or some other world that's similar."

Intrigued, I began searching our onboard intranet for details on the colony worlds. There wasn't much other than a listing for *Colonists, Beta Cygnus*.

It seemed that they'd settled on a planet less than eighty lightyears from Earth. The world was hospitable in every way: it was warm, wet and gently irradiated by a golden sun. The only trouble was Beta Cygnus was too big. The gravity was crushing. The colonists had worked on the problem for years, but it wasn't known if they'd ever come up with a solution. When solar flares knocked down our transportation network, we lost our only way to contact the colonies.

These embryos were proof to me that they had solved it.

"One riddle down, many more to go," I said aloud to myself.

"Excuse me, Skipper?"

"Rumbold, if the Betas solved their genetics problem and came up with a person who found their new planet comfortable, wouldn't it make sense to manufacture a large number of copies of that person?"

"I—I guess it might, sir. But the thought is a strange one for us."

"Yes," I agreed, "and there may be many more surprises to follow."

"What do you mean, exactly?"

"If one ship made it here, we have to assume more will come. We'll learn more about them when they do."

"Everything will change..." he said thoughtfully.

"Yes, I would suspect we're facing a series of cultural shocks. We have to expect plenty of cultural deviations if we're going to reunite with our lost colonies. Think about it: when the Betas were severed from our society, cloning was in its infancy, and Rejuv was a brand new product. They've gone their own way since then. They know nothing of our laws, our proscriptions."

Rumbold shifted in his seat and leaned closer to me. His breath was laced with stale coffee, but I was used to it and didn't twitch away.

"Are you really that certain, Captain," he said in a loud whisper, "that we've discovered colonists out here? Embryonic or otherwise?"

"Yes, that's my conclusion," I said. "But that's not the puzzle that's bothering me. What I want to know is *how* these tubes got here."

"You know what the boys in the aft section are saying about that, don't you?" he said, eyes rolling side to side to see who might be listening.

The ship was buzzing with equipment and Weaver was making a great deal of noise while Yamada helped him suit up. That distraction gave us excellent cover. Not for the first time, I wished I had a private stateroom aboard *Cutlass*.

"Tell me," I said.

"They think this ship is dangerous."

"I would say it's a harmless derelict," I said.

Rumbold waved a stubby finger at me. "No sir," he said. "That's not necessarily so. There are things about the past...well, things only old men like me know about anymore."

Giving him a puzzled look, I was about to probe for more details when my console lit up. A large contact had been detected by on our long-range sensors.

"It's *Altair*, sir," Rumbold said. "It has to be."

"Excellent. I've prepared my report. Transmit it to Singh now."

Rumbold eyed me dubiously. "Are you sure you haven't put anything in there you might come to regret later?"

"No," I said firmly. "The truth can't be regretted. The truth simply *is*—and it's my duty to report it as accurately as possible."

Rumbold started a booming laugh that ended in another coughing fit before he transmitted my file.

I glanced at him in annoyance. People often asked me to edit my findings and opinions, but it was my belief that doing so would be shirking my duty. I hadn't become a Star Guard officer to be in the business of blurring lines and covering up facts. If I'd wanted that, I could have studied at my father's side in politics.

Singh didn't contact me right away. Perhaps he was reading my report. But when he did finally open a channel, it was blinking yellow. That indicated it was both private and urgent.

I donned my mind-link and took the call privately.

"Are you out of your head, Sparhawk?" he demanded.

"If you read my report, sir, I believe you'll find it to be quite rational."

Singh stared at me. He wasn't using his eyes to see me—not exactly—and I wasn't using my eyes to see him. Instead, our optical nerves were receiving a signal that fooled our brains into believing we were seeing one another. The effect was somewhat dream-like, and I often saw background imagery that was less than distinct. It was as if the man I was talking to lived in a world of swirling mists. Even parts of his body blurred and the flesh ran at times. It was an oddity of the technology that everyone got used to eventually.

"I'm going to go over this with my techs," he assured me. "If you made a mistake—or worse, if you embellished something to make a case for yourself—"

"That's not in my character, Captain."

"No," he said thoughtfully. "I don't suppose that it is. That's a pity, because I was really hoping things wouldn't turn out like this."

Frowning, I cocked my head and studied him. "I'm not sure that I understand—"

"Good-bye, Sparhawk," he said. "I salute you for service well-rendered. I'm sure I'll be asked to say a few words at some ceremony when I get home. And I assure you that I'll make you shine like an angel with wings of gold."

My mind went cold. I couldn't believe what I was hearing—what I thought I was hearing—in my commander's voice.

"Captain Singh," I said sternly. "Don't do anything that you'll regret."

He laughed. "I regret everything—but it's too late now."

The connection broke, and I slumped back into my seat. A sudden disconnection of a mind-link was a stunning event. It felt as if I'd just been startled awake in the middle of a dream.

Looking around me, I realized it wasn't a dream. It was a nightmare.

Weaver was already outside the ship, and Yamada was just climbing into the airlock. Most of the others were suited up, but they weren't wearing helmets. I had to get them out of here.

"All hands!" I shouted. "Prepare to abandon ship. Suit-up immediately. Seal your partner's suit, this is an emergency!"

Upon hearing my announcement, the crew around me froze for a split-second before they went into furious activity. They dropped whatever they were doing and scrambled to obey my orders. They hadn't survived as veteran spacers for so many decades without responding quickly when an emergency was announced. No one even asked the nature of the trouble—they just *moved*.

In the hard vacuum that makes up the vast majority of our universe, hesitation can kill. They all knew this, and they hastened to seal themselves up in their suits. They probably were planning on asking me questions—but not right now. Later, when the unknown emergency had passed, that would be soon enough.

After slamming my own helmet onto my head, I turned to Rumbold. "Chief, topside shields up, full power!"

"Shields, sir?"

"Do it!"

He hastened to obey. The generators whined, protesting the sudden increase in power demands. Relays clacked all over the ship, and the running lights downshifted into a deep red. We were bathed in a world that was suddenly the color of blood.

"Warm the engines. We might have time."

"Time for—?"

He could not finish the question. The first bolt stabbed down from the starry sky. An iridium beam of particles could slice apart a tiny ship like *Cutlass* like shears cutting through paper. Our hastily deployed shield deflected it—barely.

Outside the ship, light and radiation were dispersed with violence. I recalled that Weaver was still out there, and Yamada had been in the airlock only moments prior to the blast.

"Weaver?" I called, flicking at my screen which had dimmed and gone out, but then came back a moment later.

"He's...he's dead, sir," Yamada said in my ear. "I can see him outside. He's been burned to a crisp. What hit us, sir? Was it one of these damned clones?"

"No," I said. "It was Singh. He called down a strike from *Altair*."

Gasps and cries of rage and dismay swept the crew.

"Fire our missile, Rumbold," I ordered. "Override the safety locks. Target *Altair*."

"But sir, it won't even get to her!"

"It doesn't matter."

"But...we can't fire on our own ship! That's a Guard vessel up there!"

"I know. Fire the missile, then turn all power to our shields. It will take time for them to cycle up the particle-bolt again. While they focus on destroying the missile and our heavily shielded pinnace, we'll have time to escape."

"Escape? Escape to where?"

"To wherever these clones came from. Where else?"

Rumbold looked at me as if I were mad, but with a trembling hand, he reached out to his board.

He activated the overrides as quickly as he could. Alarms sang. The computer spoke, displayed, and audibly warned us with various dire noises that we were breaching security protocols.

We ignored everything the ship said even though she almost begged us to change our minds. At last, overcoming her great reluctance, *Cutlass* fired on *Altair*.

-15-

We fled through the snow, plunging across the tiny world in a frozen twilight.

The sun was on the far side of the world at the moment. Each "day" here was just over an hour long. I had to wonder if I'd ever see my home star rise again.

Behind us, a second bolt struck *Cutlass*. We turned our heads away, and still the light of the released energy was as bright as an arc-welder's torch. The shield absorbed the blow, but only barely. It was dim, brown-orange and crackling. When the next bolt came, the shield would buckle entirely.

"If they've fired a missile back at us…"

"I know, Rumbold. If they have, we're dead. We'll be so much molecular dust, returning to the stars where our matter originated. But don't worry, they won't fire a missile."

"How do you *know*, sir?"

I glanced at Rumbold. Through his darkened visor I could make out his features, twisted in fear. It was a wonder that a man who was as old as he was could still fear death. Hadn't he cheated it long enough?

Or maybe, it was the precise fact that he'd lived so long that made him fear death all the more. I didn't know, and I didn't care to ask.

"If they were going to fire a missile, I think they would have already done it, and in my estimate it would have landed by now.

"If that's so, why aren't they firing a bird? It would be unstoppable. Lying here on the surface, *Cutlass* wouldn't stand a chance. The concussion would reverberate from the ground and crush her."

"Yes. But think: why are they doing this? Why is Singh doing this?"

"I've got no idea. He's mad."

"I don't think so. I think he's protecting this object. I think he wants it for himself, or he's in league with someone who does. He's also smart enough to know that if I die House Sparhawk will demand an investigation, and it's a lot harder to explain unaccounted-for missiles than particle beams."

"Singh is a traitor then?"

"Anyone who orders a ship under his command to sit on a rock then fires on them when he comes out to relieve them of their duty... Yes, I would describe Singh as a traitor."

Yamada hustled up next to me. She was carrying a bag of equipment that was almost as large as she was. Due to the ship's tiny gravitational field, she was able to bear the load easily.

"Sir," she said, "I don't know if it's safe to attempt to blow that plug and dig inside this rock. We don't know anything about the interior."

Her worries forced a chuckle out of me. "Unfortunately, we know how things are on the surface," I said. "Right now, I'm willing to take a chance."

"Understood, sir."

She fell back, and we soon reached the plug. "Blow it open," I ordered.

Yamada finished prepping the charge, but before she could detonate it a massive cascade of gas and energy flared overhead.

We threw ourselves down into the snow and planted our faceplates into it. After a few moments, realizing I was still breathing, I dared to roll onto my back.

"It was our missile," I said. "Our single missile. Nice to know the warhead was still good."

"I hope it killed Singh," Yamada said with intensity.

I glanced at her. I knew that she'd had feelings for Weaver. We all cared about one another. After spending so much time together inside *Cutlass*, we were like family. We bickered—but we cared, too.

"Detonate that charge!" I ordered.

"Everyone hug the ground!" she shouted.

Those of the crewmen who were just getting to their feet threw themselves flat again.

A silent explosion puffed into the dark sky. Ice crystals, vaporized metal-rich rock and hot gas rushed by us. We felt, rather than heard the explosion. A deep vibration came up through our bellies and our bones.

Approaching the smoking crater cautiously, we weren't overcome by a gush of tubes released from the interior. Instead, we found ourselves staring down into a dark, frozen space. The opening was obscured by floating vapor that the stabbing lights on our suits couldn't penetrate.

"Well," I said, "there's nowhere else to go."

Letting myself slide down the side of the crater, I sank feet first into the unknown. Behind me, my crewmen gasped and called out in alarm.

I didn't heed them. I let myself go. With the very low gravity, it wasn't like a plunging fall, but the sensation was alarming all the same.

The starry sky vanished overhead. Above, all I could see was a misty gray light.

In front of me was a blinding, moving cloud. My suit lights didn't penetrate the vapor, instead they were like headlights in fog, they blinded me as much as illuminated anything.

I fell for what seemed like a very long time and panic almost overwhelmed me. What if this entire object was hollow? What if it had no bottom, just a far side? I might have just killed myself in a unique fashion.

Fighting down an urge to cry out in fear, I kept drifting downward.

"Sir? Can you hear me, Captain Sparhawk?"

It was Rumbold, calling faintly over my radio.

"I can hear you. I'm still falling. Don't come in yet. Wait until I land and report back."

Rumbold chuckled. "You don't have to worry on that score!"

After a few more seconds, I touched down. It wasn't a shock, but rather a welcome jolt to my legs. My knees buckled, and I pitched forward. I put out my hands blindly, afraid I'd smash my faceplate into something hard and sharp.

Breathing hard, I got to my feet again and looked around. I was standing on a smooth surface. It was a floor—or a deck. I knew right away that it was too even to be natural. There was grit and debris, but that was probably due to the break-in far above.

"All right," I said, "come down one at a time. I'll step aside and shine a light to guide you."

"Do you see a way out, sir?" came back Rumbold's worried reply.

"No," I said, "but *Altair* will soon scan the surface and detect you. We have to get inside before they fry anyone who's exposed. Finding a way out will be our next order of business."

"Mind if we hook up a line, sir?" he asked with a hint of pleading in his voice.

I thought about it. If Singh was going to be thorough in his efforts, a hole with a line leading down might give us away. But, I didn't want to be stranded below.

"Good idea. Do it and come down now."

Soon, eight of us stood on the strange deck, looking around and almost huddling together.

"What do you think is going on up on *Altair*?" Rumbold asked me. "How do you think he got his crew to fire on us?"

"I don't know," I said. "Probably a lie or some kind of false order from Earth. In either case, I doubt he'll come down to talk to us. He wouldn't want his crew to hear our side of the story."

Rumbold slapped his hand on my shoulder. "I get it now. I was wondering before why he was communicating to you solely through the mind-link. That's good for private calls—but why would he need privacy?"

I looked at him and nodded. I was following his thoughts.

"I think you're right," I said. "He did that on purpose. He didn't want anyone else to overhear our conversations. If he'd made the call in the clear, he'd have given away evidence of his treachery."

"Yeah, at the very least, it would be easier to investigate."

"Skipper?" Jimmy said, walking toward us. He was still cradling his stump.

I felt for the man. He hadn't gotten a break since we'd left Earth.

"What is it, Jimmy?"

"I found the source of the tubes. Come over here."

Following him, I came to a shelving system loaded with thousands of tubes. They were arrayed like wine-bottles in racks. Each had a coded microdot on the rack, and on the tube itself.

"It looks like they were locked into place," Jimmy said. "See these brackets? But some kind of disruption must have occurred. Many of the brackets broke open and the tubes fell on the deck, spilling everywhere."

"That's clear," I said, eying a mass of tubes rolling around on the floor. "But what I don't understand is why they would need to label these tubes individually if they're all clones of the same being."

"That is strange," Jimmy said. "Maybe some clones are more important than others. Or maybe there are several types of clones. We only tested a few of them."

He shrugged and nudged a few rolling tubes around with his boot.

Because the vapors were clearing now, I could see the extent of the space we were in. Judging only by our suit lights and the cavernous roof, I figured it was about the size of a large gymnasium. The ceiling was less than fifty meters away. The roof gently arced overhead with the top of the hull. The walls were vertical and even. I guessed the chamber to be about a hundred meters square in floor space. Much of that area was occupied by racks of tubes.

"We're in a cargo hold," Rumbold said, walking over to me. "But I think we should keep moving. If Singh is determined enough, he'll find this hole we're hiding in."

"Has anyone found an exit?" I asked.

None of them had. I played my light up on the rim of the entry point we'd used. Snow filtered down through it in clumps.

"We're definitely inside a ship of some kind," I said, "or possibly, it's a station like Araminta. It's big enough for that. But we can't defend ourselves here. If troops drop, they'll stand up there and burn us easily from the outside."

"They wouldn't do that!" Yamada said. "Our own guardsmen? How could Singh order such a thing?"

"I don't know," I admitted, "but we have to accept that he managed to convince his crew that *Cutlass* must be destroyed. Rationally, it follows that we're to be killed as well."

The group was glum at this thought. Many had considered our predicament solved by finding shelter. Now, they weren't so sure.

Then, everything changed. Those who were peering up at the entrance far above us gasped. A light flashed, and a brilliant glare shone through the round aperture.

The destroyer *Altair* had arrived.

-16-

We scattered. It wasn't cowardice—but we were definitely driven by fear and the desire for self-preservation. If the destroyer spotted the opening and fired a beam down into this chamber, we were all as good as cooked.

"I found a way out, a big hatch over here, sir!" shouted Yamada.

I headed in her direction. Several crewmen were right behind me.

The hatch was an odd one. It wasn't man-shaped with an arched top, the way a door in a bulkhead aboard one of our vessels would have been. It was circular, perfectly rounded.

"How do we get it open?" I demanded.

Rumbold wasn't waiting around. He had his big hands on the wheel, and he was spinning for all he was worth—but it wasn't budging.

"That's a waste of strength," I said. "See the bolts at the top and bottom? This thing is sealed tight. It's a pressure door, and I bet it can withstand a lot more force than we can muster with our arms."

Rumbold slumped, sides heaving. I could hear his breath puffing over his suit's microphone, but he didn't say anything. His eyes were directed upward, to where *Altair* lurked.

"Yamada, get this door open," I said. "Hack the security."

She looked at me as if I were mad, but she moved forward to try. She worked on it for a full minute. There was a hand-plate next to the hatch. It was made for a very large hand, but she ignored that part. Instead, she worked on the wires underneath, seeking to short them out.

"I'm going to have to try to splice them in combinations, Captain," she said. "If I simply cut them, I think it will disable the door rather than open it."

"Understood. The rest of you, spread out and look for another path out of here."

While she worked and the rest searched, I eyed the opening above us. Rumbold came to stand beside me.

"No point looking away, eh, sir?" he asked.

"What?"

He pointed at the opening above us. "I mean, you're looking right up at the hole. If that ship fires a beam in here, your eyes will be burned out of their sockets and your brain will boil in your skull. But why bother trying to hide under one of these clone-racks? We're as good as dead anyway if Singh figures out we're down here."

"Actually," I said, "I was intrigued by the configuration of that hole in the roof. It's my conclusion that it isn't a hole at all. It's a door, a hatch just like the one we're trying to get through now."

He boggled at the two doors. "By damn, I think you're right! I never would have seen it—the shape is so unusual. These colonists have sure gone their own way over the last century or so."

"That's only to be expected. Yamada? How's the hack going?"

"I've spliced into the wires, and I'm running combinatorics through the lines now, sir. They use standard voltages and square-wave forms, I'm glad to see. At least our computers can talk to theirs."

"Different technological histories, but with the same roots," I said. "Further proof we're dealing with colonists."

"Won't matter much if we die down here," Jimmy said.

I looked at him sharply. "Have you found another way out?"

"No sir...sorry," he said a little sheepishly. "I don't think there is another exit. There are vents, but they seem to lead to life support pods. The ductwork is too narrow for a man to enter."

I thumped my fist against the wall beside the hatch. "I don't recognize this material, but it seems as hard and dense as granite."

"Harder, sir," Yamada said. "My instruments indicate it's a nickel-iron base, laced with collapsed matter and fullerene tubes. The whole vessel is made with this stuff. That's why the sensors registered it as good for mining."

"How's the hack going?"

She didn't answer for several seconds, then she turned to me and smiled. "I've got the first symbol. I don't know what it is, just a binary combination with a checksum. The lock isn't sophisticated, fortunately."

Nodding, I wasn't surprised. Why make a complicated lock on a cargo hold? It was only there to provide minimal security.

A shadow passed overhead. The flicker of it was vague, only showing on the deck where our pooled lights weren't shining. But it had to be *Altair*, orbiting this rock and looking for us.

"Singh wasn't fooled!" Rumbold said, staring up and whispering despite the fact no one could possibly overhear him. "He's up there, searching for survivors."

"That would seem likely," I admitted. "Team, switch off your lights. Only Yamada can use lights, if she must. There's no point giving them an easy reading."

One by one, we dimmed our lights down to near invisibility. The darkness was almost complete, and the gloom that was cast over us was eerie. Part of me began to wonder if I'd made the best choices. Perhaps if I had lifted off and charged into battle with the *Altair* that would have been best. Certainly, it would have been a hopeless act, but dying down here frozen and blue from lack of oxygen wasn't looking any better.

"Two symbols down," Yamada said. "Three to go."

"Hmm," I said, staring up at the starry sky above. As a gush of snow splashed down from the hole above to sprinkle the floor below, I was struck by a thought.

"Crew," I said. "I need everyone to look for another hand-plate like the one Yamada is working on. Do it now, do it by feel or use your com-link for illumination. Don't turn on any suit lamps."

They shuffled and moved slowly, spreading out around the hold. Rumbold kicked Jimmy in the rear. "You heard the captain!"

While they did as I'd ordered, I moved along the nearest wall, feeling for wires, a hand-plate—anything. Every few seconds I glanced up at the gray circle of starlight in the unrelenting blackness of the hold.

For about a minute, nothing happened. Then Yamada spoke again.

"Third one down, two to go."

They were fateful words. *Altair's* crew had tapped into our communications. They had been waiting for one of us to make a comment over an intercom. Two rifles flashed up above, firing power-bolts down toward Yamada.

Fortunately, the shots went wild. They couldn't see her clearly. But now we knew where they were.

"Stand down, Guardsmen!" I boomed over the open channel in the clear.

A bolt came in my direction. It smashed into the rack of tubes I was sheltering behind, sending up wisps of released gas.

"You're firing on your brothers!" I said.

"You launched a missile at *Altair*, traitor!" came a rough reply.

"Identify yourself!" I called back. "Are we under arrest?"

"Our orders are to kill the traitors."

"You damned drunken rats!" Rumbold shouted, joining the conversation. "You're the ones firing on your own crewmembers. You destroyed our ship! I should burn you down where you stand!"

The firing stopped. At that moment, I thought of a possible solution. If we could talk to the exec aboard *Altair*—I'd always thought him to be a sane man. If we accepted arrest and were taken to the bridge, I felt sure I could sort this out.

But then someone on our side fired. I wasn't sure who, but the shot struck home and took out the man in the gray circle above us. His chest a smoking ruin, he crashed down into the chamber at our feet.

More fire was exchanged in both directions. I tried to get Singh's men to calm down again, but they weren't interested in talk any longer.

Cursing, I heard Rumbold call to me. "I've found something, Captain."

"Found what?" I demanded, firing two bolts up at the circle in the roof.

We had the advantage of being spread out and having only a single target, but being below them we were more exposed than they were. Worse, we were vastly outnumbered. The destroyer had a complement of nearly two hundred crewmen. If they felt like it, they could simply roll a charge down into the hole, killing us all. I was surprised they hadn't done so yet.

"Four down," Yamada said.

"Keep working! Rumbold, I'm making my way to you along the walls."

More bolts flashed. I heard a sickening howl. I saw Jimmy's light go red inside my helmet. This time, we had no way to save him.

"Damn," I said, "this is madness."

Rumbold grabbed my elbow, and guided me to a standing position. He showed me a plate with wires running up the wall of the ship.

I knew what it was instantly. This had to be the control mechanism that controlled the upper hatch.

"Here it is, sir," Rumbold said. "I'm not sure what you want with it, but I found—oh no, sir!"

I stood and drew my saber. I'd had time to put on my shielding cloak, and my weapons belt with my sword and pistol.

The saber was a silver line that gleamed in the crossfire of weapons around us. With a single stroke, I slashed the wires that ran up the hull.

There was a grinding noise that I felt in my bones as much as heard. The heavy hatchway overhead constricted closed.

The firing stopped, and my crew staggered out from hiding, cursing and coughing.

Rumbold and I looked at one another. Our faces were shining with sweat. Our breath blew on the inside of our visors, steaming them up momentarily with each puff.

"You've sealed us in here!" he said in shock.

I nodded and sheathed my blade. "They could have killed us a dozen different ways. It was only a matter of time until they did so."

"Yeah, but now we're entombed."

We stared at one another. I didn't deny his words.

"What about that fifth symbol, Yamada?" I called out.

She didn't answer right away. For a sick moment, I thought she might have been killed. But then Rumbold and I clanked to her position and found her hard at work, her tiny computer still churning on the encoded lock.

"I don't know..." she said. "This might not work—they aren't using the same encoding set we're using. They've developed a different version, I think. The last symbol—my tablet might not have the right vocabulary."

"You'll figure it out," I said with a confidence I didn't feel.

-17-

After another ten minutes or so, Yamada finally finished the hack. The door rolled away revealing an inky-black passageway beyond.

"Well done," I said, stepping past her and cranking up the illumination cast by my suit.

We had enough battery power and oxygen to keep us going for another ten hours at best. But there was no point in lying around conserving every breath. Either we would find something aboard to keep us alive, or we wouldn't. I knew it would be best for morale to keep moving.

"What I don't understand is what Singh is up to," Rumbold said at my side. He was the second man to enter the passageway and clank along at my side.

"It's a mystery to me," I told him. "But the assassination attempt on my father was a surprise as well. People seem to be coming at me from all directions."

"You've got that right!"

"Yamada," I said, turning to my lead technician. "This region seems to be completely depressurized. Am I correct in that assumption?"

"Not quite, Captain," she said. "The passageway did have a trace of air, but it quickly escaped when we opened the hatch. We could seal it and hope the atmosphere will build back up."

I halted and watched as my crewmen filed past me, looking around. The passage was festooned with piping and hardware I didn't recognize. The piping could be part of a life support system.

"It's worth a try," I said. "Close the door once we're all inside."

"No retreat?" Rumbold asked.

"No. The hold wasn't all that much of a sanctuary, in any case."

"What about Jimmy, sir?" he asked. "We could bring him with us…"

I glanced at him, but he said no more. Was he thinking of sharing out Jimmy's air and power? Or, perhaps, even something worse?

"All right," I said. "Bring him with us."

Once everyone was inside the passage, it was a little crowded, being no more than two meters wide and three high. Yamada shut the door—and we were rewarded with a welcome surprise.

The walls lit up, at least panels along the side did, creating bright white bands of light on either side of us.

"I'm hearing something," I said, noting a rising hiss. "Is it breathable?"

Yamada studied her computer closely. "Yes sir. It's a nitrogen and oxygen mix, but it's higher in oxygen content than Earth normal. Still, I wouldn't open your faceplates yet. It's too thin to breathe at this point."

"Power, air…" I said, smiling broadly. "Looks like we're going to make it, crew!"

There were nods and relieved looks. I pretended everything was fine. Keeping up morale was an officer's job, and a big part of that job was never letting on how grim a situation really was.

"Let's see what else we can find," I said, striding down the passage in the lead.

The walkway curved gently as we walked, so we couldn't see more than fifty meters ahead or behind us. I found it somewhat alarming that the lights were only shining where we were at any given moment, switching off behind us and flickering into life as we reached a new section. I supposed the ship was conserving power, but I had no idea if that meant the supply was dangerously low, or if it was a preprogrammed function.

We passed a lot of locked, circular doors. I had Yamada try out a few of them, but unfortunately, they each had a combination that didn't match the one that had gotten us out of the cargo hold. Rather than spending another ten minutes working on a random door, I decided to press ahead and see if we could find the extent of the passage we'd discovered first.

"There are no labels on these doors," Rumbold complained. "They all look the same. How were those female giants able to find their way around?"

"See that dot over the door?" Yamada asked, pointing to a small mark that looked like the pinhead tip of a vid pickup. "That's not a camera. It's an identifying microdot of information."

"So high?" Rumbold asked, peering up at the nearest dot.

"Remember, they were tall people." I said.

"Right..."

"Yamada," I said, "can you interpret these dots? We must know where these doors lead."

"Maybe," she said. "Can you reach up there and run my tablet over the dot? I can't reach."

Taking her computer from her small hands, I reached up and brushed its sensors repeatedly over the microdot. After a few seconds, I handed the device back to her.

"Ship's stores," she said a few moments later.

"Excellent," I said. "We'll read them all until we find something useful."

"Wait a second!" Rumbold said. "Did you say ship's stores? You're sure about that interpretation? That would confirm this is a powered vessel, not some kind of abandoned station."

"The translation is over ninety-five percent certain."

I eyed the two of them and nodded. It was critical information. We'd known all along that we were inside an artificial structure of some kind, but that wasn't very definitive. If this was a ship, it stood to reason it would have engines and a bridge. If we could get the engines operating...

"Start looking for a bridge," I said. "Anything that will get us to a command sector of some kind."

"Medical," she read next.

We kept going.

"Life support."

That made me halt. After thinking for several long seconds, I gestured toward the door.

"Open it. We need air and heat more than we need anything else right now."

Yamada went to work on the door immediately. My crewmen were visibly relieved. It weighs on a spacer's mind to know he's living on borrowed time. Usually, a man walking outside a ship always knows he can scoot to a nearby airlock and find solace if he's running out of the essentials for life. Even then, one tended to check the key measurements, such as how many breaths you had left to take, every half hour or so.

But when you know you're cut off from life support, it tends to become an obsession. A man who's in trouble will check those numbers every few minutes, and the tension will grow into a great weight on his mind as time ticks away.

It was about four minutes later that Yamada broke the code on the lock. I complemented her on her improving skill. She smiled.

"It's not me, it's my computer. The algorithm is learning likely variations heuristically."

"Never turn down praise," I told her. "I couldn't have done it so quickly."

Beaming now, she led us into the chamber. Compared to the cargo hold, life support was relatively small. But I knew that beyond the tight walls around us were large machines that distributed air, water and heat.

We approached a large graphic control system. Yamada laid hands on it, and she swept her fingers over it. The interface seemed to respond reasonably to a standardized set of gestures.

"We've got power," she said after working on the system for several minutes. "But it's low. I don't think we should try to heat the whole ship. The engines are shut down completely. They're as cold as they can be, and from these diagrams it looks like they're supposed to feed the internal generators most of the time."

"The batteries are low," I said thoughtfully. "That indicates the ship has sat here for a long time. I wonder what happened to her? Any logs or computer connections?"

She showed me the console. The direct control system wasn't password protected, but when she tried to access the ship's central computer she was blocked by security. The connectivity options were set up to allow operators to do appropriate work with life support in this chamber, but not to access the ship's systems in general.

"This unit isn't going to let me get away with splicing wires and hacking," she said. "The doors were built to allow physical overrides in case of emergencies, such as the one we're in the middle of, but the central computer is protected. To get into their network, we'll have to have the right passcode."

"Fair enough. Let's see the ship's layout, if we can."

That she could display. The crew gasped as the decks and passages were laid out in colorful screens before them.

The ship was huge. It was a hundred times the size of *Altair* and more than a thousand times the size of *Cutlass*. I was impressed with the colonists, clones or not. Just building such a vessel was, by itself, a marvelous feat of engineering.

"And to think," Rumbold said, "back home they begrudge us the budget to keep six destroyers in space. This ship is fantastic! An unbelievable achievement for Beta colonists, by damn!"

I nodded, but I wasn't as elated as the others. I was thinking about the implications of this massive vessel. If the Betas had built it, they were undoubtedly our masters in the construction of shipping. That was worrisome enough, especially when adding the fact they'd figured out a way to get from their system to ours with this vessel.

But what concerned me more was that this ship had been seriously damaged somehow. On the diagrams, there were large areas displayed in red with repair requirements listed over them.

"Were those areas damaged during flight, or was this ship attacked and damaged in battle?" I asked aloud.

The group sobered as they studied the computer.

"This damaged area contains the fire control systems," Yamada explained. "Without fire control, they couldn't aim their weapons. The second damaged deck over here indicates it's a core power distribution center. If I was trying to disable a ship in battle, I might well choose the same targets. I think the fact that those two regions were damaged, plus the fact they're both on the outer rim of the ship, close to the hull itself, indicates a purposeful attack occurred."

"She's right, sir," Rumbold added. "This looks like the aftermath of battle to me. We're lucky the enemy didn't disable her engines. If we can get the generators going again, we can fly."

"Yes," I said thoughtfully. "But another point strikes me: If a group of colonists managed to build a ship of such amazing size and power—who else out there was able to build enough hardware to beat this monster in combat?"

They eyed me in concern, grasping my point immediately.

"Something must be out there that's even bigger and more powerful than this battlewagon," Yamada said quietly.

"Right," Rumbold said, leaning an elbow on the screen and scratching his face. We had our visors open now, even though the air was still a bit thin and cold. "That's got to be the way of things. It's a frightening thought. I don't think our entire fleet could stand up to this ship alone, much less whatever behemoth beat her in battle."

"Hmm," I said thoughtfully. "Chief, you asked me earlier about Captain Singh's motivations. Maybe he knows more about this ship than he's been letting on. Maybe he has a purpose to his seeming madness."

"He's a traitor! Pure and simple!"

I smiled thinly. "Hopefully we'll be able to get some straight answers out of him if we can get this vessel operating again."

My crew, given a new goal and new hope, tackled the problem with gusto.

The loss of *Cutlass* still stung my mind whenever I thought of it. I'd loved that ship, lowly though she was. I guess a commander always has a soft spot in his heart for his first command.

But rather than letting the destruction of *Cutlass* demoralize me, I was determined that it would give me purpose. Here, we had a new ship, a frighteningly powerful one that appeared to be abandoned. If we could get it into a functional state, Captain Singh may yet come to regret his recent choices.

The life support system wasn't perfect, but it functioned. We didn't have enough power to pump air and heat into every chamber aboard the vessel, but we didn't have to.

"Warm up the bridge, engineering, this section we're in and the passages in-between."

"Working on it, sir," Yamada said.

"Delegate the task to one of the engineering mates," I told her. "I'm taking you and Rumbold on a little tour."

She licked her lips nervously, but nodded in agreement. We put down our faceplates just in case and exited life support. The crew looked after us wonderingly. They were more than happy to stay inside the only comfortable chamber aboard.

Rumbold had his pistol out, I noticed. I couldn't blame him for that. Yamada walked with her face gazing down into her glowing computer screen. It was as thin as paper, and she held it rolled open with both hands. Occasionally, she spoke out loud to it.

"I noticed something on the screens as we examined them," I said as we walked the lonely passages. We moved down several decks. The ship was a maze.

"This is it," I said, stopping in front of a door like a dozen others. "What's that microdot say?"

"Uh…detention, sir. I'm pretty sure that's it."

I nodded, curious. "That's what I thought. Can you open it?"

She worked on the door for less than three minutes before she had it open.

"You're getting better and better," I told her, then I stepped inside.

The chamber was different than any of the others I'd seen so far. The ship overall was laid out very methodically. Most of the walls, passages and chambers had a certain sameness to them. Only the purpose of each region and the equipment inside provided variety.

This room was different. There were sub-chambers, a dozen of them, each effectively a cage-like structure with ribbed walls and small portholes in the sides.

"Cells?" Rumbold asked. "May I ask why we're here, sir?"

I pointed to the last cell in the line. "That cell," I said. "I noticed when we first examined the diagrams that there was power and heat down here. I didn't know it was the detention center, but it makes sense to me now."

I walked up to the cell and peered into a fogged over porthole.

Rumbold huffed and followed me. "You can't be serious!" he said. "A prison? One cell that's still functioning? No one could be alive in there!"

Rather than answering him, I tapped lightly on the metal cell wall. A ringing, reverberating sound met our ears. The cell was like a tin drum, echoing my tapping.

Suddenly, a face loomed in the glass.

Rumbold fell back, gasping. "By the gods!"

Yamada sucked in her breath, but said nothing.

For my own part, I simply stared. Her face—it was obscured somewhat by the glass, but still unmistakable. She was the woman Yamada had projected by reading the DNA in the tubes. Those clones must have been her sisters. Thousands of them.

But that wasn't the shocking part. The thing that alarmed my crewmen was her size. Her face was that of a giant. As broad and thick-boned as the largest of men.

-18-

The female giant in the cell regarded us thoughtfully. We could only see her face, but even that was impressive. Her green eyes were intelligent but wary. Her raven black hair was long and hung down to spill on her broad shoulders.

Those eyes…they shifted from one of us to the next. Often, they came to rest on the weapons we had on our belts.

"Hello," I said in Standard. "I'm Captain William Sparhawk. Who are you?"

"You are Basics?" she asked aloud, speaking Standard with a strange accent. Her voice was deep for a woman's, but not as deep as mine.

"I'm not sure what you mean by that term," I said.

"Basic stock. Old-men. That's what you are—I can tell. You're all varied in design but not for specific purposes."

"We're Earth men," I said, "and we're here to rescue you."

She studied us suspiciously for a moment longer, then a smile spread across her wide face. That smile wasn't entirely friendly, in my opinion. There was a hint of something predatory in it.

"You'll find the lock difficult to open," she said. "But there is a bypass at the guard station over there. Before you open it, please make sure the atmosphere is breathable, for my sake."

"We'll do so," I said. "Yamada, power up life support in detention, please."

"It will be a few minutes, Captain."

I turned back to the prisoner. "We have time for a few questions," I said.

"How fortunate," she said, but she didn't appear to be happy.

She wanted to get out of her cell. I could understand that, but I felt I had to know more of her situation first.

"What's your name?" I asked her.

"Betas don't have names, we have serial numbers. But those I interact with on a regular basis called me Zye—the last symbol in my serial number was Z."

"Zye...all right." I proceeded to introduce the three of us. No one looked comfortable. I could tell she didn't trust us, and we certainly didn't trust her, but the introductions seemed to help a little.

"Zye," I asked, "how is it that you're alive and everyone else aboard this ship seems to have died or abandoned her?"

"I don't know. I've been trapped in here—I don't know how long. Fortunately, the cell is automated. It has fed me, provided me with air, and removed my waste since the ship was stricken."

"Do you know what might have damaged this vessel?"

Zye shrugged. "The Betas have many enemies. It might have been the Stroj, or the Reavers. I can't be sure. The crew wasn't interested in keeping me up to date on events."

"How did you come to be imprisoned? What were the charges?"

Her mouth worked for a moment, but she didn't answer.

"I'm like you," she said at last. "That was my crime. I varied too much from the pattern. They didn't like the variation."

Frowning, I wasn't sure how to take her statements.

Rumbold cleared his throat and I glanced at him. He indicated that I might want to step away from the porthole to talk to him privately. I indulged him, connecting a channel for a privately radioed talk and turning off my external speakers.

"What is it, Chief?"

"I don't like this, sir, and I don't like her. She's obviously some kind of vicious criminal."

"We don't know that."

"Oh, come on, Captain! A man doesn't have to be a hundred and sixty to know that a prisoner is generally behind bars for damned good reasons."

"Point taken. Thank you," I said. Disconnecting the channel, I activated my external speakers again. "I'm getting good sound now, Yamada. How's the air in here?"

"Chilly, but breathable."

I removed my helmet and regarded the woman in the cell intently. She was taller than I, a full head taller. But I didn't get a feeling of menace from her. Rather, I thought she was the conniving sort.

"You're a criminal, aren't you?" I asked. "What was your crime? Theft? Deception? Violence?"

Zye stared at me for several seconds.

"Deception," she said at last. "Betas don't generally steal. We don't covet possessions, and there are few items known to us that are worth the effort in any case. We *can* be violent, but only with good reason."

"So you lied about something?" I asked. "Explain to me what kind of lie might cause someone to be imprisoned for so long."

"My crime was in being different from my countless sisters—and hiding the fact," she said. "I know that must be difficult for you to understand. You're a Basic. You're unevolved."

"You're different than the others?" I asked. "Meaning you're not a pure clone?"

"Yes, that's right."

"You look like your sisters. We projected your likely appearance into adulthood. I can't understand why you would hide a small variation in your genetics—was it a mutation?"

"Yes, a mutation. Variations are permitted when they're deemed positive. My mutation was classified as negative."

"What mutation?"

Zye looked thoughtful, almost ashamed. "It has to do with my personality. If you meet another Beta someday, you'll detect the difference very quickly. They're universally boring."

Yamada laughed. "A planet loaded with boring clones? That's a sad state of affairs."

Zye glanced at her, then turned her big eyes back to me. "Compared to myself, you Basics are the worst of misfits. By definition, you and every person from Earth is a far worse deviant than I could ever be."

This was too much for Rumbold. He stepped closer and glared up at her.

"That's enough, you," he said. "We're not deviants! What do you know about us? You're looking at three honorable guardsmen. We've never performed a crime in our lives. We've sworn to maintain the law of our world."

Zye laughed then. It was an odd, baritone sound.

"You see?" she said, still looking at me. "Your breed is too different, too varied in type. This aged individual barely comprehends what I'm talking about. I would predict that Betas and Basics will always have great difficulty in understanding one another."

Before I could calm the two of them down, the power surged and dimmed around us. The light panels in the walls flickered, and we eyed them in concern.

"A power outage?" Rumbold asked.

For the first time since we'd met her, Zye appeared to be alarmed.

"I've never seen anything like that, she said. "I've been in this cell for a year or more. What is your crew doing to the ship?"

Her statement surprised me. She'd said before she hadn't known how long she'd been in the automated cell, but now she'd said it had been a year. Which was the truth? Hadn't she said her crime was deception? I was beginning to understand why she was behind bars. Perhaps it was as Rumbold had said: there was always a good reason.

But there was no time for recriminations. I contacted the crewmen I'd left back in life support, demanding a report.

They quickly responded, indicating they were innocent. They hadn't done anything to impact the flow of power around the ship.

The lights flickered again, but this time they went out altogether. A droning hiss signaled the end of the process.

"That's life support," Yamada said. "It's gone. There's no air flowing in here anymore."

The chamber had gone dark, but our suit lights sensed this and turned themselves on. Right then the three of us reached for our helmets. I could already feel the pressure dropping.

Before we'd buckled our helmets firmly into place, a muffled booming sound began. We looked up, startled.

Zye was hammering on the metal walls of her cell. Each time her massive fist struck, the wall bulged. Her face was in the porthole, teeth revealed in a snarl. She shouted something, but I could barely hear her.

I could tell that her air was running out. Somehow, we'd depressurized this part of the ship. She was dying.

-19-

The air around us had been warming up quickly, but now the cold of space was stealing into the detention center again. The air smoked with vapor and ice crackled on the walls.

"Let's get her out of there!" I ordered.

"But sir," Rumbold objected. "We don't even know—"

"She's been in there for years, and we come along and kill her? Is that how you want our first encounter with a Beta colonist to be remembered?"

He shut up, and Yamada activated the door lock. It swung open immediately.

I was again impressed by Yamada's skills. While we'd been talking to Zye, she'd worked on hacking her cell door. Now that her efforts were critically needed, she was ready to act.

Zye fell out of her cell and crawled on her knees, wheezing and steaming. She was nude—I hadn't realized that before as I'd only seen her face through the porthole. She was uncommonly broad of shoulder and thick of bone. Her breasts hung down from her chest, and I was surprised she made no effort to cover them.

Despite her feminine charms, her sheer size was alarming. She was easily bigger than any guardsman I'd ever met. Only a few of Earth's athletes could boast her size—all of them male.

Grabbing up a suit from the locker she'd indicated earlier, I brought it to her. I jammed the helmet over her head and helped her trembling hands work the leggings up over her long, broad thighs.

Zye was shaking slightly from the cold, but she was still functioning. I checked the external pressure readings—the atmosphere was desperately thin. If these pressure readings were correct, one could quickly lose consciousness and die.

But she kept moving, slowly, numbly. Her hands reached for the straps and zippers. Fortunately, the suit had smart seals that connected and meshed on their own. I switched on the suit, and it began to pump air and heat over her body. The suit inflated around her like a crinkling balloon.

Within a minute, she was able to stand. Her eyes were bloodshot, but no capillaries had burst. I was worried about altitude sickness and other maladies from fast pressure changes, but her rate of recovery was remarkable.

Her sides heaving as she sucked in oxygen, she straightened slowly to her full height. She had to be over two meters tall.

She looked down at me with a strange expression. Her arms swept forward suddenly, and she clutched me under my arms. I was lifted into the air like a child. That baritone barking—her laughter, began again.

Rumbold's pistol was out in an instant, but I waved him off. Fortunately, Zye didn't see this interchange due to her helmet's restricted zone of sight.

Reluctantly, Rumbold lowered his gun, but he didn't holster it.

I hung in the air and managed a smile. Zye was sweating and grinning like a bear with game in her clutches.

"I'm impressed!" she boomed. "You've saved me! I will not soon forget this favor!"

She hugged me then, and I struggled not to wheeze and cough. My ribs rasped against one another as I was crushed into her massive breasts. I endured the indignity for several seconds, and she released me at last, setting me down on my feet with a gentle movement.

"I'm sorry," she said. "I see by the expressions worn by your crewmen that I've embarrassed you."

"A little gratitude is to be expected," I said, feeling myself wanting to straighten my spine to its utmost extent. Something about being towered over—it made me want to look as tall as I possibly could. Being the tallest among my crew, I wasn't used to the experience.

"No!" boomed Zye, lifting her hand into my faceplate. "Not a little gratitude. You trusted. You acted. You prolonged my existence. My own sisters have forsaken me, and they would have executed me when we returned home. My gratitude is like the ocean of space itself."

Not quite sure how to take her unexpected attitude, I decided to make the best of it.

"I accept your thanks, and I hope we can help each other survive even longer. Zye, we need your help to operate this ship. We don't have time to figure out how everything works on our own."

I quickly explained the realities of our predicament: that *Altair* stalked the space outside this ship, and that her captain wanted us dead.

Zye took this in with a frown and a nod.

"These renegades of yours must have done it," she said. "When we were hit in battle, our power couplings were damaged. I remember that much before my sisters ran from battle. That means your enemies have entered the ship through the damaged section and disconnected the power entirely."

"The ship's hull was breached in these areas?" Rumbold demanded.

"Yes, how else could the guts of a ship encased in fullerene-laced armor be damaged?"

"Right..." I said, thinking fast. "Of course. We sealed the cargo hold door, and so they looked for another entrance. They must have found the holes in the ship's hull. Their sensors are better than anything we had aboard *Cutlass*. They were able to penetrate the ice and find a breach."

"Singh and his men are aboard this vessel?" demanded Rumbold in alarm.

"Yes," I said. "We must assume so."

Rumbold turned a skeptical eye toward the Beta. "Your story shifts like mud," he said. "You told us you didn't know how long you'd been inside that cell or what had happened to this vessel. Now, you're full of details on both subjects."

Zye shrugged her massive shoulders. "Would you trust a Beta who wandered aboard your ship while you were helpless in a cell?"

"Probably not," he admitted, "but now I'm seeing why they locked you up for deception and abandoned you here."

Zye's face darkened, and I had to intervene before an argument began.

"We don't have time for this," I said firmly. "Zye, we need your help. Are you with us?"

"Yes!" she boomed. "I consider myself part of your crew. You are my captain, William Sparhawk."

"All right then. How do we repel these invaders?"

Her eyes roamed the dark ceiling. She lifted a hand after a moment of thought. Her gestures were somewhat alien to me. She was human—but not quite like an earthly woman. I tried my best to drive these unhelpful comparisons from my mind, but I kept coming back to them.

"We could gather your crew in the life support section and irradiate the passages," she said. "The reactor's cooling jacket was ruptured in battle, but it self-sealed afterward. It would take only a small effort to destabilize it again."

I thought about it, but I shook my head. "No, that's too drastic. I don't want to kill more guardsmen. Singh is misleading good men."

"No killing?" Zye asked. "That will make things much more difficult."

"I've got an idea," Yamada said. "Let's go back to life support."

We moved quickly through the ship's passages. At each junction, I looked for the suit lights of an opposing combat patrol. I felt that Singh had all the cards. He was aboard with marines, no doubt, and they outnumbered us ten to one. All I had was Zye and her knowledge of this vessel.

"Here," she said when we reached a side passage. "I assume you wish to avoid your opponents for now, correct?"

"Yes, absolutely," I said. "We can't beat them in open battle."

"Then we should go down these passages to the troop deck, then back up again to life support. If they're coming in from the power section, they'll march right through the next junction."

We followed her lead. I was impressed by what little I saw of the troop deck as we wormed our way through it. There must have been enough bunks in a series of identical chambers to hold a thousand troops—possibly more.

"Zye?" I asked as we moved. "I'm surprised to see quarters for an invasion force on a battle ship. What kind of mission was this vessel designed for?"

"S-11 is a battle cruiser, not a battle ship," she replied. "She's capable of navigating the rivers between the stars alone. Such vessels are always large and outfitted for any contingency. If an invasion is required, she can perform the mission."

"S-11?" Rumbold asked. "Is that the ship's name, or is it her class?"

"Both. All our ships are numbered."

"Oh," he said thoughtfully. "So, there's an S-10 out there somewhere?"

"Yes, unless she's been destroyed."

Rumbold rolled his eyes. I could tell he didn't think much of the Beta naming scheme. Leave it to them to give their ships numbers rather than names. I had little doubt that the "S" stood for "Ship."

"S-11..." Rumbold said thoughtfully. "Not the most inspiring name for a warship. Why not call it *Defiant*, or something?"

"That is your prerogative. She is under your control now."

I leaned forward, liking the idea. "*Defiant* it is," I said. "Thanks for the name, Chief."

Smiling, Rumbold's mood was instantly elevated. "Is this vessel the largest design you Betas have in your fleet?" he asked Zye.

Zye glanced back at him. "It's the only warship design we have. As I said before, my sisters aren't imaginative. Well, I should qualify that: they're imaginative enough, but they tend to all imagine the same thing at the same time!"

She boomed with laughter, although the joke had less of an impact on the rest of us.

I thought about the implications of her statements. There were several details that stuck out in my mind.

"Just to clarify," I said, following her up the last passage to the deck that housed life support. "This ship can follow wormholes? On Earth, we've lost that capacity."

"Yes, your routes shut down long ago. But there are plenty more. You only have to look for them. We Betas found that out long ago. Earth cut herself off from us, and you did not try to reestablish the connection. That was a mystery to us. Perhaps you could enlighten us as to why you did so?"

"I don't understand," I said. "We had a solar flare, a very large one, about a hundred and fifty years back. It was similar to something called the Carrington Event, another solar flare that damaged electrical systems on Earth in the days of telegraphs and railroads. In the Cataclysm, all of our power systems were damaged, and after we repaired them, we found we were cut off from our colonies."

"Yes, yes," Zye said, flapping a large hand over her shoulder dismissively. "We figured something like that had happened—or something worse. We suspected when your star hiccupped, it must have burned away all life on Old Earth. In any event, all you had to do was look for new pathways to the stars. There are rivers between the stars, affected by currents and eddies. What you haven't explained is why you didn't seek new paths to your colonies?"

Rumbold and I looked at one another thoughtfully.

"That's a good question," I said. "Our government always said it was impossible."

"Well then," Rumbold said, "someone's lying!"

Zye gave him an unpleasant glance. "Yes, someone *is* lying. But it can't be me."

"Why not?" demanded Rumbold.

"Because, old fool, I'm standing here before you. This ship is in the Solar System. If interstellar travel is impossible, how did *Defiant* come to be here in the first place?"

Rumbold's eyes bugged from his head, but he stayed quiet. Her words were irrefutably logical.

She was right. If *Defiant* had made the journey, it proved it could be done.

Therefore, Earth's government had lied to her people for a century and a half. And that thought alone was alarming enough. What truth had we stumbled onto that warranted the destruction of *Cutlass* and her entire crew?

More thoughts, however, tumbled unbidden into my mind following this first one. Singh's motivations now were suspect to me. Perhaps I wasn't supposed to find a way to board this ship. Perhaps I was supposed to help maintain the fiction that a vessel like this one couldn't exist.

The second, even more disturbing thought was of my father. Was it possible that he and his political friends knew the truth? Did they try to dismantle the Guard every year with fervor precisely because they didn't want to explore space and rediscover the new pathways that must exist?

I wasn't sure what I'd uncovered, but I was certain that I had yet to get to the bottom of it all.

-20-

When we reached life support, Yamada went into action. Her plan was simple but far from foolproof.

With Zye's help, she managed to gain greater control over the ship's systems. She tapped into the batteries that had been slowly recharging since we'd first gotten a few of the generators back online.

"We don't have much power, but it should be enough," Zye said. "Your plan is devious, Yamada. I applaud you. I would never have thought of it."

"It's simple enough," Yamada said. "First, we attract Singh's troops into certain regions near the outer hull by lighting them up and pressurizing them. When they move to investigate, we blow open the nearest outer hatch and let them fly out with the depressurization."

Zye nodded her big head. She tapped at the boards until a login screen arose. Planting her hand on it, she snarled when the screen turned red and shook fractionally.

"They revoked my authority!" she boomed in complaint.

"Naturally," Rumbold said. "You were a prisoner."

She showed him her teeth, then looked back at the screen. She tapped in a long series of symbols.

"What's that?" Yamada asked. "It looks like a code. May I?"

She lifted her tablet and snapped a quick shot of the password before it could disappear.

Zye laughed. "You think ahead. Now you have the chief biologist's password."

"What," I asked Zye, "are you doing with the chief biologist's password?"

"Making good use of old knowledge," she said. As she talked, menus came up and she tapped her way through them with the speed of an expert. "But I assume you're asking how I came to have an officer's password. I told you I was found to be of unacceptable type. Most aberrations such as myself are killed before adulthood, but I managed to survive. I did so by altering my own test results in the data core. It was this deception that eventually caught up to me and got me convicted of genetic variance."

"I see," I said, and I thought I was beginning to understand Zye. She was a criminal on Beta Cygnus, but to us she was a woman who'd learned to survive a harsh world. She'd done what she had to do.

As a man dedicated to upholding the law, I found her a troubling person. She'd obviously broken the laws of her people. But, if those laws were unjust, should breaking them be a crime to someone like myself? My laws were different—utterly different, in this instance. It wasn't a crime to be unlike your parents. In fact, Earth had gone the other way. It was a crime to erase any kind of genetic individuality.

Watching her work alongside Yamada, I came to a decision: I would do my best to protect Zye. As long as she served me as she'd sworn to do, I would serve her interests as well, being her commander and her guide among my people.

I could already tell that, although the Betas might be physically imposing and militarily strong, Earthlings clearly had an advantage in sophistication. We were subtle diplomats and politicians. How could a race of clones compete with an infinitely varied race in negotiations? They would all think the same, and thus, once we figured out their weaknesses, they could be collectively manipulated.

"We're ready, sir," Yamada said, breaking into my thoughts.

"Have you located them?"

"Yes, the ship's sensors are counting heartbeats. Twenty crewmen, armed presumably. They appear to be taking the bait now."

"Wait until they're all in the section to be depressurized," Rumbold said. "Get them all at once, the bastards! Once blasted out into space, with any luck, they'll achieve escape velocity and be tossed into deep space. *Altair* can have fun tracking each man down individually."

"We can only hope Captain Singh himself is among them," Yamada said.

"He won't be," I said, studying the screen. "Here they are. They're passing through the last bulkhead and into the trap now."

"Yes, I see that."

We watched tensely. The group paused when they entered the pressurized region. I had no doubt they were trying to figure out where they were and what was going on.

"Come on, come on..." Rumbold muttered.

More of them entered, but one seemed to be lingering at the entrance. Several of them were almost out of the trap, moving ahead.

"Captain," Zye said, "some of the enemy troops are about to exit the trap area."

I stared at the screen for a second longer. It was more difficult to order Zye to spring the trap than I'd realized. It seemed like trickery rather than battle. I knew some of these men might be killed. Violently hurled out into space by the pressure-release, suits might rip, faceplates might crack.

In the Star Guard Academy, they'd drilled home the goals of clean ethics and fair play. I wouldn't have had second thoughts against an alien menace, but these people weren't really the enemy. I knew them. I'd served with them. They were Singh's crewmen, guardsmen like myself following orders.

Rumbold caught my eye. "It's them or us, sir," he said, as if reading my mind.

"Seal the chamber," I ordered.

Zye's fingers were poised over the screen, waiting for this order. She tapped instantly.

"Done," she said.

"Open the external hatch," I said.

Everyone's eyes were glued on the imagery as it rapidly shifted. The contacts slid toward the exit at first—then with sudden speed they were ejected through the open hatch.

"Flushed into space!" Rumbold said. "It worked!"

My eyes crawled over the screen. "Not for that one."

We all focused on the lingering individual at the back of the line. He was very near the spot where the bulkhead had closed, sealing the trapped area.

"He's not moving," Rumbold said. "He might be hanging on by his fingertips."

"Or," Yamada said, looking at me, "he might have a hand or a foot trapped in the hatchway we shut. These doors don't have safety sensors. If you stand in the way when they close—they just close anyway."

I felt slightly sick at the thought. Had I severed a crewman's limb, or pinned him?

"Close the external hatch," I said. "Repressurize. Yamada, you're in charge here. Hold this post. Rumbold, Zye, come with me. Let's find out what happened."

They followed my orders quietly. The crew seemed as troubled as I was—all except for Zye. Her eyes were steel. She didn't seem to suffer from empathy for her fellow man's pain. Maybe that was because she didn't consider us to be her people. Or maybe, she hadn't been engineered to be the caring type.

Either way, she followed my lead. So far, she'd never argued with one of my commands. She'd said she would follow me as her captain, and I was beginning to believe her.

Moving at a bouncing trot, we made our way to the corridor where we had set the trap. Zye led the way as she knew the layout of the ship best. She didn't have a weapon, but she never hesitated to plunge ahead, regardless.

Keeping up with the woman was a challenge. Each of her sweeping strides seemed to carry her forward a distance that took me nearly two paces to match. I marveled that her long stay in captivity hadn't weakened her. Was that due to rigorous calisthenics while imprisoned or sheer vitality? I didn't know the answer, but nonetheless, it was impressive.

She opened the final bulkhead with a touch and threw herself against the wall of the passage. I barely reacted in time, myself. A power bolt sizzled through the door and melted a spot of metal on the ceiling. The three of us sought cover, huddling to either side of the open doorway.

"Ceasefire!" I shouted. "I'm Captain Sparhawk of *Cutlass*."

The man laughed and coughed. "You're captain of a slag-heap, then."

"You're outnumbered, and we're not here to harm you at any rate."

"You killed my men! "he shouted. "Let me out of here!"

I drew my pistol and fired three bolts around the edge of the doorway. I was shooting blind, and I purposefully aimed high. I wanted him to know we were armed and serious, but I didn't want to kill him in cold blood.

"I repeat," I said, "we're not here to kill you, but if you insist on shooting at us we may have to change our minds. We're guardsmen, the same as you."

"You're a traitor," he answered.

"Not I. This situation is a gross misunderstanding. *Altair* fired on our ship without warning, a mystifying act. We're still not sure how this all started, but we're determined to find out."

The man fell silent. "You should just let me out of here, Sparhawk. Open the hatch. I'll climb out to the surface, and I won't even tell them I talked to you, I swear."

"What's your name?"

"Marine Lieutenant Morris," he said with a twinge of pride in his voice.

Marines weren't common in the Guard, but each of our six destroyers carried a squad of them. They had rough reputations.

"What did Singh tell you, Morris? Why are you here chasing fellow guardsmen?"

"You should drop this game, Sparhawk. I'm getting tired of it. Either finish me or let me go."

"Are you injured?"

"Fuck you," he said tiredly.

I nodded to myself thoughtfully. No marine would admit he was injured in a situation like this.

"He's hurt," Rumbold said. "I can hear it in his voice."

Zye leaned close. "He's probably got a foot caught in the far doorway."

I contacted Yamada. "Has the target moved?"

"No sir, he's exactly where he was when the trap was sprung. I think he's probably pinned there."

"Come down here and join us, please.'"

"On my way."

I edged up to the open hatch and called through using my external speakers. "Morris, we've no wish to harm you further. I know you're hurt. If we open that hatch behind you, the blood will begin to flow. You'll probably die before *Altair* can pick you up."

"Wicked bastard," Morris muttered. "I'm not going to become your prisoner."

"All right then, we'll call you an honored guest. I'm coming out into the open now to check on your condition. If you kill me, you'll have dishonored yourself and my men will promptly shoot you in return. It's your choice."

I began to move forward, but a massive hand flew out to bar my progress. It was Zye, and her face loomed near me. She didn't want me to step into harm's way.

"Step aside," I told her evenly. "That's an order."

Reluctantly, her long arm retreated.

Holstering my pistol, I stepped boldly down the passageway.

What I saw there at the other end of it made me wince. Marine Lieutenant Morris was in a bad way. Not just his foot, but his entire left leg was clamped in the unforgiving jaws of the hatchway.

He had his rifle aimed at me, but I could tell he was struggling to keep a bead on me. His aim wavered with each ragged breath he drew.

With even steps that never faltered or appeared rushed, I walked toward him. He kept the gun on me until we were close enough that our eyes could meet through our faceplates. I could see he was younger than most guardsmen. His skin was bathed in sweat.

"You marines really are the toughest the Guard has, aren't you?" I asked conversationally.

This comment elicited a grin. "That's right, Sparhawk."

With an offhanded gesture, I suggested he lower his weapon. The muzzle drooped, and he finally set the rifle down and rolled onto his back. He lay there, stricken, staring up at the ceiling of the passageway.

"Rumbold, have you got your medical kit? We need it here. Yamada, bring your tablet. We've got to download his vitals from his suit."

"What about me, Captain?" asked Zye.

At the sound of her voice, the marine perked up. There was something different about it. A timbre that was not quite like any that earthlings were familiar with.

"Just stay there and watch for reinforcements, will you Zye?" I asked as if she were one more member of my crew. This seemed like a bad time to introduce this poor man to his first Beta.

My people advanced and we went to work on the lieutenant.

Yamada's equipment helped when it came time to open the door that was pinning his leg. She'd reprogrammed the nanites to close tightly in Morris' suit, clamping the blood flow off to his leg. We didn't want him to bleed to death.

Rumbold, during this procedure, managed to gently disarm the marine. Morris' numb fingers slipped off the trigger of his weapon reluctantly.

At that point, Zye disobeyed me and trudged forward. The marine's eyes widened, but he didn't speak. He was already in shock, I could tell.

"You want the prisoner to live?" Zye asked.

"Yes."

"If we take him to detention, my automated cell will attempt to repair him. It might not work on an Earthling, but there's no power in the medical section."

"All right. Let's go."

I reached down to pick up the marine, but found he was already cradled in Zye's massive arms. His face wore an expression of disbelief. I hoped to be there when he recovered and had to face his rescuer. Zye trotted down the passages with the marine held effortlessly aloft. The gravity aboard the ship was low, of course, but I was still impressed.

-21-

Before we reached the detention center, the lieutenant we'd captured passed out. His leg hung limply at an impossible angle. I felt responsible for his condition as I'd been the one who had ordered the hatch to be closed on him.

Pushing that thought away, I reminded myself that Singh had started this showdown, not me. I was only trying to keep my crew alive, which was my duty as an officer of the Guard.

"Open the cell door for me," Zye said, and Yamada quickly complied.

Zye placed the dying marine on a bed that was far too big for him. He wasn't a small man, but he looked like a child in her arms as she placed him on the featureless bunk.

"We have to strip off his suit and let the chamber do its work."

"How fast does this cell function?" Yamada asked. "If we take off the suit, he'll bleed out."

"You're right…not fast enough." Zye reached for a strap that circled her waist. There were several that hung from various cinch spots on her spacesuit. It was the first time I'd really taken the opportunity to examine her equipment.

"That's not a smart suit, is it?" I asked.

"No. Betas don't have such things," Zye said, tying the strap around the lieutenant's leg to form a tourniquet. "Now we can take his suit off. The medical bot won't operate if blocked by thick clothing."

I recalled that Zye had been naked in the cell, I now understood why. We stripped off Morris's suit and stepped out of the chamber. The exposed wound was grotesque. Really, his leg had been severed. It was hanging by skin and tendons alone.

As soon as we closed up the cell, it began to whir and hum. "The bot is going to work," Zye said, peering through the porthole. "He might live. We'll see."

"We did what we could," I said. "Is it all right to leave him in there?"

Zye nodded. "If he survives his injury, he'll be kept alive for years. The cell is merciless in this regard."

I glanced at her sharply as her tone had a hint of bitterness in it. Had she attempted suicide in her cell? I wouldn't have been surprised. Trapped for years in an automated cell without companionship or hope of rescue…it was a wonder, as I thought about it, that Zye was sane at all. Perhaps her resilience was a feature of her genetic design, and by inference, part of the personality of all Betas.

We moved back to the life support section. The crew there was glad to see us return alive.

"Any new developments?" I asked them.

My hydraulic engineering mate showed me that something had changed: more of the ship had come awake in our absence.

"Hmm," I said, studying the ship's diagram. "It's following some kind of script."

"The ship is programmed to add vital systems one at a time when the generators are running again," Zye explained.

Eyeing her thoughtfully, I asked her a question: "What were your duties aboard *Defiant* before you were arrested?"

"Maintenance," she said vaguely. "I kept things running. That's why I know how many of the subsystems operate."

"I see. It would seem to be in our best interest, then, to get more power flowing around the vessel. Given sufficient feed, can the ship repair itself?"

"We have no nanites," Zye said. "No smart metals that fold themselves back into shape. We never developed that technology. But we do have robotic repair units. If you can get power to the lower aft deck, you'll find the units running all over the ship, rebuilding her."

Rumbold perked up. "That should give Singh's men something to chew on!"

"Right," I said. "Yamada, stay here with an assistant to man life support and watch the screens for infiltration. We don't know how long we have before Captain Singh decides to visit us again. The rest of us will head for the power-coupling deck."

It took nearly an hour to reach the center of the power-coupling deck. In a damaged spacecraft, the going can be treacherous. Cold vacuum alone is deadly enough, but jagged twists of metal, poisonous corrosives and radioactive substances are frequent elements in any large ship's construction. We had to wind our way past these hazards and into the damaged region carefully, like a party of cave spelunkers.

When we'd reached the power couplings themselves, we found them remarkably intact. It was the massive cables that were severed, rather than the critical switching equipment that routed the power.

Rumbold and his team proved themselves to be instrumental over the following hours of hard labor. With Zye's help, they shunted and reconnected the massive cables, repairing them. I was relegated to the role of an observer and spent most of my time tapping on various control screens.

I learned that the ship's interface, although strange, wasn't unfathomable. With Zye's help, I managed to breach many security elements and access the data core.

Fascinated, I paged through the information I found there. The ship had been commissioned two decades earlier, if my understanding of their dating system was accurate. She was one of several identical massive vessels. Her class was indeed referred to as a battle cruiser, meaning she was an independent capital ship capable of performing missions in remote star systems without support vessels.

As I paged through star charts and saw various colonies mapped there, I became increasingly excited. My heart pounded in my temples. This ship was a treasure trove of critical information. Earth had been asleep for so long...

How could this have happened to us, I wondered? How could we have been so blind? We'd assumed that because our own pathways to other star systems had vanished, that the pathways between other star systems had also been destroyed. Even more foolish, we'd believed new pathways could not be found. But why?

On the surface of it, when confronted with the physical evidence, I was dumbfounded at the shortsighted nature of Earth's rulers. How could we have assumed so much, so wrongly, for so long?

Then, unbidden, darker thoughts came to my mind. Perhaps we *weren't* so stupid after all. Perhaps, at some level, government officials knew the truth, or at least they suspected it. How could they not have done so?

All my life, I'd believed the common wisdom of my fellows. I'd been certain that the colonies were cut off from us and we from them. We weren't even sure whether or not they still existed. Every teacher in every school, from kindergarten to graduate school, had professed this knowledge to me as indisputable fact. Anyone who disagreed was labeled "ignorant."

But it wasn't so. We *weren't* alone. And our isolation was due to our own disinterest. There were surviving colonies, many of them. As I continued tapping at links, looking at new worlds, I realized that there were actually more colonies than I'd ever been told of. This fact led me back to Zye with fresh questions.

"Zye," I said, "how many colonies are there in space?"

"Human colonies? About a hundred that we know of."

My eyes narrowed. "Do I take it from that statement that some of these colonies are not human?"

"That's right. There are worlds where humans share the planet with native life-forms. Creatures that weren't transplanted from Earth long ago. In addition, along the distant frontier where new colonies are still being founded, alien intelligences have been encountered from time to time."

My blood chilled in my veins. "Aliens," I said. "Real aliens, not microbes and odd scrubby plants?"

"That's right. But we Betas don't know much about them. We only have contact with a few local human colonies, all of which are hostile to us. We've never met with a real alien that I know of."

"But...if you know the pathways," I asked, "why don't you trade? There used to be a thriving trade system."

"There is some trade," she said, "but it's nothing like the old days. Remember that before the Cataclysm, all the pathways between the stars were first discovered between Earth and the colony systems. Earth was the hub, the center of commerce. You had to travel to Earth before you could get anywhere else. The colonies didn't have direct, independent trade routes. Because of this weakness, a dark age began when we were cut off."

"It was similar on Earth but possibly worse. We weren't just cut off from you, our homeworld was wounded as well. Most of our technology was wiped out during the span of a single hour due to the massive solar flare. In the years that followed, we endured starvation, wars... The fact that the old pathways between our star system and the colonies had been erased wasn't our worst trouble."

"I see," Zye said thoughtfully. "What you describe is close to what was generally assumed. We didn't know if you still lived or not. Therefore, we had to fend for ourselves. We had trouble just feeding our population at first, and when equipment from Earth broke down we often lacked the skills to repair it. We had to build new industries from scratch, replacing infrastructure that had previously existed only on Earth. Most of our population died out within the first decade. Correspondingly, the Betas decided to rebuild our race with survival in mind. We cloned a new generation of Betas, designed to survive hardship."

"You said before you were made up of females—why only females?"

"The original plan involved superior female lifespans and the ability to reproduce. We wanted to be able to quickly expand our population naturally without cloning."

"Reproduce without cloning?" I asked. "By meeting up with others...an outside group with males?"

"We have a few males," she said matter-of-factly. "They're in storage in case we need them. But you're the first male I've ever seen with my own eyes."

The more I learned of the Betas, the more disturbing I found them to be. Also, I was becoming curious as to the behavior of Zye herself. Perhaps the psychology of the situation between myself and this amazing woman was more complex than I'd imagined at first. If I was the only male she'd ever encountered, and I was also the first human face she'd seen when we'd rescued her from her cell—these facts could explain a lot. When taken together, the emotional impact of making my acquaintance might explain her apparent devotion to me.

"Thank you for being so open," I said, "we'll talk more later."

"I'm yours to command."

She walked away and continued helping Rumbold's men shunt massive cables around.

I looked after her. She'd said these last words as if they were part of a ritual. Perhaps that's how one Beta addressed another who was their leader. I found that to be an interesting concept, then I relegated the idea to the back of my mind.

Once the power-couplings were functional again, we had decisions to make.

"What part of the ship do we want to make operational first?" I asked.

"Weapons systems, sir," Rumbold told me. "What choice do we have?"

I frowned at him. "Are you suggesting we should blow *Altair* out of the sky? Wouldn't that be confirming Singh's lies about us?"

Rumbold shrugged. "I guess you could activate *Defiant's* drive. That way, we could at least fly her. Not an easy choice, I admit."

"Communications," I announced. "That makes the most sense to me. If we activate the drive, we might be able to fly, but we'd be flying blind. No sensors. Possibly, no helm control either. The drive is too interdependent, likewise the weapons systems."

"Communications then?" Zye asked.

"Do it."

Zye directed the repair crew, all of whom were sweating in their suits, to help her connect the final coupling. The collars touched, then the meshed splines locked into place. With a confident hand, she reached out and threw the massive breaker.

The lines hummed under our feet. Everyone shifted uncomfortably, aware of the unknown voltages that now coursed close to our bodies. It was one thing to work on a ship you understood, it was quite another to toy with systems on a vessel that was, for all intents and purposes alien, and many times the size of our largest ships. If not for Zye's help, I doubt we could have done it at all.

Lights flickered, dimmed, then came back up to full power. The ship adjusted to our altered pathways, funneling juice to unknown destinations. After a few tense seconds, during which we all glanced at one another with wide eyes, we began to smile.

All of us, that is, except for Zye herself. Her confidence in her own technical skills was absolute. She stepped away from the rest of the group and went to work on another damaged region.

After we were sure we weren't all going to blow up or be burnt to ash by our jury-rigged repairs, we followed her.

"There's a problem," she said, examining various readouts. "The generators are already at their peak output. That shouldn't be—but it is. I can only surmise that we've lost several generators, and that we must head down to the power deck to get more of them operational before activating more systems."

"All right, but do we have communications?" I asked Zye.

"Of course."

"How do I use them?"

"Operate any station. Access the data core as I've shown you. Link into battle command and transmit whatever you want."

"Battle command?" I asked. "Are you talking about a Beta communications network?"

"Naturally. This is a Beta military ship."

"But I wanted to talk to *Altair*. Can the system communicate with other ships using some kind of proximity broadcast?"

Zye shrugged. "Perhaps. I'm not a communications officer."

"All right then. Repair crews, carry on. Follow Zye to the generator deck and see what can be done. Rumbold, you're in charge."

"Aye, aye," he said, sighing. "Any chance of a break, sir? For food and such-like?"

I glanced at him and the others. Sometimes, I forgot they were actually quite old. Longevity treatments halted ageing, but they weren't exactly fountains of youth. Older crewmen still became tired and hungry sooner than did the young.

"Right, take a break—no more than an hour."

"I rested long enough in my cell," Zye said. "I'm not yet fatigued. Permission to keep working, Captain?"

I glanced at her. Was that an expression of disgust? Or was she just anxious to keep working for the betterment of all? It was hard to tell. Her facial cues weren't quite like ours, and she maintained a poker face most of the time anyway.

"Permission granted. The rest of you catch up to her when you can."

There were relieved sighs and grunts all around as my crew dispersed. I went up to find Yamada in life support, which we'd made our temporary headquarters.

"We've got external communications," I told her. "Let's see if we can raise *Altair*."

She lifted a thoughtful finger and shook her head. "Perhaps we should think carefully, sir," she said.

"What are you suggesting?"

"If we talk to Singh, we're likely to be ignored or banned. He doesn't know we can communicate, and I think we should play the advantage carefully."

"Okay...are you saying we should report back to Earth?"

She nodded.

"But who..." I said thoughtfully. "By now, he's alerted the Guard to his actions. He must have some kind of excuse, some kind of accusation we're unaware of. Even if we talk to an Admiral, he may or may not listen."

"Right. But there are other options. Who else can you contact who might help us?"

Instantly, I realized what she was hinting around about. "You want me to contact my father—to circumvent the chain of command."

"Exactly, I don't think we have any other choice."

The thought wasn't a pleasant one for me. I'd spent the last decade proving to myself and my father that I was independent. I was my own man now, not just another whining, seventy-percent clone living in a parental shadow.

But now, here I was, contemplating calling daddy for help.

"I don't want to do this," I said. "The very thought of it stings my pride. But I think you're right, it's the wisest course of action."

"William," she said in a lowered voice, "if it's any consolation, your crew has come to respect you for your own qualities. It's only now that I realize the burden you've been operating under. You don't want to rely on your father for anything, do you?"

"No," I said.

"Why not?"

The question was overly personal, and I thought about waving it off—but I didn't. I felt the events of the previous days gave her the right to ask it. My crew had entrusted me with their lives, and they'd performed admirably. Opening up a little wasn't always recommended for officers in the Guard, but regulations said it was up to the individual.

"My father doesn't want me to be in the Guard at all," I said. "He abhors Star Guard. He thinks of it as a fossil, a relic without a purpose, a burden on the taxpayers."

She nodded thoughtfully. "That makes sense, considering his politics, but we really didn't believe it. We thought you were one more patrician's son getting a commission he had never earned by trading with his father's name."

"What do you think now?"

"That I'm in the presence of a true patriot, an officer who believes in what he's doing. You've sacrificed more than any of us as most of us didn't have an easy life as an option."

"I'm not sure about that, but I thank you for the kind words."

Smiling, she turned her attention to the screens. She toyed with them using Zye's passcode until she found an external broadcast option and set the frequency for Earth's public communications net.

"We can spoof the system with simple packets," she said. "The Betas are using a protocol that we've abandoned, but it's still supported for legacy devices."

"But will it allow me to speak to my father?" I asked.

"The system will contact him if you type in your ID and password. It will appear to him as an odd connection from an unknown source. The real question is: would he answer such a call?"

After a moment's thought, I shook my head. "No. But I know someone who might."

Instead of typing in my father's ID, I chose instead to type in an ID I'd never utilized before…that of Chloe, of House Astra.

-22-

I'd reasoned that Chloe might be curious, rather than dismissive, of an unknown caller. She might even expect me to contact her clandestinely. Banking on her natural curiosity, I hoped she wouldn't check with her mother's security people, who'd almost certainly advise her to ignore the call.

Unfortunately, due to the distance to Earth, I couldn't make a normal real-time call. I had to record a message and transmit it all at once. The message would be more like transmitting an email than a phone call, something I was certain Rumbold could relate to.

Thinking over what I was going to say, I became uncomfortable with Yamada's scrutiny. She was already recording and looking at me expectantly.

Yamada wasn't the most indiscrete member of my crew, but I didn't want her to be tempted with private information the others would relish gossiping about. I thought about editing my message down to a purely business-like statement of fact, but Astra and I had experienced a personal moment at her father's home. How could I fail to mention that encounter in this transmission and still expect her to help me?

"Uh, could you excuse me for a moment, Ensign? I wish to make this recording privately."

She raised her eyebrows as if she were thinking about asking me a question, but then she nodded. "All right, I'll go. When you're finished, tap this save symbol that looks like an anvil, then the green send arrow at the bottom. The transmission will take over an hour to reach Earth, then we can hope for a reply an hour after that."

When she was gone, I began recording.

"Lady Astra," I said, sounding formal at first. Then I cleared my throat, let my spine curve a little into a more natural posture and smiled. "Chloe, I miss you. I'm sorry about the long absence without contact. I've been sent on a deep space mission investigating an anomaly that was thought to be a comet—but the object turned out to be a ship of colossal size."

I queued up and attached a series of still images and video. The various decks and shots of Zye herself were in the files. I made sure the most surprising features were included, as I wanted the montage to prove I wasn't lying about our discovery.

"The ship was built by colonists from Beta Cygnus—you may remember them from our history texts. The large woman in the photographs is named Zye, and she's a Beta. This must all come as a shock, but I assure you it's true. I'm betting you know enough of our history to realize how monumental this discovery is. Unfortunately, not everyone is happy about the find."

Here, I added an audio recording of Singh declaring he would destroy my ship and crew. I attached this and transmitted it as well.

"As you can see, Captain Singh is attempting to hide the truth about this ship—this battle cruiser. And now comes the hard part."

I directed the camera at me again. Looking down for a moment, I tried but failed to come up with a nice way to ask for her help. I sighed instead.

"I'm going to ask you to help me. I'm going to ask you to champion the truth over the name of House Astra. Distribute these files. Forward my message to the press and to as many outlets as you can. I know this will be a hard thing to do as our parents are part of political parties that would rather not admit this discovery is real. But it *is* real, and Singh is trying to cover it up by killing me. He's probably blaming me for some accident—maybe outright treachery."

Looking into the video pickup, I forced myself to smile again. "I enjoyed our short time together, and I hope to see you again. Regardless of your decision, farewell."

Closing the transmission, I tapped the save button, then, after a few seconds of indecision, I sent it.

The moment I'd finished, I began thinking of who else I could send the message to. My parents came to mind, of course. How could I keep them in the dark? They might never open the message, but I thought I had to at least try.

Setting up the vid pick-up again and composing myself, I began a new message directed at both my parents. One of them might be curious enough to check it and not assume it was some kind of unsolicited garbage from the grid.

Before I could finish a dozen words, however, the vessel around me shook with an impact.

The ship's lights dimmed, wavered, then went out. A moment later I was bathed in emergency red.

"Yamada!" I shouted. "Yamada, do you read me?"

Static spat from my implants. I thought I heard a buzzing, as if there were voices, but then nothing.

Getting up quickly, I drew my gun and headed for the doorway. As I did so, I glanced at the ship's diagram in the midst of the life support chamber. Part of the ship was flashing. It was the power-couplings again.

"Damn it," I said, opening the hatch and trotting through the passages.

When I got to the deck, I saw smoke hanging in blue-white twists. I couldn't smell the smoke because I had my helmet sealed, but I knew the aftermath of an electrical fire when I saw one.

"Yamada? Rumbold? Is anyone on the power-coupling deck?"

There was no answer. As I moved through the region, I almost tripped over a body. I rolled the suited fellow over—it was Alberto, one of mine. There was a blackened hole in his chest. He'd been shot with a power bolt.

I eased him back onto his face and crouched, eyes searching the scene. There was no one around. I began moving again, toward the generators, when a brilliant light flared.

A bolt had struck near my head. A pipe full of wires had been blasted open. Burning metal threw sparks in my face. The report from the strike must have been deafeningly loud, as I could clearly hear the roar of it even through my helmet.

Twisting and firing a bolt back at my attacker, I got lucky. I don't have any other explanation for it. I caught my attacker full in the gut, and he doubled over. Sprawling and convulsing on the deck, I didn't approach him to render aid. Instead, I warily circled the room full of heavy equipment, looking for any partners he might have had.

Finding no one else, I decided this ambush had been set up to catch anyone entering the chamber. Perhaps Alberto had been unlucky, showing himself first and being shot for his trouble.

As far as I could tell, the dark chamber was empty except for the two dead men. I left, heading toward the generators, but I was wary now. I didn't want to be taken by surprise again.

When I got to the power generators, I feared the worst. What if I was the last man aboard, being hunted by Singh's crew through the labyrinthine ship?

Fortunately, the scratchy buzzing sounds that tickled my auditory nerves via my implants grew more distinct and turned into human voices. Friendly voices.

"I don't get it," Yamada was saying. "I've switched on two more generators, and less power is being distributed."

"That's because they got to the couplings," I said, stepping out of the shadows.

Rumbold whirled around and for a second, I thought he might shoot me. But he controlled his surprised reaction and lowered his weapon.

"There you are, sir. Do you know what's going on?"

I explained about Alberto and the man I'd found fooling with the power-couplings.

"But," I said, "that doesn't explain the lurching sensation I felt from the ship before that. What happened? Did someone try to engage the engines?"

"No, Captain," Zye said. "It was your destroyer. They latched onto *Defiant* with some kind of beam."

"A grav-beam," Yamada said.

161

"Really?" I asked. "This ship must displace a hundred thousand metric tons. Maybe more with the ice on the hull. Singh might damage his engines trying to take us somewhere."

"Let's hope so," Rumbold said. "From what I gather, he put down a few more marines to knock out our power and began dragging us at the same time."

"Right," I said, thinking hard. "He's dragging his prize home…"

They all looked at me. The next move was my decision. Naturally, I had no idea what I should do. The situation was unprecedented. Despite that, I nodded with confidence.

"All right, fine," I said firmly. "If he wants to up the ante, so will we."

They stared for a moment, then Rumbold brightened. "Weapons? You want us to hook up the weapons systems and target locks, isn't that right, sir?"

I thought about it, staring at him for a few seconds.

Finally, I nodded and gave them a confident smile. "That's right. Let's do it. This old battlewagon must have the power to damage one aging Earth destroyer."

Yamada's hand snaked forward and she clamped it over my wrist. "But sir," she said, "we can't destroy *Altair*. It would be unconscionable."

"Don't worry, I told her firmly. You get the targeting system working with Zye's help, and we won't have to."

Spurred into action, the group set about following my orders.

While I stood guard and frequently checked the ship's diagrams for any further signs of invasive forces, I couldn't help but wonder what I'd unleashed here in space today.

I'd contacted Earth, delivering revolutionary news. I'd killed a man—my first, I realized now in retrospect—and I'd ordered my tiny crew to fire on *Altair*.

What would tomorrow possibly bring that could be more startling?

-23-

Several hours later, I'd almost forgotten about the message I'd beamed to Earth. I'd been so busy helping my crew to get a full bank of generators operating again, it had slipped my mind.

"Captain?" Yamada said. "There's a message for you, sir."

I stared at her in confusion for a second, then quickly stepped up to the boards that she indicated. The message was from Chloe's account.

"Your friend?" she asked.

"Yes, of course…thank you."

"If you'd rather take it in private, I could—"

"Don't worry," I said. "I'll view it on my retinal display."

I piped the message to my implant, and it began playing at once. A few times during the presentation, it blurred and slipped, but each time it came back into focus.

Watching Chloe Astra's body being superimposed on the world in front of me was an odd experience. She seemed to be right here among us—but she wasn't.

I was accustomed to the technology, of course, but generally it didn't have the kind of psychological impact that Chloe's form had. She wore very little—something made of gauze, or synthetic silk. It hugged her lithe frame in ways I couldn't help but notice. I gathered instantly that I'd interrupted her sleep. Out in space, stuck within a colonial battle cruiser, we'd lost track of what time it was back home.

"William," she began, "what an odd and alarming message you sent me. I miss you too, and I hope you'll be all right out there in the dark. About your request..."

She looked down, almost ashamedly, my heart sank to see it. I felt certain that she was about to tell me I was going to have to fend for myself.

But what she said next was quite possibly worse. "I'm sorry," she said. "You have to understand...I'm a seventy-percent copy, just like you. I'm an integral member of House Astra, and I always will be. Don't misunderstand, I'd like to help, I really would, but I'm taking a great risk by even speaking with you."

My despair turned to confusion. Out loud, I muttered: "But why?"

Yamada and few others gave me a curious glance. I knew I must have looked odd to them—staring at nothing with unfocussed eyes. But I didn't care about them right now, I was hanging on Chloe's every word.

"I didn't forward your message to my mother. You had essentially already sent it to her—you have to understand that. You see, I'm watched most of the time. After your visit things got worse. My communications are all monitored now, and anything interesting is immediately sent to my mother by the house AI. I am her heir, after all, and in her mind I've strayed lately..."

I was beginning to catch on. Her mother was the problem. As the leader of the Centrists, she was a dangerous political adversary for my father even though they'd seen eye to eye in regard to dismantling Star Guard.

A single tear ran down her face. "It began almost immediately. Before I even saw your message. The media are running those images you sent me—but edited versions. You're being portrayed as a renegade. A madman flying a dangerous colonial relic. A threat to all humanity. And the political advertisements are blaming your father's party. They—they twisted everything you said. You know what can be done with unsecured video."

Nodding to myself, I did know. For political opponents, such things were clay to be molded into whatever form they wished. So that was it...I was to be handed the role of scapegoat.

"Your father is already firing back, naturally. He's got a more accurate version of events playing—but the trouble is, the Navy isn't taking your side. They're backing Singh. Your father is on every news cycle, looking like his heir is a mutineer and he's trying to cover up the truth."

She shook her head and gathered herself. She was like me in that way, trained to be a master of self-control.

"You understand these things. My mother struck first. That was the first story the news people heard. Then the Guard backed her up—last came your father with a different version, but...well, the opinion polls are bad."

Chloe finally looked directly into the vid pickup. "I'm sorry," she said. "I can't do anything politically. I have no position to play, but I promise you I'll back you up if I ever do. I believe in you, William Sparhawk, even if no one else does. Come back to Earth safely, any way you can."

The message ended. I was left intently staring at nothing.

My crewmen were glancing at me and one another in concern.

"Good news, I hope?" Rumbold said half-jokingly.

"No," I said. "We're in trouble. And we're on our own."

I looked around at the faces surrounding me. Had I misplayed the situation? Had I gotten all of them listed as mutineers? Perhaps, I thought, I should give myself up right now. If Singh would accept my surrender, further bloodshed could be avoided and at least my innocent crew might be exonerated. After all, who could fault them for following the orders of their commander?

My mouth opened, but then it clamped closed again. I felt a surge of stubbornness. I wasn't going to give in to my political enemies nor those of my father.

Singh's actions had begun to make sense to me, in a twisted way. He was an opponent of my father's party. He wanted the Sparhawk family to be disgraced, to fall hard and hopefully die out entirely. Perhaps that was why he'd gone so far as to attempt to kill me and my crew.

It would not be the first time that extreme political views caused a man to behave irrationally, to turn against his own.

Standing up, I straightened my spine and looked around the questioning circle of faces. They were no longer working. They'd forgotten their tasks.

Stepping to the nearest generator, I made an adjustment and switched it on. Power thrummed in the room. I could feel the vibration and the static from it right through my boots.

"Weapons and basic sensors. I need both—and I need them now."

Rumbold's eyes were as big and round as ever. "You've got it, sir! Six more hours, that's all I ask. Then you'll have those guns and the power to drive them! For sensors, you'll have to ask Yamada."

I turned to her, and she nodded thoughtfully. "We can do it. All they need is a fraction of the power that the cannons require. I recommend we switch them on last, so the enemy doesn't knock them out right away."

"Good thinking. We'll leave them off until the critical moment. But do you really think all they need is a power supply? Are they undamaged?"

She stepped closer. "The sensor arrays aren't in the best shape, and they're covered in frost and debris—but the *Altair* is right on top of us. All we have to do is get a general directional fix. At this range we can't miss—but sir, can I have a word?"

Nodding, I stepped aside, and she followed me.

Behind us, Rumbold got the rest of the crew grunting and heaving on another generator, attaching shunts and repairing a damaged coil.

"What is it, Yamada?"

"That's what I was going to ask you," she said privately. "I saw your face. The message is from Earth, isn't it? Bad news?"

"No," I said, "not really. Our situation hasn't changed. We are in deep space, being improperly victimized by our task force leader. He's made a false report back to the capital, that's all."

She nodded thoughtfully. "A false report—which they believed?"

I forced a smile I didn't feel and laid a hand lightly on her shoulder. "Listen," I said, "we're far beyond visual range. Whatever happens out here will be explained by those who survive to tell the tale."

"You're going to kill him, aren't you?" she whispered. "You're going to take out Singh."

Right then, as she said that, I realized she might be correct. Singh might force my hand. If he wouldn't stop his attacks, what other choice did I have? To keep my crew alive, I might have to move against him with the same ruthlessness and determination that he had used. A battle couldn't be won on a purely defensive basis. At some point, you had to turn the tables on your tormentor to achieve victory.

"We'll see," I said to Yamada, "but I'd prefer to do this without destroying anything or killing anyone."

"That isn't working out. You'll have to take the fight to him."

"We'll see," I repeated firmly.

I dropped my hand from her shoulder then, and she moved away. As she left, I noticed an intense pair of eyes studying the two of us.

The eyes studying me belonged to Zye. I was startled by their intense nature. Her expression was unreadable, as always, but I got the feeling she didn't approve of my actions in regard to Yamada.

I dismissed Zye's reaction and returned to my work. I didn't have time to work out the vagaries of Beta psychology. I had a ship to repair and a public relations battle to win.

I only hoped the situation wouldn't escalate.

-24-

Despite Rumbold's promise he'd get the guns running within hours, we'd spent almost a full day working at it. There were too many unknown systems and delays. I didn't blame him as the crew was doing their best, but it was frustrating.

As every hour crept by, I feared Singh would launch some new attack, but he didn't. I suspected his defeat had permanently changed his mind on that angle.

We were moving at a pretty good clip by the time Rumbold reported the weapons systems were functional. *Altair* had been towing us the entire time, as if we were a chunk of scrap metal to be brought to Ceres for dismantlement.

We didn't know where she was towing us, but it didn't much matter. Wherever we were going, I was sure I didn't want to go there.

"Activate the external sensors," I ordered Yamada.

"Full active, sir? We'll light her up. There's no way she won't know what's coming. She'll probably knock out our array the minute we do it."

"I know," I said, "but we'll have a lock on her by that time."

"There is another option, sir," she said.

We were back in the life support section. It had become our local bridge. The real bridge had been found, but it wasn't yet operational.

Our fire control was very limited as a result. We were almost operating the ship manually. We had a data feed running from the sensors embedded in the hull down to our displays in life support. Inside the ship, relayed suit radios carried my commands to the troops in the weapons pods.

"Rumbold," I said, eyeing Yamada, "final check. Are your gunners ready?"

"Guns, one, two and three at the ready, sir. Just give the word, and we'll power up. It might take a few seconds to charge—so keep that in mind, please."

So many unknowns. It was nerve-racking enough guiding a ship I knew well through combat. Doing so while half-blind and flying a vessel I had no real understanding of was eating away at me. I hadn't slept in twenty hours, and the inside of my suit needed a good airing out.

"Zye, are the generators fully operational?"

"The ones we've got online are all in the green, sir," she said.

I would have to take her word for that. The ship was hers, after all. But we weren't her people. I was surprised and pleased that she seemed to trust us now. Perhaps it was because her own people had abandoned her.

"Yamada," I said, turning to her last, "you said something about another way? You'd better give it to me now. I'm not going to hold off much longer. It's too risky. They might detect a power surge and damage everything we've worked so hard to build back up."

"I know, Skipper. But I think you should give Singh one last chance. Contact him directly and negotiate."

Frowning at her, I considered. "No," I said a moment later. "It will only tip my hand. I'd have to threaten him to get him to listen, and that will give him the chance to react. It would endanger us too much."

"I respect your opinion, sir," she said, "but I think you should think about the aftermath."

"What aftermath? We're traitors, remember? How will it get any better or worse?"

"It doesn't have to be that way. Contact him, and we'll record his responses. When and if we get back to Earth, we'll have something to defend ourselves with—recorded proof that we did our best to remedy the situation."

"That's an interesting idea," I said. "My family is famous for such PR coups. We've traded our way to the top on them, in fact. You must realize by now how much I hate dirty tricks of that kind."

"I know you do," she said sympathetically. "But this isn't just about you. It's not even about your crew. It's about Star Guard itself. What do you think should happen, sir, in the light of this new knowledge?"

"What knowledge, specifically?"

"The fact that we're not alone in the galaxy. That our colonists are out there, building dangerous fleets, and that one of those ships managed to make it here to our system."

"I hadn't really given it a lot of thought," I admitted. "I've been focused on surviving."

"Right, well, this is our chance to change everything. We've got to do this right. We've got to help Star Guard and Earth itself."

I heaved a sigh, and checked the time. I'd wasted two minutes talking to Yamada about this. At any point, Singh could make a move on me.

Trying to think clearly, I went over my options. She was right, of course. This situation was bigger than a squabble between two Guard officers in deep space. It was about the future of the navy and humanity in general.

I sighed deeply. "Open a channel to *Altair*," I said.

Yamada whirled and put her hands on her board. She tapped three times and I could hear the call signal go out. A tone sounded, followed by silence, then the tone again. This cycle repeated six times.

"That's enough," I said. "He's not interested."

"Give him a minute, he might be taking a piss or something."

"Then his exec would answer," I said.

"Maybe he gave orders that only he could talk to you. That only makes sense given his actions, doesn't it?"

Nodding, I had to agree. Six more times, the tone sounded. Then nine. Finally, I stood up and walked over to her. "Let's cut the signal. Let him call us back if he—"

I stopped, the channel had opened and gone live.

"Sparhawk?" Singh's voice asked. "You've finally called to surrender?"

"I've called to end this conflict, Captain."

"Good. Here are my terms. You'll come to the surface in a space suit, without armament. Come alone, the rest of your people will be allowed to exit the rock when you're safely in custody. Now, as to the charges you'll be confessing to—"

"Sir," I interrupted. "I think you misunderstand the situation. I'm negotiating your surrender, not my own."

There was a moment of silence, then a stream of curses. "You got me out of bed for this? You asshole. I'm going to enjoy it when—"

"Captain Singh," I said loudly, "please listen to me, because the safety of your ship and crew require it. We've armed the main weapons battery of this vessel. Upon my order, a sensor array on the external hull of the ship will go active. It will ping and lock onto your ship. Once we have the signature, I'm sure you realize that at this range we can't miss. Your own armament doesn't have the location of our guns mapped. We will fire and disable *Altair*. I do not want to do this as I believe Earth will need every ship she has in the coming—"

"Shut up!" Singh screamed into my ear. "Of all the crazy shit—you're worse than those fake press releases we cooked up! You and your bat-shit father. We're going to do this my way, and we're going to do it now. I don't want to hear another word about imaginary weapons banks and—"

Turning my head, I signaled Yamada. Her face tightened with stress, but she relayed my order. Outside the ship, a bank of metal dishes tried to swivel, but couldn't due to the accumulated ice and debris. They were intended to sweep an entire star system and finally did manage to switch on and blast out radiation. The signals were so intense that they easily penetrated the obstacles coating them and a signature response from the *Altair* came back to us.

On the main display, an outline of *Altair* appeared. It was eerie, seeing this alien technology operate. This is how the Beta crew might have looked upon our fleet if they'd encountered it in battle.

Singh's tirade broke off. "There's something—are you doing that, Sparhawk?"

"I told you sir. We're engaging you now. Events have been set in motion. You have a very short window during which you must comply with our wishes. Otherwise—"

"Helm, hard over!" I heard Singh shout. "Evasive action. *Now*!"

"Unless you stand down now, Captain," I said. "We will fire on you. I'm not bluffing. I never bluff, sir."

There were a few moments of silence.

"You can't have done what you say you've done," Singh said. "That ship is alien to you. It's a derelict. You can't—"

"We can, and have, sir," I said loudly. "We had help. Some of the crew and repair robots were active aboard. We've done it, and now you must accept that it is you who must surrender to me. If you don't, I'll be forced to damage *Altair*. I'll give you thirty more seconds, then—"

"William!" Yamada shouted. "They've rolled over and engaged their guns. They're pumping depleted uranium rounds right down on the sensor array."

I watched as the display showed a beam of sparks which leapt from *Altair's* midsection down toward our vastly larger ship. Within the span of a second, the image of *Altair* melted.

Yamada looked up at me, her eyes huge. "You can't give them any more time. They'll gun their engines and move—they've blinded us!"

She was right. There was no more time. I took two long strides to the display and I tapped the image of the ship, which was now only an outline, a computer projection of where it had been.

"Rumbold!" I shouted. "Activate the primary cannon!"

"Only one, sir?" he asked.

"Follow orders!"

"Done sir, her clamshell is opening…she's priming…she's…"

"Sparhawk!" Singh shouted in my ear. "For God's sake, man! Don't do it!"

I heard the fear in him. I heard the full knowledge of the situation. He could see the gun. He knew what it meant, and so did I.

"I'm sorry, Captain, but I didn't start this fight."

I touched the fading diagram depicting *Altair* again.

Yamada sucked in her breath, as she'd seen the specific target I'd chosen.

The ship shivered. I knew the feel, even if I'd never experienced it before. The cannon had fired. It had released a vast amount of energy, forming a beam so powerful and accurate it could reach across the gulf of emptiness between planets and strike another vessel.

This time, however, the beam only had to go a few kilometers. It struck accurately, and *Altair* was disabled.

Yamada's eyes sought mine. "You—you took out the bridge. You deliberately selected the bridge."

I nodded slowly. "It was the only way. You said it yourself. Singh had to be stopped."

She was breathing hard. Her face was reddened as if by grief or shame.

I reached out to touch her, but she shied away from me. I immediately retreated. I'd made a mistake, allowing emotion to move me to embrace her—now could hardly be the time.

She looked at me again. "You really *are* like your father," she said.

"They fired first, Christine," I said gently.

"Sorry," she said. "Let me explain: your actions were justified. I'm not saying they weren't. But to actually *do* something like that takes courage, determination—ruthlessness. You have all those traits, apparently."

I wasn't sure whether I should be insulted or pleased, so I turned back to the screens. I was surprised to see them come to life again, showing a damaged image of *Altair*.

"The sensor array is back online?" I asked.

"There are several arrays. I only activated one initially, as I expected them to knock it out when it pinged them. I've switched on another array."

"Of course—good work."

There was a cold lump in my gut as I surveyed what I'd done. *Altair* was spinning slowly, lopsidedly. She was out of control, leaving the orbit of our larger vessel and drifting away from us. Her grav-beams were off, as were her engines. The bridge module, a section that sat forward between the primary cannons, was twisted wreckage.

"William?" Yamada asked.

"Yes?"

She came up beside me, and we surveyed the wreck that had been our mothership.

"Why did you select the target with your own hand? You touched the control bar to fire personally. Did you think that I wouldn't follow your orders if you asked me to fire on their bridge?"

"That wasn't it," I said. "I wanted to spare you the anguish—the sensation I'm feeling right now."

"Oh, I see…thank you for that."

-25-

Together we stared at *Altair* as she rolled, going through her death throes. She was venting plasma, gas and liquids which froze instantly into clouds of icy droplets.

We tried to establish communications with her, but failed. Now and then we caught a snatch of frantic radio, probably from one survivor's suit to another, but we could do little to help. We had no rescue ships, no grav-beams—nothing.

Watching *Altair* die was difficult for me. I could scarcely believe I'd done such damage to one of Earth's finest vessels.

"Open a channel in the clear," I ordered Yamada. "Broadcast it to anyone who might be able to listen."

"Channel ready, you're live."

"Crew of *Altair*," I said. "This is the battle cruiser *Defiant*. We would like to render assistance, but we have no means to do so. If you can get to the hull of our ship, we will do what we can to help."

A full minute passed. I began to lose hope. But then a faint, scratchy answer came back. I was sure it was a suit radio.

"We can't trust you, Sparhawk," said a voice.

"Yes, you can. Who am I speaking with?"

"This is Midshipman Taranto. We're not going to surrender. You'd kill the last of us if we came to you."

I knew him, and I placed a face with the voice as soon as he said his name. He was a squatty man with lamb-chop sideburns and a hawk nose.

"No surrender is required," I said, "I'm an honorable member of the Guard, the same as you are, Taranto. Listen to me: *Altair* is tumbling farther away. We can't come to your rescue. You must come to us."

"You're a renegade, a pirate—"

"Please, let's set aside this tragic conflict for now. A court of inquiry on Earth can settle any questions as to who was at fault."

There was a moment of quiet, then: "You would submit to a court martial? After what you've done?"

"I absolutely would, if such a thing is eventually ordered by CENTCOM. I swear to that on the honor of House Sparhawk."

"All right then. We'll probably be butchered, but we're coming to you. We've got no more than three hours of oxygen left in our suits, anyway."

His statement left me confused. "So little? What about the lifeboats?"

"The lifeboats weren't properly maintained."

I understood then. The poor budgets and lax maintenance schedules had claimed more victims. The supplies aboard the lifeboats had been allowed to leak away. Probably, their fuel tanks had been emptied long ago to feed *Altair's* hungry engines as well.

"All right, contact me when you've reached the outer hull. We'll guide you in."

The channel closed, and I looked at the screens thoughtfully.

"I need to regain the trust of these men," I told Yamada. "I'm going to speak with our prisoner. Is he awake yet?"

"I don't know," she said as if startled. "I'd forgotten about him in that automated cell."

Nodding, I walked toward the exit. "Now we know what happened to Zye."

When I arrived at the detention center, however, I found Marine Lieutenant Morris had not been forgotten by everyone. Zye was there, staring at him through the porthole.

"Zye? Is Morris well?"

"He's functional," she said. "The medical machinery performed surgery on his leg—it had to be removed. The system is generating a simple prosthetic."

I winced at that news. After all, I'd ordered the door shut on him.

Steeling myself, I walked up next to Zye, who went back to peering into the chamber quietly.

"Is he speaking?" I asked.

"I think he is," she replied.

I saw then that Morris was indeed talking in his cell. His lips were moving, and his face was red with anger, but I couldn't hear him.

"Why...?" I began. "Did you mute his speaker?"

"Yes. I found his speech distracting."

"I see...what exactly are you doing here, Zye?"

She looked at me for a moment. "I'm remembering. I spent a long time in that cell. Now, for the first time, I can see a prisoner from a new perspective—that of the jailor."

"Okay...do you mind if I talk to him now?"

"Not at all, Captain. Be my guest."

She retreated, and I was left alone with the lieutenant. I turned on the speaker and apologized to him.

"There's something wrong with that woman!" he told me. "I don't know where you found her, but she's a freak."

"She's a Beta," I said. "A colonist. They've been cut off from Earth for so long, their cultural norms have clearly deviated. Are you well, Lieutenant?"

He glared at me and slapped his lower leg. "Oh sure, I'm doing fine. I've just got to get used to this plastic leg!"

"I'm sorry about that. This ship isn't capable of regrowing tissue, I guess. When you get back to Earth, I'm sure they can fix that."

"Yeah, right. Six weeks in some ward full of cripples, waiting for my turn. Thanks a lot, Sparhawk."

"Would you rather be dead?"

"No, I wouldn't. I'm sorry. You've kept me alive. It's just that woman—a Beta, you say? I barely remember the long list of colonies. They taught us about them in school, but I never thought I'd meet one."

"Lieutenant, there are things we must discuss."

I told him then about the fate of *Altair*. He was shocked.

"You mean you destroyed one of our best ships?" he demanded. "You killed the bridge crew?"

"*Altair* was disabled, not destroyed. She can and will be repaired."

"With what?" he snorted. "Have you seen our budgets the last few years? She'll be scrapped."

I shook my head. "Think it through, Lieutenant. We're on a battle cruiser. If she were in prime condition, I'd bet she could take on every ship Earth has combined. In the light of this, the government will have no choice other than to increase the budget for the navy—dramatically, I should think."

"Huh," he said, staring into space. "You might be right. If the colonists have powerful vessels like this, and a few of them managed to get here, we'd have no chance. The navy will have to be rebuilt to defend the home world. Damn…the colonists might have twenty ships like this—they could conquer Earth in a week!"

"Exactly," I said, "and that brings me to my next point. Earth is going to need every vessel and guardsman she has. That would include you, me and this captured ship."

"It hasn't been captured yet," Morris said, his eyes narrowing, "you're still aboard."

"I'm not the man Singh said I was. I'm a member of Star Guard. Everything I did I was forced to do in order to save my crew."

He stared at me suspiciously. "You didn't obey orders. You declared mutiny against Singh, who was leading the task force."

"Let's go over the sequence of events. I was sent out to investigate this object. At the time, no one knew *Defiant* was a ship."

"Go on."

"When I got here and reported back that I'd found a large vessel, not a natural comet, Singh ordered me and my crew to stay here. He wanted *Cutlass* to sit on the hull of this ship so we'd be stationary targets. Then, he ordered *Altair's* gunners to destroy my vessel."

Morris looked troubled. "That was a head-scratcher. We marines were put on standby, but I heard what the gunners were chatting about. They didn't know quite why we were to fire on our own pinnace. Singh said you'd refused to obey orders—but the gunners could see the situation. They knew you were just sitting there on top of this rock that turned out to be a ship."

"Exactly. When the attack came, I ordered my people to run as there wasn't time to lift off and escape. We found our way into the ship after that. The rest you're familiar with."

"Okay, let's pretend I believe your story," he said. "Why would Singh do it? What possible reason could there be?"

"I'm not sure," I said, "but it must have to do with the fact this vessel is a warship. Perhaps he wanted full credit for the find. Or perhaps he planned to use it, or sell it. I'm sure the truth will come out in the end after a full investigation."

"I'm not so sure about that. You're a son of House Sparhawk. I think that's why Singh hated you so much."

"It was clear he disliked me personally," I said. "You knew this?"

"Everyone did. He leaned on you from day one. He gave you *Cutlass*, the worst pinnace of the lot, only because he wanted you off his decks."

Nodding, I considered the possibilities. Singh had maintained a grudge against me, that much was clear. Still, attempting to destroy my pinnace and kill my crew seemed extreme, even for him.

"It had to be related to this ship," I said. "He asked me to investigate and when I made my initial report, he ordered me to return. We were low on fuel, and he was determined to come out personally. I think he decided he had to kill me when I discovered the truth about this object—that it was a large ship. I'm thinking now that he sent all the pinnaces out to look for this ship, but when we found it he didn't want the discovery made public."

"I'm with you on that one. Say, Sparhawk, is there any chance you can let me out of this cell?"

I stared at him thoughtfully for a moment. "I'm the senior Guard officer on this ship. Do you accept that fact?"

"Yes…" he said, eyes narrowed.

"Good. Therefore, I'm in command here for now. In time I'm sure I'll be relieved—either when we return to Earth, or when other vessels arrive to perform a rescue. Do I have your word as a guardsman that you will obey my orders until that time?"

"As long as you don't ask me to do something contrary to the laws of man or nature," he said warily.

"On your honor, do you so swear?" I asked.

He sucked in a deep breath and let it out. Swearing on one's honor was a big deal to any guardsman, especially a marine.

"All right," he said at last. "You have my word. But you better not be full of shit, Sparhawk. If you are, I'll tear your guts out myself."

"I stand forewarned."

Working the detention center control board, I opened the cell door. He walked out cautiously, as if he were barely able to believe he was free.

"I owe you my life," he said, "but I also owe you death for killing my officers."

"We must put all that aside for now," I told him. "Earth itself is under threat. As you said, the Betas might have a dozen more of these vessels lurking somewhere."

He laughed unpleasantly. "If they do, we're totally screwed."

I didn't arm the lieutenant, but I did allow him to walk unrestrained at my side. We got as far as the detention area exit before we were intercepted.

An angry, looming Zye stood in the doorway when it shunted open. She had a pistol leveled at Lieutenant Morris' chest.

"Have you been coerced, Captain?" she demanded without taking her eyes off Morris.

"No," I said. "The lieutenant and I have come to an understanding. He's an honorable man, and I'm sure he will obey me until such time as I'm no longer in command of this vessel."

Her eyes flashed to me, then back to Morris, who had his hands part-way up. He was glaring, but he looked worried, too.

"I don't condone releasing an enemy combatant," Zye said. "But you're in command, as you said."

She lowered her weapon partway. By my estimate of the angle, she was now aiming at Morris's groin, rather than at his chest.

"Excellent," I said. "This way, Lieutenant."

I walked smartly down the passage. Morris followed me, favoring his false limb. I noticed that now and then he cast a glance over his shoulder at Zye.

"She's still following us," he muttered, "and she's got that gun trained on my back."

I nodded appreciatively. "An excellent bodyguard. She trusts, she obeys—but she keeps a tight watch. I approve."

Morris looked at me in confusion. "What kind of a hold do you have over her?"

"She's placed herself under my command. As you have."

"Huh. You must be some kind of sorcerer, Sparhawk!"

"I've been called worse."

Morris laughed at that. It was a real, full-bellied laugh. I couldn't help but like the man.

-26-

When I reached the life support center, I found Yamada wasn't there. She'd left a message blinking on the display. It was a map showing the current deck and the one above. She'd left a dashed line in yellow, which climbed up a shaft and to another location.

"Yamada?" I radioed, "where are you?"

"The ship's repair bots have been busy, sir," she said promptly. "I'm on the bridge. Not everything is working up here, but we've got sensors, communications and weapons control."

"I'll be right there."

Lieutenant Morris followed me, and Zye's ominous presence brought up the rear. We found the new bridge to be a hotbed of activity. There were repair bots everywhere. Two of them were setting up consoles, welding with an upper arm while two lower arms held metal slabs in place.

I was impressed by the sturdy nature of Beta construction. Unlike *Altair*, which was thin-hulled and lightly armored in comparison, everything about this vessel seemed solid and built to last. The interior structure wasn't as tough as the outer hull, but it was still fullerene-laced. The poly-alloy base material used in the decks and walls was several centimeters thick. Nothing about *Defiant* was weak.

The internal components of the bridge such as consoles and furniture were mere steel, but they were still impressive due to their precise form.

"Is this the command center?" I asked, stepping to a central raised stage and eyeing three chairs of startling size.

"Yes," Zye answered from behind me. "The captain sits in the rearward seat, overlooking the other two, which are occupied by the helmsmen and the tactical officer. All three seats can spin in any direction, including a vertical angle."

I ran my hands over the chairs, each of which was enclosed in a spherical cage of metal tubing. They were attached to the floor, but built to rotate freely. They looked almost like gyroscopes to me. I could tell they were designed to keep the bridge crew oriented in any direction they wished.

"How do these seats work, exactly?" I asked.

"The ship's inertial dampeners are designed to prevent injury caused by high-G acceleration," Zye said. "But it's possible during maneuvers to overload the dampeners. It's been determined that these chairs can prevent blackouts by always rotating so that the officers will be in an optimal position to take the centrifugal forces exerted on their bodies."

"I see…" I said, walking around the enclosed, cage-like chair in the rear of the group—the captain's chair. I put my hands on the tubing and gently spun it. To my surprise, it moved easily.

"Do you want to give it a try, Captain?" Yamada asked. She moved to the forward console Zye had identified as the helmsman's station and took a seat, smiling at me.

"Yes, why not?" I said. Feeling oddly elated, I climbed into the seat and felt it roll under me. "Can you lock it?" I asked. "It's moving too easily."

"Of course," she said.

Yamada touched her console, and my seat instantly resisted motion. I could still move it by applying pressure with my feet against the deck, but it wasn't rolling all over the place anymore.

"I like that better," I said. "The view from inside this seat is unobstructed for the most part. It's like sitting inside the cockpit of a power-lifter."

"I thought the same," she said. "The system is set up so you can turn and apply your hands directly to the rear console, or you can look over the shoulders of the helmsman and gunner."

"Zye?" I asked. "What about navigation, sensor operations and communications?"

"Those stations are arrayed along the walls," she said, pointing to the stations encircling the central three. "The ship is designed to be operated with a minimum bridge crew of three. More personnel improve responsiveness, but they're optional. These three stations can perform every function."

I looked back at her. "I'm impressed," I said. "This is a Beta design, I take it?"

"Yes—well no, not exactly."

I frowned. "What do you mean?"

Zye shifted slightly, moving her weight from one heavy hip to the other. Her long, straight black hair swung with the movement.

"Normal Betas aren't capable of innovative designs. This work was done by an Alpha."

I blinked at her. "Did you say an Alpha? So you aren't all clones?"

"We *are* clones, but we're not all equal. Slight mutations are applied to one out of every hundred embryos. The DNA is reshuffled, varied at random. Often, these special clones die as they aren't viable. But sometimes a special individual is spawned. An Alpha."

Spinning my chair around, I gestured for her to take the third seat: fire control. She did so, and she fit perfectly. In comparison I felt like a child playing in my father's favorite chair.

"You Zye," I said. "You're an Alpha, aren't you?"

"I was meant to be," she admitted. "I was a variation, an experiment. But I was a failure in the end. It was determined that my variation wasn't useful, and I was to be put down."

My mouth opened, then closed again. I nodded thoughtfully. "I see," I said. "You hid your flaws. You survived. You were eventually found out, however, and that's why you were imprisoned."

"Yes," she said, looking uncomfortable. "I'm sorry, but the subject is painful to me. It's my greatest shame."

"There's no shame in being different, Zye," I said firmly. I spread my hands wide. "Look at us. We're all variations. None of us conform to any mold. You're among your own kind here. Even if your Beta sisters rejected you, you've been accepted on this crew."

She smiled then. Her thin lips twitched up, but the expression quickly faded. I was happy to see her reaction.

"I'm glad to hear that," she said.

I thought about pressing her to reveal the nature of her "variations". How, exactly, was she unlike her fellow Betas? She'd said when we'd first met that her crime was to hide things, and clearly she'd managed to do that for a very long time. But they'd found her out in the end.

Despite my curiosity, I decided to pass on asking her more probing questions. Eventually, she'd open up and let us know more about her painful past. When she felt like telling us more, I'd be on hand to listen.

"All right then," I said, turning to Yamada, "let's go over the repair list. What are those robots up to?"

"Oh…okay," she said, taken by surprise. "I've got the list right here, sir."

She began to rattle off numbers and details. I was pleased. The repair bots were working constantly, fixing systems all over the ship. Initially there had been only two functional robots. Their top priority, apparently, had been repairing more generators so that more robots could operate. Now we had a full army of bots bustling around doing critical work. Since there were no more robots to put online, they were all working on the ship itself, and they were fixing things with startling speed.

"What about the external repairs?" I asked. "The sensor arrays and the damaged hull?"

"Are you sure you plan to give this ship up when the time comes, Sparhawk?" Lieutenant Morris asked me suddenly.

I spun my chair to face him. I'd forgotten about him, but he'd been standing near the exit watching us the entire time.

"What are you saying, Lieutenant?" I asked.

"That you seem to be entirely too comfortable in that chair. You know the Guard will never let you keep command of this vessel, don't you?"

I struggled to keep a straight face. Although his words did sting, I knew he was right—I was falling in love with this battle cruiser. I no longer cared who had built her.

Chastising myself internally, I climbed out of the captain's seat. "I suppose you're right. We need to get on with the rescue effort. Have any of the survivors from *Altair* reached our hull yet?"

"No sir," Yamada said, "but they should be arriving soon. They managed to get one of their lifeboats to operate, but all it did was give them a boost in our direction before they ran out of fuel."

Frowning, I examined the data. "Are you saying the entire crew of *Altair* is riding in a single lifeboat?"

"Not exactly. They wouldn't all fit inside. Most of them are clinging to it. What I'm saying is they used the boat's very limited fuel reserves to counter *Altair's* spin. They're without power now, and they'll crash down into the outer hull in…about twelve minutes."

"What's their velocity?"

"About thirty kilometers an hour, sir."

I thought about that. It wasn't a fatal speed, especially with a soft mass of snow to cushion the landing—but it would be enough to break bones.

"Let's go up and meet them," I said.

My crewmen looked at me. "That wasn't the arrangement you made with Taranto," Yamada said.

"You listened to that?"

"I overheard," she said quickly.

"Their speed of descent will cause injuries. I'm not going to be responsible for any more deaths if I can help it. Yamada, stay here. Zye, you come with me."

"Wait," Lieutenant Morris said. "Can I come with you?"

"Will you remember your oath? To obey my commands while aboard this vessel, until we either get back to Earth or authorities arrive?"

"Yes. If you'll save the crew and give up when the time is right—then yes. I can help convince the crew to cooperate as well."

I nodded sharply. I was pleased by his attitude, but I didn't want to show it too overtly. The truth was, I needed a man *Altair's* crew would trust to convince them not to try to kill us all and take over the ship.

We exited the ship through the same gaps in the hull that Lieutenant Morris and his men had originally used to board her. Morris led the way, in fact.

Boot tracks going the other way were commonly discovered. There were a lot of them. I realized that we'd barely won this struggle.

"What would you have done, Lieutenant," I asked, "if you'd managed to take this ship? Execute my crew?"

"What? No."

"Imagine the scenario," I pressed. "We fought hard but lost. Five or six of us survived, wounded and spent. The order comes down from Singh—kill the prisoners."

Morris looked at me as if I were mad. "Why would he do that?"

"Imagine that I'm telling the truth. That Singh was on some kind of mutinous mission of his own. He gives you that order—what do you do?"

Morris hesitated, troubled. "I don't know. I don't know if I could do it. We marines are few and far between these days. Most of the Guard is landlocked. A few fly in the navy. We're trained to follow orders—but I don't know."

"Were you technically the Marine Commander aboard *Altair*?"

"Was I? I still *am* the ship's Marine Commander—well, whatever's left of her."

"Does that position give you independent authority?"

He shrugged. "To a degree. An admiral or a captain could order me around, of course. My only discretion is how to follow their directives. Boarding ships, defending ships, that's my job. Of course, this is the first real action other than search and seizure missions involving smugglers that we've done in a century."

Nodding thoughtfully, I followed him up onto the outer hull of the ship. It was like exiting an ice-encrusted cave in the Antarctic. Overhead, the stars glittered. Jupiter was visible, and from our vantage point, the massive planet resembled a small moon. We were far closer to the gas giant than Earth had ever come in her locked orbit. I could even make out a few of the largest Jovian moons like motes of dust circling a bulb of light.

"How long?" Zye asked me.

"Until the lifeboat arrives?" I asked. "About two minutes."

She peered off into the distance. "I think I see it. Something is coming toward us. Our speeds are almost matched—but we're being overtaken."

I followed her gaze, but saw nothing.

"I can't see the boat!" Morris said, moving restlessly and peering into space. "Can you see if it's tumbling?"

"I don't think so," Zye said, staring.

I could only surmise that her eyes were better than ours. It made sense—if you were going to clone thousands of giants, filling an entire star system with them, you might as well design them with excellent vision.

"Zye," I asked. "Is there any chance they'll hit us?"

"I can't tell. We should stand inside the rip in the ship's hull. We can take shelter at the last moment if necessary."

We waited for two long, tense minutes. At last, I could see the tiny lifeboat, as well. It was tumbling, but gently. A spray of smaller objects, silhouetted by the light of the distant Sun, leapt free from her at the last moment and sent themselves off in random directions.

"They're jumping off," Zye said, "so the ship doesn't crush them."

"Taranto!" I shouted. "We're here, we see you're inbound. We'll come to render aid as soon as you impact. Please identify your most seriously injured people, so we can take them to our medical facilities first."

"Sparhawk? Is that you—?"

The message cut off as the group crash landed. I could see, all around us, bodies striking the snow. They sent up puffs of ice crystals in a dozen individual geysers.

Then, the lifeboat hit. There was a flash, and a jet of gas was released in a steamy puff. The boat rolled three times, then came to a halt. Fortunately, lifeboats were built solidly. It had stayed intact.

"I'm in the lifeboat," Taranto said. "I'm okay, the others are reporting in—"

I heard them then. Taranto must have ordered them to switch channels. They were transmitting in the clear.

The survivors were groaning. Some cried out in agony. They had broken bones and a few had problems with suit integrity.

We scrambled out of our cavern and plowed into the ice. The nearest body was only thirty meters away, and it was moving feebly.

The next hour was difficult for everyone, but we managed to get them all into our vessel. No one shot at us, fortunately. They were too stressed and shocked by the manner of their arrival for that. They welcomed emergency people rushing to their aid, it was only human.

Zye, however, did give a number of them pause. They shrank from her huge hands, but she plucked them up and carried them off like naughty children. Some of their startled reactions were comical.

When the worst of the wounded were finally inside cells in the detention center, medical robots went to work on them. Taranto came to my side. He was uninjured as the lifeboat had taken the rough landing in stride.

"Sparhawk," he said, clapping me on the shoulder. "You're a man of your word, whatever else you might be."

"Thank you, Midshipman," I said. "I only wish I could have saved more."

Taranto stared at me with squinting eyes. "I can't figure you out, man," he said. "Do you really think you're going to get away with this? The destruction of a fleet vessel? The killing of your own commanding officer?"

"The truth will see me through to justice, sir," I said.

He nodded, bemused.

"I'll speak at your trial," he said. "I'll tell them what you did here. I owe you that much—but Sparhawk?"

I turned to look at Taranto. It was then that I saw the pistol in his hand. He'd carried it in a pouch, I surmised. He had it aimed at my side.

"You gave your word, Midshipman," I said.

"That I did," he said ruefully, "and that pains me, it really does."

-27-

Taranto's treachery took me by surprise. I suppose that was a character flaw in my make-up. As a man of commitment, I am sometimes blind to the possibility of duplicity in others.

Zye, however, had no such failings. She'd been operating the detention center cells, setting them into automatic mode so they could go to work on the most injured men in their embrace. The general medical deck was, as yet, still inoperable.

Even before Taranto made his play, she'd sensed his intent. She moved behind him, and her large hand clamped over his, directing the pistol downward.

A power bolt cracked the air and melted a puddle of poly-alloy on the deck. Zye had managed to aim the gun away from my person.

A brief struggle ensued—very brief. Taranto, red-faced and wide-eyed, struggled with both his hands on the gun.

Zye seemed unimpressed. The gun didn't waver from its position, aiming at the deck. Her other hand, however, snaked up and around his throat. She constricted his neck—and it was over. Soundlessly, he slid to the floor.

Several crewmen, both mine and those from *Altair* swung around to look at us in shock.

"He's injured himself," Zye stated loudly. "I must provide aid to him."

She picked up Taranto's limp form and carried him to an empty cell. Stripping off his clothes as a mother might a baby, she left him there and slammed the door.

The others watched with confused frowns as the surgical bot went to work. They cast suspicious glances at us. I exited the center quickly, giving them a nod and a reassuring smile.

Zye followed me, as usual. When we were alone in the passageway, I confronted her.

"He's injured himself?" I asked. "That was the best you could do?"

"Among Betas, I'm considered a masterful liar."

She said this with such flat confidence that I was unable to do anything other than believe her. "I'll take your word for that," I said. "Did you use tactics such as that to hide your status from your own people?"

"Yes. I told them I was normal—that I wasn't an Alpha at all. For many years, I acted as normally as I could, behaving as others did. Eventually, however, I made mistakes. I told lies that were found out. They knew then that I could not be a Beta—you see, Betas do not lie."

"Ah," I said, smiling. "There's an old saying on Earth to the effect that in a kingdom of the blind, the one-eyed man is king."

Zye frowned. "I do not understand the connection."

"Never mind then," I said.

I wasn't surprised by her lack of comprehension. Zye's people weren't a subtle, introspective group.

The rest of the visiting crewmen, now leaderless, seemed less rebellious. It helped that their former Marine Commander was committed to following my orders. The rest of them followed his lead. Many of them were too injured to fight, anyway.

What I found most disturbing was the number of crewmen I'd saved. Out of a complement of nearly two hundred, only thirty had made it to us alive. That fact haunted me. I wondered if I could have done anything differently—maybe if I'd let Singh win…

I brought up the idea to Yamada, who laughed at the thought.

"You're asking me if I'd rather be dead instead of them? Because that's what would have happened. My answer to that is definitely 'no.'"

"But we've killed a hundred and fifty men to keep the ten of us alive."

"That's true," she said, "and it's tragic. But there's more to this situation than that, William."

"How so?"

"Let's imagine that Singh had won the battle and this ship. What would he have done with it?"

"I don't know...maybe taken it home to Earth as a prize?"

She shook her head. "You're as blind as Zye in a way," she said. "You graduated at the top of your class in the Academy, didn't you?"

"Yes, but I don't see—"

"Then let's use that big brain of yours."

I looked around to make sure that none of the others were listening. Only Zye was keeping an eye on us, as always. The rest were repairing bridge functions or were somewhere else on the ship. Most of the repair bots and my crewmen were working on the engines now.

"What are you suggesting?" I asked. "Out with it, Ensign."

"Just this, sir," she said, "I think Singh was planning to take this ship for his own."

"To what purpose?"

She shrugged. "Do you think Earth's entire arsenal could stop this battle cruiser?"

"Maybe—well, no. The more I see of her capabilities, I think our fleet would have been at a disadvantage."

"Exactly. This battle cruiser would have cut through the rest of our destroyers like butter. Earth has some antiquated missile batteries on the Moon and in orbit, but this vessel has tremendous range, from what I've seen. She'd stand off at range, striking by surprise and knocking out all defenses."

Shaking my head, I had trouble believing it. "But why?" I demanded. "And, there's a big hole in your theory: his crew. They went along with firing on my pinnace, but they'd never attack Earth."

Yamada nodded. "I've been thinking about that. I've got a bigger computer than you do, and I've been working the database on crew histories."

"Yes?"

"Singh was originally from the rocks."

I stared at her. "So? Lots of spacers start out like that. The service is a relative vacation for them."

"Yes, but what if he held separatist beliefs? There are a lot of rock rats that resent Earth."

"An interesting theory," I said, "but it's only that."

She shook her head. "Unfortunately, it isn't. I've been going over *Altair's* logs."

"How?"

"When the ship was hit, the onboard systems automatically downloaded everything to the lifeboats. It's a black-box system."

"I didn't know that. What did you discover?"

"Singh made several encrypted transmissions—and he received replies."

"Let me guess. These transmissions were directed toward the outlying system? Toward the rocks?"

"Yes. He did this after we found the Beta ship, before he attacked us. I think he got some kind of go-ahead from allies out here."

"Miners? Plotting rebellion?"

She shrugged. "How else do you explain his actions? He could have just flown out to the battle cruiser and assumed control of her—but instead, he blasted *Cutlass* to atoms. I think that was just his first move."

Frowning, I was beginning to wonder if Yamada was right. Could Singh have been involved in such a monstrous plot? It was so audacious, so ill-conceived…

"His first move," I echoed. "His next move would have been to kill his own crew. That's what you're saying, isn't it?"

She nodded grimly. "I think so. He called his friends out in the rocks. He summoned them to help him. Destroying us in our tiny pinnace—that was the beginning. But you derailed his plans by not dying. Do you see now why I say you did the right thing? The thing you had to do?"

"But I had no idea he was going to try something so insane."

"No, but you knew he was up to something and that he was going to kill us. You had to stop that. Your first duty as a captain is to your ship and your crew."

"All right," I said, letting myself be convinced. "Unfortunately, we might never know for sure if your assumptions were correct."

Yamada smiled and touched the main displays. I looked on with interest. Unlike the ship's diagrams shown within the life support module, the bridge had a full tactical display.

The screen showed a region spanning something like a fifth of the Solar System.

"We just picked this up," Yamada said. "See this green triangle? That's us. These tiny yellow dots over here are unknown contacts. From their behavior, I've concluded they're small ships."

As she spoke, more and more dots appeared. The battle computer was spotting them and extrapolating their trajectories.

"This is much better data than the sensor arrays were giving us a few hours ago," I said.

"Yes. I directed some of the repair bots to fix the arrays. They went up there on the outer hull and cleared off the ice. They also connected up the sensors. The dishes are moving now, scanning the star system automatically and feeding information to the battle computer."

Taking it all in, I reached out and tapped a swarm of yellow contacts that were fairly close to our location.

"What are these ships? Plot their trajectory."

Wordlessly, Yamada obeyed. Zye came up to look over our shoulders, which she could do easily.

"That's the formation of ships I wanted you to see," Yamada said. "They appear to be in-bound to our position. The readout gives us two hours before they intersect with our location—but they'll be in weapons range long before that."

"They are enemies," Zye said firmly.

Her breath puffed into my hair. She was such a large person, she moved a lot of air when she breathed nearby without her helmet on. I ignored the fact and tried to stay focused on the problem at hand.

"Analysis, Yamada?"

"Zye's probably right," Yamada said. "They're coming directly toward us, moving fast. Given their angle of attack, I think we know who they are."

"Rock rats," I said, "militia ships, probably. They aren't even supposed to be out here—especially in such numbers."

Zye loomed closer. I could feel her body heat on my back. I wondered then if perhaps Betas were accustomed to standing close to one another. Zye seemed to have no concept of personal space.

"Militia ships?" she asked. "Rock rats? What are these creatures and why do they threaten us?"

"The rock rats—sorry," I said. "I shouldn't call them that. They're independent miners, officially. They provide most of Earth's metals and other raw materials. Unfortunately, due to their remoteness, the Guard is unable to police them properly. They've got problems with pirates, claim-jumpers, smugglers and the like. Over time, they've built up their own militia forces to handle the lawlessness of the outer reaches of the Solar System."

Zye looked annoyed. "That's unacceptable," she said. "I can't imagine such a thing happening among Betas."

"No, it probably wouldn't. But in this system…well, you should think of Earthlings as a mix of Alphas and rogues. We don't have too many Betas, really."

"Chaotic," she muttered and retreated.

"What if we contact them, warn them off?" Yamada asked.

"We'll try it," I said, "but they look determined. I'm concerned that they haven't attempted to contact us yet."

"They may simply attack," Yamada said.

"Yes," I agreed with reluctance in my heart. "They're the new crew. Singh promised them this ship. It's the only thing that makes sense of his actions. We found this vessel for them, and he plotted to deliver it. Now, they're coming to collect."

We all stared at the screens for a few seconds. The swarm of yellow dots edged infinitesimally closer.

"What are your orders, Captain?" Zye asked.

"Redirect the cannons," I said. "Lock on their lead vessel."

Zye worked her console eagerly. "Should I fire?" she asked.

I could hear in her voice that she wanted to. She didn't like the rock rats, and I couldn't blame her. They were popular only among people who'd romanticized their existence. Like the pirates of centuries past, they lived grim lives on the fringe of society.

"No," I said. "Don't fire yet. We'll warn them first."

Zye stared at me in disbelief. "That is not the optimal strategy."

"No," I admitted with a tight smile, "I don't suppose that it is. Yamada, do we have helm controls yet?"

"Not yet—no engines, no directional jets."

"Then running is out of the question," I said. "Call Rumbold to the bridge. While he's en route, realign our communications dish to direct a beam straight into their formation. Transmit a message indicating we're a Star Guard vessel, and that they're entering restricted space. Tell them they must turn back."

Yamada turned to her console and contacted Rumbold first. Then she recorded and transmitted my message. I knew it would go out as a blip of light to be caught and pondered by the people aboard those tiny ships. I only hoped they would listen as I had no desire to do any more killing today.

-28-

When Rumbold arrived on the bridge, he looked around with a gleam in his eye.

"Now *this* is a ship!" he laughed. "I can't believe how quickly these eight-armed robots have gotten things put right. Zye, your people are to be commended for their efficiency."

"Your compliment honors us both," she said in a formal tone.

Rumbold's eyebrows performed a quick up-down movement, indicating surprise, but he said nothing further. The crew seemed to be getting used to Zye's odd responses.

Clapping his hands together loudly, Rumbold mounted the central stage with the three rotating command chairs.

"Where do I sit, Captain Sparhawk?"

Smiling, I indicated the helmsman's spot. Yamada was stationed there at the moment, but she got up without complaint. She knew Rumbold was our best pilot. Her skills were more technical in nature.

"You have the conn, Chief," she said, ushering him into the seat.

"Whoa!" he cried, rolling around in the spinning chair. "This isn't a chair, it's a roller coaster!"

Zye reached over and increased the friction settings on his chair so that it would only move with a deliberate effort.

"That's better," he said. "Thanks."

Once settled, he seemed to finally notice that Zye was seated next to him.

"Excuse me, Captain," he said, frowning and nodding sideways at the Beta woman. "Do we have new bridge personnel?"

"Yes, we do," I said. "Zye knows the ship better than any of us. She'll be handling the tactical controls. Yamada, sit at that station over there. You'll take over communications and operate the tactical display coming from the battle computer."

"Will do, sir," she said.

Rumbold looked troubled, but he shrugged and put his hands on the console in front of him. Almost immediately, it began beeping error codes.

"Not like that," Zye said. "The helm controls aren't hooked up, but the computer will still respond as if they are. You can't just tap at anything you feel like."

"Oh...I see," Rumbold said, lifting his hands gingerly. "The layout isn't that strange—it's based on the same intuitive gestures as our own consoles. But what's this circular widget here?"

Zye and Rumbold were soon deep in a discussion of the finer points of the ship's piloting controls. I dared to smile while I watched them. Rumbold naturally didn't trust Zye—but we needed her. She was our interpreter, our guide.

Betas were technically human, and all their technology could be traced back to Earth designs. That said, more than a century had passed on both worlds. Despite the fact there hadn't been many advances during the dark years of separation after the Cataclysm, there had been *some* change. Divergence of social and technological norms could only be expected.

Before Rumbold had learned more than the basics, a gruff male voice began speaking. The words boomed, reverberating from the walls of the bridge.

"To the trespassers aboard the salvaged vessel," the voice said. "You are hereby advised and commanded to vacate the premises. The Independent Miners Confederation has laid claim to the ship you now illegally occupy, and we've formally filed with Earth Central for all salvage rights. Do not, I repeat, *do not* take anything with you when you leave. To do so would put you in danger of prosecution, conviction, and summary execution."

Our eyes rose upward, searching for the source of the voice. There had to be speakers somewhere—but I couldn't see them.

"I'm sorry," Yamada said, battling her communications controls. "I must have left the com system set up to play messages aloud after I sent your statement."

"That's not a problem, Ensign," I said with a calm I didn't feel. "Are we now squelched?"

"Yes. The channel is closed in both directions for now. We'll record any further messages they send—but I won't play them out loud."

Getting up, I walked over to her consoles and looked over her settings. Zye accompanied me.

Yamada appeared embarrassed that we obviously didn't trust her ability to operate her assigned station.

"I'm sorry," I said, noticing her discomfort, "but it would be a disaster if we broadcast our entire battle plan out to the approaching ships right now."

"She's done it correctly," Zye pronounced and returned to her seat.

"Very good," I said, returning to mine. I decided I'd have to take Zye's word for it. I couldn't operate this vast ship alone. The crew had to carry their share of the weight.

"What's our response going to be, Captain?" Yamada asked me a minute or so later.

"Hmm? Well, I'm thinking that over. They've made their play with their absurd claims. Now, they have to be wondering why we're not responding."

"Do you think they'll really fire on us, sir?" Yamada asked.

"That they will!" Rumbold said. "If we look weak, they'll swoop in and steal this ship. They're jackals, scavengers. They only respect strength. Fire a shot into their midst, that's what I say. You've got to show them you're serious, sir."

My attention shifted to Zye. "Have you got a target and a firing solution?"

"Possibly," she said. "We don't have triangulated data, which lowers our hit probability significantly. Normally, our ships place probes around a system in which a battle is about to occur. To fire at a moving target accurately over great distances is difficult. To raise the odds of a hit when the enemy is within a cone of probability, we use multiple sources of targeting data."

"Right," I said, having studied such tactics at the Academy years ago. "They're small ships, and highly maneuverable. They'll dance around, and since they're so far away, we can only see them as they were several seconds ago. That's the hard part about long range battles with mobile targets."

"The longer we wait, the closer they'll get." Rumbold said. "We'll be at the effective edge of their weapons range soon. Best to stop them as far away as we can."

"You're right, but I don't think they'll actually fire. They want to capture this ship, not destroy it."

"But sir—"

"We've got a launch!" Yamada interrupted. "Four missiles incoming—make that six now. I'll display them…damn it…there they are. Do you guys see that?"

We did. She'd relayed the data to every screen, showing us what the battle computer was showing her.

I stared at the incoming missiles, my heart pounding. It was startling because, to the best of my knowledge, militia ships like these weren't equipped with long range missiles. Such a configuration was illegal.

"Zye," I said. "Fire just outside their likely positions. Put a shot across their bow to warn them."

"Locked…firing," she said.

We felt the ship shudder a little as the big batteries above us unleashed beams into space. The force of the recoil was enough to put us into a slow spin.

"Can we counter that spin?" I demanded.

"No sir," Zye said. "Not without helm control."

"Damn. When we fired on *Altair* we didn't go into a spin."

"No, but the angle was different then."

"Right. We'll have to deal with it. Has the beam reached them yet?"

"Yes, but we don't have the data—there. A hit."

My face froze. "A hit? Zye, you *hit* the rock rat ships?"

"Yes," she said with a hint of pride. "An excellent shot, especially since it was my first."

Rotating my seat around, I regarded her sternly. "I ordered you to put a shot over their bows, a shot outside the likely cone of—"

"Take a look," Yamada said. "The miners have been spreading out. Their new positioning got them killed. They fanned out to make it harder to hit them, so when Zye fired off-center, she still got one."

"Two," Zye corrected. "That's confirmed, the battle computer has completed the new count."

"Two…" I said in shock. "Two ships with a crew of five men each, on average? We just killed ten miners."

"Ten rebels, you mean!" Rumbold interjected. It was clear where his sympathies lay.

"I don't understand how you hit two with one beam," I said. "That's pushing the odds, Zye."

"I took the step of widening the aperture on the cannons. The beams were broad and diffuse. I reasoned that option would work best against these targets as they're small and widely spread out."

My face was a mask of displeasure. "Cannons? As in plural? Am I getting this right? You fired multiple cannons with a wide dispersion? I ordered a single shot!"

Zye blinked. "Perhaps you aren't yet completely familiar with Beta weapons systems. When a battery of cannons fire, they *all* fire. There is no option to fire a single gun. That would disrupt the automatic gas dispersion, reloading pressure systems, and the—"

As she spoke, I realized then how we'd hit *Altair* so hard. We'd fired a full battery of cannons right into the bridge. It was no wonder we'd knocked out the ship in one punch. I had to be more careful. There were bound to be mistakes made when operating a captured ship like this.

"All right, all right," I said. "Forget it. Let's deal with the situation at hand. We've just blasted a full-bore barrage into them and taken out two ships."

"Sir?" Yamada said. "There's another incoming message. Do you want to hear it privately, or…?"

"Play it on the PA again. You might as well."

"...butchery! Never again will the Independent Contractors trust the Guard! You're all fiends, arrogant thieves! There will be repercussions, I assure you. We'll not be cowed so easily next time!"

The transmission ended. I was left with a desire to close my eyes and rub my temples, which I indulged.

"Sir...they're breaking off," Yamada said. "They're splitting up into squadrons and flying away in every direction."

"Just like rats swarming out of a garbage dump!" Rumbold laughed. He kept laughing until he coughed and hacked.

"How long until their missiles impact our hull?" I asked with my eyes still closed. I was tired, I realized. How long had it been since we'd slept? I wasn't sure.

"They won't hit us," Zye said.

I opened my eyes again and looked at her. "Don't tell me you managed to blast their missiles out of the sky with that single barrage as well."

"No Captain—but the missile contacts have disappeared. I believe our attackers ordered them to self-destruct."

"You see?" Rumbold crowed, getting up out of his rotating chair after a brief struggle. "They ran away the moment you blasted them. They even blew up their own missiles out of fear, so you wouldn't have an excuse to keep firing! You gave them a hard knock on the nose, Captain. Don't be sorry for that. You had no choice. That's what rats understand."

"There's another interpretation," Yamada said. "Maybe the missiles were a bluff all along. Perhaps they were dummies, or maybe they planned to have them miss at the last moment."

"Why would you think that?" I asked her.

"Because they want this ship intact, remember? They don't want to damage her, not really."

I nodded thoughtfully. "I tend to agree with your assessment, Ensign. But that doesn't leave me resting easily. The miners want this ship badly enough to kill us all and rebel against Earth. They won't give up so quickly next time."

"Singh wanted this ship badly enough to betray both the Guard and Earth itself," Yamada said. "That indicates other factions might feel the same way. To what lengths might they go to capture *Defiant*?"

"It's hard to know," I said, "but I have a feeling our confrontations have only just begun."

Our conversation died. My crew went back to their screens in a dark mood.

Only Zye seemed happy. I could see it in her demeanor. For the first time in her life she'd slain two ships and ten men. That seemed to please her like nothing else we'd experienced together so far.

Given that she was a Beta clone, I could only surmise that the rest of her people were similar in personality. I imagined an entire planet full of grim, warlike giants. They were loyal, but they were also killers, through and through.

That didn't bode well for our future interactions with them.

-29-

When there were no approaching dangers on our tactical displays, I felt a deep sense of relief. I also felt a deep weariness.

"Crew," I announced, "I think we've all earned a break. Let's stand down and—"

"If you don't mind, Captain," Zye said. "I'll man the bridge in your absence."

I looked at her thoughtfully, then nodded. "All right. Zye, you have the helm—or at least you're standing watch."

I stood up, took off my helmet and ruffled my hair. "I'm going to look for a shower," I said.

"I'll join your search," Yamada said, yawning and stretching.

Zye and Rumbold eyed her speculatively. Rumbold's eyes were boggling.

"What?" she asked. "Oh—no, I don't mean like that!"

She walked off the bridge, embarrassed.

"Captain, sir," Rumbold said. "If you don't mind, I'll stay awake here with Zye until you're back. Two watch-standers is customary, after all."

My eyes slid from him to Zye, then back again. I knew the story immediately: he didn't trust Zye. Who could blame him? Maybe she had plans of her own now that we'd repaired much of her ship. I thought she was loyal, but I was willing to hedge my bet.

"I believe this ship needs a dozen crewmen on the bridge to operate smoothly," I said. "Very well, I'll see you when I wake up. But at that point, you're going to take your turn in a bunk, Chief."

"No arguments there."

I walked off the bridge, found a shower and climbed in. I wasn't even sure how to operate it, or even if it would work due to damage and neglect. I gave a howl of pain when the hot water finally did come, right out of the reactor's cooling jacket by the feel of it. Full of phosphates, I was half-scalded by the time I'd figured out how to get the temperature down to a tolerable level.

After I'd mastered the fixtures, I found the water luxurious. I hadn't had a real shower for a month. The sensation was indescribable.

Afterward, I found a quiet bunk in an empty dormitory. The officers' quarters weren't pressurized yet, so I couldn't go there. It was just as well, I figured. There were a lot of people on this ship I didn't entirely trust yet. Taranto might have accomplices or at the very least sympathizers, and I couldn't take the risk of being a target yet again. I was beginning to understand what my father must have gone through all the time.

Sleep overcame me quickly. I dreamed of gigantic invading troops wielding lasers and axes—and then of Chloe Astra. The second dream was much more pleasant. She was wearing her sea foam dress. My sleeping mind seemed to have forgotten that the dress had been worn by an android copy of Chloe, not the flesh and blood version.

By the time my implants woke me up, the dream-Chloe and I were making love.

Rolling out of my bunk stiffly, I searched for breakfast. I found it with a group of desultory crewmen from *Altair*.

We ate what the ship's automatic mess hall produced for us from its flash-frozen stores. The fare was heavy and unforgiving for my guts. Apparently Betas ate gamey, red meats full of spices and preservatives. There was almost no vegetation or any drink other than water to be had. Was this due to the natural tastes of the Betas, or had the vegetables all wilted? I didn't know, but I was glad we had something solid to eat.

The crewmen from *Altair* eyed me and muttered among themselves. I saw a few familiar faces, but none that I would have called friend. They seemed content to sit among their own, and I didn't break in on the party.

From my training as an officer, I knew that I should try to bridge the gulf between us, but it was difficult. For years, I'd been assigned to *Cutlass* and independent operations. Singh hadn't really wanted me aboard his destroyer, and I'd become comfortable with my exile. *Cutlass* had been a tiny command, but she'd been mine to rule as I'd wished.

Fortunately, no one in the group was an officer to challenge my rank. The only living man in that capacity was Taranto, and he was still in the detention center.

When I'd almost finished chewing what tasted like a sausage made from dried wild boar meat, Marine Lieutenant Morris came in. He saw me, and after filling his plate, came to sit with me.

The rest of the crewmen stared at us. Neither Morris or I returned their scrutiny.

"Good morning, Captain."

"Lieutenant Morris," I said. "I hope you slept well."

"Hell no," he said. "How about you?"

"Actually, I was so tired I overcame my adrenaline drenched bloodstream and fell hard."

He nodded. "Good to hear, and understandable. If those rock rats come back, we'll need you on the bridge again, bright-eyed and ready to fight."

Morris was speaking in an overly loud voice. I knew immediately why he was doing so: he wanted the others to hear the truth. He wanted them to believe I was needed and trustworthy. I appreciated the effort, and I hoped it worked. The crewmen were aware that I was a Guard officer, but Singh had probably never given them reason to like or trust me. Worse, I'd recently killed Singh and imprisoned his replacement.

"I heard you shot Taranto," Morris said conversationally. "I bet he deserved it."

This statement startled me. I glanced at Morris, who gave me a flat stare in return.

Perhaps I had a political mindset inherited from my father, but whatever the case I understood quickly what was going on. Apparently, there was a rumor among the crew that I'd done away with the last fleet officer aboard.

"No, not at all," I said. "Taranto is fine. He was injured accidentally and our best medical equipment is inside the detention center, strangely enough. The regular medical facilities aboard this ship aren't yet repaired."

"Ah, just a misunderstanding then, excellent," Morris said, flashing me a smile. "You going to eat that last chunk of sausage? At least I hope it's sausage…otherwise, I don't want to know. But we shouldn't let food go to waste. Who knows how long we'll be stuck on this ship without supplies?"

"Be my guest."

He speared it with a fork and actually ate it with gusto. I had to wonder what they'd fed the marines under Singh's gentle care.

We talked about pleasantries after that, and soon the other crewmen left, having finished their meals. When the last of them was gone, Morris leaned toward me, frowning.

"Sparhawk, can I ask you to stand up right here and spread your legs for me?" he demanded with sudden vehemence.

"Uh…what for?"

"Because I want to kick you in the nuts, that's why!"

I snorted in laughter. "You wouldn't be the first to profess such a heartfelt desire," I admitted. "But if I might make a request: don't use your plastic foot."

He glared at me for a moment. "Where's that hulking female gorilla of yours?"

"She's standing watch on the bridge, making sure we aren't killed in our sleep by the rock rats."

He nodded. "That's an important duty, but if I were you, I'd keep her on your six with a gun in her hand. You killed Captain Singh, remember? Then the moment they arrived, you cold-cocked the only officer they had left. They aren't going to start loving your patrician ass anytime soon."

Shrugging, I confessed he had a point. "I'm glad you're not in their camp," I said.

"If I was, you'd already be dead, fancy House name or not."

I found myself liking Morris. He was a rough, brash man, but he was clearly on my side.

"Tell me," I asked, "what converted you to my point of view in this conflict?"

Morris looked thoughtful. "It wasn't your looks," he said. "Nor your silver-tongued talk, that's for sure. No, let me tell you the truth: we're in a dangerous situation, here. If the wrong party gets ahold of this ship…that could spell disaster."

"Such as Singh? Or our mining friends?"

"Exactly. Just think about it: a madman running this monster? It would be like having a T-Rex loose in a henhouse. The forces of Earth are good men for the most part, but they wouldn't stand a chance. From what I've seen, this vessel will outclass the entire fleet once it's up to speed."

I nodded. "I agree. What do you think I should do with this ship now, Lieutenant?"

"Well sir, the way I see it, there are only two options. You could turn it over to the navy to become our new flagship. Barring that, you could scuttle her. That might be the safest course, in the end."

I frowned. "Honestly, that idea had never even occurred to me. Why would you suggest such drastic action?"

He leaned over his plate, but he was no longer eating his food.

"Because this thing is frightening," he said. "It's like the first nuclear weapon back in Earth's history. In the wrong hands it could lay waste to Earth—or make a man into a king."

"Your concerns match my own," I said. "But I don't think destroying her is a viable option."

"Why not?"

"Because, Lieutenant, she has sister ships. A dozen of them at least. Worse, she was clearly beaten in combat. That means that as powerful as this vessel is, some other force out there bested her. So there must be at least two powers in our region of space that presumably could arrive any day in our star system and display overwhelming force."

Morris frowned in real concern. "A dozen ships like this? The Betas have that many?"

"Yes. That's what Zye said, and I have no reason to doubt her. Why would they build only one? And even if she's lying, *someone* blasted holes in the sides of this vessel. There must be a ship or a fleet out there that can defeat her."

"Yeah, I see your point. We need this ship. That makes things worse than I thought. There's no easy solution."

"No," I said. "Earth will have to grow up. It's as if we've been dreaming for the last century, while our colonies have become adults. They have vigor. They'll be tougher than us when we meet them again."

"If Zye is any example, I can't argue with you there."

Finished with our meals, we got up, shook hands, and headed for the exit.

"I've got your back, Sparhawk," Morris said. "But there's only so much I can do. Try to come up with some kind of demonstration that lets the men know you're a trustworthy officer, and that they need to keep you breathing—if you get my drift."

"I'll do what I can."

We parted ways, and I made my way to the bridge. My discussion with Morris had been disturbing.

-30-

Following Morris' advice, I began searching for Zye. I was getting to know the ship by now, and what had once seemed like a maze of passages was mapped out in my mind.

When I finally found her, she was in the cargo hold. It was still freezing cold down there—and dark. She was standing among the racks of tubes, examining them with a careful tenderness. I supposed that to her, they were children.

Walking up to her, I tapped her on her broad back. That was a mistake. In spacesuits and near vacuum conditions, it was impossible to hear another person approaching.

Her reaction was swift and violent. She whirled, eyes blazing. Sparks flashed, as something struck my personal shield.

I'd had the foresight to turn it on after Morris' warning. It was a good thing I had. The shield absorbed her wild slash, leaving only a bright tracery of afterimages on our retinas to show it had passed at all.

"Sorry," I said, staggering back a step. "Didn't mean to startle you."

"Captain?" she asked as if dazed. Her sides were heaving, her shoulders hunched for battle.

I was impressed by her reflexes. In less than a second, she'd shifted from calm introspection and private thoughts about the embryos into a killer rage. I filed this fact away for later consideration.

"Sorry," I said again. She seemed to hear me this time. "I was wondering what you were doing down here."

She stared at me for a moment. It was the sort of stare a snake might give to any animal that surprises it. Slowly, she calmed down with a visible effort.

"It would be best," she said, gulping for air and closing her eyes, "that you don't surprise a Beta."

"I can see that. When we first discovered your ship, we found tubes like these floating in space around it. Did you know that?"

I had her full attention again. "No."

"It's true. Our best guess is that the original miners who discovered the vessel opened the hatch to this hold. The action depressurized the chamber violently. Some of these vials must have been unsecured as they were blasted out into space."

"Such a crime," she said, looking around the room slowly. "I'd calculated that there were missing embryos—but I'd hoped they'd been removed when my people abandoned the ship. They must not have had time."

Studying her for a moment, I decided not to tell her about the smuggler I'd found with a few dozen samples in Earth's orbit. That couldn't possibly improve her mood.

"Why is this ship carrying so many embryos?" I asked her. "What's the purpose?"

She looked at me in puzzlement. "I would have thought that was self-evident. This vessel was prepared for colonization, should a suitable planet be found."

"Ah," I said, understanding the situation immediately. "That makes sense. It is equipped with a star drive, after all. Are all your cruisers built with star drives?"

"No, not all. They are difficult to build. We only have a few. They open a way for the others. But this ship—we were traveling alone, prepared for whatever we met up with. At least, that's what we thought."

"Do you know what damaged your ship?"

"Enemy fire."

I smiled. "Of course, yes, but *who* was responsible? You said the Betas have many enemies."

"I've been looking into the data core. There's little there in the way of recorded logs at the time of the battle. But what I did find has led me to believe it was the Stroj. They are a savage people. Aggressive beings who will attack anyone they meet, heedless of losses."

Nodding, I took a mental note.

"Stroj," I said thoughtfully. "Human splinter colonists like the Betas, I assume?"

"Human, yes. But like us? That's insulting. I will ignore your statement and assume it was made out of gross ignorance."

"Thank you," I said. "I meant no offense."

I couldn't recall having heard of a colonist group called the Stroj, but that didn't mean they didn't exist.

There was so much we didn't know about this new universe in which we'd found ourselves. An entire interstellar community lived around us, and we knew next to nothing about it.

Looking around the hold, I was struck with a new thought. "How many Betas are here—as frozen embryos?"

"I haven't performed a count," she said.

"Do you know how many there were originally?"

"Ten thousand Betas, and one hundred Alphas. Most of the Alphas would turn out to be culls, of course, but a few of them would grow up to lead the rest."

"Culls?" I asked. "You mean rogues and mutations?"

"Yes."

"One would think that you might have come up with a more precise system than random chance to create superior Betas."

She shrugged. "An Alpha makes such an attempt from time to time, if it is in their nature. So far, none have succeeded."

"I think I'm beginning to understand," I said. "In a way, your similarity is a weakness. You are what you are, you can't innovate very well as that isn't a strong point of your design."

"Exactly. We've found that the randomness of evolutionary mutations isn't completely dispensable. That's why we have the Alphas. They create all our advances, make all major decisions. They're few in number, but they're critical."

"How was the first Alpha created?"

"Our Mother, the original woman who created us all, was the last survivor of the colonists who settled on our planet. Our world is a harsh one, with fierce gravity, tidal shifts and deadly wildlife. When she realized the colony was going to die out, she worked to create a singular being that could thrive on that world."

"I see…and the Alphas?"

"Mother *was* the first Alpha—can you not see that?"

"Of course. She made Betas as an improvement upon her own design. A people more cooperative than pure clones of herself."

Zye nodded. "You do understand. I'm impressed."

"But why spoil a perfect solution? Why did she make more of Alphas?"

"She lived long enough to realize the Betas would stagnate. On her deathbed, she ordered the variation to be implemented in every hundredth embryo. We've followed her command from that day to this, with excellent results."

"You have much to be proud of," I said. "Your people were designed to survive where mine perished."

My words made her happy, as I thought they might.

"One last question, Zye," I said. "Would you say you're any more or less clever than your average Beta?"

"I'm definitely more cunning than they are. That's how I managed to live for many years in their midst, unsuspected."

"That's what I thought."

If I had to guess, I'd say Zye's intelligence quotient was an approximate match to human normal. If she was considerably smarter than the average Beta, that helped explain their lack of imagination. Despite all their strengths, the Betas needed Alphas to act as their leaders.

I knew that if leaders were such a rarity among Earthlings, it wouldn't work out well. A company of soldiers needed many more leaders—sergeants, lieutenants and the like—to operate effectively. One person leading a thousand? It would be chaos. But possibly, since Betas were all obedient clones that thought alike anyway, they could cooperate effectively.

Thinking as an officer, I believed it might be rather nice to not have to deal with a shipload of personalities. You could definitely get more done if your crew invariably did as they were told.

On the flipside, it sounded like it would be extremely dull. I shuddered to think what Beta dinnertime conversation sounded like.

We left the cargo hold together. Zye began asking me about my personal shielding. Apparently, Betas didn't possess such technology.

"I wouldn't expect Betas to have portable shields," I said. "We only invented them on Earth about fifty years ago. That would be long after your colony was separated from us."

"So many ideas," Zye said, musing. "Your people are like chattering marsh-water. A lake being struck by a million drops of rain all at once. No voice ever matches any of the others. No shared thought. Chaotic."

"You might like it," I told her. "Our cities are very stimulating. There's new entertainment every hour in Capital City. It never stops."

"There's no set quiet-time?" she asked, frowning.

"No. People do as they wish. If you're hungry at midnight, you can get up, drive your air car to a restaurant and order whatever you want to eat. It's called freedom, Zye. I recommend it highly."

"What about males?" she asked me. "Are there many of your sex available?"

"Ah…yes, of course. About half the population is male. There are billions of us."

"Billions…are there any large males?"

I shook my head sadly. "Among my kind, I'm considered larger than average. There are few that are as large as you are, Zye."

"A pity, but I suppose one must take what one can get."

The conversation had taken a somewhat unexpected turn. I'd always believed she was interested in men, but I found her straightforward approach to the topic alarming.

-31-

The engines were operable eight days later. By that time, I was no longer worried that *Altair's* crewmen would assassinate me. There was no love lost between us, but they'd come to accept I was their new captain. I was a usurper, certainly, and not to be trusted. But I was also a Star Guard officer, and their years of conditioning and discipline allowed me to lead them.

There was a new, darker source of dread growing within me, however. A shadow lay over everything we were doing to help get the battle cruiser safely home to Araminta Station.

It had to do with our attempted communications with Earth—we just weren't getting through.

"Yamada, anything on the frequency range?" I asked as I walked the bridge back and forth—some might call it pacing. There was plenty of room for the activity between the various stations as everything was built and sized for Betas.

"No change, sir. Just silence."

"Analysis?"

"We're either being jammed or Earth has been destroyed."

She chuckled at her joke, but I didn't join her. "Jammed? Shouldn't we be hearing static, then?"

"No sir, not necessarily. It's an active, intelligent jamming. If I had to guess, I'd say some station is in-between our location and the dish we're trying to talk to. When we transmit a signal, the interrupting device picks it up and adds in confusing data on its own, turning our message into a mess. It's a technique rather like shining a powerful spotlight onto a dim light bulb to wash it out."

I nodded thoughtfully. "And who, in your opinion, would possess that kind of technology?"

She shrugged. "It's not all that sophisticated or rare. Could be the rock rats, or anyone else with a budget and the mind to do it."

"Great," I said, settling into my chair.

A week had gone by, and I'd not been able to communicate with Star Guard command or my parents—no one. For all I knew, none of them had any idea I was out here in dire need of assistance. They probably all still thought I'd gone rogue somewhere in the out-system and attacked my own comrades.

My skeleton bridge crew had gathered together when they'd heard the engines had been marked as "operable" by the robotic repair systems.

"These robots are amazing," I told Zye when she walked in. "I suspect they're better than anything we've got for this task back on Earth."

"Hey now," Rumbold protested. "Let's not forget about the dozen broken backs that have been laboring double-shifts to get this bird flying again."

"You're right, Chief," I said. "Much of the credit must go to my crew. But Zye, who built these robots? Did you ever tell me that?"

She glanced at me, then looked back at her boards. "They weren't built by my people. We do not design such things—not even our best Alphas are able to."

"I see. How did you get them, then?"

"We captured a few in battle. After discovering they were highly useful, we traded for more."

"Hmm," I said. "You defeated their owners in combat? Why not press on and enslave the makers?"

"Interstellar invasion is difficult. We didn't have a thousand ships and millions of Betas to spare. Instead, our Alphas reasoned it would be easier to trade for what we wanted."

"That's a very rational viewpoint. Who created the robots, then?"

"The Stroj."

I looked at her in alarm. "Your enemy?"

"We've since had a falling out."

"I've been doing what I could to research these people Zye calls 'the Stroj,'" Yamada said. "I believe they started out as a scientific expedition, but they were lost after the Cataclysm. They were the crew of the colony ship *Inquisitive*."

"You're correct," Zye said. "They were stranded in an M-Class star system. They were forced to colonize a local world circling a cool, dim star."

"Huh," Rumbold said, "I think I do recall such a ship. They left just before the lanes shut down. They must have been an unhappy lot after they arrived and found the ER bridge had slammed closed behind them."

Zye frowned at us. "What's an ER bridge?" she asked.

"That's the official term for the interstellar pathways you described," Yamada explained. "It stands for Einstein-Rosen bridge. Some call these bridges wormholes, an entanglement of two spots in the continuum."

"We must have forgotten the official term for them..." Zye said thoughtfully. "Or else Mother didn't think it was worth remembering."

"She probably had a lot of things to teach to her first thousand daughters," I said.

"The concept of an ER-bridge was first described in 1935," Rumbold said. "We learned that back in school. It seemed very important then...without the bridges, it would take a century to travel between the nearest of our colonies."

"Zye," I asked, "have the robots repaired the ship's ER bridge drive, or only her local drive?"

"The bridge drive is not yet operational," she replied. "We only have conventional engines with intra-system mobility. To engage the bridge drive, as you call it, would first require that we locate an open ER bridge."

Rumbold and I looked at one another. Yamada, who had been working her console steadily while we talked, looked up to listen.

"Can this ship do that? Can it find a new bridge?" I asked. It was the question all of us wanted to ask.

"Yes," Zye said.

We stared at her, then glanced excitedly at one another.

"Let me get this straight," Rumbold said. "This ship, by itself, is capable of ferreting out new pathways to the stars?"

"Yes," Zye said again, in the exact same tone.

"Is that function repaired?" I asked.

"It was never damaged."

"Let me guess why you never said anything about it, then," Yamada said, jumping in.

Zye looked at her flatly. "Because I was never asked."

"That's what I thought," Yamada said. She shook her head in disbelief. She turned to me. "Imagine, William, what this might mean to Earth. We not only have a way to get to the stars again, we have a ship that's capable of finding her own way to anywhere we want to go."

"That isn't true—not exactly," Zye said. "In theory, you can go anywhere, but you have to find the correct path first. The trouble is that you can't determine the end point of a thread—we call the pathways threads—without traversing it."

"So, you're flying blind?" I asked. "Every time?"

"When you explore a new path, yes. Once it is known and mapped, it's much safer."

Zye was describing a frightening prospect, and it dampened our enthusiasm. We would have to jump blindly, not knowing if we'd come out trapped in the gravitational grip of a black hole, or doomed in some other fashion.

"I see now why your people went out ready to colonize but ended up having to abandon this ship. They jumped blindly, came out in a dangerous region, and were promptly ambushed. In order to escape, perhaps they jumped again."

"Several times, I'd estimate," Zye said.

"But that wouldn't necessarily allow them to escape. You said this ship can open a path for others. The enemy must have pursued them."

"It's the only logical conclusion," Yamada agreed. I could hear the rising excitement in her voice. "The Stroj chased the battle cruiser. Eventually, the officers aboard this ship must have realized that they couldn't escape. So they abandoned her and sent her off into space on a fresh course."

"And that final leg led her here," I said. "But there's one thing that I don't get. If these Stroj were following the ship, and they wanted to capture her, why didn't they follow to this system and take the ship? After all, she'd been abandoned and badly damaged by that time."

"There is only one plausible reason I can think of," Zye said, "but it is unpleasant to contemplate."

We looked at her curiously.

"They might have decided," she said, "to go after the fleeing crew instead of the ship."

That was a grim thought. What kind of enemy would rather lose the ship than let the crew escape? I was beginning to hope I never met up with the vile Stroj personally.

"So," I said, "the ship came here on automatic pilot, abandoned. In that case, who knocked out her engines when she arrived?"

Zye had no answer for that one.

Rumbold shrugged in confusion and disinterest.

"The fact is they're gone," he said, "and the ship was left here, floating in the dark for years. No one was aboard except for Zye. It's a wonder you didn't go mad, girl."

Zye looked at him dismissively. "Betas do not experience madness. It's not in our design."

I had my doubts about that, but I didn't mention them. I had no doubt she was strong-minded, but there had been a certain degree of hunger in her eyes when she looked at me. She was human after all, and she had to be tremendously lonely for all that time, not knowing if she would grow old and die in an automated cell.

"I have an idea…" Yamada said. She'd been working on her console steadily while I mused about Zye and her fate. "I think I know how it could have happened. The engines weren't excessively damaged at the end of the battle when the crew decided to abandon her."

Zye looked at Yamada suddenly. "You've accessed the logs?"

"Yes, I've figured out how over the last week. You aren't the only one with hacking skills aboard this vessel."

"But you admit you withheld this critical information until now? A Beta would be punished for such an omission."

Yamada's face darkened. "Let's get something straight, Zye," she said. "I'm a Star Guard officer, and you're a civilian from another star system. I answer only to the Captain. As far as I'm concerned—"

"Ensign," I said, intervening, "perhaps it would be best if you just informed us of your findings."

Yamada flicked her eyes back and forth between my face and Zye's stony mask.

"All right," she said, "I think the ship was programmed to jump as Zye says. It did so, after the crew abandoned her. She was damaged, but still flying due to inertial effects. Looking at the sequence of events, It appears the ship crossed a bridge between star systems on autopilot and ended up here. But while she flew, her engines died. They were already damaged, and the primary ignition chamber burned through during those final hours. It's a wonder she didn't blow up."

Zye nodded thoughtfully. I could see in her eyes she was playing out the scene in her mind. "The Stroj decided to process the crew, rather than to capture the ship. The engines detected the catastrophic fault and shut down. The ship would have fired braking jets and gone into hibernation without further programming."

"We may never know the exact details," I said, "but the scenario you two have come up with makes good sense. When we return to Earth, I'm going to enter it into my report and credit you both with the investigation effort."

This seemed to mollify them both. They went back to their duties, which consisted of systems checks. If we were going to try to fly this vessel again, we had to make sure she wouldn't explode upon applying her first kilo-Newtons of thrust.

First, we had to stoke the core, which took guts in and of itself. A few hours later, we felt brave enough and confident enough to ignite the primary engine chambers.

Squinting, despite the fact I knew it wouldn't protect my eyes, I ordered Rumbold to begin the process.

"Are you sure, Captain?" he asked worriedly.

"Just do it, Rumbold. We'll die quickly if the chambers rupture."

"That's quite a comfort!"

He finally applied his thumb to his board, then made a spinning motion around it, touching his index finger to the correct control.

Zye had read the instructions to figure out how to perform that particular maneuver. I took it that it wasn't general knowledge, and that some Alpha designer of the past had wisely made the touch-sequence an awkward gesture that couldn't be performed accidentally. It wouldn't do to have someone sit on the console and fire up the core by simply leaning on it.

An intense rumbling rolled through the ship. We felt it in our bones. It was like an earthquake—but it was more of a deep vibration than a rolling or jolting. If I hadn't been clenching my teeth, they might have clacked together.

"Status?" I said loudly.

"We're good here," Yamada answered.

"No breach shown," Zye said.

"The panel is all green," Rumbold said, "but that might mean we're dead anyway."

I gave him a silent "thank-you" and gazed at my supervisory panels. Apparently, a ship's captain didn't deserve the most detailed information feed in Beta systems design. What I saw was a diagram of the ship with vital systems blinking and interacting.

Most of the systems were still green, with a few yellow and red exceptions. Not everything on the ship had been repaired yet, such as the medical facilities. We'd focused on weapons first, then the engines. Frills could wait until we saw the blue-white sphere of Earth under us.

"Yamada, tell the crew to buckle up. We're going to do this. I was planning to just warm the engines for a test-firing, but it's my belief letting them go cold again while they're damaged is more of a risk. We'll press on and make our way back to Earth, starting now."

Rumbold clapped his hands together and whooped. I smiled at him.

For the next few minutes, while the primary engine kept stoking itself up, we watched every instrument obsessively.

"Sir!" Rumbold shouted suddenly, making me jump. "I think—yes! We're moving, Skipper!"

"Excellent, Chief," I said, forcing my tensed muscles to relax. Rumbold had a way of generating excitement within himself and sharing it with anyone else who was listening.

"Confirmed," Zye said. "We're going to start feeling it soon. What thrust level do you wish to allow?"

I spun my chair slightly to look at her. "What's the maximum?"

"Approximately thirty-Gs," she said calmly. "But I wouldn't recommend that kind of acceleration. My analysis of your cardiovascular structure indicates—"

"Cap it at two Gs for now, Zye," I said, alarmed. Thirty Gs might be survivable for a Beta, but any Earth man would be crushed.

Before she eased off, I could feel myself getting heavy. The effects magnified until I was laboring to take a breath. Two Gs, after weeks of near weightlessness, felt like rib-crushing pressure. We were all gasping within five minutes.

"We're at two Gs," Zye said calmly. "Are you sure you want to ease off on the acceleration?"

"Yes, please," I said through gritted teeth. "We're used to being pressed into our seats, but this flight is going to be a long one."

Zye shrugged. "It will be even longer if we crawl along—but we've leveled off."

Rumbold looked at me balefully. He was feeling it, I could tell. Longevity treatments didn't completely erase the aches and pains that always accompany age.

-32-

The door to the bridge swished open ten minutes into the flight. Our acceleration level still stood at exactly two Gs. A struggling Lieutenant Morris gripped the doorway with his face twisted into a tormented mask.

"What's going on up here?" he demanded.

"Sorry Lieutenant," I said. "We sounded the klaxons and ordered everyone to their crash seats. Is someone injured?"

He shook his head. "They're alive, but they're bitching up a storm below decks. Are you crazy, Sparhawk? Who would apply this kind of thrust in a ship that's barely operable?"

"These thrust levels are exceedingly low, Lieutenant," Zye said. "I assure you, S-11 was designed to take far more."

He looked at her suspiciously, then turned back to me. "You're taking an alien's advice on everything now?"

It was a stinging remark, and I shook my head slowly at him. "Zye isn't an alien, she's human. And yes, I'm taking her advice. No one else knows much about this vessel, Lieutenant. I'm glad to have her aboard to help us."

Grumbling, Morris turned to go, but paused to ask a question over one hunched shoulder. "At least tell me where we're going."

"Earth, of course."

Morris looked startled. "Is that wise, sir?"

"Where else would you have me go?"

He shook his head. "I don't know. I doubt there's a safe harbor for this ship anywhere in the system."

I looked after him as he staggered away, weighed down by the G-forces. The door closed behind him, and I was still frowning at it.

"Huh. That's a long walk with two Gs on your shoulders," Rumbold said. "He could have crawled, but he's too proud for that, I'd wager. Even with that plastic leg of his."

"Hmm?" I asked. "Ah yes, probably so... Rumbold, what do you think Earth's reaction will be when we return home with our prize?"

He looked thoughtful. "They'll panic, I'd bet. We need to talk to them before we park in orbit. We'll look like an invasion force otherwise."

It occurred to me that Rumbold was right. If we flew silently into orbit around Earth, well, it would look pretty scary from the ground. They might even fire missiles at us, and I wasn't sure I could take them all out.

"All right," I said, spinning to face Yamada. "Do we have long range communications working properly yet? We must get through to CENTCOM."

"Negative, sir," Yamada said. "We're getting nothing through. For all I know, they're beaming messages to us as well—but I'm not hearing a thing."

"Helmsman, program a more circuitous route. If we can get out of line with whoever is jamming us, maybe we can get a message through."

"Will do," Rumbold said, "but this navigational software sucks."

Zye spun around in her chair. "What's the meaning of that term in this context?" she asked.

"What term...you mean 'sucks?'" Rumbold asked. "It means something is substandard, garbage, irritating. Doesn't make sense, I know, but that's how Earthlings use the word."

She gave him a hostile look. "It was programmed by two gifted Alphas," she said. "There is no better design. It does not suck."

"Yes it does," Rumbold said, working the boards and grumbling.

I decided not to get between them. I took it as a good sign that Rumbold was now willing to injure Zye's sensitivities without apology. It had always been his habit to do so with regular crewmen, and he was only demonstrating she was just one more member of the group to him.

Zye, on the other hand, was harder to read. Was she deeply upset by his words, or only mystified? It could have been either. She rarely showed much in the way of emotion on her face, and when she did, it was with a cold, predatory demeanor everyone else found disturbing. It was like teasing a large shark—you couldn't tell if you were pissing it off or just making it hungry. An unfortunate scenario in either case.

When we were up to a full two Gs of thrust, we leveled off and maintained without any issue. After two full hours we were up to an impressive cruising speed, and I had Zye reduce our acceleration levels to one G.

The crew sighed in relief. Everyone was sore and tired—except for Zye herself. She seemed utterly unperturbed by the experience. Even while the added force had been at its worst, she'd shown no signs of discomfort.

"What's the standard gravity like on your home world, Zye?" I asked her.

"Slightly more than two Gs," she said.

Nodding, I thought that over. "In that case, our recent acceleration was an easy vacation to you. Is that right?"

She frowned slightly and shook her head. "No, it wasn't as easy as it should have been. I performed a regular routine of calisthenics in my cell at every eating period, but I still have atrophied significantly. A Beta native, fresh out of our gravity well, would break me easily on a sparring mat in my current condition."

"Unless you tricked them, right?" I asked, smiling.

Zye eyed me for a moment, as if checking to see if she was being insulted again. Seeing my smile, she nodded confidently.

"I excel at unexpected tricks, it's true. It's nice to know someone who appreciates my gifts. I've lived my whole life hiding my greatest abilities."

After giving her another reassuring nod, I stood up and stretched. My chair rolled away behind me, empty and spinning slowly. The whole deck was currently canted at about a twenty degree angle, as we were banking now, moving us off our initial course.

"Still no luck with the jamming?" I asked Yamada.

"I was just resending a message," she said. "I'll write a script to ping away at a list of relay satellites. I'm starting to see acknowledgements now and then—signals indicating we've gotten through the first layer of the handshaking protocol. But we're still being jammed, I bet, because we can't establish a working channel. They keep collapsing."

"Keep working on it. Whatever is out there jamming us must have a range limit. We'll escape them yet."

Two days passed, during which we banked again, getting back onto course for Earth. Looking at the star charts, we hadn't really managed to change the angle between Earth and our position that much. If the jamming source was close to Earth, we'd have to move halfway around to the other side of the Solar System to get an angle that would avoid this active jamming.

Accordingly, I'd ordered my crew to change course again, coming about and plotting a direct path to Earth—or at least to where Earth would be when we got there. We were traveling at such a tremendous speed now that we'd be there in less than a week.

We passed the rocks, then the orbit of Mars, before anything surprising happened. With about a hundred thousand kilometers to go, incoming contacts appeared on our boards.

I was sleeping when the klaxons went off, and I rolled out of bed onto the floor—or rather, I shot across the room. The ship was gliding now, with the big engines idling. The only gravity was the minimal pull the ship itself had due to its extreme mass.

Unused to the light gravity, instead of sliding out of bed I'd actually vaulted into the air and landed on the far wall. My elbow stung, but I was otherwise fine.

Muttering curses, I donned a fresh suit quickly and contacted the bridge.

"Rumbold? Yamada? Who set off the alarm?"

"It's Zye here, Captain," Zye's calm voice came into my earpiece. "We've detected a group of ships on an intercept vector to our position."

"How long do we have before they're in weapons range?"

"About fifty minutes, sir, barring further course or speed adjustments on either side."

"All right, you did well to sound the alarm," I told her. "Contact Yamada and Rumbold, we need them on the bridge."

"They've reported in and are on the way, Captain."

I closed the connection and rushed to the bridge. I checked the time—it was three thirty in the morning on ship's time. We hadn't been maintaining round the clock watch-standers. We were understaffed, and not much had been happening for the last week of flight. The result was we'd all be bleary-eyed and fuzzy tonight.

When I reached the bridge, I was gratified to see I wasn't the last man to get there. Rumbold followed me by a full minute. He looked like he'd been up all night drinking—which was entirely possible. His normally bloodshot eyes were like two red coals.

With a wordless grunt, he heaved himself into his seat and began slapping at the controls.

"Those aren't attacking ships," he said after examining the data. "They're Star Guard ships. Don't you know your own allies, Yamada?"

She cast him back a sour glance. "Zye sounded the alarm, not me."

I spoke with crewmen who'd rushed to their battle stations here and there around the ship, telling them to maintain a ready stance. Then I turned to Rumbold.

"Earth ships?" I asked. "Size, configuration?"

"Destroyers, sir."

"How many?"

"All of them, apparently. I've got five large contacts and a dozen or so screening vessels. Pinnaces like old *Cutlass*."

His explanation didn't satisfy me. "Rumbold," I said, "you've been in Star Guard for many more years than I have. When has CENTCOM ever put all their ships into one task force?"

He looked thoughtful for a moment. "I was going to say during an exercise or a parade—but no. They've never done so, to the best of my knowledge."

"That's right. It's against the Admiralty's doctrine to do so. They've never wanted to put all their eggs into one basket, so to speak."

Rubbing at my face for a moment, I tried to think. I needed a shower and breakfast—but I doubted I had time for either.

"What's the status of our defensive systems?" I asked Yamada.

She looked at me in alarm. "You don't think they'll fire on us, do you?"

I made a waving gesture, suggesting she should answer my question.

"We don't have much," Yamada said. "We spent all our time getting the engines, helm and navigational systems working. Since then, I've focused the repair robots on improving sensors and communications."

Turning to Zye, I looked at her. She returned my gaze with unblinking seriousness.

"We might be able to get some point-defense cannons operable in the next hour," she said. "I've had a few robots working on armament since the beginning."

"That was never approved by my station," Yamada said.

"No," I said, "but it appears to have been a smart play. Let's inspect these systems."

"They're on the hull—forward and aft," Zye said. "The robots could be ordered to focus solely on them, but—"

"Do it, Zye. Then you and I are going out there to have a look. I want to see the hull integrity for myself, and the state of our guns."

I transferred the bridge to Rumbold's capable hands, urging him not to make any sudden maneuvers without warning us. We'd be cast off into space if he did.

Zye followed me stoically to the airlock. "She doesn't like me," she said.

"What? You mean Yamada?"

"Of course. She never approves of any action I take. She assumes the worst intent on all my decisions."

"Why do you think that's the case?"

"I'm a threat to her."

I thought about that for a moment. But then the airlock finished its cycle and opened up onto a scene of stars and planets.

The sun hung like a brilliant search beam over the prow. Our visors dimmed automatically to keep us from being blinded, and our radiation counters began to tick loudly. There must have been a small storm in the region.

What was most shocking was the near total lack of ice on our hull. It had almost all melted away now as we were much closer to the heat of the sun. Our engines had warmed up the hull as well, finishing the job.

The ship's hull was starkly exposed. It had transformed into a vessel of stained metallic gold.

"Why do you think you're a threat to Yamada?" I asked Zye.

"Because she likes to be the smartest person on the bridge. The one with all the answers. She fancies herself to be an Alpha."

I smiled at that as I led the way across the hull. We had our magnetic boots activated, and each step clicked and clanked.

"She does pride herself on her technical competency," I admitted. "But I hardly see how—"

"Not only that," Zye said. "She sees me as a sexual rival as well."

I took a misstep and almost pitched onto my face. Zye's massive gauntlet reached out quickly, caught my elbow, and righted me.

"You should be careful," she said. "There are many cables and pipes on the outer hull."

"Right," I said, "about your last comment…"

"Let's forget about it. Isn't that what Earthlings would say? Further discussion would only embarrass both of us."

"Consider it forgotten, then," I said.

Two hundred halting steps took us to the prow, where a cluster of guns stood aiming at nothing. They were arrayed on a bulbous pod, looking like a sea anemone that had lost most of its spines.

"Here we are," I said, examining the pod. "They look operable, but there are only six cannons? That's the whole forward cluster?"

"No," Zye said. "There are four such pods. Another is opposite this one on the prow. Then there are two more on the fantail."

"Let's have a look."

By the time our little inspection tour was done on the prow, I'd found the robot team. They were working like ants on the second forward pod. They had a chain going, carting materials and tools back and forth with furious intensity. Each of the multi-limbed bots seemed capable of welding, lifting and placing elements at the same time.

"Before the enemy ships are in range," Zye said. "We should have both the forward pods working. That's only fifty percent of our armament, but it will have to do."

"Enemy?" I asked. "Those are Star Guard destroyers out there—Earth's finest. They aren't our enemies."

"Call them what you wish," Zye said. "Everyone aboard knows they're going to fire on us."

"Let's go below," I said, clanking quickly back toward the airlock.

"There are other options," Zye said as I left her behind.

"What are you talking about?"

"You've got the bots working on defensive systems only. Maybe you should put them onto refurbishing the missile tubes. We could get them ready to fire within another hour or so."

I stared at her for a moment. Was she bloodthirsty or just practical? I wasn't sure, but I thought it was a little of both.

"Keep the bots working on the defensive pods," I said.

"What will your next move be?" she asked me.

"I have to talk to them. To get them to see reason."

"I don't have much hope for your chances," Zye said. "If they were Betas, they wouldn't even reply. They would destroy you without compunction."

"Well, they aren't Betas. I'm going to give it a try."

-33-

Back on the bridge, I asked Yamada to open a channel with the destroyers. The connection opened immediately. I suspected the source of the jamming didn't mind allowing me to talk to this flotilla.

"This is Captain William Sparhawk," I said, "in command of the newly captured battle cruiser, *Defiant*. We couldn't help but notice Star Guard has seen fit to send out an escort to render aid and guide us to Earth. If you would be so kind as to coordinate with my navigator to make this go smoothly, I'd appreciate it."

There was an expected delay as my ship and theirs were still over twenty light-seconds apart.

"Sir..." Yamada said. "They're braking."

"They're moving to intercept," Zye said with certainty. "They can't very well destroy us on a single high-speed pass."

I lifted a finger in her direction. "We don't know their intentions yet, Zye. Relax."

She looked anything but relaxed. I purposefully sat in a somewhat slouched position. When a commander isn't worried, his crew tends to be calm as well. The trick is to be convincing.

Sliding my eyes around the bridge crew, I calculated that my ruse was only partly successful. Zye looked like she was gearing up for a boxing match. Rumbold was sweating, and Yamada kept glancing over her boards every second or so with quick movements.

"Sparhawk, this is Rear Admiral Hedon," said a rumbly old voice at last. He didn't sound happy—but then to my knowledge he never had. "You're hereby ordered to match our course and speed. You'll be boarded and we'll take it from there. I thank you in advance for your cooperation in this matter."

Without meaning to, I heaved a sigh. There it was, out in the open. They had no intention of letting me fly this ship home.

On the surface of it, the orders seemed like a reasonable precaution on their part. The trouble I had was the small matter of a perceived mutiny in my recent past.

"Yamada," I said, spinning my chair so I could make eye contact with her. "We've found the source of the jamming, haven't we? It's the task force closing with us."

She nodded her head. "Definitely. I'm still trying to transmit to Earth, and I can't get a byte past them. The fact that our signal is crystal clear with the destroyers—well, there's no other explanation."

I rotated around slowly and faced the vid pickups. "Put me on screen. I want to see the admiral, if possible."

"Active."

At this point I was transmitting video, but we were still getting only audio in return.

"Admiral," I said as affably as I could while talking to a blank wall, "please understand that my crew and I have suffered a variety of attacks and false allegations. In that light, can you explain why your ships are jamming all our communications with Earth?"

The delay was slightly shorter this time. "Sparhawk, stand down. That's all you have to worry about. You'll be relieved and processed accordingly. You'll get your day in court—all of you."

Before answering, I turned to Yamada. "Bring Lieutenant Morris to the bridge. I want him standing at my side."

She nodded and quickly relayed the summons.

Turning back to the cameras, I activated the transmit button again. I forced a smile I didn't feel in the slightest. "Admiral, you have not answered my question. Why are you jamming us?

I've been trying to contact CENTCOM and report my status for many days. I have critical intel on dangers that involve all Earth."

When the next response came in, the Admiral finally sent video as well.

I saw *Rigel's* bridge. Admiral Hedon stood in the center of the scene with his hands behind his back, staring at me from under bushy eyebrows. He looked pissed off. Behind him, his crew craned their necks and gaped at the interior of my ship.

In comparison with *Rigel*, *Defiant's* bridge was cavernous. Also, there was Zye, who was attracting a lot of attention.

"Sparhawk," Hedon said. "I gather you're refusing to follow my orders. That saddens me. I know you come from a good family, boy, so I'm going to lay my cards on the table. Maybe your breeding will win through, and you'll do the right thing. I've been ordered to stop you from returning to Earth. You're not going to be allowed to communicate with possible coconspirators back home."

Hedon paused to look around my bridge. Possibly, he'd only just begun to notice the details. He frowned in confusion. "What kind of a ship is that—?" he asked someone off-screen. "And who is that hulking woman back there—is she even human?"

I turned toward Zye with a smile. I beckoned to her. "Come stand here beside my command chair, Zye."

She did as I asked immediately. She towered over me, especially as I was sitting down.

"I'll be God damned..." the Admiral said, gawking.

As if on cue, Lieutenant Morris stepped onto the bridge. I waved him up to the central stage area. He came up warily, eyeing the forward screens. He didn't look happy to have his face on camera.

"Admiral," I said, "let me introduce you to two important people. This woman is Zye. She's a Beta—a colonist. Her people built this amazing ship, and she's helped us to get it underway again. On my other side is Lieutenant Morris. He was the Marine Commander aboard *Altair* and previously served under Captain Singh."

Admiral Hedon looked at the two in bafflement. From his point of view, both were impossible. How could Singh's Marine Commander be aboard my ship? How could a colonist exist in the Solar System at all?

The Admiral shook his head and threw up his hands. "This conspiracy is beyond anything anyone's presented to me, even in conjecture!" he said. "I didn't believe it then, Sparhawk—and I don't want to believe it now. But you've gone and presented living evidence and given me little choice."

My eyes narrowed and my teeth clenched. I wasn't sure what he was talking about, but I was sure this wasn't going the way I'd hoped. I'd thought that if I showed him that this ship was a legitimate colonist vessel, an intelligence miracle, he'd listen to me. The fact I had rescued Singh's crew, and they were now working with me to help Earth wasn't doing the trick, either. None of that seemed to matter.

"This is going dreadfully," Hedon said, almost talking to himself. "You're in league with alien colonists, you somehow colluded with mutineers aboard *Altair*, and you managed to destroy not one but *two* Star Guard ships."

He faced the vid pickup angrily. "Your own ship, man? How could you? A Star Guard Captain's sworn duty is to his ship and crew, and you destroyed one and corrupted the other. There's no other explanation."

It was my turn to throw up my hands when he finally stopped talking. "Sir, your account is inaccurate. Singh ordered *Altair's* gunners to fire on *Cutlass*. That wasn't my doing."

Hedon's brows bushed up and he glowered at me. "Twisting the story and standing on details won't save you," he said. "What matters to Earth is the loss of the destroyer, naturally. No one has been able to figure out how you managed to destroy Singh's ship with a derelict wreck—the answer is now clear. You had inside help. It was sabotage, I'd wager my head on it!"

He leveled an accusatory finger at Lieutenant Morris, who stood at my side.

"I see you have the traitor beside you! Don't bother to deny it. Anything else is unthinkable. I have to admit, I hadn't thought a Sparhawk would sink so low, but I was clearly wrong."

"Admiral," I said patiently. "I found the ship as a derelict, you're correct. But the Betas have excellent repair technology. Zye here was in dire straits, stranded aboard and unable to help herself. We rescued her and in turn she helped us get this ship going again."

I gestured toward Lieutenant Morris, who was white-faced.

"Morris served on *Altair*. He and his men survived the attack we were forced to launch upon *Altair* when Singh attempted to kill my crew. Since that time, he's joined me and become my supporter."

Turning back to the cameras, I forced another smile. "Look, Admiral, all we want to do is bring this ship home to Earth. Let our people examine her and learn from her technology. We have to be able to build our own capital ships—otherwise when more colonists return to Earth, they'll find us weak."

There, I'd made my case as best I could. Surely, he had to see reason.

"It's worse than I thought," the admiral said on his next, and last, transmission. "It pains me to tell you, Sparhawk, that I must now follow my contingency orders. We will not come in close and dock with you—that is no longer an option. Since you destroyed Singh's ship, you might be inclined to take down another. In case you're still considering hostile action, let me assure you that my crew is completely loyal to myself and Star Guard. You will have no saboteurs here to help you this time!"

He paced a bit, shaking his head. "No, I don't see any way out. Your surrender is no longer sufficient. I can't let you get close to my vessels. I won't be bamboozled by your trickery, endangering our last five ships. I'm going to have to destroy you at range, Sparhawk. Everything changed when you provided me such direct evidence of mutiny, conspiracy and even treachery with that—that monstrous alien of yours. If you have any decency, any shred of loyalty to Earth left, you'll abandon ship and hope I'm allowed by CENTCOM to pick you up for trial. Admiral Hedon, out."

Gawking at the screen, I couldn't believe it. After a moment, it dimmed and went black.

"Open the channel again," I snapped at Yamada.

"I'm trying sir—no response."

"What about Earth?"

"They're still jamming us, sir. We can't get a byte past them."

"They've opened their gun ports," Zye boomed, interrupting our conversation. "I have missiles inbound. I repeat, missile launches detected. Six…eight…fourteen—sir, should I light up our weapons systems?"

I felt slightly ill. I stared at the dark screen facing me.

There was a horrible choice before me now, lying at my feet. Should I fight them, or let them destroy the battle cruiser?

At that moment, I honestly didn't know which path I would ultimately choose.

-34-

The crushing weight of defeat. I'd read about it, but I'd never experienced it before. As a naval officer, I was relatively untested. Certainly, I'd done brief battle with *Altair*—but that had amounted to a single surprise shot. No such ruse would work to win the day this time.

That entire line of thinking begged the question in any regard. Should I fight at all? The man commanding those destroyers was my legitimate superior. He'd informed me that my ship was to be destroyed. *My ship.*

Admiral Hedon was right about one thing, it was a Captain's sworn duty to protect his ship and crew. On my honor, this time I would do both or die in the attempt.

My mind unfroze about ten seconds after Hedon had announced his intentions. Everyone on the bridge was looking at me to make a decision—any decision.

Zye was the only person who wasn't doubting my leadership. She was focused on her boards, reading off the data that her commander needed. I struggled to listen. It was the least I could do.

"Forty missiles in total, Captain," she said. "That appears to be all of them. We're going to be within range of their cannons soon as well."

Eight missiles from each destroyer. That was everything they had. For some reason, that gave me an idea.

"Yamada, plot us an escape course."

"Already done. Considering our forward inertia, we'd do best to accelerate and flash right past them."

"We'll take a full blast from Hedon's cannons if we do that!" Rumbold objected loudly.

"There's no choice—other than to abandon ship and let them destroy us. Fools!" I hammered at my cage-like seat. "Hedon doesn't see it. He doesn't value this ship, he only sees it as a threat."

"Your orders, sir?" Yamada said.

This was it. The moment I'd been dreading. I was going to have to disobey my superiors again—but I hesitated. I had no pretext. My mind raced, trying to come up with—

"Zye," I said. "Do we have any life pods aboard?"

"Negative. My people took them all when they abandoned her."

"Right. Anything else? A small pinnace, perhaps? A launch for carrying officers?"

"Nothing."

Whirling around to Yamada, who looked at me in disbelief, I waved for her attention. "What kind of yield do these warheads have collectively? How big of a blast radius?"

She worked her board, but Zye at tactical came back with the answer first. "There's no chance we'd survive. Even though we're in hard vacuum the explosions would be relatively small in range, but the radiation would fry us for a number of kilometers. We can't escape."

I nodded, grinning savagely. My crewmen suspected I was mad, I could tell, but I didn't care.

"That's it!" I said. "He's given me no choice. I don't have to obey him if he orders me to stand and be annihilated. No trial, no due process—nothing. Admiral Hedon's orders are null and void."

"That's very comforting, Captain," Rumbold said, "but what are we going to do to keep breathing?"

"Helm," I said. "Put the hammer down. Maximum acceleration. Blow right by them—now!"

Rumbold immediately complied. He must have had his finger on the button already.

The pressure was intense. I could hardly breathe. My nose began to bleed, then my eyes and cheeks wouldn't stay closed.

"Zye," I croaked, "take over. If we black out, it's okay. But keep flying. Don't kill us—but keep flying."

"Taking the helm," she said in a remarkably natural voice.

Things were a blur after that—literally. My eyes were compressed somewhat and I could barely move my head to see the instruments.

The destroyers were taken by surprise. Their missiles were left targeting empty space. We'd leapt ahead of them, and they whizzed by. They turned to follow, but we knew they would run out of fuel long before they could overtake our vessel.

Their cannons, however, were a different story. Beams lanced out, connecting our ship with theirs briefly.

I felt and heard impacts. The ship shook and the walls rang as if giants were beating upon the hull.

"Permission to return fire, sir?" Zye asked.

I shook my head. I tried to say no, but I couldn't get the words out.

With great effort, I looked around the bridge. Rumbold was out. Yamada—she was still moving weakly, but she couldn't even touch the boards. Lieutenant Morris had wisely fled the bridge and sought a crash seat somewhere.

Zye came into my vision as I used the automated chair to spin me around.

She was upright. Her hunched shoulders were the only sign she was feeling the strain.

I could see in her eyes that she wanted to fire our cannons. She wanted to blast the destroyers out of the sky.

Struggling to suck in a breath, I wheezed out a few words.

"No, Zye," I said. "Don't fire on them. We'll make it. Our armor will hold."

She showed me her clenched teeth, but then she turned back to her boards and worked them.

I desperately hoped she would follow my orders, for everyone's sake.

That was my last thought before I succumbed to the low blood pressure in my brain and blacked out.

* * *

When I awoke, I felt a touch on my forehead. My eyes fluttered open. Zye loomed over me, her face filled with concern.

"Can you speak?" she asked me.

"Yes," I managed to croak. "But I've got a huge headache."

"That's normal. What's my name?" she asked.

"Zye."

"What ship do you command?"

"Uh…" I hesitated. I almost said *Cutlass*, but I corrected myself. "*Defiant*," I said firmly.

She smiled tightly. "Good. Your brain is functioning."

With a degree of effort, I straightened up and looked around. Despite my throbbing head, I seemed uninjured. Rumbold was still unconscious, however, and Yamada was stirring and making mewling sounds.

"See to her," I said to Zye.

"You should rest," she said.

"No time," I said. "What about the destroyers? Are they still firing on us?"

"We're out of their effective range. Their missiles have run out of fuel, and I changed course, so they can never reach us."

"Good, right," I said, checking on Rumbold. He wasn't waking up. "He's an old man," I said. "I hope he recovers."

"How old?" Zye asked me.

I turned around, and I saw honest curiosity on her face.

"About a hundred and sixty, I believe," I said. "When he was a child, the colony ships were still flying. He said the huge, spherical vessels were like small silver moons in Earth's orbit before they broke away and left the Solar System."

Zye cocked her head, clearly astonished. "How can he be so old and still serving in the military? No Beta has ever lived so long."

"Well, we have longevity treatments," I said. "But they're not perfect. He could easily tear an arterial wall—causing a stroke, or blood clots. They're real dangers after the first century of life."

Zye moved to Rumbold's chair and knelt, examining him. She put her hand to his throat to feel his pulse. Then she brought out instruments.

"I might have killed him," she said. "I didn't know he was so frail. I'm sorry, Captain."

"It's all right," I said. "You followed my orders and saved the rest of us. Besides, Rumbold is as tough as nails. He might surprise you."

I lightly touched Zye's back as I walked past. It was an automatic gesture of comfort.

She didn't stiffen in alarm, but she did turn her head in my direction and give me a quizzical look. I got the feeling that Betas didn't go around touching one another when they felt bad.

Checking on Yamada, I found she was sick. She vomited, then tried to stand. I urged her to stay in her chair.

The door swished open and Lieutenant Morris walked onto the deck. He looked more fit than any of us, except for Zye herself.

"Did you do it?" he asked. "All the boys are betting on it down below."

There was an odd look on his face, and a pistol in his hand. I glanced at the gun, then back at him.

Zye caught on a moment later. She stood quickly and moved to draw her weapon. I raised a hand, directing her to stop.

"What's the problem, Morris?" I asked.

"You did it, didn't you?" he asked, glaring at me. "You destroyed our last ships."

"No," I said, "I didn't. Did you notice that extreme bout of acceleration? We outran them, that's all."

He frowned, looking back and forth between Zye and myself.

"I blacked out during the maneuvers," he said, letting his hand slip from the butt of his pistol.

I noticed Zye kept her hand on her weapon, and I didn't admonish her.

"We all blacked out," I said. "Except for Zye."

Morris looked at her with fresh suspicion. "Then why didn't she shoot back?" he asked. "She's always quick on the draw."

"That's true," I said, "but I ordered her not to. She knows how to follow orders."

Morris snorted. "That's nice for her. Maybe you should try doing the same, occasionally."

"If you're referring to Admiral Hedon's orders, they were illegal."

"How's that?"

"You can't order a friendly ship to stand still while you destroy her and her crew—especially without any cause or trial. There was no investigation, no due process, nothing. We hadn't fired a shot at them, so they couldn't claim self-defense."

Morris worked his lips for a moment, wiped his mouth with his hand, and nodded. "That does go against regs," he admitted.

"That's why we ran. We were within our rights to do so. Unless, of course, you and the rest of *Altair's* crew would rather I had followed the good Admirals orders and had us jettisoned into space in hopes of being picked up—if we survived the blast radius of this ship?"

"Okay, okay—but what now? CENTCOM isn't going to stand for this."

"We'll explain it to them."

He laughed bitterly, found a chair and flopped tiredly into it. He dug out a flask of what I assumed to be whiskey and took a drink. He offered me some.

At first I refused, but then I thought the better of it and took a gulp. It was hot, body-warm, and tasted like gasoline.

"Good stuff, huh?" Morris asked.

I nodded, unable to speak.

"Is he okay?" Morris asked, pointing at Rumbold.

Zye was bending over him, applying a medical scanner. All the lights on it were yellow. I assumed that wasn't a good sign.

"He'll probably pull through," I said.

"Good, I like that old guy."

"Lieutenant," I said to Morris, "what would you have done if I'd said we *had* fired on the destroyers?"

He took another drink. "I think I would have blown my brains out."

I eyed him in surprise. "That's not what I expected you to say."

"No? You ever been involved with a court-martial?"

"I can't say that I have."

"Me either," he said, "and I don't intend to—ever. It would kill my old man. He was in the Guard for fifty years. I couldn't do that to him. I'd rather put myself down and be accounted as a man who died doing his duty."

"I see... What do you think we should do next?"

"I'm not the Captain," he answered gruffly.

"No, but I'm still asking for your advice."

He appeared thoughtful. "I'd fly this bird home and park her in orbit. Then give CENTCOM the keys to her on your terms. They'll have to take them. What else can they do? This is the biggest thing that's happened to Star Guard since the Cataclysm itself."

"That's good advice, thank you."

Standing, I went to check on Rumbold again. Yamada was working on him now. She had her portable medical kit out. The lights were now half-green and half-yellow, which was an improvement.

"I think he's going to pull through," she said. "He had some internal bleeding, but with a transfusion and a dose of surgical nanites in his veins, he should be okay in a few hours."

"Where's Zye?" I asked.

"Right here, Captain."

I turned and saw she had positioned herself behind Morris.

The lieutenant stood up and looked at her. "You're as quiet as a cat when you want to be," he said, laughing.

Zye just stared at him. She didn't take her eyes off him or his gun for the next hour—not until he finally left the bridge.

"She's like a cat staring down a canary all right!" Rumbold croaked after the lieutenant was gone.

Surprised, I turned to see he was awake but still lying groggily in his chair. I nodded my thanks to Yamada.

"He'll pull through," she said again. "He's a tough old bird."

"What's a cat?" Zye demanded suddenly.

I glanced at her, and I found she was watching us intently.

"A cat is a quiet, predatory animal," I told her.

Zye's face flickered. A smile? It was hard to tell.

"I accept your comparison without taking offense," she told Rumbold gravely.

Rumbold rolled his eyes. They were the only part of him that was moving freely.

Fortunately, Zye didn't react to the eye-roll. She might not have known what the gesture meant.

-35-

A full day passed that was relatively uneventful. Outrunning the destroyers on our way to Earth had proved to be an easy task, but they weren't far behind me.

It wasn't until we were quite close to Earth that the jamming finally stopped. As soon as it did, we attempted communication with our superiors.

Unfortunately, CENTCOM wasn't pleased with the situation. In fact, I came to realize they were terrified.

"Unknown vessel, you are hereby ordered to halt," said the CENTCOM dispatcher. "Your approach to Earth is an act of war and will be met with deadly force."

I turned to Yamada. "What's the signal delay from this range?"

"We're about two million kilometers out. The Moon is on the far side of Earth, but we've got satellites to bounce through—I'd say we've got a ten light-second lag."

"All right, try to open a regular channel with whoever has the conn down there."

Yamada worked the controls. At last, a person I knew to be Admiral Cunningham appeared. She was only slightly younger-looking than Admiral Hedon had been, but looks could be deceiving when longevity treatments were involved. It all depended on the critical point at which a person began taking them. Often, women opted to start the treatments early, which allowed them to hold onto the end of their youth.

Consequently, Admiral Cunningham appeared to be in her late forties.

"To whom am I speaking?" she demanded.

"Admiral Cunningham," I said, "I'm Lieutenant Commander William Sparhawk. I'm the acting captain of this battle cruiser, *Defiant*."

She was silent for some time as the information was transmitted and relayed around the cosmos. During that time, her eyes roved over the scene on my bridge. As Hedon had done, she soon fixated upon Zye.

"You're incorrect, Sparhawk," she said at last. "You're not a captain. You've been relieved. You're actions are inexplicable, and they've been classified as hostile. Now, listen to me: you'll stand down, allowing your ship to be boarded. You'll be arrested and removed. Do you understand me, Commander?"

Despite my determination, I felt stressed. It wasn't every day a mid-ranking officer faced a series of angry members of the highest brass.

"I will do as you command, Admiral," I said. "I feel compelled to explain my actions, however. Admiral Hedon did not simply order me to stand down. He informed me he was going to fire on my ship and destroy her. Ordering a ship and crew to idly stand their posts while they are destroyed is an illegal act. I therefore refused to follow his orders."

We waited through the lag. Admiral Cunningham frowned as she listened to my transmission, then she replied.

"You're defying orders again?" she demanded. "All the while you banter with me, you're approaching at high speed. We have no choice but to assume that you're going to attack Earth. Our missile batteries are on high alert. I'll fire if I have to, Sparhawk, and we only have a few minutes before I have to make that call."

I sighed, letting the air out of my lungs in a long, drawn out manner. Turning to Yamada, I made a spinning motion with my index finger. She cut the feed to the screens.

"Send her the evidence," I told her. We'd long ago edited a file showing Admiral Hedon's statements clearly. "Rumbold, slow us down. Don't let the destroyers catch up, but make a good show of braking."

"On it, sir," he said.

"Zye, you know what to do if we start to black out."

"I understand," she said.

We turned the screens back on and waited for Admiral Cunningham to receive the file.

She frowned, viewing the recording we'd sent. She looked up sharply when she heard Hedon say we had to be destroyed, that he couldn't afford to take the chance to board us.

"I see," she said. "Hedon didn't follow his orders—but I can understand his reasoning. I can also understand yours…it's a delicate situation."

"There's nothing to fear, Admiral," I said firmly. "I'm coming home, that's all. I'm delivering a prize undreamed of. Please don't ask me to stand still and die. I'm an officer of the Guard. I've comported myself honorably throughout this difficult mission. I would ask that you accept that. I will surrender this ship to you personally when I arrive."

She looked troubled. I could see the indecision.

"You're asking me to take too big of a gamble, Sparhawk," she said. "Try to see this from my point of view: You're approaching with sufficient firepower to level our cities. We have to fire our missiles. There just isn't any other way."

It was my turn to become intense. "You can't order me to die without cause, Admiral," I said. "I'll be forced to defend myself and my crew. It's my sworn duty."

"A threat!" she said, perking up. "That's the first time you've shown your hand, Sparhawk. You *do* intend to dominate our world with this alien battlewagon of yours, don't you? And to think you come from a family of means. I've been charged with defending this planet, and I—"

She went on after that, but I talked over her, not listening.

"Admiral, please," I said. "I'm slowing down, surely you can see that. I think we might come to an accord. Order Hedon to stop chasing us. We'll stay at range. Then, you can come up here and inspect this prize personally. I'll give you command of her upon your arrival."

Finally, Admiral Cunningham stopped talking. She was getting my message. We were only about seven light-seconds apart now.

She appeared to be alarmed at my suggestion.

"A hostage? You expect me to give you a hostage, is that it?"

I released another sigh. "No, madam. I do not. I expect you to take command of the greatest prize Earth's ever been offered—"

I got no further. I realized she was no longer listening to me. She turned back to the screen after having spoken to subordinates.

"I'm sorry Sparhawk. You've crossed the line. We can't allow you to come any closer."

"Sir!" Yamada said. "We've got multiple launches...Fort Luna and the Lagrange Five Guardian Platform—they've both released a barrage!"

Everyone on the bridge fell silent around me. They were staring at their boards in shock. Dozens of red contacts appeared, then dozens more. They were converging slowly on our position from two angles.

My lips worked for a moment, but I was speechless. I honestly hadn't thought they would take it this far.

Admiral Cunningham stood at attention and saluted me on screen.

"I'll put the best possible face on it when I inform your next of kin, Commander," she said solemnly. "Cunningham out."

The channel closed, and we were left staring at a blank screen.

"Your orders, sir?" Zye asked several long seconds later.

Her voice was calm. I envied her ice-cold mind.

"Stand down," I said. "All engines stop."

They looked at one another. Everyone except Zye appeared to be sweating. Rumbold responded first.

"All engines stop," he announced. "It's been good serving, Skipper."

"Thank you, Chief," I said, "but we're not done yet."

Spinning my gyroscopic chair around, I faced Zye. "Activate our point defenses."

"Already done."

I snorted. She'd acted without orders—but then, I hadn't ordered her *not* to turn on the gun pods, and she was in charge of the ship's tactical weaponry.

"Zye," I said, "are all our pods operational now?"

"Yes. Reconstruction was never stopped. The repair bots finished the task some hours ago. They've since moved on to repairing the medical bay."

"Do you have any estimates as to how many missiles it would take to overload our defensive guns?"

"No," she said, "I'm not formally trained as a weapons officer."

"Of course…but you've read up on the systems, right?"

"Naturally," said Zye. "This situation is unprecedented in the documentation, however. All damage estimates include factors such as evasive maneuvers on our part. To stand still—it's suicide, sir."

Nodding, I couldn't argue with her. "It's meant to look that way."

"Why?" Yamada asked me suddenly.

"I'm hoping they'll reconsider. I'm hoping they'll self-destruct those missiles at the last minute when they realize what a monumental error they're making."

Rumbold sighed and pushed back from his station. "Sir, if I may speak plainly?"

"I can't conceive of a better moment for plain talk."

"They won't back down. They'll hit us with everything they've got. They're afraid, sir, and frightened people do thoughtless things."

I nodded slowly. "I know that. But I can't think of any other path for us."

"We could press forward," Zye said. "We could slip into orbit—a low orbit. With our main batteries poised over defenseless cities, we could demand they destroy those missiles they've launched against us. I've done the math—we could reach Earth before those missiles reach us. All I need is your order, sir."

Zye had given me a grim choice. I thought about giving the order to press ahead—I honestly did. But at last, I shook my head.

"No," I said. "We'll sit here, and we'll ride it out. What will hit us first, the destroyers or the missile barrage?"

"The missiles—they'll be here in about two hours."

"Okay. Move everyone to the internal chambers. Create some baffles along the outer hull regions to absorb shock. Check and double-check every point-defense gun."

White-faced, Rumbold and Yamada moved to follow my orders. Zye got up, and I looked at her questioningly.

"I'm going to check on the status of the cannons personally. Please don't let that Marine Commander onto the bridge, sir."

I chuckled. "He's the least of my concerns—but all right."

She left, and I looked after her.

I had to wonder what they were thinking down there on Earth. What kind of panic there was in the streets? By now, they had to know we were approaching. The news people had cameras, nano-spies and paid informants everywhere. The government was like a sieve when it came to withholding important information. Earth hadn't faced a real worldwide crisis of this magnitude in more than a century—perhaps never. There was no way they could keep a story this big from breaking down there.

That meant my parents were aware of the situation. They had to be watching. It was a disturbing thought. Quite possibly, they were going to learn of my death by witnessing my transformation into a floating heap of radioactive slag.

Two hours is a long time to wait for death.

During that time, we busied ourselves with preparations. We did what we could, shoring up our hull, creating blast-barriers and test-firing the countermeasures. We donned our helmets and pumped the air out of the pressurized regions of the ship. That was to help prevent blast-transference. Without air inside the ship, concussive blast waves would be much weaker and less dangerous.

For the most part, it was all an exercise designed to keep our minds off the fateful future. I think most of the crew knew that the shielding and hull would either hold or they wouldn't.

Only Zye seemed unperturbed by the situation. She followed every order with mechanical attention to detail.

At last, the final minutes came. I ordered everyone aboard into a crash seat and spoke to them through my implants.

"Crew, this is the moment of truth. We're standing, ready to take this attack launched by Earth, but we're not defenseless. There are less than a hundred missiles incoming. Unlike previous cases, we're not going to be able to dodge them all. Our defensive guns, countermeasures and the incredibly dense hull of this vessel will have to prove their worth."

Pausing, I checked the readouts. The ship shuddered as the first decoys were launched automatically. They would mimic the signature of our ship and provide diversionary targets for the incoming birds.

"I want everyone to brace themselves. We've shown we mean no harm—but CENTCOM clearly isn't convinced. They're not bluffing. They've launched missiles, which clearly demonstrates their intent as well as the level of misunderstanding we're facing. We'll be undergoing evasive actions now. Captain Sparhawk, out."

I heard a cheering response and a babble of rising voices as I left the channel. I let them chat a while. Talking to others about positive developments could only raise morale—besides, my crewmen deserved to die with hope.

"Permission to evade, sir?" Zye prompted me.

"Do your best—but don't kill us in the process."

In retrospect, I should have been more specific in my instructions. I might have said, for instance: 'do not drive us to unconsciousness, internal bleeding or break our bones.'"

But I hadn't thought to be that specific.

Left to her own devices, Zye was abusive. It all started with a gut-wrenching lurch. I regretted my last meal, then I felt that meal seemingly press upward, intent on entering my skull and sharing that limited space with my brain.

The direction and momentum shifted, and now it was as if someone of great weight was hanging from my legs, pulling them from my hip sockets, dislocating, tendons stretching—

We reversed again. I would have vomited, but my stomach had locked up into a tight ball of muscle that felt like a stone in my guts.

My chair, throughout this ordeal, spun around and around. I'd never much enjoyed carnival rides, and after the next two minutes passed, I was sure I'd never so abuse myself again.

Most of my crew lost consciousness. Two died, in fact, asphyxiating on their own vomit. Zye seemed oblivious to the red blinking names of these casualties—there was too much going on.

The ship was unloading ordnance. Counter missiles, fast-tracking laser beams and tanks of chaff were pumped out to flow in our wake.

Many of the missiles darted after our mimics. These exploded harmlessly—but the others learned. These were intelligent missiles. They were implacable, and they adjusted almost as rapidly as their brethren were destroyed.

The surviving missiles bore in on us. They ignored our mimics. They dodged our beams, our tiny intercepting missiles and, in their final plunge, the main cannons themselves. These last fired with a broad scope, dilated open to their maximum aperture. They gushed energy in short-ranged, powerful blasts like searchlights stabbing at swooping moths.

Less than one in ten made it to our hull. Would that be enough to destroy us? I didn't know immediately.

The hammering shocks carried through the hull into the interior walls. They folded the ships internal structures despite the fact the warheads hadn't breached the armor itself. The deck of the bridge seemed to buck and ripple under me.

A final, vicious lurch caused my helmet to be dashed into the ball of steel tubing that encased my seat.

The visor cracked, and my air began to escape right in front of my eyes.

I'd been undone by the fact that the seat was designed for a Beta. Like a child in a harness that's too big, I slipped free and my faceplate had shattered. The vacuum that I'd personally ordered to be created on the bridge sucked the air out of my suit, and it deflated tightly against my skin like a falling tent.

With conscious thought, I let the air out of my lungs. It was an easy thing to do; I simply opened my mouth and let the vacuum steal my breath from me like a ghoul in the night.

Holding one's breath under such conditions is a natural instinct—but a deadly one. The pressure difference will burst every sack in your lungs, giving you no chance at all.

So I let go of my last breath, and I prayed with those final shreds of my mind which still operated that I'd survive to see another day.

-36-

A face loomed into my blurry field of vision. It was too large to be credible, and at first I thought I was dreaming.

I blinked and then realized I was looking at Zye. She moved her hands over my cracked faceplate—and my vision blurred further.

I realized she'd been busy slapping translucent plastic patches over my broken faceplate. It was an emergency measure, but it was working. I could feel the air pumping into my suit, filling it again like a deflated balloon.

The pressure was thin. I couldn't catch a solid breath at first. But there were strong hands on my chest, pressing rhythmically—Zye's hands.

"I'm—I'm okay," I said in a wheeze. "I can breathe. Tend to the others."

Her stern face appeared again. It was blurred, but still visible in the red emergency lights. She flicked her eyes over my body until she seemed satisfied. Then she moved away.

I tried to turn my head to see where she went, but the task was almost beyond my capacities. Allowing my aching eyes to close again, I began to shiver. The cause was mixed: I was both freezing cold and in shock. My body had been chilled by the perfect stillness of the void. Who knew what other damage rapid depressurization might have caused? I would probably get the bends—or I might die of an embolism.

With so much to look forward to, I activated my implant.

"Damage report, all decks," I ordered.

For a moment there was quiet, but a storm of sound soon came. People were chattering, crying and gasping in pain.

"Crew," I said with a sternness I didn't feel. "We're still alive. We rode out the attack. Well done, everyone!"

This had some effect. Most quieted, and I began to get a trickle of reports. We'd lost people—seven in total. Even though many had come from Singh's crew, I considered them all to be my crewmen. I wasn't proud of my losses, but in battle, people tended to die.

"Pull yourselves together," I said. "Let me relay what I've learned: the hull wasn't breached. I repeat, despite the fact that two missile bases launched over ninety birds at us in an unprovoked attack, the hull of this ship never cracked. We've taken their worst, and we lived."

There wasn't any cheering but there were some sighs of relief. Some gave thanks to God, and a few sobbed. That was all.

I closed the general channel and opened my command channel. I contacted Zye directly since she didn't have an implant. She'd connected her helmet's old-fashioned headset into our com system.

"Well done, Zye," I said.

"Nothing was well done," she said, "I failed you."

My blood ran cold for a moment. In my heart, I believed she meant there were more missiles incoming. Steeling myself, I asked her the next question, the one I had to.

"Is there another attack coming?"

"No. I meant…you ordered me not to let anyone die. You Earthmen are so fragile. I miscalculated."

Relief flooded through me. Zye was right, of course. She'd miscalculated several times.

"Is Rumbold still alive?" I asked.

"Yes. He did better than you did this time."

"I slipped in my harness. It's too big for me."

"Perhaps Rumbold's corpulence saved him."

I laughed, but it ended in a coughing fit.

"Yamada," I said, "you there?"

"Here, Captain."

"Is there anything else coming at us?"

"No sir. Not even the destroyers. They're hanging back. I believe they want to make sure we're dead. We're drifting in space. Zye cut the engines."

"Right. They're like jackals circling a dying predator, hoping we'll expire soon but unwilling to be the first to take a bite."

"Uh…right, sir."

"Repressurize the internal chambers," I ordered, feeling stronger. My body ached and my sinuses burned, but I felt certain I could function. "Check for leaks first."

"That process is already underway," Yamada said. "We'll have the bridge full of air again in about six minutes. It'll be cold air—but you'll be able to trade that cracked helmet for a good one."

I waited the six minutes, then four more for good measure. When at last it was deemed safe, I opened my visor and sucked in the cold, cold air.

It was so frosty, so dry and so searingly cold I had another coughing fit and had to wait a few more minutes. Upon my recovery, I inspected the bridge carefully. A few consoles were cracked, but my panel had survived intact, as had the forward screen.

"All right," I told my crew. "I want everyone to get into their seats. I want every light on, and all damage concealed. This bridge has to look exactly like it did before the attack."

They climbed to their feet, groaning, and worked to achieve the effect I'd demanded. When we were finished hauling away a few broken consoles and a crash seat that was stuck in an inverted position, we assumed our places. I ran my fingers through my matted hair and toweled the sweat from my face.

Even Zye was sweating now, I noticed.

"Turn down the heat—that's warm enough."

When the illusion of an unaffected bridge was complete, I contacted CENTCOM again. After several long seconds, the pale face of Admiral Cunningham appeared.

"Admiral," I said. "We've been struck by several missiles, but we're still space-worthy."

"I see that," she said, her face unreadable. Her nostrils flared. I could see her chest rise and fall rapidly—fear or anger? Perhaps both.

"Can I assume you're now convinced that we mean no harm? Will you allow me to approach Earth and slide into orbit over her?"

"Commander Sparhawk, you may approach Earth," she said after a pause. "We have no way to stop you as I'm sure you're well aware. I urge you to remember your oath of office. I order…no that's wrong. I *request* that you remember who you are and resist any temptation to take advantage of this situation."

"I've never had any other intention, madam," I said. "I'm an honorable officer of the Guard."

She stared at me, as if truly seeing me for the first time.

"If that's true, Commander…well…we owe you an apology."

"Yes Admiral, I believe you do."

The channel closed, and we made our way without further mishap into Earth orbit. In our wake, the five quiet destroyers commanded by Admiral Hedon lurked. They were following us at a safe distance.

I knew that we'd only managed to get this close to Earth because they'd had no options left. We'd beaten them. We'd taken everything they could throw at us and survived, without even throwing a punch back.

The realities of the situation were disturbing. If it had been the Betas that had commanded this vessel, how would things have gone for Earth? The destruction that a ship like this could deliver upon a defenseless world was too grim to contemplate.

* * *

When we docked with Araminta Station, everyone aboard was tense. I figured the station crews themselves were nervous as well, since our ship was nearly as big as the Araminta itself.

Rumbold accompanied me to the docking airlock, and he urged me to action with every step.

"Captain, sir," he said in a harsh whisper. "We can't just open the doors, for pity's sake?"

"What else would you suggest we do, Chief?" I asked as I strode down the final passageway.

Ahead, the arching sheets of metal that formed the airlock loomed. They were huge since Betas and their equipment were all oversized. The universal collars that docked ships to the station had strained mightily to clamp on and create a tight seal.

"You could say it's jammed," he said. "Stall for time. Get assurances that we'll be treated well. That they'll arrest us rather than shoot us out of hand."

My eyes swept to meet his, then flashed back to the airlock controls. I pressed the pressurization button, and we heard hisses and rhythmic pumping sounds. The Beta ship began to equalize the pressure, temperature and oxygen levels automatically.

"Rumbold," I said, "I appreciate your concerns. But I'm not going to lie to or evade my superiors any longer."

"But they might just shoot you in the head the moment they open that door!" he said emphatically.

Troubled, I looked at the steel sheets in front of me. "It's possible," I said. "But if that's the case, I've signed onto the wrong service. I refuse to believe it. We've done as we promised. We've delivered a great prize to Earth. There's no reason for them to react irrationally."

"The real world doesn't always work the way it's supposed to." he said. There was a note of pleading in his voice that I found irritating. "Remember Hedon? He was hell-bent on taking everything we did in the worst possible light."

"True," I said, "but now, we're facing more than a single officer. I find it unlikely they've all turned against us."

Rumbold crossed his arms and sighed. "You're as stubborn as your old man. You know that, don't you?"

I glanced at him. "Disrespectful—but accurate. Have faith Rumbold. After all, I've kept us breathing for this long."

He finally fell silent, and we waited out the lengthy repressurization process. When the doors opened at last, we were greeted by none other than Admiral Cunningham herself.

She looked the two of us up and down, but she didn't smile. Not even faintly.

"Follow me, gentlemen. Have the rest of your crew report to Guard headquarters on deck three."

We followed her onto the busy station. I got the feeling that we were the talk of the post. As we passed by shops, offices and bars, everyone stopped what they were doing long enough to stare.

On deck three, at the end of a long, dark hallway, I was separated from Rumbold. Each of us went into separate debriefing chambers.

In the past, I'd been debriefed by hostile officers—several times in fact. Captain Singh had always had a special place in his heart when it came to abusing me.

But this time was different. Instead of anger and invective, I was met with respect—even deference.

As I went through the process at Araminta Station, I recalled courses in psychology that I'd taken at the Academy. It was natural human behavior to respect someone who has been previously deemed a threat but who has turned out not to be. Probably due to a sense of relief. In addition, I noticed a certain sheepishness among the brass. They'd been wrong about me—horribly wrong—and they knew it.

They didn't show these feelings openly, of course. But they were revealed in subtle ways during our discourse. Rather than grilling me harshly about every aspect of my journey back to Earth, they accepted my initial tale with only a few requests for embellishment.

Satisfied almost immediately, they moved on to other things.

"Lieutenant Commander Sparhawk," Admiral Cunningham said, "what is your assessment of our tactical situation?"

I blinked. "In regard to what, madam?"

"Compare our fleet to that of the Betas."

Nodding, I thought it over. "Tactically, if our fleet were to engage theirs—even with this battle cruiser as our flagship—we would be quickly destroyed."

They nodded, not even bothering to look up. Apparently, my conclusions matched their own.

"What, in your opinion, should be done to rectify this situation?" she asked.

"I'm hardly the one to make such decisions, Admiral."

"No. But you've spent time with a Beta. You've been commanding a Beta ship for weeks. No one is more qualified to make a suggestion."

I glanced at her two companions, both of whom were rear admirals. They'd been statues most of the time, only nodding now and then. I knew they were here to listen, not to speak. Cunningham was the only one doing the talking. Perhaps they'd planned it that way. It was hard to be sure.

Deciding to take a chance, I leaned forward. "Rebuild Earth's fleet. Copy this battle cruiser as quickly as you can and design improvements. We have technology they don't have, and they have secrets we've lost or never possessed. While you're doing that, prepare a diplomatic delegation and strategy. If more Beta ships come—or others do—we must be ready to talk or fight."

"That's good advice," she said, "and not just because it matches our own. What obstacles do you foresee in achieving these goals?"

"To be honest, it will all be political. My father leads a coalition that's made a policy plank out of short-changing the Guard. We can try to make the Servants see reason."

She cocked her head and nodded. "You're not like your father, are you?"

"I wouldn't say that. I'm a seventy-percent clone. I'm not his copy, but I'm quite similar. The primary difference is one of goals, rather than capability or attitude."

"Well said." She leaned back and tapped at a tablet. Her eyes unfocussed, and I knew she was consulting through her implants. Data was no doubt flashing into her field of vision, superimposed between the two of us.

"Continue," she said. "You know this person...Zye is the name, I believe. What do you think of her?"

"She's competent, loyal, and extremely tough in both mental and physical terms. According to her, there are many ships like this one. Those ships are identical in capability as are most of the Betas themselves."

I proceeded at length to discuss Alphas, rogues and what I knew of Beta society.

"Sparhawk, we have a special mission for you," Cunningham said at last.

"What mission, Admiral?" I asked.

"We want you to stick close to Zye. We're sending you down to Earth. Show her around. Be her escort. She trusts you, and she should learn about our culture. If the Betas do show up, we'll need her to talk for us."

Already, I could see a critical flaw in their plan. They didn't understand Beta culture, or at least they hadn't quite grasped the absolute nature of it. I'd described her as a rogue, an outcast, but they didn't seem to understand what that meant.

With an effort of will, I decided to omit my objections. Zye deserved to be treated like some kind of ambassador. Without her, the battle cruiser might have been destroyed, or fallen into the hands of the rock rats.

"What about the miners?" I asked.

Cunningham made a dismissive gesture. "They're no threat," she said. "If they'd captured the battle cruiser—well then, we'd be in danger. But as it is, they've been neutralized. In fact, Admiral Hedon's flotilla is heading out there even now to crush their ridiculous rebellion."

I tried not to frown, but failed. Frowning and nodding at the same time, I accepted her pronouncement, even though I disagreed with it. I'd told them the miners had plans, that they clearly had allies somewhere on Earth. But no one took my warning seriously.

Admiral Cunningham stood up suddenly. The two other Admirals and I did the same, taken by surprise.

"There will be celebrations in your honor—a lot of them. You'll be required to attend. Take Zye with you. See that nothing happens to her—nothing unpleasant, that is."

"Uh...I'm confused, sir. Have I not been depicted as some sort of demon in the press?"

Her face was haunted by a smile, but only briefly.

"What you say is partially true. We couldn't hide the ship's existence from the public—not entirely. But we did manage to hide our worst fears. We chose to portray you as a hero as you approached. The miner's league was depicted as the primary villain. You're going to have to continue to play your part now, Sparhawk. Do you think you can do it?"

This development surprised me, but after thinking it over, I understood. "So, in the official version of events, I was never attacked by Star Guard ships?"

"No. Can you imagine the embarrassment?"

I frowned. "It's a lie. That troubles me."

She folded her hands together in front of her. "Let's think about the goals you stated earlier, such as the rebuilding of the fleet. Do you think the political class will be more or less inclined to help a military structure that spent the last week attacking its own members?"

"Hmm, I see your point."

"Good. Follow the fiction. Keep it simple, and don't embellish. All you really have to do is omit certain unfortunate events. No lying will be required."

"I'll do my best to support you, Admiral."

"Good. We're ready to adjourn. Do you have any questions for us?"

I looked from one of them to the next. The two officers flanking Cunningham were as silent as ever.

"There's one thing that puzzles me: why did Singh do it?"

"He was sympathetic with the Miner's League. He was born out in the rocks, you know."

"Yes, many spacers have the same background. That doesn't automatically turn them all into rebels."

She awarded me an indulgent smile. "Maybe it was a matter of discovering an opportunity. When he found the ship, or his rat friends did, he formulated a plan. He was an egomaniac. The evidence is quite clear in that regard. Now, will that be all?"

I thought about mentioning my suspicion that Singh had allies here on Earth, but I could tell she didn't want to hear about that. It was my job to play the part of the hero, and all she wanted from me was a commitment to the role.

"Very well, Admiral," I said. "I'm committed to serve Earth. Thank you."

The briefing ended, and I left the chamber.

That is when I remembered a critical detail. I raced after the Admiral. "Admiral, one last thing."

"Yes, Commander?"

"Zye mentioned another race of colonists. One that's clearly more powerful than the Betas. They nearly destroyed the Beta ship. She called them the Stroj—they're out there. That's who we really need to worry about."

The Admiral gave me a grim look.

"That's all, sir. I just thought you needed to know. And I am sorry for the bad news."

Within a remarkably short time I was ordered to exit the station itself. A flood of scientists and technicians were boarding *Defiant* even as I went in the opposite direction. They were eager, with a light almost akin to greed in their eyes. I could have told them they weren't going to be disappointed. The ship was just as miraculous as they hoped it would be.

But I didn't talk to them at all. Instead, I carried my duffle to the sky-lift.

There, I met up with Zye. She was standing alongside two marines who looked uncomfortable with their duty. She was at least a head taller than either of them.

We took the next lift down into the thick atmosphere of Earth. Above us, in the dark, was Araminta Station. Docked to her was the magnificent axe-head shape of *Defiant*.

"She's so big," I said, "so stark and powerful-looking. With all the ice melted away, the ship looks like a shark among minnows."

Zye stared up into the heavens with me.

"I hate that ship," she said flatly. "But I also feel a pang of regret to leave her. She's all I have left of my world here."

"Don't worry," I said, "you'll like it here. We have countless conveniences and amenities that your world lacks. We're a luxury-minded folk. Enjoy yourself for a time, Zye. You've earned it."

She looked uncomfortable at the mere thought.

"I will follow you," she said ambiguously.

-37-

Following the tradition of returning sailors for countless centuries past, when I returned home, my first thought was of romance. I'm not sure why that was, but it definitely applied to me. I supposed that after a long journey through space, a man's thoughts inevitably focused on those he'd left behind.

Before I could contact Chloe Astra, however, there were my parents to contend with. My implants began singing with a flood of input, a great deal of which came from my father and mother. The messages had apparently been buffered over the preceding weeks while I was in deep space and jammed by Admiral Hedon's destroyers.

Even after I'd reached Araminta Station, Star Guard had seen fit to block all personal incoming traffic until after my briefing. Presumably, this was to keep me from revealing the truth about my journey home to anyone in the public.

I fended off my parents with assurances I would visit them soon. I repeatedly claimed I was uninjured and healthy. All of my responses were partially true. I was merely hiding critical details.

When it came to transmitting my own messages, there was only one person I was interested in contacting. As the sky-lift reached ground, I sought to open a channel with Chloe. When we exited the massive doors and stepped out into the crowded concourse, the channel finally opened.

"Commander Sparhawk?" she asked in surprise. "Is it really you?"

"Yes," I said.

I wasn't sure why I was unable to see her this time, but I could hear her voice perfectly. The technology of our implants was quite amazing at times. I noticed the power of this modern miracle most clearly when making contact with someone who had an emotional impact upon me. Lady Astra the Younger was just such a person.

It was as if she were present and speaking into my ear. Her words weren't a reproduction of sound, created crudely via vibrating bits of paper and magnets. Speakers could never capture the real feel of another human voice.

Instead, my auditory nerves were treated to a perfect simulation of her presence, an effect so close to that of the real thing as to be indistinguishable from reality. The sound of her voice was so pleasant to me…it caused a wave of happiness to surge into my mind without warning. I stopped walking on the concourse, closed my eyes and allowed myself to enjoy the experience.

It was a silly thing, I cautioned myself. I had only met this woman briefly. To be so taken with her, to have been thinking of her for months—it wasn't my normal mode of operation.

Trying to pull myself together, I made an effort to sound breezy and in control.

"Lady Astra!" I said. "It's so good to hear your voice, but why can't I see you? My eyes are getting no input at all."

"I'm not dressed at the moment."

"Oh…never mind then," I said, feeling slightly embarrassed. "I didn't mean—"

"It's quite all right. Just a second—there."

I could see her now, her visual presence was overlaid upon my optical nerves. She was effectively superimposed upon the carpeted floor of the concourse lift in front of me. She stood wrapped in a mauve towel. Her hair was soaked, and it hung lank and dark down her bare back.

Physically, I froze. Zye stood next to me and stared at me in concern. She looked around, as if suspecting I'd spotted some kind of threat. I waved my hand at her, and we stepped out of the way of the flowing crowds to a wall. There, I was able to lean back and take in Lady Astra in all her glory.

"Can you see me?" she asked.

"Yes, I can see you now. Can you see me?"

"Of course. Is that the sky-port?"

"I've just come down on the lift."

"Who's that person next to you? She's so tall! Can that be—is that the Beta girl?"

"Yes, this is Zye."

Zye looked around as if expecting to see the person I was introducing her to. If she'd had an implant of her own, that would have been possible. But I was glad, in this case, that she couldn't see Chloe. I didn't need Zye to make unwarranted assumptions based on Chloe's state of undress.

"Who are you talking to?" Zye finally demanded.

"A friend," I said. "Here, surf the grid while you wait."

I gave her a handheld scroll, which she took and tapped at with only the vaguest interest. The grid didn't hold her attention the way it did most Earth people. She was a physical being who took the greatest interest in those who were immediately present.

Turning back to Chloe, I smiled involuntarily. "When can we meet?" I blurted.

Chloe blinked in surprise. "You want to see me?"

"That's why I called."

"Yes…well, my mother…" she said.

"Are there any social events you've got on your schedule?"

"Always," she said. "I'm booked solid this week."

"What are you doing tonight?"

"Another dinner. At the Commerce Ministry this time. The Capital can be so boring. Mother loves to parade me at such affairs. Sometimes she doesn't even show up herself."

"I'll meet you there," I said.

She looked startled. "How? Do you have an invitation?"

"No, but I'll get one."

She smiled, and she suddenly appeared shy. "I'm closing the channel. I have a lot of work to do to get ready."

"Don't worry, if you showed up in nothing but that towel you'd be sure to dazzle them all."

She laughed and disconnected.

Shortly thereafter I noticed Zye was staring at me. There was a deeply suspicious frown on her face.

In my time with this single Beta, I'd learned her kind didn't often express emotions. But when they did, there was no way to mistake them.

"What's wrong?" I asked her.

"Who were you talking to?"

"A woman. Lady Chloe of Astra. Her mother is a Servant, as is my father."

"I see. Your parents are both Alphas on this planet?"

I thought about it, then nodded. "Yes. That's a fair assessment. Public Servants are the servants of the people. They make our laws and policy decisions."

"They rule you. Like Alphas."

"That's one way of looking at it."

She eyed me as we continued to walk through the concourse.

"The female you were speaking to—you said something about a towel?"

"I might have."

"Are you intimate with this woman?"

I stopped and sighed. "Zye, we need to get some things straight. Asking probing personal questions is considered rude on Earth. Don't you have protocols regarding privacy on Beta Cygnus?"

"There is no privacy on Beta Cygnus."

"Hmm. What about sexual contact, mating rituals, that sort of thing? Don't you keep such behavior confidential?"

"These things you describe don't exist for Betas. Only Alphas are allowed to mate, and only upon rare occasions. Males are extremely rare."

"Well, on Earth we have a balance of men and women. For the most part, we procreate the old-fashioned way."

She stared at me disapprovingly.

"You have excellent cloning technology," she said. "I know you do. Why would you—?"

"Look, Zye," I said. "There are going to be a lot of things you'll find surprising here. Try to keep an open mind and learn as we go along. Now and then I'll explain things we encounter, I promise."

Once I had Zye's odd mixture of suspicion, curiosity, jealousy and incomprehension under control, I devoted myself to getting invited to the event at the Commerce Ministry.

The task proved to be more difficult than I'd anticipated. I started off with a series of calls, talking to my parents—who weren't very helpful. They had no intention of going to the Commerce Ministry, where other Houses held sway.

Worse, they wasted a considerable amount of my time by requesting me to attend a long list of events that supported *their* causes and political allies. Now that I was ostensibly a hero, I was in demand, and therefore, I represented a commodity my father wanted to exploit.

Finally, after I escaped Tannish and my parents, I called House Astra directly. Perhaps Chloe knew how I could gain an invitation.

Having selected Chloe's home ID, I fully expected to gain access to her directly. I was rudely surprised.

"William Sparhawk?" a voice said.

I knew the voice. It was that of Servant Astra, Chloe's ancient mother.

"Servant?" I asked. "Is that you? I'm so sorry to disturb."

"Why are you contacting my daughter, Sparhawk?"

I hesitated. My reasons were beyond obvious, but I was nevertheless reluctant to admit to them.

"There's an event tonight at the Commerce Ministry. I was seeking an invitation."

Whatever she'd expected me to say, this wasn't it. She appeared suddenly, occluding my vision.

Lady Astra the Elder had once been a beauty, but those days were countless decades past. Now, she resembled a caricature of living flesh rather than the real thing. She was wrapped in the best of intelligent garments, but she'd done little to repair her face. As I understood it, cosmetic injections interfered with certain longevity treatments. Many people could only tolerate one or the other.

Lady Astra had clearly chosen long life over beauty.

"You..." she said incredulously. "Our newly hatched hero from space...*you* wish to attend an event at the Commerce Ministry? Why?"

"Well, madam, I—"

"No, don't bother to utter your lies. I understand implicitly. The answer to most inexplicable behavior is easy to see in retrospect. You're a Sparhawk, and you've managed to gain newfound fame. Therefore, you're looking for a way to capitalize on your gain."

Barely knowing what to say, I stammered. "Madam, I assure you—"

"I see it all now!" she pronounced suddenly. "You're invading new territory. Well, forget it, Sparhawk. I can guarantee you won't find any political converts at the Commerce Ministry!"

"Your suppositions couldn't be further from my goals."

"Save it, Sparhawk," she said bitterly. "Your family lacks all sense of decorum or subtlety. Regardless, you can come. I want to watch you as you attempt to pry away my supporters. I welcome the challenge."

"Uh...thank you, madam. I accept your invitation, but I think there's a misunderstanding—"

"We'll see. But one more thing, hero, about my daughter. I would urge you toward caution. I don't take personal intrusions lightly. Chloe is inexperienced, but she's closely watched. You won't gain the kind of information you're looking for through seduction. I won't have that."

I flushed in embarrassment. It was a horrible misunderstanding, indeed. For the thousandth time in my life, I wished my parents had been laborers, known only for their punctuality, rather than for duplicity and manipulation.

"I assure you again, madam, that my intentions—"

The words died away in my throat. The vision of Lady Astra the Elder, with all her finery wrapped around mummified flesh, had vanished. She'd hung up on me.

"What a woman," I muttered.

"You're displeased with your mate?" Zye asked.

"She's not my mate—and anyway, I was talking to her mother. She's quite determined to keep us apart."

Zye thought that over for a time. "Good," she pronounced at last.

-38-

When I arrived at the Commerce Ministry dinner with Zye in tow, I found myself to be inexplicably worried about what I would say when I met Chloe.

I knew it was absurd. I'd faced down swarms of nuclear missiles mere days earlier. Knowing that did give me a certain sense of distance and confidence in my station, but I still didn't feel completely at ease in personal situations.

The feeling ratcheted up with the arrival of Lady Astra the Younger. Her stunning presence did intoxicating work upon my mind.

Dressed in a blue so deep it was almost black, her dress sparkled with stars—literal stars. There were constellations any spacer would recognize displayed on her flowing garment. Orion the Hunter rode one thigh, and Leo gripped her right breast. I was entranced.

So, apparently, were most of the patrons at the gathering. They clapped politely, and they rushed to greet her. But before they could escort her to her seat at the table of honor, her mother arrived.

I have to say that when she was properly attired and made over, her mother cut a fine figure herself. Her skin may have been parchment, but her trim body moved without the stiffness of age in a brilliant, sun-yellow dress. She was like an advertisement for the wonder and mystery of a dozen brands of longevity treatments on display. Her musculature and bones had been preserved, along with her critical organs, presumably.

Only the skin on her face and extremities betrayed her great age.

For my own part, I'd arrived early and taken up a station near the kitchen doors. As auto-waiters glided in and out of the doors and hurried through the crowds, I was presented with numerous chances to snatch drinks from their uplifted trays.

By the time the Astra family was seated, I'd consumed five varied beverages that had been ordered, no doubt, by other people. These drinks hadn't completely put my mind at ease, but they'd given me a glowing smile.

Zye watched me with concern.

"Are you inebriated?" she asked.

"Direct and to the point as always," I answered. "As a matter of fact, I am a little drunk."

She frowned at me for several seconds then turned her head to see where I was looking. Chloe was seated now, her dress shifting over her body with every motion as she smiled, nodded, hugged, and patted the dozens who clamored for her attention.

"Why don't you approach her?" Zye asked.

"Do you want me to?"

"No."

I laughed. "Then you should be happy I'm standing here, but I can see by your expression you're not. Why's that, Zye?"

She stared at me for several long seconds, considering her response. "Our mission here is a social one. You're not performing as expected."

I snorted at that. Leave it to Zye to urge others to follow orders, whether she disliked them or not.

"You're not even part of Star Guard," I said. "At least, not officially. What do you care if I do what the brass wants or not?"

"I—I'm tied to you," she said awkwardly. "Your failure is my failure. I don't like failure. No Beta does."

For the first time since the Astra family had entered, I turned to face Zye. "You are a puzzle, you know that?"

"Why does this particular female disturb you so much?" Zye asked. "Is it her appearance, or are there hidden events between the two of you?"

I could tell the question was asked in earnest, so I tried to answer it honestly.

"Both," I admitted. "We met under strange circumstances before I left Earth. I've thought of her often during my long voyage. She became lovelier in my memory each time I did so, rather than fading in importance."

"Strange," Zye said. "When I look at her, I feel only antipathy."

Shaking my head, I found myself smiling again. In many ways, Zye was an innocent. "That's jealousy, Zye. It's a natural emotion. Come, it's time to make our move."

I strode away from the kitchen door. The robot waiters flowed around me expertly. I was barely aware of them.

But as I walked, I realized I was drunk. Sometimes sudden movement after holding still for a time proved this to a man. Narco-drinks are powerful, and I rarely drank them. I had no tolerance built up like these society types.

Letting out a hiss, I fumbled with my implants, seeking to stimulate them with my mind. Implants were rather like organs that one could control directly with nerve-endings as one might control a muscle. Unfortunately, being drunk made the task more difficult, just as it made walking more difficult.

Focusing on the task, I worked to increase my blood-filtering levels. I wanted to remove excess intoxicants. Probably, I should have done so before stepping forward on this quest—but then I might never have moved from my spot leaning against the wall.

Unfortunately, before I could begin clearing my bloodstream, I was spotted and recognized by Servant Klieger. He was a portly man from the orbital habs. He approached me, carried by a robot that simulated a pair of walking legs. Like most people who spent the majority of their lives in zero-G, Klieger was unable to walk unaided in the grip of Earth's gravity. I grimaced as he clapped his hands over mine.

"I'll be!" he exclaimed. "Sparhawk the Younger, isn't it? Of course it is. The resemblance is uncanny—but then it should be!"

He found this uproariously funny, and I managed to chuckle. I was glad for my intoxicants all over again.

"The Hero of the Guard," Klieger said. "That's what they're calling you, you know. Imagine it! Just because you chased off a swarm of rock rats with a captured ship or something."

"It was a bit more involved than that," I said, trying to keep a civil expression on my face.

Klieger sniffed. "The news reports were vague."

"I'm sorry about that. Now, if it's not too much trouble, could you direct me toward the snack table? I'd be—"

"Hold on," he said, his eyes narrowing. His sweaty hands gripped mine like two wet balloons. "Why would a Sparhawk—*any* Sparhawk—be caught here? Don't tell me you're here to recruit! This is Centrist Party territory, after all. We'll not have you poaching our junior members!"

"Nothing like that, sir," I managed. "I was invited by Lady Astra—the Elder."

"I see," he said, rolling his eyes in her direction. "Have you seen her heiress? The comparison is stunning, isn't it? You wouldn't think age could do so much to a woman's face, but there it is."

"Yes, well, if I might be—"

"Hold on," he said. "Lady Astra!" He cried out in a powerful voice that belied his noodle-like limbs. Apparently, his low-gravity lifestyle had done nothing to weaken his diaphragm.

At this inopportune moment, Zye decided to intervene. Her powerful hands reached down and removed Klieger's swollen fingers from my person. He boggled at her, noticing her for the first time. His auto-legs backpedalled, and I pushed Zye gently back.

"What's this?" Klieger asked. "A bodyguard? Is that a female, or do my eyes deceive?"

"She's a Beta, sir," I said as gently as I could.

Zye wasn't helping. She glowered at the man with all the gentle demeanor of a genetically engineered attack-dog.

Fortunately, Lady Astra called down, having recognized us. "This way, Sparhawk," she said. "I've saved a spot for you at my table."

I walked away from Klieger in relief. Zye followed, looming over my shoulder.

"Who is this...person?" Lady Astra asked in surprise, eyeing Zye with a mixture of curiosity, astonishment and alarm.

Behind her a bodyguard team tensed. Like all important people, she maintained a private security force. After my father had been nearly assassinated, the higher ranking Servants in every party were on edge.

"She's one of my crew members," I said.

Lady Astra smiled. Her face crinkled like paper as she did so. "I get it. She's your bodyguard. Impressive. No one else on Earth has a Beta following them around."

The intoxicants in my bloodstream had ebbed slightly, but I wasn't in the clear yet. Possibly, if they'd been entirely absent, I would have restrained myself from making the remark I did next.

"She's no robotic assassin with breakaway arms," I said, "but I find her most helpful."

Astra's face tightened at the mention of the assassin. "Take a seat, Sparhawk, before you pitch onto your face."

I did so, and Zye sat beside me. Chloe turned in our direction then. She sat at her mother's side, across the table from Zye and myself.

Her face lit up when she saw me, and I couldn't help but brighten in response.

"William!" she said. "I'm so glad you could make it."

"Your mother insisted."

Lady Astra the Elder pushed back her chair suddenly.

"Excuse me," she said. "I must see what's holding up the kitchen."

She moved away swiftly, her feet carrying her through the crowd with expert movements. She didn't have to sidestep often, as most people darted to get out of her way when they saw who was approaching.

"Introduce me to your friend, William," Chloe said.

I did as she asked, and explained that Zye was a Beta. This fascinated Chloe. The two attempted to converse, but the talk soon died out. Zye wasn't known for chatting.

In time, Lady Astra returned, and in her wake came an army of serving robots. They piled food before every guest according to the menu choices we'd made via our implants during the social period.

The entire affair struck me as artificially rapid and lockstep. Was this due to Lady Astra's poor attitude? I wasn't sure. She was in charge of the host political group, and therefore the party was hers to orchestrate—but it seemed odd that she would carry her agitation so far as to inconvenience important guests.

After our meal, I took a gamble. I asked Chloe to dance.

She lit up with a smile that I found more than entrancing.

"I thought you'd never ask."

I took her hand, and while her mother and Zye watched disapprovingly, we moved to the dance floor. Throughout the dinner, gentle, rhythmic music had been playing. The musicians were living clones trained in classical era music but given the freedom to be creative with the works of that time. Dances akin to a complex waltz were the rage these days and quite exclusive. Leave it to Lady Astra to spare no expense.

We joined a half-dozen couples who were from various Houses and began an organized series of practiced steps. Modern dance was more staid than it had been in the past. There were no wild gyrations or exposing of flesh during a state dance in this day and age. Many of the oldsters referred to the complex processions of the young as overly stuffy yet still enjoyed them. I suspected that throughout history, the courtship of the dance was thrilling to most participants, no matter the details.

"You dance very well," Chloe told me. "But I would expect nothing less from a Sparhawk."

"Your instructor is to be congratulated as well," I said formally.

The music shifted a moment later, and she suddenly ducked close to me. We found ourselves in a clutch. I felt a rush of both embarrassment and excitement at her nearness. She was warm and vital in my arms. I could feel the rippling of her intelligent dress as it sought to slip between exposed spots of her bare flesh and my hands, no doubt following its programming.

The other dancers had moved closer now as well as the current composition had entered its fourth movement which was meant to be slower and more intimate.

"I'm finally in your arms again," Chloe said in my ear.

"It's been too long."

"Do you think we might slip away together?"

Startled, I looked down into her face to see if she was serious. I could see by her eyes that she was.

My heart pounded. "I...we can try."

"Here's my plan," she said in a husky voice. "I've been thinking about it all day. Mother will never take her eyes off me—except when she starts to make her speech."

"She's going to make a speech?"

She looked at me as if I were simple. "She always makes a speech. Doesn't your father?"

"Yes. Yes, I suppose he does."

We made our plans as the fourth and fifth movements waxed and waned. I'd thought gripping her person would be the highlight of the evening, but now I realized that was just the beginning. Neither of us brought up what we might do after we left the party together—but that part was easy to imagine.

Whatever misgivings I might have had about coming to this social event had long since faded. I was certain I'd made the right decision.

Events took an unexpected turn, however, as we returned to the dinner table.

Our hands were clasped, but we were trying not to look conspiratorial. I'd been so enamored with Chloe that I'd never thought to look back at my hostess. I'd never thought to check on Zye's activities, either.

That's why when Lady Astra the Elder pitched forward onto the table croaking like a gigged frog, knocking over after-dinner drinks, I was taken utterly by surprise.

Her eyes were shockingly wide, and they bulged in a manner that was difficult to believe. The back of her lovely yellow dress was splashed bright red. In the center of the red region were three dark spots—puncture wounds.

Zye was standing tall over the dying woman. A gun was in her hand.

For a brief, horrible moment, she was like a giantess amid a gaggle of stunned, screaming children. Then she aimed her oversized pistol into the crowd and fired repeatedly. The reports were deafening.

-39-

Although my understanding of the situation was incomplete, I knew what had to happen next.

Lady Astra's private security force was nearby, wearing formal black suits and watching the crowd. It was always easy to pick out security personnel—they were the ones that weren't eating, drinking or talking to anyone.

Three rapid strides brought me to the table, where I jumped onto Zye's back, my cloak swirling around her form.

A storm of gunfire erupted. My cloak unfurled like a banner, generating my personal shield. I'd switched it on as soon as I'd seen Lady Astra fall. It was reflex, just as was the surge of adrenaline and other stimulants which now oozed from my implants.

Why did I seek to protect Zye? Because I knew she would surely die if I didn't. It wasn't a matter of thinking—it was instinct. When moments like this came, there was only has a second or so in which to act. If I'd stood by blinking in confusion, they would have shot her down.

"Get away from the alien, Mr. Sparhawk!" ordered the security chief.

I couldn't answer right away. Zye had reached up and wrapped thick fingers around my throat. They were squeezing, and the world was going rapidly black.

"William?" she asked in surprise.

She let go of me.

I rasped, coughed, and managed to speak. "Zye, drop your weapon. That's an order."

Her pistol clanked heavily onto the table beside Lady Astra, who was still squirming. I was vaguely surprised. The woman should have been dead by now.

The security people rushed Zye.

"Let them arrest you!" I ordered, feeling her muscles tense up.

"I'm innocent. I shot the killer."

"She shot one of my best men!" the security team leader said between clenched teeth. She was angry and there was murder in her eyes.

"Surrender, Zye," I said.

Switching off my shield, I let them approach and disarm us. That was when I saw Chloe. She was draped over her mother, weeping and trying to help her. A medical crew came into sight soon afterward. The Centrist Party seemed much more alert than my father's party had been when an assassination attempt had been made upon his life. Quite possibly, my father's experience had caused them to anticipate such an attack.

The room around us had mostly cleared by now. The initial panic had subsided into a rapid retreat. Soon, only security people, Zye, and the two women of House Astra were present.

Zye and I tried to explain what had happened to the security team leader, but she paid no attention. Holding up a hand for silence, the head of Astra's security unfocussed her eyes and stared into the distance.

"I'm reviewing the video," she said. Several long seconds passed, during which I waited tensely.

"It was Thompson," she said. "I can't believe it."

"Check the body," Zye said. "It's not flesh. Not all of it, at least."

The security people did as Zye suggested, frowning.

"A robot?" one of the security agents said incredulously. "Polymer bones wrapped in flesh?"

"They grow flesh over mechanical components to hide them," Zye said, "and they dispose of the original, in most cases. Your Thompson is most likely dead. I've seen it many times."

I turned to her in astonishment. "You have?"

"Yes," she said. "That thing I shot is a Stroj agent."

"A Stroj?" I said, stunned.

The security people demanded an explanation. I gave them the information I had learned from Zye.

"They come from a colony," I said, "one that was established after Earth was separated from her fledgling worlds."

"This proves that Stroj ships disabled mine," Zye said. "I'm not surprised they're here."

The series of revelations left me speechless. Chloe came to me then, and she touched my uniform with bloody hands. She'd walked her mother to the flying ambulance outside while we'd spoken with the security team.

"She has to live," she said. "Mother has to pull through. They say she has a chance. She had alterations made—internal alterations."

I nodded, unsurprised. The woman was a tough old bird. One that had demonstrated she was fixated upon long term survival.

"I'm glad it wasn't you, or Zye," Chloe said. Her eyes were brimming with tears, as I tried to comfort her.

"Zye," I said, "you need to help us hunt down these Stroj creatures and eliminate them. What do you think they're trying to do here on Earth?"

"Stroj agents are commonly dispatched to a new world before conquest. They infiltrate, learn critical intelligence, then move into their secondary stage."

"Which is?"

Zye shrugged. "To foment strife and rebellion. To make every woman mistrust her own sister. They're methodical and often successful."

"I take it they came to Beta Cygnus. How did you stop them?"

"We examined every member of our population. Those that failed to meet the norm were easily isolated and destroyed."

"But…" Chloe said. "Surely, you must have killed innocent members of your own population in such a sweep."

Zye shrugged disinterestedly. "We excised the cancer. That's the most important detail."

I turned to Zye. "Why didn't you tell us that the Stroj were here? Weren't you debriefed?"

"Yes," she said. "I waited for appropriate techniques to be applied, but your intelligence people are quite lax. I was never tortured, threatened or otherwise coerced."

"So you withheld information? About a mutual enemy?"

She looked at me, puzzled. "I was not ordered to comply with the interrogators. Naturally, I withheld information."

I let out a long sigh. "Who would you accept such orders from?"

"You, of course."

Nodding and unsurprised, I recalled that Zye and I had been quickly separated after our return to Earth. They'd debriefed us separately, and quite politely. Apparently, their gentle treatment had been viewed with scorn by Zye.

"All right then," I said. "From now on, Zye, cooperate with guardsmen. Answer their questions."

"As you wish."

The next hour consisted of an interrogation by House Astra security. I couldn't blame them. I only wished Zye had been more forthcoming earlier.

The truth was we'd all been taken by surprise. Earth was only just coming to grips with the idea we were back in touch with other worlds. We'd thought of ourselves as singular and unique for so long…the colonies had almost faded into the status of myths.

At one point during the proceedings, Chloe came close to me, kissed me on the cheek and left. She wanted to go to the hospital on her estate, where her mother was in critical condition. It wasn't the sort of ending to the evening I'd envisioned with her, but I urged her to go home.

I tried to plan my next step. Star Guard had to be informed about all of this. We'd thought someone on Earth had manufactured a robotic assassin and clothed it in human flesh—but we'd never suspected that colonist spies were the ones building these monstrosities.

"Captain," I said, addressing the leader of the Astra security detail. "In my official capacity as an officer of Star Guard, I'm confiscating the corpse of the assassin. Please transport it to CENTCOM."

She looked irritated, but nodded. "We'll do it."

"Zye, accompany me please."

"Hold on," the agent leader said. "We haven't exonerated her as yet."

"She's a member of my crew. I'm not going to press charges against you for firing on her, and you're not going to detain her and hinder our investigation. These creatures threaten our whole planet. That elevates the matter, and it's officially under the jurisdiction of the Guard."

Again, the captain looked annoyed, but she nodded.

Times were changing. Not too long ago, a personal security force leader might have stood up to a guardsman, confident that the machinery of government would back her up. The Guard had long been toothless and almost irrelevant.

Events were propelling us forward. Everyone could feel it. Earth had a threat from the skies again. Humanity needed to stand united, and we all knew we had to band together. Centralized authority was usually born from necessity, and this occasion was no different than countless similar moments in history.

"Zye, let's go," I said.

She loomed over my shoulder, and security people melted from our path as we strode from the scene. I was glad I'd turned on my blood filters some time ago. They were doing their job. By the time we reached CENTCOM, I'd only have a faint headache to remind me of my excesses.

We climbed into a hired air car. After a violent launch, I was impressed. The driver had taken my urging to rush seriously.

My implants buzzed in my head. Printed on my retina was the name of the caller: William Sparhawk, the Elder.

"Father?" I answered.

"William..." he said. "I hardly know what to say. How can you be involved in two tragic events within such a short span? The suggestion it's all a coincidence strains credulity."

His directness took me off-guard. A part of me had dared hope a congratulatory word had been earned. But my father wasn't one to focus on the best elements. Instead, he tended to find the flaws in any effort.

"I take it you're talking about two assassination attempts?"

"Yes, of course. Not to mention a rebellion in space. How is it you're the center of this unrelenting sequence of disasters?"

The question annoyed me, but I had to admit he had a point. "Have there been any other assassinations of note? Any other signs of discord among the populace?"

"What a question...but of course, you've been out of touch. The answer is yes. We've had a number of labor riots. The cities are demanding better power rations, and the sea farming unions are on strike. Is that the sort of thing you mean?"

"Maybe. You see, according to the Beta colonist Zye, we're under attack worldwide."

"How so?"

I proceeded to relate Zye's report on the Stroj. "These beings have shifted, according to her, from spying to sabotage. That indicates they're prepping us for invasion."

My father was the one who sat in stunned silence this time. He finally revealed himself to me, sending video to match the audio transmissions.

I was surprised at his appearance. He was still in medical garb. He was lying on his back in bed, staring up at the vid pick-up.

"You haven't made a full recovery yet?" I asked.

"No...and keep the information quiet, will you? My rivals are already getting ideas."

"Certainly. But what's your condition, exactly?"

"There were certain toxins in the artificial being that attacked me. She injected me with mal-bots—nanites that are still rupturing cells throughout my body on a daily basis. Antibodies and surgical bots are doing battle with them in my guts at this very moment."

"That would seem to indicate the assassination attempt came from a technologically advanced group," I said.

"Connect me to this Zye person," he demanded.

"I can't," I said. "She doesn't have an implant."

"Well then...can you forward your nerve data to me directly?"

"I'll patch you into the feed."

Performing this trick was a mental effort, but I was finally able to gain the attention of my implant's processing core. It had a necessarily simplistic interface. Soon, the feed from my eyes and ears was being transmitted and reproduced with minor lag inside my father's brain. Not everyone had an implant capable of such things, but being the heir to House Sparhawk did have its advantages.

Zye looked at me dubiously.

"Who am I talking to?" she asked. "You or your father?"

"Both, after a fashion," I admitted. "We're both listening."

"So strange..." she said, clearly uncomfortable with the technology.

"Just forget my father is listening. Speak to me as if we were alone."

"That's not possible. You've just informed me we're not."

"I mean pretend—never mind." I realized that she might not be imaginative enough to "pretend" anything, and besides, time was wasting. "Please make your report."

"Very well. There are many colony worlds. Not all of them are in contact with one another. But one planet that has successfully attacked several others is possessed by a group known as the Stroj."

"Tell me about them," I prompted.

"They are no longer completely human. I think that's at the basis of their difficulties with other human colonists. They don't empathize with Basics such as you—or Betas like me, for that matter."

"Basics?" my father said. Zye couldn't hear his questions so I repeated query.

Zye looked at me quizzically for a moment. "Your father asked the question, correct?"

"Yes."

"Bizarre... Basics are what colonists call Earthlings. You're our basic stock. Some worlds still exist that are

286

populated purely by Basics, but most have differentiated physically and culturally."

"Go on. What about the Stroj?"

"They were one of the last groups to leave Earth. They were of Eastern European stock, as I understand it. Because of the Cataclysm, they weren't able to find their way to their target world. They wandered, spurned by other colonies, until they found a dim red dwarf with a planet barely able to support life."

"What kind of climate do they have?"

"The world is small and murky. Subtropical, I think you'd call it. But the climate isn't the trouble. The planet was overgrown with organics when they got there."

"Plants? Animals?"

"Yes, and they're all highly toxic to Basics. The atmosphere was dangerous too, full of heavy metals due to frequent violent volcanic eruptions."

"That does sound grim," I said. "I suppose they adapted their bodies to survive."

"Yes, drastically. They started off with cybernetic alterations. In time, the cybernetics became dominant, and their flesh became optional. Some don't bother to grow it anymore, except for sensory organs and sub-brains."

I tried to envision a race of cybernetic creatures that were partly human but mostly machine. They sounded unpleasant in the extreme.

"The key to understanding them is to accept they are all unique blends of machine and flesh," Zye went on. "They design and redesign themselves to fit their missions. One Stroj might appear as a robot. Another might have only a few parts that are machine-based. They're all slightly different in configuration. To them, flesh is like clothing to a Basic. Most importantly, they can subsume the flesh of a person and take it over—as you or I might put on a jacket."

"I see…" my father said, and I repeated his words to Zye. "How are such strange beings operating in our midst?"

"They can mimic other races. No colony is safe from their spies. They're masters of disguise."

Lifting a hand, I stopped the conversation. "I've had a sudden thought," I said. "Before Singh ordered me out on the deep-orbit mission to find the Beta battle cruiser, I apprehended a smuggler over Antarctica. Singh tried to stop me, but I persisted and caught the man. He behaved strangely, and he had in his possession a number of Beta embryos in tubes. He'd clearly stolen them from *Defiant*."

Zye was upset. "Did you execute him?"

"No…Captain Singh didn't even want me to chase him down. He said the embryos were to be sold to the miners. I was forced to let him go."

"We must find him!" Zye burst out.

"We will, Zye. We will," I said with all the certainty I could muster.

"William," my father said inside my head. "I'm going to disconnect and make inquiries. I want you to come home immediately. We'll talk face to face."

"Father, I'm returning to CENTCOM. I report to Admiral Cunningham now, remember?"

"I'll make inquiries," he repeated cryptically.

The channel closed, and I turned to Zye. "He's gone."

"That's a relief," she said. "I find it disturbing to have two males looking at me with a single pair of eyes."

Before we reached CENTCOM, Admiral Cunningham contacted me.

"Yes, Admiral?" I answered.

Zye looked at me and rolled her eyes. I was staring off into space again.

"Commander Sparhawk," Cunningham said in an irritated tone. "There's been a change of plans. I want you to proceed to House Sparhawk and brief Servant Sparhawk in person."

I frowned. Clearly, my father had been throwing his weight around.

"Admiral," I said. "I'm a guardsman first and foremost. I would like to report personally to *you*."

"It's a reasonable request, but it puts me in a delicate position."

"How so?"

"Must I spell out the situation to you?" she asked. Then she sighed. "I see that I must. Your father is in charge of the appropriations committee. He's long stood in opposition to the Guard, keeping our budgetary requirements from being met. If he were to change his mind on that topic, in light of these new developments..."

"I see," I said, and I *did* see. My father had contacted her and either threatened or offered to reward her—it was one and the same among the political class. "The avoidance of this type of situation was precisely why I joined the Guard."

"A noble ambition," she said without an ounce of sarcasm. "But we're all forced to live within the boundaries of certain realities. And as you, yourself have made quite clear, we are once again no longer alone in the universe."

"Very well," I said. "I'll do as you ask. But first let me relay to you what I've learned."

At length, I discussed the presence of the Stroj, their apparent violation of our star system, and their infiltration into our midst.

"I'm upset to learn these details," Cunningham said when I finished, "but I'm not surprised. There have been a number of odd events. The idea that some kind of outside influence has been behind these incidents goes a long way toward explaining them."

"Glad I could be of assistance, Madam. We must find a way to detect these Stroj infiltrators and catch them."

"Agreed. Now, return to your father at House Sparhawk. That's an order."

Redirecting the air car onto a new course, we soon landed at House Sparhawk. My mother greeted me with enthusiasm on the pad—but she seemed alarmed by my apparent body guard.

"Who is this...?" she asked.

"Mother, this is Zye, a Beta. She's a friend and a loyal crew member."

After the introductions were made, I took Zye to meet my father in person.

The old man looked to be in bad shape. He was wearing an oxygen mask, and tendrils of tubing crisscrossed his prone form.

"You didn't look this bad in the projections you sent me," I protested.

"No, sorry. I edit all the impressions and even the nerve-feeds that I send out. I'd stand a chance of losing my chairmanship if I let anyone see how seriously ill I really am."

"Poison?" Zye asked, leaning forward in concern. "Stroj poison?"

"Yes," my father said, sighing. "That's what it must be. Ever since that wicked machine cut me."

"It's not exactly a machine," Zye said. "Not in the traditional sense. It's a hybrid form. Alive and dead at the same time."

"Yes, well, whatever poison it used is killing me."

"Have you tried an EMP burst?" Zye asked.

My father nodded. "The nanites seem to be shielded."

"Then you must move on to more extreme measures," she advised. "Stroj poison is always fatal if unchecked."

"What do you suggest?"

"Electric shock. Two thousand volts should be sufficient."

"At what amperage?" my father asked dubiously.

"Five amps should be do it. A duration of approximately ten seconds is required."

My father's eyes widened. He looked in my direction.

"Is this your way of getting your inheritance early? I'll surely die!"

"Resuscitation is generally needed afterward," Zye admitted. "But tissue damage is minimal with proper grounding."

My father suffered a bout of coughing after that. His coughs were wet and thick. I saw blood at the corners of his mouth when he finished. With a trembling hand, he reached up to wipe at them with a cloth.

"All right," he said. "None of my physicians have managed to do a thing. They've prodded and irradiated me half-to-death. Their latest scheme was to attempt a reprogramming of the swarm by injecting fresh nanites to infect the rest."

Zye shook her head. "We've tried that. Stroj poisons are resistant to such techniques."

Father heaved a sigh. He summoned engineers and explained what needed to be done. After arguing with his medical staff, he ordered them all to leave until the procedure was over.

As engineers wired his pale wrists with cuffs and cords, he looked at me squarely.

"Sparhawk the Younger," he said. "In a way, I'm unsurprised to find you in the midst of all this. I'd long believed you were a failed clone, a mismatch, but now it seems that you *are* like me. You've simply chosen a different organization to strive within."

"Father, it sounds like you might come to accept my decision to join the Guard?"

"Never," he said, "but I might learn to live with it eventually. We'll need good men in powerful ships if even half the things this Beta has told us are true."

At last, the engineers were finished. We were ushered to a safe distance before the transformer was connected to the contacts.

I nodded to my father, and he nodded back.

Then, they flipped the switch.

-40-

It would be fair to say that my father and I had never been close. But in that moment, as I watched him die thrashing about in agony, I felt kinship with him.

His face was very similar to my own, after all, if many years older. His mouth opened as the voltage hummed and surged, and some random frequency of the alternating current must have matched that which causes fine muscular movement. His eyes were blinking open and closed very rapidly, as if a machine were driving them.

"That's enough," Zye said.

"You said fifteen seconds," I pointed out.

"Yes—but he's already dead."

They killed the power, and the technicians fled. In their place, a squad of scandalized doctors and nurses rushed to replace them. They cast glares in our direction.

"What was the point of that?" demanded the head physician. "You might have set his hair on fire!"

"It wasn't perfectly done," Zye admitted. "But he has either been cured or his death has been hastened. It's up to you which it will be."

I was too upset to speak, but I maintained a rigid expression. Nothing less was expected of a member of the Sparhawk household under such circumstances.

We watched as they worked on Father for several minutes. His breathing and pulse were reestablished, but they were artificially maintained. His brain wasn't providing his body with nerve impulses. They were being delivered through emergency implants that sat here and there on his body like glimmering leaches.

"His internal implant has melted," complained a doctor. "He'll need a new one."

"That can wait," I said.

The head physician approached me with an expression of distaste. "As strange as it may seem, you're in charge of the House now, William the Younger. What are your orders?"

"Revive my father," I commanded without hesitation.

"We're trying. We might succeed, or fail—or he might turn out to have been reduced to a vegetative state. In any case, as long as he's unconscious you're the Servant of House Sparhawk."

My face tightened. This was a moment I'd never looked forward to, and I'd certainly never expected it to come so soon.

Zye looked confused. "You're taking over for your father? I expected there would be a new election."

I regarded her quizzically. "Elections for open seats are extremely rare. Ascendancy to power as a Public Servant is a life-long appointment."

"Your system of governance is hereditary?" Zye asked. "I hadn't learned that in my studies."

"You're mistaken," I said. "My father was *elected*, not born into the position."

"And what about you? What's your claim to power based upon?"

"Our legal scholars reasoned long ago that since I'm a copy of him, I was essentially, by inference, elected as well."

"But you're not even a pure clone!"

"Pure clones are illegal here."

Zye stared at me for several seconds, then she did something I'd never seen her do before. She laughed. It was an odd, clipped sound. Almost as if she were imitating a person laughing.

"What's amusing?" I asked.

"You Basics are delusional," she said. "Your governmental system is hereditary, but you hide behind technicalities."

I shrugged, losing interest in the topic. "In any case, that's how it works on Earth."

"What about your mother?" she asked. "Isn't she the head of the House before you?"

"My father was elected as a Public Servant long ago," I explained. "My mother never ran for that office. As I'm my father's heir, the duty falls to me. My mother has her accounts and properties—but no political power."

"Bizarre," Zye said under her breath.

"Let's go. We must inform Mother personally."

We left the bustling medical people to their grim work. They were poking fresh needles into my father's gray flesh, and I didn't want to watch any further.

Mother was understandably distraught. At least she didn't blame me.

"It was the only way? Shocking him to death?"

"Yes," I admitted, "he did die. But if we can revive him, he should begin healing."

She shook her head. "It's so horrible. Who are these Stroj creatures? Why do they want to come here and bother us?"

"They're predatory," Zye said. "They believe in a strict evolutionary doctrine. As they're masterful adapters, they consider themselves superior forms of sentience."

"Superior? According to whom?"

"The cosmos. If they can slay or subjugate all others they encounter, they feel they will have proven their point. We Betas, however, have thus far beaten them back."

There was a certain note of pride in Zye's voice. My mother looked her over closely.

"You stopped them—but other worlds haven't. Is that right?"

"Yes."

"How many other worlds have been conquered?"

Zye shrugged. "The Stroj aren't forthcoming. They tell us nothing other than lies and platitudes. We have directly witnessed three worlds fall to their aggression, however."

"What happens to these worlds?" I asked. "When they surrender?"

Zye stared at us. "Isn't that obvious? The civilians are consumed by the Stroj after the fighters die. The fallen are like clothes of flesh for the Stroj. They dress themselves with the dead, as a hunter might clothe himself with the skins of animals."

My mother nodded. She looked worn and beaten. I embraced her, and she returned the hug with feeling. It was a rare moment for both of us.

Zye watched us in quiet curiosity. Betas clearly didn't hug one another.

"You must excuse our emotionalism," Mother told her. "We're not accustomed to such grim circumstances."

"Yes," Zye agreed. "I've noticed that. Basics seem to have become soft and indolent due to years of isolation."

"You'll find the Guard is ready to defend Earth," I said with a certainty that I didn't feel. "We'll rebuild. We'll recruit. We'll fill the skies with ships. We have more population than all the colonies combined, I'd bet."

Deciding there was nothing further I could do at home, I headed for the roof. Numerous air cars awaited my orders. It was strange, not having to ask anyone's permission to take whichever one I wanted.

I climbed into the back of the finest vehicle in my father's fleet. It was a Duranto-95, in excellent condition. Zye climbed in beside me, and I ordered the driver to lift off.

"Where to, sir?" he asked.

"CENTCOM. We're going to the offices of the Admiralty."

We were whisked away into the sky with alarming acceleration. I was reminded of the power *Cutlass* had exerted when I'd pressed her.

"I feel compelled to point out, sir," my driver said, "that everyone at CENTCOM is likely to have left for the day."

"I'll check," I said, noting the westering sun outside the tinted windows.

After trying to contact Admiral Cunningham directly for several minutes, I sighed. The central office was open, but Cunningham had retired for the night. At least that indicated there weren't any further emergencies.

"All right," I said. "Head for the city."

"Where are we going now?" Zye asked.

"I thought we might have dinner in Capital City."

"Aren't there kitchens at your home?"

"Of course. But you haven't been able to enjoy much of Earth yet. I thought we could see the town."

She thought that over. "Your father is on his deathbed. Don't you care?"

My jaws clenched. "Of course I do," I said, "but I can't do anything about that. Do you want to see the city or not?"

"No," she said.

This caught me by surprise. "You don't? You aren't curious about it?"

"I'd rather go back to our ship. I feel more at home there."

Nodding, I thought I understood. Betas were ill-equipped for the spice of life. She might well be experiencing cultural shock. After all, for the last several years of her life, she'd been locked inside a cell in that ship.

"Okay, I'll—just a moment."

My implant was buzzing. With trepidation, I answered the call. Was my father dead or in a vegetative state? I didn't think it could be possible that he'd recovered so quickly.

"William?" came a familiar voice.

I felt a wave of recognition and well-being. The voice belonged to Chloe.

"Chloe? Where are you?"

"I'm home."

"No visuals?"

"Mother left the com system in a partially disabled state. It's all I can do to get word out to you."

My mind raced. "Chloe," I said gently, "you do realize that with your mother disabled, you're the head of House Astra."

She was quiet for several seconds. "I hadn't thought of that, but you're right," she said. "It's strange, I've spent years being groomed for this moment, and yet now that it's here, I don't feel ready."

"My point is you can bypass your mother's security today—if you wish to."

After a few moments, she appeared to me. She seemed to be in the back of my air car, sitting to Zye's left.

"What's your mother's status?" I asked her.

Zye looked to her left, frowning. But of course, there was nothing there she could see. She crossed her arms in frustration. I wondered if she'd learned that gesture from Earthlings. I'd never seen her do it before.

"Mother's condition is grave but improving. She'll probably be conscious by morning."

"What about nanites?" I asked. "Have they discovered an infection of microscopic bots in her bloodstream?"

"They did say something about it. But our physicians are very competent. Some might even say ruthless. They excised the affected organs. New ones are being grown and grafted."

I gave a little shudder. It was horrible, but I now wished we'd had the foresight to do the same. If we'd done so, my father would not be on the edge of death now.

"My father is in a similar state," I said. "There have been attacks on other Houses as well. I've been studying the news feeds. All over the world, Servants are being assassinated."

"It's the rock rats," Chloe said with vehemence. "We should never ship them seeds again. Let them die out there when their hydroponics give out."

"I'm not so sure the miners are the source of the problem," I said. I proceeded to explain about the Stroj. Now and then, Zye threw in details, even though she couldn't see or hear Chloe. She was learning.

Throughout the explanation, Chloe became increasingly apprehensive.

"Come see me," she said at last. "I'll let you in. Tonight, no one can stop us."

I thought about that, and I realized she was right.

"All right," I said. "We're on our way."

I closed the channel and directed the driver to House Astra. He said nothing, but merely veered onto the appropriate course.

Looking at the back of his head, I thought I noticed a familiar cant to it. The way his hair shone—it was almost a glossy black.

"Miles? Miles Tannish?" I asked. "Is that you?"

"It is indeed, sir," he said.

"Why are you playing the part of a chauffeur?"

He shrugged. "You're the Servant now, sir. You must be protected—whether you like it or not."

I nodded and sat back in the plush seats, defeated.

"Where are we going?" Zye asked suspiciously.

"To the House of a friend," I said.

"Chloe Astra?"

"Yes. She needs comforting."

Zye glowered, but she didn't ask any more about my goals. She probably knew what they were.

When the mountaintop mansion came into view below us, I reflected that being in charge of one's own destiny now and then was a pleasant thing.

-41-

House Astra appeared in the dark forest under our air car. We landed, and I found myself greeted in an utterly different manner than I had been the first time I'd arrived here.

Instead of a group of servants attempting to direct us to the tradesman's entrance at the back of the building, we were greeted by an anxious squadron of people in uniform. They wore the livery of House Astra, blue on black, and many of them were security agents.

This time, rather than attempting to assault me, they flanked Zye and me and led the way to the front entrance. We mounted the laser-carved steps in grand style.

The doors swung open silently to allow us entry. There, off to one side, stood the same elderly doorman who'd greeted me previously in a dismissive manner. Tonight was very different.

"This way, Servant Sparhawk," he said, bowing low.

I was surprised his back didn't creak when he leaned forward so far, but obviously he'd partaken of treatments to keep his flexibility despite his age. We followed the man into the grand foyer and then into the parlors beyond.

He paused at a large locker. "Please leave your pistols here."

Reluctantly, Zye and I put our primary weapons into the locker. I felt fortunate to still be able to carry a blade in House Astra. Many people considered any kind of sword or knife to be harmless—but they were wrong.

In the next parlor, Chloe greeted me in person. She was smiling broadly, and I couldn't help but return the expression. Zye looked on, as if studying a mysterious ritual—one that she definitely didn't approve of.

Chloe turned to Zye and gave her a courteous nod, of which Zye made no acknowledgement.

"I know you two met at the dinner," I said, clearing my throat. "But I don't think you were able to become acquainted. Lady Astra, this is Zye, my crewman and confidant."

"I'm in your debt, Zye," Chloe said. "All of House Astra owes you our thanks. We've reviewed every recording. You may have saved the life of my mother, and anyone else that might have been injured if that Stroj creature had survived a moment longer."

"Yes," Zye said. "Your analysis is correct. The Stroj are at their most dangerous in their final moments when they deem their primary task to be complete."

I frowned at that, not fully understanding her meaning. But I was too fascinated by Chloe to ponder it further. I felt as if our evening had been rudely interrupted hours ago, and I wished to pick up where we'd left off.

"Chloe, perhaps you can show us to our quarters for the night," I suggested.

"You'll be staying?"

"I think so. Zye is sure to be fatigued after her long day."

Zye looked at me, startled, but she didn't object. Chloe smoothly led us upstairs to show us where we could spend the night. She first stopped at a suite fit for a queen.

"Here's what I have for you, Zye. I hope it will be acceptable."

Zye ran her eyes over the vast, sumptuous room in bewilderment. "I'll be lost in here. Where's the bed?"

Uttering the word "bed" caused a couch to transform itself into a sleeping platform. Sheets rustled as they unfurled themselves. In a few moments, they were spread perfectly—wrinkle-free and taut.

"Will this do?" Chloe asked.

Zye looked at us. We were standing out in the hallway. Zye was in the room. She frowned.

"Are you sure you'll be all right?" she asked me.

"Yes, of course. Don't worry. You can retire for the evening. Food will be brought up. There are a dozen genetically bred security agents between us and any threat."

Reluctantly, Zye retreated and closed the door. The last thing I saw as the door closed was her watchful, suspicious left eye.

Chloe made a face the second the thick door shut. She beckoned me to follow. Her manner had changed immediately to a playful one.

I followed, smiling.

"Is she always like that?" Chloe asked.

"Protective? Yes."

"It's like having a hulking agent following you around. A female one—but you probably like that, don't you?"

Bemused by her attitude, I didn't answer. She led me to another room on the next floor up. This one was even more sumptuous than the one she'd put Zye into. I looked around, impressed. The chamber was done in gentle umber, a purple so deep that it resembled shadows in a forest.

There were sky vanes overhead, showing the heavens. It was impossible to tell if the scene depicted was real or not, such was the resolution of the effect.

"Is that the actual sky?" I asked.

"Of course not," she said, amused. "It would rain right into our faces at night!"

That was the moment when I realized what was going on. This wasn't another guest room. It was Chloe's personal room.

I looked at her in surprise. "Where am I to sleep?" I asked.

She moved closer to me and looked into my eyes. "Where do you *wish* to sleep?"

That was enough teasing for me. I took her in my arms. She melted, and I realized that I hadn't wanted anything more than this—not since I'd first laid eyes upon her.

I did my best to play the part of the gentleman, but it was difficult. I'd not been with many women. My work in the Guard took me off-world for months at a time. Relationships with female members of my crew were either frowned upon or outright forbidden, depending on their rank.

On Earth, I'd met and enjoyed the company of several women, but they'd never managed to wait for me to return from space. By the time I came home and looked them up again, they'd always moved on.

Chloe was different on so many levels. She was my peer—literally. For this single night, under the perfect projection of a thousand stars, we were able to make love as two adults. Technically, we were two recently-elevated officers of government. No one could tell us we were making a mistake, or causing a political problem. Our lives were our own.

We ate food brought up by servants and bathed ourselves in scented waters. We were able to abandon our worries for a time, feeling it was likely our parents would recover. Nano surgery could do amazing things. We trusted our doctors, they were the best Earth had to offer.

When our parents regained their strength, however, we expected they would retake the reins of power from our youthful hands. Knowing that didn't make my time with Chloe any less savory, but it did make matters seem more urgent.

We made love repeatedly, gently at first, then wantonly as dawn approached. I slept in fits, but I didn't seem to feel tired when the sunrise pinked the skies outside.

A thumping sound came at our door as we lounged and yawned awake in the mid-morning sun.

Chloe got up, wrapping a sheet around herself. It snaked up over her shoulders, so she didn't have to hold it there. Before she could open the door, the thumping came again, louder this time.

Concerned, I got up and put my hands on her shoulders. She looked up at me worriedly.

"Does that sound like one of your servants?" I asked.

She shook her head. Her eyes were big, but they weren't yet frightened.

I drew my saber and stepped to the door. She watched in concern, but she didn't protest. So much had happened lately that hadn't seemed possible. We could no longer sneer at the idea of taking precautions.

Opening the door a crack, I saw it was none other than my driver, Miles Tannish. I lowered my blade.

"Servant Sparhawk, sir?" he asked. "Will you be needing my services any longer? I spent half the night in the car..."

His eyes angled past mine, toward the Lady Astra, who stepped quickly away and out of his sight. I saw his tongue flash out as if to lick his lips, but then he let it retreat.

"No, Miles," I said. "You can go. I'll get a ride in one of the Astra cars."

"I see," Miles said. "May I have a word, sir?"

I scowled lightly, certain I was about to be scolded for my actions, however gently.

Sighing, I stepped outside the room. It was then that I saw something very unexpected.

The elderly doorman, Tobias lay on the floor. His throat had been slashed open. His haunted eyes stared upward, dead but filled with horror. Why wouldn't Tannish have mentioned this detail?

Just then, I whirled toward Miles, who had stepped behind me. He was now armed with a stiletto. The narrow blade gave off a strange, gleaming light.

-42-

I lifted the tip of my saber just in time to catch his thrust. I deflected it and reached my free hand up to the clasp at my throat—but my cloak wasn't there. I had no personal shield this time.

Miles made another attack, lightning quick. I caught his wrist and twisted, but he kept hold of his weapon. We were in a clinch for a moment, struggling.

He seemed alarmingly strong. He'd always been smaller than I, and though I'd assumed he was fit, I was surprised at his physical power.

He threw me backward. I instantly upgraded my estimation of his strength—it was phenomenal. I was dashed against the wall.

I regained my feet and managed to get my blade between us again. He dared not rush in as I would have skewered him. He advanced with caution instead. Putting my back to the stairway, I let him come on.

He slashed methodically as he followed me down the steps. Now and then, I gave him stop-thrusts and hacking counters toward the head, which he ducked with agility.

Continuing to retreat, I led him away from Chloe's door. I wanted to get him as far from there as I could. I waited calling for the Astra agents—I wanted him away from Chloe first. If she heard me and came out now, he might take her hostage. Things would become infinitely more complex at that point.

"Miles," I said calmly, "you fight moderately well. Where did you learn to spar this way?"

He showed me his teeth. His demeanor wasn't entirely sane. He wasn't behaving like the Miles I knew at all.

He came on harder. I was truly impressed. I'd been taught how to handle myself with a great variety of weapons all my life, but I'd always preferred swords and pistols. With a saber in my hand, I felt confident I could best any man who wielded a knife—but Miles was surprising me. He caught my blade with his, despite my great advantage in reach. He ducked, whirled, and came back in, slashing after beating my longer weapon aside.

Despite the natural advantages a sword has over a shorter blade, I found myself on the defensive most of the time. The vibrant glow of his weapon worried me too. I dared not let him touch me with it. I thought it likely that even the slightest tap might turn out to be fatal.

He wasn't so cautious, however. As I retreated to the bottom of a sweeping staircase, I decided to put his carelessness to good use.

Disengaging our two blades with a twist, I managed to cut him. It was little more than a gash a few centimeters long in his right bicep. Blood ran, thick and red. He seemed not to notice.

Growing bold, I stopped retreating, feinted in *quatre* and thrust. He took a stab in the thigh that time—but still, he kept coming. He showed no sign of pain, no hint of fear.

Finally, the true nature of the situation dawned on me.

"Stroj..." I said, naming him. "You're not human at all."

"Not true, Earthling Basic," he said, drawing back for a moment and grinning at me. "See the floor? I bleed, the same as you do."

"No," I said with utter certainty. "You're a soulless construct. A being without conscience. Your kind isn't human anymore."

For some reason, my words upset him. I hadn't known that Stroj could become angry. The first one I'd seen had moved like a robot. The second—well, Zye had finished the creature off so quickly I hadn't been able to talk to it. But I'd been in the company of these beings before.

"You merely fear that which you don't understand," he said. "Don't worry, I'll educate you."

"You bleed," I said quickly, before he could attack again, "but that's just dead flesh wrapped around an artificial frame. It's like clothing, merely a vanity. Why don't you creatures shed your flesh entirely? Why not stand naked, all whirring gears and buzzing belts?"

"You've been listening to the Beta, haven't you?" he asked. "We're not all like that. We vary. Some, like me, have an organic brain still. I can no more shed my flesh than—"

I used the Stroj's moment of distraction to strike. As quickly as I could, I thrust for the head. His dagger came up—but he was a fraction too late. I laid open his scalp to the bone. Blood ran over his left eye, blinding it. Still, he stared at me. There was no pain in his expression, nor fear—but there was now rage. Perhaps he was more human than I'd thought.

"You can't penetrate my skull with a sword, fool," he said. "It's a poly alloy, harder than steel or stone."

I frowned. "It was worth a try."

We sparred another dozen steps. I was still retreating. At last, I passed the door I'd been looking for. Zye's door. With a quick motion, I rapped the pommel of my sword on the wall.

Miles—or the creature that had been posing as Miles—cocked its gory head. It was an almost human gesture. He was puzzling out why I'd rapped on the wall.

The door popped open behind him a moment later. Zye's massive hands reached for Miles. Her arms seemed impossibly long. They couldn't be stopped.

The Stroj ducked low, bending over backward, so that his legs were almost flat. The stiletto flashed at Zye's unprotected leg.

"No!" I roared.

But it was too late. Zye took the blade in her thigh.

That didn't stop her, however. She grabbed his neck, and she wrung it, like the neck of a fowl. The spine snapped, and the thing that had been both Miles and a Stroj to me flopped on the floor, sputtering.

Zye stumbled back, stricken. I rushed to her side. The Stroj, for its part, watched from the floor. Its eyes rolled around in its head, but it seemed to be paralyzed.

"Zye," I said. "I'm so sorry."

"The lamp," she said, croaking. "Don't let them spread."

For a moment, I didn't know what she was talking about. Then I laid eyes on an antique floor lamp that sat nearby. Knowing what she wanted, I grabbed the lamp in one hand, cut the cord with my saber, and ripped the two live copper filaments apart.

"Show me the wound," I said.

Zye gripped her pants and ripped them apart. Two lengths of smart cloth flapped hopelessly, trying to repair the damage made by the ripping.

Without thinking about it, I applied the exposed copper to her person, attempting to place each pole on either side of the wound in her thigh.

There was a snapping sound and a tiny flash. Zye stiffened, gasped, and almost fell to the floor.

"Take a seat," I said. "He's not going anywhere."

Mile's eyes rolled around watching the two of us with interest. His mouth worked, but he could not speak. His throat had been crushed. How he was still operating at all was a mystery to me.

"Again, quickly," Zye said.

"Are you sure—"

"Immediately! I can feel the nanites entering my bloodstream. Already they—"

Snap!

I'd applied the cord again. She stopped talking, and a wisp of hot steam rose from her wound. I was effectively cauterizing it. The acrid smell of seared flesh filled the hallway.

"Good," Zye gasped several seconds later. She struggled to her feet. "We must take him to Lady Astra now."

I glanced at Miles. His eyes were like two bloody marbles. The lids no longer bothered keeping up with the pretense of needing to blink. His orbs rolled and stared alertly, following our actions.

"I will carry him," Zye said. "You follow. Do not stray!"

Baffled and beginning to wonder if Zye were in shock, I did as she asked. She picked up the bloody mess that was Miles and began to walk stiff-leggedly down the hall with him.

"This isn't the way—" I began.

"Lady Astra is *this* way!" Zye boomed. "We will meet her shortly. Follow me. Do not stray."

Frowning, I followed along. A hundred steps passed, and Zye managed to make them all without collapsing. We approached the end of a long hallway, which terminated in a window and a balcony.

"Where—?" I began.

"The Lady contacted me. She's on that balcony ahead. She wishes to examine this creature in person."

I caught sight of Miles' eyes then. They seemed excited. They strained, rolling to the limits of their range of motion, almost as if he wished to look through the back of his own skull.

We stepped out onto the balcony. A drop of a thousand feet was revealed. House Astra clutched a mountaintop, and the morning view might have been lovely under different circumstances.

"Lady Astra, are you here?" Zye asked loudly. She kept walking toward the balcony's edge.

A gust of wind blew up into our faces. Zye's long black hair formed a wild, flying mass.

I stopped walking, and I shook my head. "Clearly, you're in some kind of shock, Zye. I don't think—"

Zye ignored me. She walked to the carved stone railing and without any warning or ceremony dropped Miles over the edge.

I caught one last surprised roll of his eyes—then he was gone.

"What in the holy—"

Boom!

A flash rolled up from over the railing. Zye and I were staggered, but uninjured.

"What was that?" I demanded. "What's wrong with you?"

Zye turned to me pridefully.

"I told you," she said. "I am a rogue. A master of deceit."

I looked over the edge while Zye shuffled painfully back into the house. The cliff face was scorched and decorated with shreds of flesh.

"Miles blew himself up?" I demanded, still confused.

"Of course. The Stroj often do so as a final act, when they calculate they can't cause more damage any other way. I had to fool him. I indicated falsely that we would take him to Lady Astra."

"Ah…" I said, catching on. "You wanted me to stay close, so Miles would imagine he could take all of us out at the same time."

"Exactly. Were you impressed?"

I blinked at her for a second, then I recovered. "Oh yes, of course. Very much so. That was excellent trickery, Zye. I was totally taken in."

She nodded, clearly very pleased with herself, and continued limping away.

Shaking my head, I followed her into the mansion.

-43-

Chloe met us inside. She was surrounded by a trio of her agents. They snarled at Zye and myself, lifting weapons distrustfully.

"They're friends," Chloe said.

"They let the assassin into the House," the agent leader argued.

I thought I recognized him, but I couldn't be sure. They were all the same breed.

"The assassin?" I asked. "Are you talking about Miles? He's dead. Zye here killed him. Did he injure anyone else?"

"Seven of my men lie dead around the house," the leader said. "They were taken by surprise in most cases. He wandered the halls, indicating he needed help. The moment anyone turned their back, he struck without hesitation."

"That must be why security never came to my aid," I said. "I'm sorry for your losses. He was probably searching for me. He did find me in the end, but at that point he paid for his evil with his life."

The leader of the agents was clearly unsatisfied. He stepped between Chloe and I.

"Why did a man from your House attack Astra agents, Sparhawk?" he demanded.

"His plan was to kill government officials. As several of them were here tonight, he wanted to slay both the Lady Astra and myself. More importantly, however, he wasn't a man of House Sparhawk."

"Nonsense. We have on vid file—"

"He was an infiltrator," I said, interrupting. "A Stroj assassin like the one that ambushed Lady Astra the Elder or the one that attacked my father during his speech months ago."

The agents were understandably upset, but Chloe managed to placate them in time. After several minutes of explanations, they allowed her to accompany me to the kitchens. They followed us in a pack. Zye walked among their number, watching them even as they watched her.

"I'm sorry I left you," I told Chloe.

"It's all right," she said. "I understand your motives. You wanted to lead the Stroj away, didn't you?"

"Yes, but the plan almost didn't work. These creatures are very difficult to destroy."

"You shouldn't have left my room without this," she said, returning my cloak.

I took it and swept it over my shoulders.

Behind us, the agents and Zye listened to our words in dismay. I don't think any of them were happy to learn Chloe and I had shared a bed last night—but no one complained aloud.

We ate in the kitchens, serving ourselves as the mansion had largely been abandoned by the staff. There was no one in the breezy building other than agents, dead men and us.

Before I could finish my meal, I was contacted via my implant. With some degree of irritation, I answered the call.

"Lieutenant Commander Sparhawk?" a familiar voice asked. "You're to report to CENTCOM immediately."

"Admiral Cunningham?" I asked in surprise. "What's this all about?"

She didn't answer. The channel had closed as quickly as it had opened. I frowned into the distance.

"What's wrong?" Chloe asked.

"I'm not sure, but I've been summoned by the Guard."

"Must you leave so soon?"

I turned to her and smiled. "I don't want to, but I must."

Zye shifted uncomfortably. Her eyes traveled from Chloe to myself and back again.

"Allow no one unexpected to enter the house," I told Chloe. "Have your Guardians check the identity of every visitor. I would go so far as to suggest you invest in a fluoroscope. You may be able to penetrate the veneer of these creatures. Unless they copy every bone so accurately—"

"They don't," Zye interrupted. "There are bulbs on their bones at the joints, protuberances...you can detect them that way."

"All right then," I said, standing. "I must take my leave."

Chloe embraced me suddenly. Zye and the agents shifted uncomfortably. None of them liked to see us touch. I felt self-conscious, and I found myself annoyed that the Stroj had decided to reveal themselves right when I most wanted personal privacy.

A few minutes later, I was flying up into the sky aboard my air car. It was odd to think that I was piloting a vehicle that had so recently been driven by an alien being.

"The Stroj seem to be everywhere," I said to Zye. "How can we defeat them if they are already hiding among us?"

"There aren't many," she said. "I would guess there are no more than a few thousand in the star system. According to reports on the net, many have already struck. Seventy-nine of your Public Servants were attacked in the last twenty four hours."

I turned to her, stunned. "Seventy-nine? How many survived?"

"Six, including you."

"They must be finishing their mission, then," I said. "Moving into their final phase. Otherwise, they wouldn't have revealed themselves all over the globe."

"I agree."

We flew on toward CENTCOM at the air car's top speed. In less than an hour, I landed on the roof. A dozen guardsmen, cloaks flapping, came out to greet me. They encircled the aircraft with their pistols drawn.

Stern faces regarded us through the canopy from every direction.

"Zye," I said, "do not reveal your weapons. Do not behave in a hostile fashion. They're paranoid after all the attacks."

"I understand their motivation, but their attitude is upsetting me as well."

"Act as naturally as you can—wait, on second thought, act like a normal Basic human from Earth."

"I'm not sure I can do that."

"Try," I ordered, releasing the canopy and standing up with my hands on my head.

Zye followed my lead. The guardsmen recoiled upon seeing her great size and stern demeanor.

After a period of confusion, various methods of identification were employed. We were led at gunpoint into the bowels of the building.

The elevator hummed, taking us down with sickening speed. It moved almost as far and as fast as the sky-lift itself.

In time, Zye turned to me in alarm. "We're below the surface of the Earth," she said. "We have to be."

"Yes. CENTCOM is like an iceberg. It's much larger underground than it is above."

"I thought the Guard had no budget."

I shrugged. "Most of the building is empty," I admitted, "but we still use as much of it as we need to. Ships cost much more money to maintain than buildings, so this place was never dismantled or reassigned."

"When was this structure built?"

"CENTCOM predates the Cataclysm. Back then, there was a lot of traffic to manage and protect. Thousands of naval vessels were directed from this building."

Impressed, Zye stopped talking. We finally reached the level the elevator had in mind, and it slowed.

The truth was, I was as impressed as Zye herself. I'd been to CENTCOM of course, but never below ground where the brass lived exclusively. The upper levels were dedicated to equipment and to the Academy. These institutions were the pride of Star Guard. They exhibited the last vestiges of the power that Earth's military had once wielded.

When we exited the elevator at last, we were searched again. I was weaponless, and I felt naked. What if the Stroj had penetrated this, our only fortress?

Making the best of it, I walked out into the tactical galleries. Most of the big chambers were dark, but one had been lit. Inside, Admiral Cunningham and a circle of her officers stood around a sparkling display.

A three-dimensional representation of the Solar System was depicted in fantastic resolution. The display loomed high, with no visible means of projection. Earth and Luna seemed to hover in the air. The missile platforms were also displayed.

Admiral Cunningham was talking as we approached.

"We lost too much ordnance against the battle cruiser," she said. "We used our best missiles—a mistake. The warheads in the rest are old. Half the payloads we have left may not even detonate if they reach their targets."

"The warheads will go off," argued another, older male. He wore the insignia of a vice admiral.

"The half-life of plutonium is an implacable enemy," Cunningham insisted. "Those warheads haven't been recharged for thirty years."

"Yes, they should be up for maintenance and rotation every seven years," the older man said patiently. "But there's a better than fifty-percent chance of detonation—"

Admiral Cunningham cut him off with a gesture. They'd noticed my approach.

"Lieutenant Commander," the older man said. "I'm so glad you could make it in to see us today."

I detected the sarcasm in his voice, but I didn't understand it.

"Sorry sir," I said. "I wasn't expecting to be summoned to CENTCOM. I was on leave and—"

"Yes, yes," the vice admiral interrupted. He turned back toward Cunningham. "This is the man, is it? I must say that before I met him, I didn't think you were serious. Now, I'm frankly shocked."

Confused, I looked from one of them to the other. I had the feeling something of great importance was going on, but I had no idea what it was.

"I'm always serious, Halsey," Cunningham said. "This is the man. We don't have anyone else."

Admiral Halsey made a sweeping gesture with his arm. "On the contrary, there must be a hundred more qualified officers in this building right now!"

It was then that I noted a figure standing in Halsey's shadow. His face was familiar—but I wasn't happy to recognize him. He was Midshipman Taranto. The last I'd seen of him, he'd been locked in a cell aboard *Defiant*. Apparently, they'd let him loose when I'd handed over the ship at Araminta Station.

"No, we don't have a hundred qualified commanders for this ship," Admiral Cunningham said, shaking her head. "The technology is too divergent from our own. Perhaps you'd be right if we had the time to train them. But we don't. We don't even know *how* to train them."

"Excuse me, sirs?" I said, unable to stay silent any longer. "May I ask what's going on? Is this related to the assassinations sweeping Earth?"

They looked at me. "Yes, and no," Cunningham said. "We have an even bigger problem now."

"That's on a need-to-know basis!" Halsey objected.

"He needs to know."

Halsey glowered and shuffled from foot to foot. Taranto cast dark looks at me from behind the admiral's bulk.

Cunningham turned toward me again. "The rock rats—excuse me, the Independent Miner's League, have announced war on Earth."

I would have laughed aloud, but they didn't look amused. Every face was sour, worried.

"I don't understand," I said. "I know they have a militia consisting of a few dozen small ships, but—"

Cunningham made a sweeping gesture with her arm. The display that hung in the air between and above us shimmered, changing. It showed a large number of red contacts on the very upper edge of its range.

"They're about fifteen million kilometers out," she said. "They're coming in quietly, gliding from deep space."

"Fifteen million kilometers from Earth?" I demanded. "That's well beyond legal limits. They're in violation of numerous laws."

"Exactly. We're fortunate in one respect, however. They're approaching at a relatively slow pace. I don't think they intended for us to spot them. They're not burning their engines."

Admiral Halsey interrupted. "We've done all the math. They'll turn and perform a hard acceleration once they pass Luna. After that, they'll be all over us."

He touched the display controls, and the image spun. Reflecting Earth's rotation and Luna's orbit, time was sped up and the progress of the miner's fleet was theoretically predicted. The red contacts slid in close, braked, and curved into a low orbit over Earth.

"How many ships?" I asked.

"Over three hundred contacts have been identified," Cunningham said.

"Three hundred…? They can't have that many militia ships!"

"They do. They've apparently converted most of their mining vessels into small warships. They're operating as long range fighters, essentially."

"What about our destroyers?" I demanded. "Where's Admiral Hedon and his task force?"

Halsey swept weary eyes toward Cunningham. "That's a good question. Perhaps you'd like to explain, Admiral?"

He crossed his arms and waited. Cunningham shook her head.

"We knew the miners were a threat. It's been kept quiet, but over the last few months, the shipments of ore from the rocks have slowed to a standstill. So, we sent Hedon out on a patrol in force. He reached Ceres just yesterday—"

"Only to discover it was virtually empty," Halsey finished for her. "That's when we began looking for this incoming fleet."

"Proving," Cunningham said loudly, "that sending the fleet to the rocks was a wise move in the first place. We wouldn't have known they were attacking if we hadn't sent them."

Halsey shook his head. "But we left Earth open in the meantime."

Cunningham sucked in a breath and released it slowly. "Yes," she admitted. "The question now is what to do about it."

"The answer is obvious," Zye said.

Everyone looked at her in surprise. I felt my face burn slightly. She wasn't supposed to speak at such a meeting. Hell, I should have been keeping my mouth shut as well.

"Go on, Zye," Cunningham prompted.

"We must use *Defiant*. There is no other effective defense. Send the battle cruiser out to stop them. Miners in converted craft won't stand a chance against her."

There was a certain note of pride in Zye's voice, and I couldn't fault her for that.

"That's what we've concluded," Cunningham said. "But the trouble is we don't know how to fly her. Our technicians have begun the work, but to take a colonist ship into battle—we don't have time to figure out its operation and train a crew. The flotilla from the rocks will be here in two days."

I sensed this was my moment. I sucked in a large breath, then plunged ahead.

"Admiral," I said. "I hereby volunteer to captain *Defiant* and take her into battle against the rock rat fleet."

Everyone looked at me. None of them spoke for a moment. Even Halsey seemed impressed, if annoyed.

Halsey had clearly wanted one of his captains to command the battle cruiser. But since all his seasoned veterans were off-planet with Admiral Hedon, that wasn't an option. They were searching the rocks for an enemy that had already left.

"And now you know why I called you here, Commander Sparhawk," Cunningham said.

Halsey jumped back into the conversation. He appeared flustered.

"It can't be done," he said. "In fact, I hereby demand that Sparhawk be removed from CENTCOM entirely. His presence here is a constitutional violation."

Everyone stared at him for a moment.

"What are you talking about, Halsey?" Cunningham asked.

"You *know* what I'm talking about. He's a sitting Public Servant. It's illegal for a Servant to hold an active military rank at the same time he's in office. Check the amendments, if you must."

"I don't need to reread our constitution," Cunningham said tightly. "I know it by heart. Sparhawk is the son of a Servant, an heir to power, yes, but—"

"No!" shouted Halsey suddenly. He was smiling now. "I'd hoped it wouldn't come to this. I'd hoped you'd see reason and put one of our better men aboard *Defiant*. But you've forced my hand. I apologize for any embarrassment this may cause, but—"

"Halsey, explain yourself or shut up."

"Very well," he said primly. "Sparhawk's father is ill. He is, in fact, legally in a coma at this moment. That makes Sparhawk the Younger the acting Servant."

I swallowed hard. He was right. He was a full-fledged bastard for bringing it up, but he was right.

Cunningham turned at me, frowning. "Is this true?"

"The last time I checked with House Sparhawk, my father was in the state he describes. He is expected to recover, however. I didn't—"

"Your family is a pack of budget-slashing, power-hungry hacks, Sparhawk!" Halsey snarled. "You can't know how much your commission irritates the upper echelon of CENTCOM. You should have been drummed out of the Guard entirely—"

"You forget yourself, Halsey!" Cunningham barked.

Halsey shut up and glowered at the screens.

She turned to me. "I'm sorry," she said. "I was unaware of your status. Please accept my apologies for our rudeness, but Halsey is correct. Your commission is suspended until your Father recovers. My condolences are with you and your family. Many have died in this rash of assassinations."

Stunned, I was at a loss as to what to say. I'd been so preoccupied with *Defiant*, and Chloe, and everything else—I'd forgotten the rules.

They were right, of course. It was a technicality, and as far as I knew, it had never come up before. But no one could be *both* a supreme member of the governing body and a member of Star Guard at the same time. As I recalled from civics classes, our world leaders had specified that restriction.

The founders had formed a government from ashes after the Cataclysm, and they'd feared a military dictatorship. It had been a wise move—but right now, it was a major disappointment to me personally.

The admirals immediately fell to wrangling about who should fly *Defiant* instead of me. I was heartsick to hear them.

Finally, Halsey turned toward me and Zye. "Sparhawk? Are you still here? You have to leave, man. Was that somehow not made clear?"

"Yes sir," I said.

"And on the way out, surrender that uniform—please."

"Of course, Admiral."

"Wait!" Cunningham said as I moved toward the exit in stunned silence.

I halted, and I dared to hope, turning back toward the group.

"We need the Beta," she said. "Could you direct her to serve another in your stead?"

My mouth opened, and then it closed again.

"I guess—I think I could—"

"It's the wrong decision," Zye said to me loudly. "These officers are fools. No one knows how to command *Defiant* better than you do."

"Zye," Halsey said. "We'll give you a commission. You'll be an accepted officer in the fleet. What can we make her, Admiral? A lieutenant? It's a battlefield promotion, after all."

"I suppose," Cunningham said. She wasn't looking at me any longer. She sounded disappointed.

Halsey, on the other hand, seemed almost gleeful. He threw out a half-dozen names. All of them were favored staffers of his, I had no doubt.

Right then, I realized I had a very difficult decision to make. During the span of several thoughtful seconds I made a choice, and I told myself I could never look back.

"Admiral?" I asked, stepping up to Cunningham and standing at attention.

"What is it, Sparhawk?" she asked. "We're very busy here."

"Madam, I could do a lot of good for the navy as a Servant," I said. "I could help secure the emergency budget you need. But that's a long term solution to Earth's problems."

"Could you get to the point, son?" Halsey demanded. He was glowering at me again. "And then get out?"

Admiral Cunningham raised her hand, halting Halsey's attack.

"Go on," she said to me.

"I think I can do more for the war effort directly, right now. After careful consideration, I've decided to serve the Guard rather than the public at large. I hereby resign my seat in the Ministry, effective immediately. I'm no longer a Public Servant. I'm now willing and able to serve the Guard in whatever capacity the Admiralty sees fit."

They all stared at me. Halsey's jaw hung low. Taranto was noticeably angry.

Only Admiral Cunningham smiled. It was the first time I'd seen her do so since I'd arrived.

"I accept your generous offer, Lieutenant Commander," she said. "You are hereby directed to take the sky-lift up to *Defiant* and take command of her. You'll be relieving—"

"Think, man!" Halsey interrupted. "You're giving up your father's seat? House Sparhawk will crumble!"

I didn't even look at him. "Admiral Halsey, if you value my father's seat so highly, you can run for it yourself in the elections next spring."

There were a few rude laughs from the assembled officers. Halsey reddened, and I knew I hadn't made a friend. But then again, I sensed he was never going to be my friend anyway.

"William Sparhawk, I hereby promote you to the rank of Captain," Admiral Cunningham said gravely. "Your new rank comes with all the honors, responsibilities, and prerequisites thus granted."

"Thank you, Admiral. Now if you'll excuse me, I must stop an invasion."

I turned on one heel and walked smartly away. Zye followed me closely.

"That was strange," she said in a whisper. "I can't imagine that level of disagreement and discord in a similar meeting among Alphas. They would most likely all agree on the best course. And if our written rules threatened our survival—we'd change them immediately and unanimously."

Nodding, I understood her bewilderment. "You see, Zye, Earthlings don't always get along. Not even with our closest comrades. But at times strength can be found in arguments. When a set of conflicting ideas is presented to a group, they will often choose the best option in the end."

"Yes Captain. I see your point, they chose you and that was the best option."

That hadn't been what I was getting at, but I liked her conclusion, so I didn't argue with it.

"In this instance Zye, I hope you're right for all our sakes."

-44-

We traveled to the base of the sky-lift then rode upward in the first available car. Strangely, the entire platform was vacant except for a few other uniformed guardsmen.

As the ride took several minutes, I decided to take the opportunity to talk to the other passengers.

"Zye, could you stay here by the window, please?"

"Certainly," she said. "You can't get far in this contrivance."

I walked away from her, but then I glanced back. Sometimes, her attitude was improper, in my opinion. She seemed to view me as some kind of infant in constant need of care.

"Gentlemen," I said to a trio of officers. "I couldn't help but notice we're the only personnel aboard the sky-lift. I can only assume the station has been closed to civilians, is that right?"

The group looked me over briefly. The leader among them was a commander named Durris.

"That's right," Commander Durris said. "We're on our way up to man that wreck of a battle cruiser, if you can believe that."

"Really? Is it ready to fly?"

He snorted. "No. Not if half of what I hear is accurate. It was damaged or something on the way to Earth. What's the point of even trying to fly an alien ship into battle against a pack of rabble? That's what I want to know. A team of pinnaces could clean up these rats in twenty minutes."

I nodded gravely. It was always good to hear honest words from new crewmen before they knew who they were talking to. My cloak had covered up my nametag, but not my rank which rode on my cap. The rank was incorrect, of course, as I hadn't had time to refit myself. I'd planned on doing so when I reached the station.

"Go on," I said, "I happen to be assigned to the same ship."

Durris leaned toward me conspiratorially. "That's not the worst of it. From what I hear, they just assigned a green captain to command her. Talk about a waste of talent. They might as well leave us here on the station, swabbing the decks with the yard-dogs and bots."

"An interesting situation," I said. "Do you know what's wrong with the ship?"

"Not really. I've just heard that they can't get it to fly. Not at all. The computer is locked up or something."

I frowned. I'd flown *Defiant* without difficulties. Sure, we'd been hit hard and suffered damage, but the ship had been left space-worthy.

Zye took that opportunity to walk up and join the group. The officers gaped. Apparently, they hadn't seen her full size until now. She'd been sitting next to me near the glass.

"Gentlemen," I said with a sweep of my arm. "Allow me to introduce one of my bridge officers. This is Lieutenant Zye—newly commissioned."

"She's—you're the Beta, aren't you?"

"She is indeed a Beta," I said. "She'll get this ship flying, rest assured."

They looked at me again with a new expression. "You're Sparhawk?" Commander Durris asked.

"Yes. I'm Captain Sparhawk—newly promoted. When you get to the station, gentlemen, don't dawdle in a bar. We're leaving within three hours after arrival. I want all hands aboard and ready to fly her."

"Yes…yes, sir!" they stammered. After that, they quickly retreated.

Zye looked at me with a glow of pride on her face. "I see that I have had some positive influence on you. Your deception was admirable." She nodded with approval.

The lift was reaching its apogee. Zye stared upward as the station loomed. This time, we were entirely within the shadow of Earth, and the station was as black as pitch. Only a few running lights outlined the hulking form.

Next to the station, *Defiant* herself floated. There was a wand-thin tube connecting the station to the ship. I expected traffic between the two to be constant. I was surprised that I didn't see the pods zipping back and forth, carrying new crewmen, supplies and the like aboard.

"That's our ship," I said. "She's a pleasure to behold, isn't she, Zye?"

"In a way," she said. "In comparison to Earth, I will feel at home aboard her. But she was also my prison in space, familiar or not."

I looked at Zye with upraised eyebrows. She rarely made such a thoughtful speech.

She returned my scrutiny. "Although I admired your skill when hiding your rank and tricking those men," she said. "I'm still puzzling as to your purpose. Why did you do it?"

"To gain information. The lower ranks often hide their true feelings from their superiors. I wanted to hear what they really thought."

Zye shook her head. "So odd. A Beta wouldn't want to know what an underling thought—not unless the underling was an Alpha or a rogue like myself. Even then, an officer would probably have no curiosity about the honest opinions of others."

"Well, you'll get used to us in time, I suppose."

"Yes. If these rebels don't destroy us all."

"They won't—not with your help."

She looked at me thoughtfully. "What do you mean, Captain?"

"You disabled the battle cruiser somehow, didn't you? When we left? That's why they can't fly her without our help."

She looked troubled. "I didn't think you'd figure that out."

I laughed. "You might be subtle and tricky, Zye, but I'm beginning to know you pretty well."

The truth was that Zye's "tricks" were often ham-handed stunts. She pulled them off mostly through the application of sheer gall. I thought that her high rate of her success when attempting deceptions had to be due to her normally stolid demeanor. People just didn't expect anything but very flat-footed behavior from her. She was the ultimate straight-man—except when she wasn't.

Zye looked down into my face wearing an odd expression. Was she blushing or was it just the angle of the light?

The sky-lift's great calipers were applied. A groaning, screeching sound was created, and the floor vibrated under our feet. Less than a minute later, we docked with the station.

The doors swept open, revealing a group of very serious technicians. They were mostly yard-dogs—bosun mechanics and bosun's mates.

Among the group was a single individual who put a smile on my face. It was none other than Rumbold.

"Captain Sparhawk, sir!" he said, stepping forward. "If you could follow me—there's literally no time to waste."

"Agreed. Let's go."

We marched in a large group around the outer torus of the station. Here, the centrifugal gravity was stronger than at the center of the disk-like station where the ships were docked. When we reached the correct spoke of the central wheel, we moved inward.

When we reached the pier where *Defiant* was docked, it looked like the dock itself was under construction. There were welding-bots, laser cutters and panels with exposed wires lying everywhere in the workspace outside the primary airlock.

"Here she is," Rumbold said with a flourish. "Pier 39. Would you like to do the honors, sir?"

He waved vaguely at the heavy hexagonal doorway. I frowned at him.

"What do you mean 'do the honors?'" I demanded. "Open the door, Rumbold."

He took in a deep breath. He and the other techs eyed one another in defeat.

"Honestly, sir, we were hoping...the truth is we can no longer get past the door."

"What are you talking about?"

Rumbold's demeanor switched from sheepish to angry in one second, a behavior pattern of his I was very familiar with.

"It's the ship's damnable AI, Captain! I don't understand it. We were working at a good pace, repairing systems, taking those battle scars off the hull—but then the computer took over and kicked us all out! It won't even allow pressurization of the docking tube, and the collar at the other end indicates it's been decoupled. I've never—"

To stop his tirade I put up my hand, palm out.

"I see," I said.

And I *did* see. When we'd arrived down here at Pier 39, I'd been under the impression the pier itself was under some kind of construction. Now I realized the ship was obstructing them, and the techs had been attempting to dismantle the ship-to-ship universal interface from the station's side.

"Did you try a space-walk?" I asked, surveying their efforts.

"Of course," Rumbold huffed. "We did that in the first hour. Nearly lost two good men in the attempt. The frigging thing just shut us out. Every time we get close to one of its external hatches, it shuts the damned thing closed tighter than a—"

"I understand," I said.

Pretending it was only an afterthought, I turned at last to Zye.

She loomed quietly nearby. She'd remained silent up until now. I didn't want anyone to discover and report her sabotage, so I hoped she'd be smart enough to play along at this point.

"Zye," I said, "do you have any suggestions?"

"I must approach the interface," she said.

The technicians had formed a throng around us. They were clearly in a bad mood, but they let her walk past them and up a ramp to the open control panels. She began to look them over closely.

While she did so, I engaged the crew in conversation. "So, Rumbold, have you been assigned to *Defiant's* crew?"

"No sir," he said sadly, "I'm working the station yard like the rest of these sad-sacks. But if you were to put in a kind word, that might change."

Suddenly, the huge door Zye had been fooling with sprung open behind us. There was a sucking sound as the vacuum in the tube was filled from the station's air supply.

"That crazy bitch!" Rumbold shouted.

Zye and I both looked at him, startled.

"Uh, sorry sirs. I meant the computer. She let you right in, didn't she? What was it, a password?"

"You have to initiate the procedural steps to docking with a Beta ship in a specific order," Zye said. "The AI is programmed to detect any pattern other than the one that's required. A misstep will shut down all systems."

Rumbold's eyes narrowed to slits. "*What?* What specific order? All we ever do is attach the tube, marry the universal collars and pressurize the tube!"

"Ah," Zye said, putting up a large finger. "I see the problem already. You're supposed to depressurize the tube after pressurizing it—cycling the air in and out twice."

Rumbold's jaw sagged. "That's insane, wasteful and downright dangerous. Explain to me why any ship would require such a procedure!"

I took a step forward, interceding myself between them. "Let's keep in mind the door is now open. With luck, the AI will stop obstructing us."

"I don't get it," muttered Rumbold. "Something funny is going on around here."

My mind raced. The other yard-dogs, and more importantly the trio of officers who'd been observing from the back, were all looking suspicious. Commander Durris, in particular looked like he smelled a rat. Leave it to Rumbold to not let something go.

"I will explain," Zye said, stepping forward. "The ship is trying to keep out the Stroj."

"The *what?*"

"The Stroj are creatures," Zye explained, "cybernetic beings. They were behind the rash of assassinations on Earth."

The men looked from one to another, confused and alarmed.

"We haven't heard of any such beings, sir," said Commander Durris from the back. He was addressing me, rather than Zye. "As far as we know, the rock rats are behind the attacks on officials as part of a general rebellion."

I nodded sagely. "That's the cover story. But I've personally met and fought with the Stroj. The Betas—like Zye here—are constantly under attack from their worlds."

Rumbold gawked at me. "That robot thing! The one that attacked your father! That was a Stroj, wasn't it?"

"Yes," I said.

Zye spoke up again. "My point is that my people have had to go to great lengths to make sure we're not infiltrated. We have patterns, codes of behavior the Stroj don't know about. If an enemy were to attempt to enter this ship, for example—"

"I get it," Rumbold said excitedly. "They'd be identified. It's like a passcode. A behavioral passcode."

"That's right," Zye said.

Commander Durris stepped up to Zye. "Is that true, Lieutenant?" he asked. "This ship has behavioral security?"

"Yes," Zye said flatly.

"Then why didn't you inform us? Our crew has wasted days fooling around—"

"She's been with me, Commander," I said, intervening. "We've been battling the Stroj on Earth, in fact."

That got everyone to shut up. Before they could ask any more incriminating questions, I herded them aboard the battle cruiser. I kept telling them there was no more time to waste, and there would be a thorough investigation later.

I didn't like to mislead people, but sometimes it was necessary when the stakes were so high.

-45-

With trepidation, the work crews followed Zye and me aboard the ship. I could tell they were worried that *Defiant* might still be engaged in some sort of elaborate trickery. They clearly believed the ship was dangerous.

As I was far more at ease than the rest, I followed her with a confident step. For her part, Zye was all business. She fearlessly marched straight to the bridge.

There were no problems until we passed the junction deck, where my crew had worked so hard to connect power cables weeks earlier.

"Those robots," Rumbold said warily as we approached a standing phalanx of automatons carrying tools. "Excuse me, Captain, but I feel I must warn you. These welding bots became particularly hostile the last time we were aboard. Maybe we should—"

"Nonsense, Rumbold. Look! Zye fears nothing. Let's try to keep up with her."

Reluctantly, he followed in my wake. Behind him came several others. They had power-wrenches and laser-torches in their hands, holding them at the ready like rifles. Every time a hatch swished shut behind us, all the techs jumped.

We passed the bots and eventually reached the bridge. Zye stepped to her station, sat down, and began engaging systems.

"The self-diagnostics protocol has begun," she informed us. "It will be a few minutes until the ship is flight-worthy. After the diagnostics are complete, we'll be able to see if any problem areas remain."

"A few minutes?" demanded Rumbold. "Problem areas? What are you talking about? There was massive damage!"

"Yes," Zye said, "there was. But the repair bots have been working since rebuilding the ship. The fact we found them all lined up and idle indicates they've finished their work. If you'd simply given them the raw materials they needed instead of attempting to do the work yourselves, your time and effort would have been much better spent."

The techs sputtered at that. "They didn't obey us!" Rumbold complained. "We saw them working, but no amount of fooling with their instruction queues changed a thing!"

Zye turned back to her boards. "Ah," she said after approximately two seconds of looking at a pull-down menu. "I have discovered the difficulty. You see this checkmark on the rotational options list?"

"Uh...you mean that dot? What is that, a bad pixel?"

"No. That is the "frozen" option. That's why the dot is blue. I'll change it to green by logging in and resetting the fields...there."

By now, the techs and the officers were crowding around, frowning at Zye's screen.

"What did that do?" asked Commander Durris.

"That allows the work queue to be altered," Zye explained. "It was frozen before—as I said."

"That's *it*?" demanded Rumbold, scandalized. "All that time we spent—what an insane interface you Betas came up with. It's almost as if you were trying to make it obscure and confusing."

"What you suggest is insulting," Zye said.

Grumbling, the techs milled around. They poked at the screens. Several items around the bridge now seemed to have unlocked. I suspected that Zye had removed some kind of obstacle which had served to impede them at every step.

Slapping my hands together loudly, I made everyone except for Zye jump.

"All right then, twenty minutes until the diagnostics are complete? Is that what you said, Zye? How about you familiarize the flight crew here with the operational controls while we're waiting."

The group moved to other terminals. I could tell the officers from CENTCOM were game, but they had almost no idea what they were doing.

"Where's the rest of my flight crew?" I demanded.

"Flight crew?" Commander Durris asked. "It was assumed we'd spend today working on the ship—in fact, no one has been able to even board her—"

"That's been solved," I interrupted. "I need experienced people. At the very least, I want Ensign Yamada and Marine Lieutenant Morris. Get them here as soon as possible, Commander Durris. Sooner, if you can."

He stared at me for a half-second. "But sir, we need more qualified bridge personnel. I served as an XO on the destroyer, *Centauri*. If you'd allow me to show you the roster of individuals CENTCOM has recommended—"

I put my hand up and forced a smile. "I do want to see it. And I want you to get them aboard as well. But put a priority on finding the two individuals I just requested."

Turning, I headed for the exit.

"Sir? Where are you going, if you don't mind my asking?"

Glancing over my shoulder, I gave him a disapproving look. I could tell already this commander they'd saddled me with might become a problem. He seemed to think he should be in charge of the ship. It was true that yesterday, he'd outranked me—but that was yesterday.

"I'm heading to the ship's stores. I checked the manifest, and I noted that they have a selection of uniforms and other equipment. I need to change my rank insignia before the rest of the crew arrives."

"Oh, right," he said, nodding. "I hope they have your size."

I stared at him for a moment longer. Had his comment been made in earnest, or had it been some kind of slight? I wasn't sure. I disregarded it and left the bridge.

When I found my Captain's bars at last and pressed them to the fabric of my uniform, they adhered there, linking the nano-fiber surfaces together. To part them would either take a ripping force, or a series of gentle taps that would reprogram the fibers.

Smiling in a reflective screen, I observed myself. I'd officially reached the rank of captain, and I'd only been in the Guard for a decade. To my knowledge, no one had reached such a rank in so short a time since the Cataclysm. I allowed myself to feel a modicum of pleasure in the achievement. Even my father might be forced to experience a certain degree of pride, should he awaken from his coma.

Thinking of my family caused me a pang. I hadn't checked on them for hours. Glancing at the time, I saw that I had several minutes to spare. I touched the stateroom mirror, transforming it into a communications device, and then I called my mother. I could have used my implant, but warships and space stations were programmed to intercept such traffic.

My mother opened the channel quickly. She looked startled to see me.

"William?" she asked. "Where are you—that isn't *Cutlass* behind you."

"No, my old ship was destroyed, remember?"

"Yes, of course. You must be calling about your father. You'll be happy to hear he's stabilized. He's not awake yet, but he should make some kind of recovery."

"That's excellent news, Mother."

She stared at me. "I've heard a rumor, William," she said. "There's talk of political difficulties. The Sparhawk family has enemies—I know you don't need me to tell you that."

"Go on."

"Well, I heard that CENTCOM may pressure you to resign. I didn't know quite how to tell you about it, but I thought you might be better prepared if the moment does come."

I looked at her thoughtfully. I knew what she was going to say, but I didn't want to hurt her feelings. Not yet.

"Why would they do that, Mother?" I asked.

"Because of a constitutional conflict. You can't be an officer in the Guard and a Public Servant at the same time. You should know that."

"Yes, of course," I murmured. I realized I *had* to tell her what had happened, but it wasn't easy for me. My parents had invested everything in their political position. To abandon that—well, it would be unthinkable to them. Either of them.

"I just wanted to get that out in the open," she said. "I'm so sorry to even worry you about it. I know how much you love the Guard, but you surely have always known this day must come. There's no shame in resigning from the military to step up to a higher level position. Don't let any of your friends tell you otherwise. In fact—"

"Mother," I said suddenly, unable to listen to her any longer. "There's something I must tell you."

"What is it?"

My instinct was to look down, to not meet her eyes as I told her the news. But I forced myself to gaze directly into her face instead.

"They did press me to resign," I said. "And I did so. They summoned me to CENTCOM and forced my hand."

"Oh, that's awful!" she said, completely misunderstanding the situation. "I'm sorry, Will. Don't worry, government work can be exciting too. You'll see—"

"Mother, I resigned my seat in the Ministry—not my officer's commission."

She was beyond stunned. Her jaw sagged, and she stared at me for several seconds. Finally, regaining her composure, she took in a breath and clasped her hands in front of her.

"We can fix this," she said. "We've faced worse—not since you were born, mind you—but Heaven and Earth can be moved when House Sparhawk—"

"I'm not changing my mind, Mother," I said quietly. "I'm not going into politics. I am where I belong—in the Guard. They've given me a Captaincy. I'm commanding Earth's one and only battle cruiser, *Defiant*."

She stared. I didn't think she was really hearing me anymore, but I kept on talking.

"As you said, no one planned this sequence of events. I feel—no, I *know* that I can serve Earth better in space than I can by sitting in some dusty building on the surface, holding endless meetings and giving speeches. I'm commanding the greatest ship in history. A ship that's needed to defend Earth right now."

Finally, her mind seemed to kick back on. "William," she said urgently. "You don't know what you're saying. If your father doesn't recover—"

"Yes, I know. House Sparhawk will lose their seat in the Ministry."

"How can you stand there and say that? You sound as if it doesn't even matter to you!"

"It does Mother. It really does. But I can't live my life waiting for Father to die. I don't want his job in any case. I don't think I ever did."

"But...but Will...we can't have another clone. You're it. Another clone would be illegal, and too young..."

"That's right, Mom. There's no time for another clone. If Father dies, we'll lose the seat, or..."

"Or what?" she asked with sudden hope in her eyes.

"Or, you could run for the seat. You could try to recapture our glory. You could garner sympathetic votes and continue the legacy."

"I don't know how to run a campaign!" she shouted with sudden vehemence. "I only know how to govern—to support your father. That's all I know. You're pushing your entire family off a cliff in order to pursue a juvenile fantasy of heroism!"

"No mother, it's no fantasy."

"Tell me then! Tell me what you're doing up in space right now!"

I wanted to explain it all. I really did. But my orders were not to discuss my mission. My service to Earth had suffered several mishaps already, and I felt I could ill afford another.

"I can't tell you about my mission," I said, "but I can tell you I'm engaged in a matter of the utmost importance to Earth."

She stared at me, her eyes narrowed to slits. "Father spoke of this—before he succumbed to the poisons. He said something about an exploratory mission. They offered you a command and a heroic assignment, didn't they? We must have more vicious enemies in the Ministry than I would ever have believed. They've done the impossible. They've brought down House Sparhawk."

"I assure you, Mother, that isn't true. I'll explain it all when I can. Until then, take care of Father and..."

I stopped talking because the screen had transformed back into a mirror again. The face that looked back at me was my own. In all my years, I couldn't recall my mother ever having hung up on me before.

After straightening my uniform into crisp lines, I strode determinedly back to the bridge.

There was work to be done.

-46-

When I reached the bridge, there was a throng waiting for me. Commander Durris was at the front of the pack.

"This is most unusual, Sparhawk," he said.

"What's that?"

He caught sight of my rank insignia, and did a quick double-take. Then his eyes drifted back up to meet mine. I was immediately under the impression he hadn't quite believed in my promotion until now.

Taking a deep breath, he seemed to recover. "Captain," he said, "the ship is almost fully operational. The techs and the rest of us...we're at a loss to explain it."

I nodded, taking it all in. "This is a Beta ship, Durris," I said firmly. "The vessel has technological capacities you'll find surprising. In some ways, it's quite advanced. In other ways, it's lacking some basic capacities we take for granted. What matters now is if she's ready to do battle. The Stroj will be here in approximately thirty-nine hours."

"We have less time than that, sir," he said. "We've got to go out and intercept them. CENTCOM briefed me on that point earlier."

"They did, did they?" I asked. "Why can't we prepare now and meet them in Earth orbit?"

"CENTCOM is worried that the enemy will launch attacks on our cities if we let them get in too close. We simply don't know what they're planning."

Assuming the Stroj were leading the miners, as Singh had led his crew of guardsmen, I was surprised they were attacking in force. I didn't think rock rats were that bloodthirsty. With an effort, I pushed these thoughts from my mind. I was only supposed to run one ship, not the war.

"Have you got our strategic orders?" I asked. "I was only ordered to get to this ship and man it immediately. I don't have a tactical battle plan in my hands."

Durris handed over a computer scroll. I read it carefully. He was right. We'd been directed to meet the enemy as far from Earth as possible.

Durris didn't elaborate on why he'd been briefed on command matters regarding *Defiant*, but I thought I knew the truth.

"Tell me, Commander," I said, "were you briefed at CENTCOM by Admiral Halsey?"

He met my eyes. "Yes, as a matter of fact I was."

I nodded. Now I was sure that Durris was one of Halsey's men. Despite that, I'd begun to like him. Sure, he'd had a high level advocate pulling to get him aboard this ship. Another Captain must have also been groomed to take command, and Durris was supposed to be his XO. That hadn't worked out for Halsey or Durris.

Some men might have been angry and resentful about their plans going awry, but Durris didn't seem to be openly obstructing me. He was surprised, yes, but he wasn't undermining me or being snide. He was a good guardsman, in my estimation, for these reasons alone. The very opposite of a man like Singh.

After reading through the roster of officers, I handed the computer scroll back to Durris.

"Excellent," I said. "I'm glad you're up to speed on the situation. The Guard did something right sending you here to help me."

Durris blinked once then nodded, accepting the unexpected praise.

"After examining the roster," I said. "I want you to be my first officer. Do you accept this appointment?"

"Yes sir!"

"Good. I'm replacing the suggested helmsman, however. Rumbold will fly the ship."

He cleared his throat.

"What is it?"

"Normally, sir, a ship of this class would have an officer at the helm."

"Good point," I said, "I'll put in a formal request to commission him—if we should be so fortunate as to survive this mission."

I knew that wasn't what he'd meant, but he didn't press the issue.

"Now," I continued, "Yamada will run the sensors, but I need a good man on strategic navigation and communications. Can you cover both posts on my bridge?"

He frowned.

"Captain," he said, glancing over his shoulder at Zye. "The first officer generally operates the tactical consoles."

I shook my head. "That doesn't work for me. I've fought two actions with Zye on tactical ops. I've got no intention of changing that now. We simply don't have the time to retrain you. Do you want the navigational post or not?"

Durris edged closer and lowered his voice. "Do you think it's a good idea, sir, to have a foreign national running the most powerful weapons in the system?"

I thought it over for a second or two. Then I nodded.

"Yes," I said. "I think it's an excellent idea. You have to understand, Commander, that Zye knows this ship better than any of us. She has sworn her loyalty to me. And, she's the only crewmember who can tolerate all the G-forces this vessel can exert upon a human body."

"Excuse me, sir?" he asked in confusion.

I took the computer scroll back out of his hand and made a series of rapid edits.

"Never mind," I told him. "You'll find out about this ship's acceleration curve soon enough."

I handed the altered roster back to him. He looked at it dubiously, but then spun around and began hammering out orders. People were up and out of their chairs, switching to new locations. The tech people were banished below decks, where there was still plenty of work to be done.

All the techs retreated except for Rumbold. He was befuddled by his return to the position of helmsman.

"I haven't earned this, Captain," he told me. "Truth is, I'm better at repairing ships than I am at flying them."

He was right, but I brushed away his objections.

"There's no time to train anyone else, Chief," I said. "And Zye can't man every post. I'll tell you what: if we live, I'll make you my damage control officer."

"That would be fine!"

"Good, but for now, I need an experienced hand on the tiller. Can you do it?"

"Sure—at least until Zye flies us into the Sun or something and I pass out again."

I patted him on the back, and he took his seat.

"First Officer Durris, have we got an ETA on Yamada and Sergeant Morris?"

"Yes sir. I got confirmations while you were off the bridge. They'll be here in less than an hour."

"All right then, let's go over our ordnance. What have we got in the hold? Are the batteries fully charged?"

We got down into the nuts and bolts after that, going through scrolls depicting lists of numbers. The needed materials were flowing aboard now. The biggest problem came in the missile department.

"Our birds simply aren't compatible with the tubes and magazines on this Beta ship," First Officer Durris complained. "We've got eighty warheads in the forward magazine, thirty in the aft, but we can't get them onto a delivery system that will fit."

"Hmm," I said thoughtfully. "The team was probably so busy trying to do basic repairs they never managed to solve that technical problem."

"I've got an idea, Captain," Rumbold said.

"Let's hear it."

"We can turn those warheads into mines with a simple proximity fuse—or a remote detonation receiver. Either way, we can lay them out in front of the enemy in a pinch."

Heaving a sigh, I nodded. "Give them both," I said. "They'll be better than nothing that way."

Looking over the ship's armament, it came down to three primary elements. The particle cannons were our primary offensive weapons. They had excellent range and killing power. Unfortunately, there weren't many of them and they had a slow rate of fire.

Our secondary defenses were essentially point-defense cannons, which I'd used to good effect against Earth's missiles previously.

The last item on the list was the mines. They might turn out to be useless, as the odds of hitting a ship with a mine in space were low. We might as well throw rocks at the enemy ships, hoping to damage them with kinetic force. Still, under the right circumstances, they might be useful.

Several hours passed, during which Yamada arrived. She looked around with a stunned expression.

"Welcome aboard, Ensign," I said.

"Thank you…Captain?"

"That's right. I've been promoted and given command of *Defiant*."

Yamada stared for a few seconds. "I honestly never thought we'd step aboard this ship again," she said. "The Admiralty was so annoyed with our tactics…did you know they debriefed me for nine straight hours?"

"Flag officers don't like to be embarrassed. That's what this ship did. We embarrassed them."

"Well sir, do you have a post for me?"

I directed her to the sensor management console. She took her seat without complaint. She looked, in fact, elated to be back on *Defiant's* bridge.

"Connect me with the Admiralty," I told Durris.

He tapped for a few moments, then the channel opened. The forward screen displayed a familiar face: that of Admiral Halsey.

"Excuse me Admiral," I said. "Captain Sparhawk, reporting in. Would you like a status report on *Defiant's* readiness?"

Halsey's eyes narrowed as he ran them over the scene around me. Everywhere, people were bustling and working on controls. They were testing, configuring and adjusting settings.

"Are you on the bridge, Sparhawk?"

"That's correct, sir."

"How the hell did you get aboard?" he demanded.

"Through the docking tube, sir."

He stared at me, full of suspicion and malice.

"Never mind, then. We need you out there intercepting the rock rat fleet. What is your status? How long do you need before launch?"

"We'll be ready in ninety minutes, Admiral," I said firmly.

This caused his eyebrows to shoot up and ride high. "What? Are you joking? That ship was a wreck not—"

"The ship is self-repairing, sir. Once we managed to gain access, we found most of the systems were operational."

"Really? Well, in that case don't waste any more time, Sparhawk. Get out there and defeat the enemy. Halsey out."

"One moment, Admiral," I said quickly. "We need supporting ships. What can CENTCOM give us? A few squadrons of screening vessels would go a long way to help."

Halsey's expression became predatory. "We're holding those in reserve."

"Reserve for what, sir?"

"In case the enemy breaks past you. We can't leave Earth's skies empty. Our destroyers are on their way back. If you can delay the militia fleet for a day or two, or better yet defeat them, we'll have our full complement back in orbit to defend us."

I sat in stony silence. The other crewmen around me had fallen quiet as well. We had all been assuming this would be an all-out effort. Putting the fleet into a single powerful force would meet the enemy with the greatest possible strength all at once. Instead, it appeared Halsey planned to use us as a distraction to buy time.

"I assume, sir, that you've got CENTCOM ops right now?"

"That's right," Halsey said. "Admiral Cunningham is off for the night. You've got to deal with me, and I'm telling you to get out there and stop those miners."

I realized my ship was expendable to Halsey. In his mind, the real fleet was centered round the destroyers. Until they returned to Earth, the planet was vulnerable as far as the Admiralty was concerned.

That was a generous interpretation of the situation. A less charitable observer might have believed he was hoping for my defeat.

Halsey misinterpreted my hesitation.

"Come now, Sparhawk," he said. "Don't tell me you're afraid of a pack of miners! Get out there with that monster ship of yours. I'm sure they'll turn tail and run when they see you on their scopes."

"Thanks for the advice, Admiral," I said. "I'll get underway as soon as possible. Sparhawk out."

The channel closed, and I sat thoughtfully while everyone worked around me. They were all so busy, and so near, but I felt as though I were a thousand kilometers from all of them.

In my mind, I was calculating our odds of success. We were going to face an unknown force alone. With luck, we'd smash a few of them and the rest would scatter. But if it didn't work out that way…

I reflected that the job of command could indeed be a lonely one.

-47-

Marine Lieutenant Morris arrived, and we prepared to cast off. By that time, we'd loaded all the fuel, power, food and ammunition we would need.

Zye came to me shortly before launch time with a worried expression on her face.

"What is it, Zye?"

"Sir, the holds have been emptied of their original contents."

"Yes? Well, we needed the space. We're carrying warheads, food stuffs, depleted uranium shells for the point defense cannons—a thousand things. What's the problem?"

"Do you know what's become of the children, sir?"

I froze. Only after a moment's thought did I grasp what she was talking about. I launched up out of my command chair.

"Let's go find out," I said.

Zye fell into step behind me without a word. I felt her presence, and her hidden anxiety. To a Beta, the frozen embryos in their steel tubes were infants. I felt I had to respect that—and I needed Zye to be as focused as possible during the upcoming battle.

We reached the hold within a minute or two. It was true. All the tubes had been removed. And the temperature in the room was no longer freezing.

"Spacer," I called to the nearest man in a blue jumpsuit.

"Yes, Captain?"

"What happened to the original contents of this cargo hold?"

"The alien artifacts? They were removed."

"Yes," I said patiently. "Where did they go?"

"Beats me, sir. They might have hauled them all into the station. Or, they may have ejected them into orbit. The Chief said they didn't have any value."

I felt Zye's smoldering presence behind me. I didn't look over my shoulder to see her reaction. I didn't have to.

"Where's your chief?" I asked the man.

He led me to his superior. The petty officer in charge looked up in shock when he saw who I was and read the insignia on my collar.

"Captain! What can we do for you, sir?"

"You can find the tubes that were here in this hold and assure me they're being handled with care and respect."

His eyes blinked once, then twice before he answered. "Uh…okay. I can try at least. They were pulled out of here to make room for all our equipment. This is a big ship, but the hold is really not as—"

"Chief," I interrupted. "I'm on a short timetable. Where are the tubes?"

"Back on the station, sir. That's where they went last I saw, anyway."

"When were they removed?"

"About two hours back."

I took a deep breath, and I nodded. "Okay. That might not be a disaster. Do you have a manifest? A signature?"

"Yes, sir. They were handed over to a local trader. He said he wanted them, and he was willing to pay, too. You know how the Guard is always on the lookout for a sucker to sell our junk to."

I frowned. "A trader?"

"His name should be on the manifest—yes, right there."

I held up an unfurled computer scroll. By running my fingers over it, I was able to get the document to scroll down to display the final line.

It turned out to be a bill of lading. The name at the bottom was known to me: Edvar Janik.

"By God," I said. "It's the smuggler."

Zye grabbed the document from me, glaring at it without comprehension. "What smuggler?"

I turned to her, troubled. "A man I ran down above Antarctica months ago. He had several of these tubes in his possession then. He claimed the tubes held embryos to be sold to rock rats."

"Sold?" she demanded, eyes storming. "Who would dare barter and trade with Beta infants?"

"More importantly," I said, "who would be interested in buying them, and why?"

"We have to get them back," Zye said. She turned to the petty officer. "You, underling, order this Edvar Janik to return the children."

The petty officer looked stunned. "Return the what…?" he asked. "I can't. He's gone. He had a ship docked at this station—but if you touch his name, it will navigate to a location program. See? Oh…apparently he's gone out of range."

Zye made a growling sound of frustration.

"He's right," I said, looking it over. "Smugglers, small-time traders—they're one and the same on the fringes of the system. Once they get about a million kilometers out from Earth, you can't be sure where—wait a moment."

I engaged my internal implant, connecting my retina to the net. I then navigated to a commerce database maintained by the Guard. My new rank allowed me to get data from CENTCOM directly.

"The files indicate that the ship isn't flying back out to the rocks," I said, working my implant as fast as I could. "It vanished on Earth. It was tracked to the Antarctic again, where it went down and off the grid."

Zye looked relieved when I turned and focused my eyes on her again.

"That's good," she said. "It's cold there, right?"

"Yes, very."

"Then we can go down and capture this fiend."

"Well, Zye," I said. "All we know is that he bought the embryos and transported them to Earth. We can't be sure that he's—"

"He's a Stroj, William," she said. "I know by the name. That sort of name—they choose them often. They were from Eastern Europe originally. I told you that, you remember?"

"Yes, right," I said thoughtfully. "You did."

"Let's go! We must fly there directly."

She turned and took a single step toward the hatch. I put a hand out and gently caught her elbow. She turned back reluctantly.

"Zye," I said, "there isn't time. We can't go down there, find him, and return before we must get underway."

"But the children, Captain!"

"I know," I said, "they're of great value. But everyone on Earth will be overrun by this incoming fleet if we don't stop them. We're talking about twenty-one billion people."

"Twenty-one billion Basics," she growled.

I removed my hand from her elbow. "I understand how you feel. I will give you leave to go down there and chase this man if you wish. But I ask you to stay—to fight with us. The embryos might be on Earth, remember. We need you. Everyone does."

Zye stood still. Her sides heaved as she took great breaths. Indecision was difficult for a person like her.

"It would be better that you ordered me to stay," she said. "I would infinitely prefer it that way."

"I don't want you to resent me. You must make this decision on your own."

She looked at me, eyes glowering, enraged and despairing all at once. "You want it all. My help, my loyalty and my gratitude all at once."

"Of course I do."

"Ruthless… You make a fine leader. I hate you right now—but I will serve you."

That said, she walked back toward the bridge. I followed. I thought of a million nice things to say, but I kept my mouth shut. When dealing with an angry, confused Beta, sometimes staying quiet was the best policy.

By the time we'd reached the bridge, the final preparations were underway. The ship was fully loaded with personnel, weaponry and supplies. We cast off the umbilical-like docking cord and sealed every hatch on both sides.

A long checklist began. Every station operator on the bridge checked and double-checked their status indicators.

I was amazed how well the ship had recovered. Defiant's technology was truly superior to Earth's when it came to rebuilding herself.

The navigational gear, however, was still less effective than the equipment aboard a standard Guard destroyer. The Betas, it seemed, had made few improvements in that regard.

They'd focused exclusively on power, weapons and survivability. Given the nature of the contest I was about to face, I couldn't find any fault with their strategic decisions.

Thirty-seven minutes before I'd promised Vice Admiral Halsey we'd be ready, we launched. The first moments were nerve-wracking. The fuel pump indicators dipped, and the power on the bridge dimmed, then brightened again.

"Just the couplings," chuckled Rumbold nervously. "She'll be right as rain when we get her up to speed."

I wasn't sure if he was giving voice to his opinions or his fantasies. A few minutes later, however, he proved to be right. The ship straightened out, stopped stuttering, and began to thrum with power.

"We don't have to do a hard acceleration," I said. "Let's get out there at a steady two Gs. Who's watching the incoming contacts?"

"I've got them, sir," First Officer Durris said. He was standing at his post, moving his hands above the over-sized boards and trying to control everything with gestures as he'd been directed. Nonetheless, he looked like a child at a bay window. Any Beta operator would have dwarfed him. "I'm putting them on the forward display now," he said.

The screen flickered into life. A dozen red points gleamed—then a hundred—then a thousand.

"Can that be right?" I demanded. "Give me a count."

"Uh...the tally should be in the lower left now, sir."

A red number read one thousand, seventy-one. My tongue seemed to thicken up in my mouth.

"How could they have that many ships?" I asked in a low, desperate tone. "There can't be that many interplanetary craft registered on all the rocks combined."

"They aren't your ships, Captain," Zye said with sudden authority. "They are *all* manned by the Stroj. The enemy has clearly captured your rocks—and your rock rats. They're no longer human Basics. They've been transformed."

I looked at her, but she was staring at the globular swarm of ships that were approaching us. So was the rest of my crew.

The swarm shifted as they came in at a cautious pace. They were about ten times farther out than Luna, but they would be here all too soon.

"Plot a course around Luna," I said. "If they don't react, we'll hit them in their flank in…navigational estimate, Durris?"

He plotted, and a spiraling curve appeared on the screen. A yellow course line intersected the enemy swarm.

"Assuming they plow on straight ahead," he said, "we'll come into weapons range in seven hours."

"Good enough," I said.

"But Captain," Rumbold piped up. "What if they see what we're doing and speed up? They could charge toward Earth, and we'd be out of position."

"Yes," I admitted, "and at that point, we'll have to unleash the full capabilities of our engines to catch up."

Rumbold groaned. "I've only just knitted my guts back together after the last time!" he said loudly.

Several of the bridge crew, those who'd experienced what *Defiant* could do, responded with grim chuckles. Durris and others who were new to the ship looked confused and concerned.

-48-

We accelerated smoothly toward Luna and did a banking turn around her, skimming close to the surface of the airless moon. Hours later, when we came around on the other side, we discovered the enemy had made a course adjustment—but not toward Earth.

"Sir, they're plowing right toward us!" Rumbold exclaimed.

Inwardly, I felt my guts twist. Outwardly, I hid my worries. I forced a tight smile, in fact, and nodded.

"Exactly," I said. They want to intercept us, rather than letting us hit their flank."

"They obviously think they can win," Rumbold pointed out, "with plenty of strength left over for Earth afterward."

"And that will be their downfall," I said, hiding my concern.

This was, I reflected, the singular moment during which the commanding officer of any warship had to exhibit complete confidence. I knew nothing about the approaching flotilla or its capabilities. But I knew that we had to stop them, or Earth would be attacked.

In this kind of situation, misleading statements from a ship's captain were practically expected. I couldn't very well tell my crew we were all flying to our collective doom. That would only serve to increase the odds of such a prophesy coming true.

My crewmembers needed to keep their morale high, and I was determined to help them, regardless of how it grated on me personally to be deceitful. Accordingly, I told myself there was no dishonor in a little bit of undeserved bravado.

"Remember," I said, "we rode out a strike containing a hundred warheads not long ago. We weren't even firing back then—this time, there will be no mercy. We'll blast them from the sky, if they won't turn back."

Zye perked up when I said these words.

"If they won't turn back?" she asked. "Surely, that doesn't mean you plan to give them a chance to retreat, does it Captain?"

I glanced at her. "It's my job to keep the enemy from reaching Earth. I'll do whatever I must to accomplish that goal."

"But sir...these creatures can't be dealt with. They are the Stroj. You've met them in personal combat. Surely—"

"Zye," I said, "please return to your post."

She had left her station and taken two sweeping strides in my direction. After pausing for a moment, she returned to her boards and hunched over them. She was clearly upset.

"First Officer Durris," I said. "How long until we're within effective weapons range?"

"We're converging...looks like five hours, if nothing changes."

"Good enough. Yamada, open a channel to the approaching fleet. Put them on screen."

She worked her controls for a lengthy period, but finally looked up and shook her head. "It's no good, sir. We can't get through."

"Why not?"

"I don't know...they have to be hearing us. I don't see any evidence of jamming. But they're not answering."

"Keep trying to establish contact."

A few hours passed while we planned tactical scenarios and watched our sensors. I felt as if we were charging into battle with an unknown enemy—because we were.

"Captain!" Yamada said suddenly. "We've got activity—looks like they're launching something."

"Missiles?" I asked, stepping to the tactical screens.

"No sir...well, maybe. Small craft, independently guided. I can't tell from this distance, but they aren't acting like missiles."

"Could you be more specific?"

"They're flying in formation. A loose wedge, about ten kilometers wide. Normal missile barrages would be a large swarm, or a stream following one another."

I nodded. "Do we have optical yet?"

"I can only get the computer to project their course. Any visual data would be conjecture at this range."

"Right, put them up on the forward display."

The bridge became quiet as we watched the data create a visual map. Still far from Earth, the enemy fleet approached at a steady pace. There were over a thousand small craft—a startling number.

Ahead of that force another wedge-shaped formation of tiny contacts appeared. There were sixty-four of these.

"They've got to be missiles," Rumbold said.

"Maybe. First Officer Durris, will they reach Earth before we can intercept them?"

"Plotting now...no."

I glanced at him. He looked troubled. "Display the course, Durris."

"Certainly," he said, and the screen shifted. Tiny red lines grew from every one of these unknown threats. They coalesced into one thicker red line—which ran directly into the green line that projected our current course.

"These new contacts are headed for *us*, sir," Durris confirmed. "Not Earth."

"Zye, are our point-defenses fully operational?"

"Yes sir. Ready to fire when the targets come into range."

"Excellent. How long do we have, Durris?"

"Difficult to say. The contacts are accelerating now, but their rate of acceleration is dropping. I'm not sure if they're going to slam into us at their top speed, or what."

"Give me your best guess."

He fooled with the numbers, and I stepped over to join him at the navigational boards. I could see he was having a few problems. He was using all his own calculations, rather than the ship's AI.

"Zye, could you step over here please?"

She appeared in an instant. I could tell by the way she loomed over Durris, frowning, that she was wondering if he might need arresting—or something similarly drastic.

"Could you help the First Officer get the AI to give us its best guess as to the timing of this conflict?" I asked her, keeping my tone neutral.

Zye reached a long, thick arm between us and tapped the board firmly. "There, right there. It's on the display already."

Durris and I looked in confusion. "Hmm," I said, "but that's only the projected moment, given their current course and speed."

"Exactly."

"I was hoping for something more. An intelligent projection of likely outcomes…?"

Zye looked baffled. "Beta computers don't speculate about anything. If they did, we'd turn them off."

She went back to her board and sat down.

Durris and I exchanged glances. "No AI data interpolation?" I asked.

He shook his head. "That doesn't fit with Beta design thinking, sir," he said. "That's why I was doing the calculations by hand on my personal computer."

"All right. Can we feed the data back to CENTCOM and see what they can come up with?"

He shook his head again. "We've got basic communications, but there's no format match. Our files are all different. Even our transfer protocols are barely compatible. We're on our own for data analysis."

"Contact CENTCOM anyway," I said. "They should be able to see what we're seeing. Let them run the numbers for us."

"Will do."

I walked away, thinking hard. We actually knew very little about *Defiant's* design. There were bound to be difficulties like this. A century and half had passed since we'd been in contact

352

with the Betas, and technological divergence was only to be expected. I hoped against hope it wouldn't screw me later on.

As we grew closer to these two groups of contacts, I became increasingly anxious. Naturally, I did my best to hide it.

After checking on every member of the bridge crew at least three times, I went back to my seat and forced myself to park there. It would be another forty minutes before anything came within extreme range.

"Captain!" Durris said suddenly. "I've got a channel open with the approaching fleet!"

"The primary group or this smaller force?"

"The primary group, sir."

"Everyone look calm. Durris, put them on screen."

The tactical map faded and was replaced with an almost human face. The skin was there, as were the teeth and the eyes. There were things missing, however. The being before me had no hair—and no ears.

That wasn't what shocked me about the person who looked upon us with obvious curiosity. What I almost couldn't accept was the fact that I recognized the face. It was none other than Captain Singh of the destroyer *Altair*.

"Captain Singh?" I asked.

"I'll be a monkey's uncle," breathed Rumbold. "That's him!"

The thing turned its head, regarding each of us in turn. I saw then, as it rotated its head that there were holes where the ears should have been.

Dark openings with flaps of skin hanging over them were located on each side of the skull. Inside those openings I saw a dull, metallic gleam. Could its skull be metal?

"Is that you, Captain Singh?" I asked again.

"Identify yourself," the person said.

"I'm Captain William Sparhawk. This is the Star Guard ship, *Defiant*."

Singh—if he truly was Singh—continued to look around at the bridge crew.

"That, Captain," Zye said, "is a Stroj in its natural form."

I looked at her, then back at the screen. It was disturbing. The creature regarding us *looked* human, but the cues it gave off were all wrong. In a way, I thought I might feel more at ease if I'd been faced with some kind of intelligent insect.

-49-

The being that resembled Captain Singh finally looked up and addressed me, after having apparently studied each person on the bridge.

"Why have you contacted the Stroj?" he demanded suddenly.

"We hailed your ships to warn you off."

"A threat? You're wasting my time."

He moved as if to disconnect the channel. I put my hand up quickly.

"Wait!" I said. "Let's talk."

"You wish to surrender?"

"No, that wasn't my first order of business."

"We would prefer that you surrender. The captured Beta ship has value. Your flesh has value. We would prefer not to destroy either."

"All right then," I said, feeling my way through the conversation. "Let's talk. Are you Captain Singh?"

"No."

"I've identified myself. I would ask that you do the same."

The Stroj fell silent for a time. Its head moved in small jerks and twists. It seemed to want to scan each of us, focusing on every face in turn, over and over. Or, maybe it was gathering information concerning our equipment and bridge modifications. This seemed more likely and I had to hope I hadn't given too much away.

I realized I was no longer thinking of the Stroj as masculine, nor even as a human. The strange creature had become an "it" in my mind.

"The unit you knew as Captain Singh was not worthy of his skin and has been destroyed," it said finally. "I'm of similar design."

"And your name is…?"

"Call me Kaur," it said at last. "Admiral Kaur."

"Excellent. Now Admiral Kaur, if you would—"

"All data of value has been collected," Kaur said. "I sense no further point to this communication. Are you willing to discuss your surrender now?"

"No," I said firmly. "I wish to discuss a peaceful resolution to our…"

I trailed off. The screen had gone dark. The display representing our converging forces returned.

"Charming fellow, isn't he?" Rumbold asked.

"That was an untrained Stroj," Zye said. "Stroj agents are programmed to blend in with whatever culture they're infiltrating. That unit was typical of what they're like in their natural state."

"How long until we can fire on them?" I asked.

Zye perked up at that. "The leading wave of assault pods will be in range of our guns in eighteen minutes. We might be unable to damage them at that distance, however."

Swiftly, I rotated my seat around to face Zye.

"Assault pods?" I demanded.

"Yes. I'm talking about the smaller contacts that are closing with our position. They clearly mean to board and take this ship. Then we'll be processed and transformed."

I was flabbergasted. "Zye, why didn't you tell us what they were if you knew?"

"I don't *know*. I'm surmising from past experience—and also, I wasn't asked."

I looked at her in frustration. Was she being evasive because she was annoyed? Or was she just being Zye? Or, was she possibly engaged in one of her odd "tricks?" I really didn't know which it was, but I was exasperated nonetheless.

"If you have an insight concerning any enemy action that we don't seem to understand," I said, "please inform us immediately."

"Yes, Captain."

Heaving a sigh, I spun away from her. "First Officer Durris," I said. "I think we should fire our big guns when they get well within our range."

"Why not fire the moment we can hit them?" he asked.

"Because they're bunched up. The armament on this ship can fire a variable spread of particles. If they stay close together, we can hope to hit more than one with each shot. I don't want to fire early, warn them, then have them split apart."

"Excellent thinking. We'll be within an eighty percent hit-probability range in twenty-five minutes. Shall I queue up our first salvo for that moment?"

"Yes. Do it," I said.

We waited. It was difficult, and I had to turn down my suit air conditioners twice. The enemy "assault pods" as Zye called them, came within our maximum range and pressed closer. It was hard not to fire.

I watched as our hit-probabilities increased steadily, forcing myself to be patient.

"Sir, the enemy configuration is changing," Yamada said.

"What? Are they spreading out?"

"Not exactly, sir," she said, "they—"

I felt a surge of near panic. Could they know we were about to fire on them?

"Zye, fire!"

"Firing primary cannons, bank one," she said.

The deck rocked under us. We heard the distant rumble of the guns carried through the ship's structure to the bridge.

"Should I fire bank two, sir?" Zye asked.

"Hold on. Damage report, Yamada?"

"I can't tell. There's some kind of deflection matter—chaff. Or a cloud of particles."

I felt the battle slipping away from me at that moment. It struck me all at once. Here I was, a junior officer in charge of a ship I barely knew how to fly, facing an enemy I knew nothing about. I felt a fluttering sensation in my guts, and it was hard to think.

"Zye, what are they doing?"

"I can only conjecture. I've never been on the bridge during combat with the Stroj before. I was maintenance personnel and in my cell prior to our last encounter."

"All right," I said, "that's fine. Just tell me what you *think* they're doing."

"The Stroj have developed countermeasures to our weaponry. That's all I know. Do you want me to fire the second bank of cannons now? We're in the eighty percent zone."

"Hold your fire," I said. I turned to Yamada. "Ensign? Talk to me."

"I just can't tell you if we'll hit them or not. There's some kind of obscuring cloud. I can't see the ships anymore. Look at the display."

I was looking. The sixty-four contacts had now merged into one amorphous blob. At least it was still vaguely wedge-shaped.

"First Officer Durris," I said. "I need advice. What are we facing?"

He stepped down from his post and stood near my chair. He peered thoughtfully at the forward screens. I had to admit, he appeared to be cooler than I was at that moment. I told myself I had to pull it together. Clear thinking under fire—that was one of the key principles I'd been taught at the Academy.

"I'd say we're looking at some kind of aerogel or thick gas," he said. "I recommend we tighten our beam diameter and try to punch through it on our next salvo."

"We can no longer see individual pods," I said. "They're probably spreading out as well. If we narrow the focus of the cannons, we'll miss."

"There is one other option. We could increase the duration of each projection. That will burn through the obstacle even with a wide pattern of fire. But, we might overheat our guns."

I allowed myself one second to think. I nodded my head.

"That's it. Zye, double the duration of fire…fire at will."

There were several seconds of delay, then the ship shuddered again.

"Bank two, firing," Zye said.

"Hold banks one and three in reserve," I ordered. "Keep firing with bank two, unless there is a failure. Give them extra time to cool down between shots."

There was an excruciatingly long delay before the ship shuddered again.

"Bank two, firing," Zye said.

"That took nearly ninety seconds," I complained.

"The heat in the chambers was intense due to the longer burn-time."

"Right. Keep going. Anything yet, Yamada?"

"Yes…yes, I think we've burned a hole through the cloud."

"Give me a visual!"

She tapped at her console. Our optical systems were finally within range. We could see the approaching force with extreme magnification and computer extrapolation.

"We've punched a hole right through the middle of their formation," Yamada said happily.

A few of the bridge crew whooped, but I crouched in my chair, fuming. "Why am I not seeing any of their pods in that hole?"

"Because we destroyed them?" Yamada suggested.

"Maybe. Or maybe they scooted off to the sides. Shift our fire to an obscured area, Zye. Fire when ready."

Time passed. We blew chunks in the cloud, but it still kept coming at us. Suddenly, the point defense guns began to chatter on their own.

"What are they shooting at?" I demanded.

"Not sure. They're seeing contacts—but they could be decoys."

"Visual on the hull!"

The screen lit up and I saw a half-dozen automated guns swinging this way and that with alarming rapidity. They were almost a blur of motion as they rotated, dipped and fired in every direction at once.

"What are they shooting at?" I demanded again.

No one answered me. Suddenly, the screen went gray. It was the fog, gel, whatever. It had enveloped *Defiant*. A split second later, we broke through onto the other side.

Then, I saw them, and I immediately wished I could "unsee" them.

Pods. Triangular shapes with flaring jets, each of which burned blue-white. They were slowing down, swooping close.

Our cannons jerked and fired streams of rounds—spraying all of space with depleted uranium pellets.

Several of the pods were hit. Some flipped, smashed into one another, and exploded. Each time one went down, I couldn't help but cheer.

But soon the invaders were down too low, too close to the hull to be hit. The battle cruiser's exterior was pockmarked with places troops could hide.

"They're down, sir."

"How many?"

"The computer counted thirty one hits—I'd say no more than thirty three got through."

There was a moment of silence on the bridge. We all looked up at the bulkhead over us. Would the armor hold?

"First Officer Durris," I said. "Contact Marine Lieutenant Morris. Is he ready to repel invaders?"

"He wants to talk to you, sir."

I contacted Morris with my implant. His voice filled my brain.

"Captain? What kind of boarding party are you expecting?"

"Thirty-three pods got to the hull. They'll be armed, and they'll be some kind of machine organic mix of varying degrees. Do not let them through your personal defenses. They use highly toxic nanite-treated weapons."

He was quiet for a second while he absorbed that.

"Any clue how many troops are in each pod?"

"Not sure…one to four, if I had to guess by their size."

"You said they're partial flesh? So, if we kill their meaty parts—will that stop them?"

I sighed. "Probably not. I've fought them a few times face to face. They're pretty tough."

"That's just grand, sir. Do you know how many marines I have aboard?"

I blinked. I didn't know. Before we'd shipped out, I'd spent all my time working on the ship's systems.

"Tell me, Lieutenant."

"I've got seventeen troops, including myself. That's it."

"Noted. I'll organize the crew to support you. We'll arm everyone."

"Thank you, sir. Just tell them I'm in command when the shit starts to fly."

"Will do—and Morris?"

"Yes sir?"

"Thanks for signing back on with me."

He laughed. "Dumbest damned thing I ever did!"

The connection closed, and I wondered if he was right.

-50-

"They can't get in here, surely," First Officer Durris said, staring at the vid pickups.

The invasion craft on our hull were opening and disgorging troops. They were in bulky suits, and they appeared to be large individuals. They carried heavy packs full of gear, moving with deliberate methodical steps.

Rumbold cleared his throat. Durris looked at him. "They might just get in," he said.

"How?" asked Durris. "The outer hull is a ferrous polyalloy. It's partly collapsed matter, very tough. It would take a nuclear blast to break through."

Rumbold shrugged. "They're rock miners, remember? They also managed to break into *Defiant* before we even began to investigate this craft."

First Officer Durris looked unusually pale.

"They *will* break in," Zye said, staring at the streaming video. It flashed and flickered, but it was unmistakable. Troops were crawling all over our hull like ants. "They are Stroj, and they would not have landed on the hull if they weren't sure they could board us."

"Wait a minute," I said, spinning my chair around to face Durris. "What did you say about a blast?"

"About the hull, Captain? That it's partially collapsed matter?"

"No, no…about nuclear blasts…I'm a fool."

I jumped up and waved to Rumbold. "Get a work crew suited up. Send all of them to the missile launch bays."

"Yes sir!"

"Durris, you have the bridge."

We were rushing through the passages a moment later. Rumbold was right on my heels.

"You're thinking of the warheads, aren't you Captain?" he asked me, huffing.

"Yes. I've been a fool. I should have spread them out in a pattern to stop these invaders before they even reached the hull. I can't believe I didn't think of it."

"You haven't had much battle experience yet, sir," he said. "If it's any consolation, very few other Earthlings alive today have faced enemy ships in a serious fight."

We opened the last hatch, and we rushed into the missile bays. There were no launch vehicles—only warheads.

Each of the devices was shaped like a pyramid. They were designed to go into a missile—but as our missiles were incompatible with the *Defiant's* launch tubes, we had only the modified warheads.

I looked them over, seeing the kind of detonators my crew had attached. As I did so, a dozen men in black spacer suits filed in. They were enlisted men, hard-eyed and serious.

"How can we help, sir?" ask a petty officer.

I waved him forward. "We can't use proximity fuses, or timers. The only way to do this is with a radio-signal. Set up the warheads—all of them."

The spacers climbed all over the stack of warheads, adjusting them manually. There was no hesitation in them, no backtalk or questioning. This was real, and they knew it.

"Listen up," I said. "There were three enemy invaders in every pod out there. That means an estimated one hundred enemy troops are crawling over our hull, looking for a way in. We've got to use these warheads as mines to blast them off the exterior hull, without killing ourselves or our ship."

They looked at me quietly. I noticed they all had at least a pistol on their hip. That was something—not much—but something.

"Each man is to take a warhead. Line up at the tubes. We'll shove one in, eject it, then the moment the outer blast door over the tube is closed, we'll detonate it."

"That's the plan?" Rumbold demanded suddenly.

"Yes," I said. "In its entirety. You there, approach the tube. You two, open the chamber and load his warhead into it. Rumbold, you handle the ejection. I will signal the detonation personally."

They did as I asked, but they were grumbling now. Evidently, the haphazard nature of my plan didn't sit well with them. I didn't have time to reprimand them for their lack of confidence and decorum. I didn't have time to explain that this plan was the best we had at the moment, either.

Using my implant, I contacted Zye. "Give me a tactical feed, please," I asked her.

"All I have is visual data—images from the hull that are about two minutes old. The Stroj are knocking out all of our vid pickups as they find them."

After wasting a few precious moments cursing, I tried to think. To detonate a warhead on the assumption it was in position—that was going to take a lot of guts. I steeled myself. I was going to have to do this on intuition.

"Warhead loaded, sir," Rumbold said. "But it's just sitting in there. No form of propellant at all."

"Wrong," I said. "The chamber is still pressurized, right?"

"Yes."

"Well, when we open the missile tube doors, the pressure should push the warhead out into space. We'll detonate it as soon as it's clear."

"How will we know when it's outside the ship?" Rumbold demanded. "What if it hooks up, or what if the outer doors open slowly? The warhead will be just sitting there. It will rip a hole right through—"

"I know," I said, "but I don't have a better way, Chief. We're going to have to chance it."

"I know a better way," he said.

Frowning, I turned to see him opening the tube hatch again. Before I could stop him, he climbed into the tube.

"What the hell are you doing, Rumbold?"

"I'll provide visual confirmation," he said. "I'm tethered now. Open the tube. If I have to, I'll push the damned bomb out myself."

"You'll be killed."

"We're going to die anyway if you keep delaying!" he complained.

I hesitated. The rest of the spacers looked at me, uncertain.

"All right. Zye, open gun port six. Talk to me, Rumbold."

"It's opening…it's too slow, sir! The gas all rushed out, and it's gone. The warhead is still sitting in the tube with me!"

"Let's abort," I said. "We'll think of something else."

I stepped over to the tube into which Rumbold had vanished. Two men stood ready to drag him back out of there.

"Hold on, I think I can push it out," Rumbold said, grunting with effort. "I've got it! It's floating free. Detonate it, man!"

"Zye, close the tube door," I ordered.

"There's no time for that!" Rumbold shouted. "Just blow it up before it floats too far off. The Stroj—oh God sir, they've seen me and the warhead. They're coming my way."

"Zye, is that missile port closed yet?"

"Almost."

"Dammit, Sparhawk!" Rumbold shouted. "Blow the thing—!"

I depressed the detonator.

I didn't want to do it. Rumbold had been a friend of mine, a loyal man who'd served for years under me. He'd taught me more than I'd ever taught him about flying a ship in the void.

A burst of released energy hit *Defiant's* hull. The force of it caused a booming sound as it smashed into the hull. It wasn't a shockwave, as there was no atmosphere to carry such a physical effect, but we were so close that the hull was battered. Inside the ship, there was a sound like that of a massive hammer striking an equally massive bell.

We were thrown off our feet, but we climbed back up quickly.

"Get the tube open!" I ordered, but I needn't have.

The spacers were already working to spin the wheel. The automatic drive on the system had been damaged.

When we had it open, a shocking thing happened—the chamber began to depressurize around us. The two men who'd opened it were sucked out into space.

I managed to grab hold of the wheel and hang on. After a few seconds, the atmosphere in the hold was gone, and the bulkheads had sealed automatically to keep the rest of the ship's air from jetting into space.

Crawling hand-over-hand to the base of the tube, I looked inside.

The two men who'd been trying to open the tube were gone. But Rumbold was still there, still secured by a tether.

He was surely dead. He wasn't moving, and his suit was scorched and gouged. Beyond him, there was only a gaping hole. Had the blast weakened the gun port so that it had flown off into space? I wasn't sure.

Reeling Rumbold in, hand over hand, I pulled him back down into the ship. My breath puffed in my ears with the effort.

Two crewmen came up to help me. They pulled on the straps, and Rumbold tumbled into our arms.

"Sir!" one of the spacers said, pointing over my shoulder.

I turned, looking upward.

There, at the open end of the tube, was an invader.

The figure was huge, hulking. I was shocked by its size. Then I caught a brief glimpse of the face, and I understood.

The Stroj wore a face that was very familiar to me. It was Zye—or at least it had adopted a suit of flesh that looked like her. The Stroj was in the skin of a Beta.

"Withdraw!" I shouted.

During this brief moment of recognition, the Stroj had methodically unlimbered her weapon. A rifle big enough for a giant her size to use swung off her shoulder and aimed unhurriedly down the missile tube directly into our surprised faces.

I dove away, but one of the spacers, a petty officer with a thin build, was burned by the bolt the Stroj fired. It struck him with such force that his shoulder, his helmet, and half his chest cavity were blown apart into a mass of vapor and fast-freezing blood.

It was as if someone had thrown a bucket of gore over my suit and flash-frozen it all. With Rumbold tucked under my arm, I scrambled away from the missile tube. Around me, the surviving spacers fled as well.

"Take Rumbold!" I ordered, stopping a spacer physically and shoving my burden into his arms.

He took the chief's limp form then continued to flee. Most of the spacers had dropped their pistols as they fled. They'd been unnerved.

Using handholds on the walls, I pulled myself toward the nearest warhead, activated it, and escaped.

Before I reached the hatch, another bolt made the metal wall near my head melt and flare white. The heat of it dissipated rapidly, but it left an afterimage on my retinas.

The bulkhead didn't want to let us pass, but when it finally did open, I saw a half-dozen marines led by Lieutenant Morris on the other side. He was a sight for sore eyes.

They grabbed me immediately and hauled me through the door. A moment later, a hail of bolts flew past in both directions.

"Close the hatch!" I ordered.

They did so, and we leaned against it, panting. "One of you spacers carry Rumbold to the detention center. Let the robots work on him."

I turned to Lieutenant Morris. "They're in the ship."

"Indeed they are, sir," he said. "I thought we'd worked out a protocol."

"What protocol?" I asked.

"That when the enemy was encountered, ship's personnel would call for me and not engage until I was there to command the action."

I nodded. "I guess I forgot that part. How many did you count in there?"

"There were three of them in the chamber, sir," he said, "but we put one down before we withdrew."

"Good," I lifted the detonator that was still in my grip.

Morris looked at it in alarm. "Is that what I think it is, sir?"

I nodded. "One of the warheads in that room is live," I said. "If I set this off, we could kill everyone in the room."

He stared at me, then the detonator. "You'll probably kill us, too."

"Maybe," I admitted.

"It's your call, sir," he said.

"Yes. Yes it is."

-51-

"Zye?" I called, feeling sweat trickle down over my face.

The inside of my helmet was steamy. I was breathing too hard. My air conditioner couldn't keep up.

"Zye?" I repeated.

"What is it, Captain?"

"What if I set off a warhead inside this ship?" I asked. "Will the interior bulkheads withstand the blast?"

"What's the yield?"

"No more than five kilotons."

She made a grunting sound. "No," she said. "Every surface in *Defiant* is fullerene-laced, but the outer hull is denser and much thicker. The interior walls can't withstand that kind of force. We'll lose approximately…twenty percent of the pressurized zones of the ship. The explosion might also rupture critical ships components, such as—"

"All right," I said, still sweating. The tickle of it was enough to drive a man to madness when trapped inside a helmet. "Forget it. We'll have to fight them with hand weapons."

Zye fell quiet for a second. "Sir, are you aware these enemy Stroj are based on Beta biotic matter?"

"Yes, I figured that out."

"I would suggest, then, that you come up with another plan. Human troops would have to outnumber them by four to one, by my estimates, to defeat them."

I cleared my throat. I didn't argue. She was probably right. Hell, my spacers had dropped their guns when faced by a single invader.

Star Guard personnel didn't join the service to participate in gun-battles. For most spacers this was a job, more than anything else. We'd grown soft over the years, forgetting our original purpose.

"Do you have another plan, Zye?" I asked.

"Yes. It's a modified version of your plan."

"Explain—quickly."

While we'd been talking, the bulkhead behind me had begun to glow. The sealed hatch between the compartment I was in and the missile launching bays was being cut open from the other side.

"I'll take a warhead out onto the hull's surface," said Zye. "I'll use one of the external hatches. When I'm in the midst of the enemy, I'll detonate it."

I had to smile. The plan was so straightforward, so audacious, it might work.

"How will you get back inside?"

"I'm not sure. But I'll try."

"Why you? Why not send me or Durris?"

"Several reasons come to mind. But the most compelling is that I look exactly like the enemy. I'm therefore more likely to infiltrate their ranks."

I had to admit, she had me there.

"All right," I said. "Do it—but make sure you get your ass back into the ship before you set off that bomb."

"I will do my best."

She broke the connection, and I immediately regretted approving her action. It was insane—but then, we were getting desperate. The bulkhead in front of us was already smoking. Molten metal dripped onto the deck. I could hear the whistling sound of escaping gases, traveling from our pressurized compartment into the missile bay.

"Lieutenant Morris," I said. "Withdraw your men. We won't make our stand here. Pull back, keep battening down every hatch. We'll delay them as long as we can."

"I thought I was in charge," he said.

I looked at him. "You want to stand your ground here? Without cover?"

"The best time to repel an enemy is when they first breach your perimeter. If we let them get deep into the guts of the ship, we'll have a harder fight on our hands."

"Zye has a plan. She's hitting them in the flank."

"Outside? On the ship's hull?"

"Yes."

He whistled. "Wow. She's got big ones. Okay, we'll pull back to the next hatch."

The marines withdrew into the next compartment, but they left the hatch ajar. They set up an ambush, with their guns aimed at the far door, waiting for the enemy to burn through.

I watched them, letting Morris run the show his way. I found it difficult to do.

When the door to the missile launch bay clanged down, the Stroj surged forward. All the marines fired at once. They'd been waiting for this very moment.

The eager invaders were bunched up, and they didn't have a clear target. Morris and his men had the drop on them. Three invaders went down before they could take cover. Morris withdrew quickly and slammed the hatch shut.

He grinned at me. "Thanks for letting me do it my way, sir."

"Well played. Keep slowing them down. Make them pay for every step, but don't commit to making a stand unless you have to. I'll be on the bridge."

I walked away feeling better about my marines. They knew what they were doing. With any luck, we wouldn't need Zye's crazy plan to win this fight.

Telling myself that and believing it were two different things, unfortunately. And by the time I got to the bridge, Zye had already left.

We'd placed the warheads in two locations aboard the ship. She went to the aft section and took what she needed. Then she used an emergency exit to leave the ship.

The vid stream of her progress came up on my screen as we were able to access her body cams. All of us watched tensely as Zye approached a group of Beta troops. Correction, I thought to myself, those were *Stroj* troops.

They looked and acted very much like Zye. The same bulk. The same pace of motion and deliberate demeanor.

As she got close to them, she did not wave. She did nothing to greet them. They approached and spread out, and I felt certain Zye was going to die before my eyes.

"They've spotted her," Durris said. "Brave, foolish girl. She's going to have to set off her bomb in a suicide move."

"Maybe that was her plan all along," Yamada said. "I've noticed she's not always truthful concerning her intentions."

I looked from one to the other of them, then back to the screen. I shared their concerns. I didn't see how she was going to get out of this one.

"Where is the warhead?" I asked. "I don't see it."

The others shook their heads. She'd put it down, somewhere.

"What's she doing now?" Durris demanded. "Slapping at her helmet?"

"Oh, she can't be serious," Yamada said. "She's trying to tell them her transmitter isn't working?"

I couldn't help but smile. There was Zye, using another of her childish "tricks" on the Stroj. She was proud of things any eight year-old on Earth would roll their eyes at.

To my surprise, the Stroj seemed to fall for it. They gestured for her to join their group. We watched as she followed from the rear of a group of six. They led her to a wound in the ship's hull.

The hole in *Defiant's* armor was sparking and blistering with plasma. A laser drill had been rigged up on an anchored tripod, pointing down into the stew of burning metal.

"They're burning their way in somewhere," I said, sitting upright. "Where is that? Locate it, Yamada."

"Just over the engine room. They're trying to drill their way into our propulsion systems."

"Damn. These Stroj never quit."

We continued to watch the vid stream from Zye's perspective. She was looking this way and that as Stroj moved away from her.

"She's going to do something," Yamada said.

I frowned. I had the same impression.

Suddenly, Zye moved with purpose. We watched as she grabbed hold of the laser drill and shot the nearest invader in the back. The Stroj's suit burned open, and the escaping gas caused the trooper to go into a spin, lifting it off the surface of the hull. The creature struggled long after a human would have been dead, but it was unable to fight back.

Zye jumped down into the molten pit of metal, which had already cooled to slag in the freezing absolute zero of open, shaded vacuum.

We felt the blast then throughout the ship. Zye had set off her warhead somewhere on the hull.

The rumbling sound of an impact on the ship's armor was familiar to me now, but it still set my teeth on edge.

"Damage report!" I ordered.

Yamada read her sensory data carefully. She was in charge of the internal and external readings analysis.

"No breaches. She put that warhead on top of something strong. We've lost her vid streaming, however. She might be gone—we can't be certain."

"That crater was a pretty thin hiding place," Durris said. "I wouldn't want to be facing thousands of rads huddling in a two-meter hole."

"She might still make it," Yamada said. "In space, the radiation will burst, not spread. They'll be no shockwave, either. It will only kill whatever is directly in its path without cover—by the way, sir, Rumbold lives."

"That's excellent news," I said.

"I think Zye might be alive, too," she said hopefully. "If the warhead went off just thirty meters away, the hull curvature alone might have been enough to block the released energy."

"Yes," Durris said. "She might have made it. The scheme wouldn't work that way on an Earth ship with a normal titanium hull, but this ship is built from tougher stuff. The hull is dense enough to stop radiation like lead shielding."

Figuring we'd have to wait and see, I contacted my marines.

"Morris?" I asked. "How's it going down there?"

"We've got them retreating, sir," he said.

I could hear the sounds of battle around him, muffled through his helmet microphone.

"Explain," I ordered.

"They were coming on hard, but then they pulled back after that blast on the roof. I think they lost their reinforcements. We've killed eight ourselves. How many can there be?"

"Keep pushing," I ordered. "I want those damn things kicked off my ship."

"Will do."

I turned my chair to face Durris. "What about the main Stroj fleet? How long until we reach extreme range against them?"

"The main Stroj fleet will be in range within the hour, sir," he said. "The trouble is the assault troops on the outer hull have knocked out two of our primary cannons."

I gritted my teeth. "When did that happen?"

"Just now, in the last few minutes."

"Those cannons are on the port side, right?"

"Yes sir."

"I can see what they're doing," I said, staring at a diagram of *Defiant's* external armament. "At first, they thought they had enough troops to capture the ship cleanly. Now we've hurt the boarding party enough that they've decided to disarm us and use their primary fleet of small ships to batter us into submission."

Yamada and Durris gave me worried looks. Neither offered an idea as to how to get out of the situation.

"The port side..." I said, heading toward Zye's station. When I got there, I sat in the overly large chair and addressed her boards. I broadcast to Zye, or I attempted to.

"Zye," I said, "if you can hear me, take hold of something—anything—and don't let go."

I set off the crash-klaxons to warn the crew, then I put my hands on the tactical battle controls. All around me, my bridge personnel were buckling in. I let smart-straps grip me as well.

My first action was to kill the auto-stabilizers and put the ship under fully manual control. Seeing this, Yamada doubled up on her smart-straps and closed her eyes.

Next, I killed our main engines. Flexing my fingers once and squinching up my eyes, I tapped, causing the steering jets to fire. A hard burst of thrust began on *Defiant's* port side. The ship slewed to starboard, and we went into a spin. It felt almost as if we'd been struck by another hammering warhead.

Outside the ship, I could only imagine the scene. The enemy was out there, maneuvering, trying to destroy our guns while crawling over the hull like ants.

But now the ship was bucking under them, throwing them off into space.

Hanging on with my hands shaped like claws, I fought not to black out or vomit. The ship spun and spun. After perhaps twenty revolutions, I double-tapped the auto-stabilizers, turning them back on.

The ship shook and underwent a half-dozen course corrections. It straightened itself out and resumed its trajectory.

"What the hell was that?" Durris demanded.

I looked at him with seasick eyes. "Hopefully, the Stroj were caught off guard. Without pitons sunk into the hull, they should have hurled off into space."

"Maybe," he said, shaking his head.

Morris checked in a moment later.

"Captain? Thanks for the ride."

"You're welcome. Get out onto the hull and mop up. I'll keep from spinning the ship around until you report back to me."

After that, we waited for about ten minutes. Finally, Morris contacted me again.

"Sir, we've got some trouble out here. One of the invaders made it into an aft airlock. Oddly enough, it seems to be unarmed. We can't get to it though, because it jammed the hatch."

"Wait a minute," I said. "Are you sure that's a Stroj?"

"Pretty sure. It looks like one. Female, as big as an outhouse and twice as mean."

"Listen, Morris. It might be Zye. Give her a thumbs-up in the portal. I taught her the meaning of that gesture last week. See what she does."

I waited tensely. At last, my helmet crackled, and Morris came back online.

"Sir, you're not going to believe this. She gave me a thumbs-down in return."

I grinned. Zye had made it.

-52-

As the second stage of the battle began, I felt far more confident than I had during the first. We flew on into the teeth of the enemy, undaunted by their tiny ships.

"Admiral Cunningham wishes to speak with you, Captain," First Officer Durris informed me.

I looked over the tactical data before accepting the call. The enemy fleet was still another hour away. I had time to listen to the brass.

"Admiral," I said, opening up a direct connection into my implants. "What can I do for you?"

"Captain Sparhawk," she said sternly. "When I assigned you to command *Defiant*, I hadn't envisioned you would turn it into a circus act. Can you explain your recent actions?"

We spent the next several minutes going over my strategic maneuvers. She seemed exasperated, but she became more congenial as the conversation went on.

"We've never seen tactics like this," she said, going over vid data and diagrams transmitted with my report. "The enemy landed on your hull, and they attacked your weapons systems?"

"That's right, madam. It was like battling an invasion of roaches. We finally stamped out the last of them less than an hour ago."

"All right," she said. "Halsey was ready to court-martial you when we watched your ship go into a spin—but let's put that behind us. We've got a surprise for you—a good one. We've launched a missile barrage from Luna. It's not much, most of their birds were fired on *Defiant* last week. But they sent what they had left."

Frowning, I turned back to the tactical boards. Zye still wasn't on station. She'd been injured during her spacewalk, and I'd sent her to medical.

There were new contacts moments later, confirming the admiral's words. Tiny dots appeared with a questioning yellow color assigned to them. They were pulsing, moving closer every minute.

"Thanks for the update," I said. "That will certainly give the Stroj fleet something new to worry about. Now, Admiral, if I might be allowed to continue the battle."

"Sparhawk, hold on," she said. "You've got to tell me what you plan to do. Give me your battle plan. The politicians and the brass here are demanding to know what's going to happen. The whole planet is watching this battle on live feed, and the news people are speculating wildly."

After hesitating several seconds, I came up with an answer for her.

"Admiral," I said, "I can't tell you that. The enemy has infiltrated our government, remember? They could be spying even now?"

She stared at me, her lips tightly drawn. "I'm under a lot of pressure—Public Servants, the press, my own staff. Can't you give me something?"

Thinking for a moment, I smiled. Zye's tricks had inspired me. Normally, I hated deceit. But in this case, it was a critical part of battle. Every Academy professor had stressed the importance of misleading the enemy.

"The key to our attack will be our missiles," I said. "We've married Earth warheads to Beta missiles successfully. We plan to combine our birds with those from Luna, and we'll destroy the entire Stroj fleet from a safe distance without loss."

Admiral Cunningham appeared to be confused, but she smiled after thinking it over. "Thank you, Captain. I'll pass this on as a classified report to be released only on a need-to-know basis."

"Excellent," I said. I felt certain the report would spread like wildfire, and I thought she must have known that.

Closing the channel, I went back to running my ship. I checked on the status of Rumbold and Zye. They were both undergoing "biological repair" as the ship liked to call medical procedures.

Looking at our damage reports, I calculated we needed time to repair our cannons on the hull. I turned toward Durris. "Begin braking. Give us more time."

"Reduced speed will make us an easier target, Captain," Durris pointed out.

"I know, but we need every cannon in action when we get close enough to hit them. I want as many kills as I can get before they are in range with their smaller weapons."

"As you wish, sir," Durris said, moving from station to station. With Zye and Rumbold off the bridge, he was responsible for operating more systems. I also allowed him to bring in junior officers to help. They were little more than trainees, but we needed them.

We adjusted our course and began braking. We would still intercept the enemy formation, but at a reduced speed.

Repair bots flooded the ship. We'd kept them corralled while the invaders were crawling into the missile ports, but now that they were gone, we let the bots loose. Automatically, they rushed to every damaged area and went to work. Soon, regions that had been blinking red on my overview diagrams went yellow, and eventually green.

Zye returned to duty during this process. I eyed her closely as she limped to her seat and sat down hard.

"Are you all right, Lieutenant?" I asked.

"I'm functional," she said. "I underwent surgery, and it was successful."

Getting up, I went to her side and looked her over. "Is that a broken femur you're walking on?"

"Yes. Your medical people clamped an internal polymer splint onto the bone. The pain is manageable."

"I see..."

Durris looked at me, as did Yamada. I got the feeling they wanted me to order Zye to a sick bed. I knew she had more than just a broken leg. She had to have radiation burns and God knew what else.

But I didn't order her off the bridge. Zye was tough, and I didn't know anyone better to operate her station. With luck, the battle would be over within hours.

"You'll get some much needed rest when this engagement is over," I told her, "one way or the other."

After a moment's consideration, my words struck Zye as funny. She provided us with a huffing laugh. I realized then she was probably on some kind of pain medication. I told myself I'd have to watch her performance closely.

"Zye," I asked her, "how did you manage to trick the Stroj?"

She looked up at me proudly. Her eyes were bloodshot. I could tell that some of her capillaries were broken and bleeding just under the surface of her sclera. I resisted the urge to wince and squint in horror.

"I was fortunate," she said. "The Stroj must have been in a hurry when they transformed my sisters into fighters. They used Beta brain matter for most of the intellect in their constructs. The enemy troops were therefore unimaginative and easy to mislead."

I forced a smile. "Well done. Carry on."

Returning to my station, I began what turned out to be a short wait. The enemy came within range of our guns before we'd managed to repair all the ship's damaged systems.

"We're in range, Captain," Durris said. "Should we hit them now, or wait?"

"Zye, do you think the Stroj will know our maximum range? What will they do if—"

"Sir," Yamada interrupted, looking at her screens. "The enemy ships are spreading out."

"There's your answer," Durris said. "They know exactly how far a Beta battle cruiser can reach."

"The First Officer is right," Zye said. "We've done battle with the Stroj on many occasions. Nothing this ship can do will be a surprise to them."

"And every battle cruiser is more or less identical," I said thoughtfully. "Zye, what would an Alpha commander do right now?"

She shrugged. "She would commence firing and close with the enemy."

"Of course. We'll do something else, then. We'll drive in at flank speed and hold our fire. Helm, all ahead full."

Durris had seated himself at the helm, I noted. I didn't say anything. He'd wanted to man that station since the first moment he'd stepped onto this bridge. Now that Rumbold was out of the way, he'd seen his chance and seized upon it.

The ship wheeled, and we were soon pressed back into our seats. The G-forces increased steadily, until it was difficult to breathe.

"That's good enough," I wheezed. "Zye, I thought this ship had inertial dampeners that would decrease the stress on our bodies."

"They're online and active, sir."

Puzzled, I looked at the iconic gauges. We weren't pulling two or three Gs, as I'd assumed. We were doing thirteen Gs. I was impressed. The stress on my body was no longer beyond my capacity to tolerate.

"How long until we reach optimal range?" I demanded.

"At this acceleration level," Durris answered, "we've got ninety-six seconds to go."

"When we get to optimal range, ease off and start firing everything we've got. I want to get in there and nail them before they can spread out any more."

"Seventy-two seconds," Zye said. Her voice was calm and gave no hint of distress. To her, the G-forces seemed normal.

"Sir, the enemy is firing," Durris said. "We must be within their effective range."

"What kind of armament?"

"Missiles and rail guns. Light pellets—probably accelerated slugs."

"Helm, take us into an evasive pattern. Shift us a few degrees at random. Make their guns work a bit to get a strike. Have we got any force fields over our bow?"

"Meteor repelling systems are fully active," Zye said. "No strikes registered yet."

At this speed, kinetic forces such as those generated by a bullet could do grievous damage even to our thick-hulled ship.

Even a rock could hit as hard as a nuclear warhead if it collided with enough velocity.

"Optimal firing range reached," Durris said.

"Engines full stop!" I ordered. "Fire the main cannons on my mark, give me a wide spread cone on each...Mark!"

The ship shuddered as all our batteries opened up. Particle beams lanced out, the cannons fired in a chained sequence. Overheating symbols flashed up almost immediately.

"I don't think the damaged bank of cannons is going to be able to keep up, Captain," Yamada said.

"Confirmed," Zye said. "The repair bots didn't completely rebuild them. They need a full overhaul back at the station."

"Cease firing on battery three. Dammit, can we take the damaged units offline and use only the cannons that work?"

Zye shook her head. "Beta batteries aren't designed that way. The venting chains together. The pressures would damage the other cannons."

"She's right sir," Durris said, pulling up diagrams and studying them. "Zye knows her ship. The cannons are kind of like pistons in a combustion engine. You can't just stop using a few of them. They're not designed for that. The whole system will shut down."

Cursing, I ordered the robots to work on the battery. We were down to two banks of cannons.

"We're registering hits," Yamada said. "Sensors indicate...see for yourself."

The forward wall flickered, and we all looked at the screen. Great gouts of energy were striking the enemy line. Groups of ships that hadn't had time to get away from one another were being blasted apart all at once.

Durris whooped. "We're burning three or four at a pop!"

"How many of the enemy ships are still in the fight?" I asked.

"Six hundred or so," Yamada said. "Make that five hundred ninety. We're still getting good hits in, but they're spreading out."

"Hit the brakes," I ordered. "We'll stand at this range and wipe them out."

For the next two minutes, my plan worked brilliantly. We'd rushed in closer than they'd expected, faster than they'd expected, and we'd caught them in a tight formation. They were now paying a grim price for their rigid thinking.

Everyone on the bridge was smiling—but it was short lived. A storm of small strikes began drumming on our forward shielding. At first, it was like the patter of raindrops. But after a full minute had passed, it was as if we were in a monsoon.

"Forward shield is red-lining, sir," Zye said.

"Can we turn our belly toward them?"

She looked at me as if I were mad. "Why?"

"There must be another deflection shield down there. We can power it up and—"

"No," she said. "Beta ships are designed to fly in one direction. There is no belly shield."

I nodded, unsurprised. "All right then. Durris, dive us down out of this storm of fire."

"That will cause one of our weapons banks to be out of alignment with the enemy," Zye protested.

"Do it, Durris," I said.

We felt our guts come up into our throats as he performed the maneuver. The storm of pellets hitting our front shield lessened, but didn't dissipate entirely.

"Level off and keep firing."

He did so, and for a few minutes, the shields slowly brightened to yellow again. But the Stroj countered and the storm again intensified.

"How many ships do they have left?"

"Two hundred ninety-eight, sir," Yamada said. "They've taken a beating."

"We're about to do the same. Durris, slew to starboard this time. We'll get out of—"

"Sir, the missiles from Luna..." Yamada said.

"What about them, Ensign?"

"They've changed course... They're now heading directly toward our flank."

We looked at one another in astonishment.

"How close?"

383

"We've got seconds left before impact. They came right up on us, sir, but I thought they were going to plow into the Stroj line, I—"

"Never mind, Ensign. Helm, hard to starboard. Put our forward shield between us and those missiles. Activate all our point-defense cannons, and override their friend-or-foe programming!"

The rainstorm of pellets changed pitch even as we wheeled to face the new threat. The pellets became a deadly hailstorm. I knew they were chewing into our armor and damaging our exterior systems.

But I didn't know what else to do.

-53-

"Our point-defense systems are firing!" Yamada said.

Her statement was unnecessary. We could all feel the vibration of the small guns hammering at the incoming missiles.

I activated the ship-wide address system with my implant.

"All hands, this is the captain speaking. Prepare for impact. All damage crews be ready to report to the forward sections."

Twenty seconds crawled by. At the last moment, the missile contacts merged with our ship. A moment after that, the deck heaved below our feet.

Bridge power cut out and emergency power took over. Only the most critical systems were active.

Worse, the inertial dampeners had died somehow. I could feel a sickening sensation as my stomach was pulled in two directions at once.

"Engine one, out!" Yamada shouted.

"We're in a flat spin, Captain," Durris complained. He was holding onto his console for dear life.

The wisdom of our spinning gyroscopic seats was now clear. Durris, Zye and myself were being thrown around, but we weren't being dashed onto the deck.

"Helm, get this spin under control. Damage report, Yamada."

"The impact of the missiles buckled the forward shield," she said. "I think Engine One was knocked out by pellets, but it's hard to be sure. We're getting hammered, sir."

"I'm well aware of that. Durris, get us straightened out or I'm giving the helm to Zye."

"Yes sir," he grunted uncomfortably.

Over the next thirty seconds, he managed to get our bow aimed at the enemy formation again. The forward shield was blinking red, but at least it was aiming in the direction of incoming fire.

"Have we got any primary cannons left?" I asked Zye.

"Yes Captain. One bank."

"Well, why aren't they firing?"

"They couldn't lock on while we were spinning...we're back in position."

I felt that now-familiar bucking that indicated a heavy weapons stream was on its way to the enemy. It made me feel good. As long as we still had effective armament, we weren't out of this fight.

"Who the hell hit us in the butt with our own missiles?" Yamada demanded. "That's what I want to know."

"I want an answer to that as well," I said.

Grimly, I ordered the lieutenant that Durris had replaced himself with at the communications boards to connect me with CENTCOM. They were going to hear directly from me.

When I finally established contact, however, it wasn't with Admiral Cunningham. Instead, when I activated my implants, it was Halsey's face that stared at me.

"Admiral Halsey," I said. "Are you aware that in the middle of a critical battle, Luna launched missiles at my ship?"

"Yes, Captain Sparhawk," he said, gritting his teeth. "I..." he lifted a hand and looked at it. Blood coated his fingers.

It was then that I noticed he was injured and standing oddly. He'd been shot or cut in the side. But he was still on his feet.

"Sparhawk," he said. "Keep flying that ship. I've been watching you handle her like a pro. I'm very impressed."

I frowned in confusion. "You're injured, Halsey," I said. "What's going on? Can I speak with Admiral Cunningham?"

"No, you can't. She's dead."

"Dead? When? How?"

"That depends on your point of view. I would hazard to guess that the real Admiral Cunningham died a year or so ago. She was a Stroj, Captain. An infiltrator. I should have suspected it. She's made countless poor decisions over the last year."

I stared at him in disbelief. "So, she put me in command of this ship to screw Star Guard? Is that what you're saying?"

Halsey nodded. "Yes, I believe so. She thought a junior officer—well, she was a Stroj. Who knows what she thought? About twenty minutes ago, after it was discovered that Luna had launched missiles in your direction, she broke cover. Two of her closest staffers were Stroj, as well. Taranto is dead. So are seven other officers here at CENTCOM. We finally took them down, but it wasn't easy."

I swallowed hard. I'd counted on Admiral Cunningham's support. It was difficult to accept that she'd helped me gain command of *Defiant* because she thought such a move was the worst possible one Earth could make. It was, in fact, humiliating.

"Sparhawk," Halsey said, "I think we both owe each other an apology. I underestimated you, and you probably thought I was some kind of monster hell-bent on derailing your career. Let me assure you, all I wanted was to put the best man we had in command of that ship."

"I see."

"Yes, you're right. That means I thought you were a poor choice. I was wrong. Keep fighting. Report back to us when you can. Halsey out."

I found myself back in my chair on the bridge of *Defiant*. I was stunned. Cunningham had been the Stroj? I'd felt an inkling, a faint suspicion, that it could be Halsey, but I'd never suspected...

"Sir?" Yamada said. "Sir, the enemy is changing formation again. They're going into a wedge formation, and they're increasing speed."

Taking a deep breath, I forced all my looming self-doubts away. "Increasing speed? On what course?"

"Directly toward us, sir."

"How many ships do they have left?"

"One hundred sixty-two now," Yamada said. "About fifteen percent of what they started with."

I shook my head. "Why don't they break off? They can't win now. Surely, they can see that."

Zye shook her head. "No, they can't," she said, "and it wouldn't matter if they could. The Stroj never give up. They never surrender, and they very rarely run from battle."

"Cease fire. Let's contact them. Open a channel, Durris."

After a few seconds passed, the Stroj I knew as Kaur appeared on our screen.

"What is the purpose of this communication?" it asked.

"Admiral Kaur," I said, "I believe this battle is over. You have lost, sir. Surrender, and you will be treated well."

Kaur looked around our bridge again. Our faces were haggard. There were signs of damage, but he couldn't help but notice we were still very much in command of our vessel and still in this fight.

"Stroj do not surrender," it said. The screen went blank.

I stared at it wonderingly. "What are they doing now?"

"They're still speeding up, as I said. They're getting tighter, converging...Sir, I think they mean to ram us."

"Time until impact?"

"Eighteen minutes."

"Eighteen minutes? They'll never make it to us."

"Your orders, sir?"

For a time, I sat there quietly, staring at the screen. The Stroj were colonists, after all. They were creatures that were partly human, or who had once been human. To order the deaths of a thousand Stroj...

"Seventeen minutes, sir."

"Destroy them," I said, in a voice that seemed not to be my own. "Destroy them all."

Defiant's cannons began firing again.

Six minutes later, the last Stroj ship was annihilated.

* * *

The return journey to Earth was a slow one in comparison. To give all the injured a chance to heal, I ordered that we proceed with no more than half a G in applied acceleration.

The multi-armed repair-bots were ubiquitous, but I noted some of them were damaged. I asked Zye about it when she returned to duty on the second day. She'd been lying in medical, fuming, since I'd relieved her at the end of the battle.

"The bots don't repair themselves," she said, her tone indicating I was a half-wit for asking.

"Why not?"

"Because they weren't programmed to do so."

"You can't change their programming?" I asked.

"The repair bots were purchased from the Stroj before war broke out. Only the Stroj can reprogram them."

Thinking about that, I wondered if the "trade-good" known as a repair-bot was perhaps a form of trick played upon the Betas. Perhaps the Stroj had planned to make the Betas reliant on these robots. Then, when the robots broke down, the Stroj could refuse to repair them.

I decided not to reveal my thoughts on the matter to Zye. She would only think I didn't understand the way of things, or worse, she might take offense. After all, the implication was that the Betas weren't too smart in their dealings with the extremely dangerous Stroj.

When we docked at last at Araminta Station, everyone aboard was worn out and happy to be home. There was something about a combat mission that was utterly unlike a dull patrol cruise through local space. After facing the unknown and possible death, all the energy had drained from my crew.

The first order of business at the station was to hold services. Many had died. My crew had numbered two hundred and sixty-five when we left home. Thirty-nine had not returned.

As the captain, I found myself in the unaccustomed position of officiating over their funerals. Many prominent guardsmen came to the ceremony, which was held on the uppermost level of the docking wheel.

When Admiral Halsey himself, arrived, I thought perhaps he'd take over the speeching—but that didn't happen. Instead, he insisted on allowing me to say whatever words of comfort came to my mind to the families and crewmembers that had gathered.

I chose a traditional route. I quoted Lincoln, Samos and Tacitus. The group listened closely, and when we were done, the bodies were draped in the midnight-blue flags of Star Guard and shot into space. Their orbits would decay within hours, and the bodies would burn up in the troposphere. It was a tradition that was two centuries old, and predated the Cataclysm itself.

Asked to make closing remarks, I took a deep breath and stepped to the lectern again.

That was when I saw a new group come into the echoing hold. They were civilians, surrounded by wary agents. Three people in the center of the group caught my attention, and they froze my heart and mind briefly.

Lady Astra the Younger moved like a radiant queen at the left of the trio. I was captivated by her eyes, her smile and the beams cast off by the jewels in her hair.

Forcing my gaze from her person, I was gratified further to note that my father was riding a drone, which ghosted over the floor making a whispering sound. At my father's side was my mother. They both nodded to me. There was pride in their eyes, I thought. I could not recall having seen that emotion on their faces before.

Turning back to the waiting crowd, I began to speak.

"Today we honor our fallen. It's only natural to suffer grief at such a moment, but I would argue that none of us here should lament the sacrifice of these guardsmen. Each of my crewmembers who died in space saved millions of lives. Think upon the significance of that.

"Why, you may ask, did this day have to come? Why did our colonists, the long-lost children of Earth, return to attack us? I would argue that they're no longer the same people. At least, not all of them. Time, technology, and countless dark desperate days have transformed them. They've descended into a new form of savagery."

The group stared at me. Some, particularly the admirals, were taken aback. Perhaps they'd thought I would stick to a mundane script praising the Guard, the constitution, and Earth in general. I felt I'd done enough of that during the eulogy.

"People of Earth, we must wake up," I said. "Today was a close call, and it will not be the last. We must rebuild our defenses so the light that is Earth never again comes so close to being extinguished. As the Romans said, '*si vis pacem, para bellum*'which translates to: if you want peace, you must prepare for war."

I concluded my speech, and the gathering broke up into small knots. As soon as I was able, I moved to the trio at the back of the chamber.

My mother's face was hard, but she hugged me. "I'm glad you lived, my son," she said.

"And I'm glad my father still breathes!" I said, falling to one knee beside him.

His medical drone buzzed as he drifted closer.

"William," he said in a wheezy voice, "that was a fine speech—even if it was a refutation of my entire career."

"It wasn't meant to be, father," I said. "It was spoken in earnest."

He put out a trembling hand and clasped mine.

"These are difficult times," he said. "A war has been thrust upon us. There are times when peaceful behavior will not save the lamb from the lion. I think this is such a day. It will rip my party to pieces, but I'm going to push for the budget you and the rest of Star Guard must have."

A smile lit my face. My mother still looked tense, but I was rejoicing inside. I had my father convinced. It was a day I'd never thought would come.

"Now," my father said, "give your attention to the member of this party who interests you most. Hell, she's even got my eye, and I'm half dead."

My mother slapped him lightly on the shoulder and urged the drone into a buzzing retreat.

I approached Lady Astra. My face was beaming—but I saw in her a sadness. A pain unspoken.

Could this be a difficult moment for her? Had she found another so quickly? Or was she perhaps less committed to her beliefs than I was, and more willing to go with the flow of her family's wishes? She was still young and untested after all.

Full of conflicting emotions, I stepped close to her. The agents surrounding us fidgeted, but they allowed it.

"William," she said, "I'm so glad to see you. The news reports—it was so grim. Your ship, when it started to spin—I thought it would blow up."

"Never," I said. "*Defiant* is indestructible. I know, as I've done my damnedest to wreck her."

She smiled faintly, but she didn't laugh.

"Why the long face?" I asked her quietly. "What's wrong?"

"It's my mother—she didn't make it. The damage to her organs was too great. She was an oldster, you know. Their tissues can't be regenerated easily."

She broke off into tears, and we embraced.

The agents leaned closer, but I tried to ignore them. I wanted to shout at them to be gone, but I knew they were just doing their jobs. After all, they'd failed to keep Chloe's mother alive. Who could blame them for exhibiting paranoia now?

"Another victim of the Stroj," I said when we parted. "I'm so sorry for your loss."

We comforted one another until Admiral Halsey approached and cleared his throat. He gave me a smirk, completely misunderstanding the situation.

"Always good to see a young man return to his girl," he said, laughing. "She's broken up over you, I can tell. Don't tell me you've injured her heart!"

"No sir," I said.

"Good, good. Well, it just so happens I'm in charge of CENTCOM now, and there is a small but important matter for us to discuss. Please report to headquarters after the gathering."

"Tonight, sir?"

"Yes, tonight. It's important."

He left me then. I frowned after him.

"Go," Chloe said. "I'll wait in the city for you—if you want me to."

I smiled. "Of course I do."

Leaving the chamber, I was unsurprised to see Zye hobble toward me in the passageway near the sky-lift. I shook my head at her.

"Zye, get back to medical. Your leg is broken, woman!"

"I'm well. I came to check on you."

"The battle is over," I insisted. "I'll be fine."

"Are you sure?"

"Yes, of course."

"And the children?" she asked. "What about the children?"

"I haven't forgotten, Zye but we need you healed. Until then I will investigate. I'll be sure to use all the tricks you've taught me."

That seemed to settle her down. I walked her back to the station's hospital and left her there. She wasn't happy, but she was resigned. She had to take the time to heal. While I was there, I visited with Rumbold. He had new radiation scars and parts of his face were a livid red.

"You look good, Rumbold," I lied.

"Right," he huffed. "You've been learning how to lie from Zye, haven't you?"

"Am I as unbelievable as all that?"

"Worse."

We laughed together, and I looked over his prognosis. I was surprised to see that he was expected to recover. He was far over his allotted lifetime budget in healthcare costs. Someone in the accounting department must have had a heart. Star Guard was doing its best for him. Knowing that made me proud to serve the Guard.

Taking the sky-lift down to the capital, an hour or so later, was a glorious experience. The city seemed so full of life and hope. It was night, and every light in town was burning.

When I reached the ground, I realized the people were in the streets celebrating. They'd all watched the battle in the skies, and they were rejoicing because our side had won—this time.

It took me nearly two hours to get through traffic to CENTCOM. I found a grim-faced Admiral Halsey waiting for me.

"You took your sweet time, Sparhawk."

"Everyone in the city is cheering in the streets, sir."

"Hmph, that may well be, but it won't affect the outcome of this hearing."

I frowned. "What hearing, sir?"

I looked around me, and I saw a number of high level staffers were present. They'd gathered into a circle around a central display stack. They were as quiet as pall-bearers carrying a casket.

"What's this about, Admiral?" I asked. "I thought we'd resolved our disagreements."

"That makes no difference," Halsey said. "This is an official matter."

"Concerning what?" I demanded, becoming exasperated.

"Concerning your promotion to the rank of captain. It was illegitimate, as it was performed by a nonperson. An infiltrator. A Stroj spy."

Suddenly, I understood. Halsey had fallen back upon a technicality. He'd found a way to defrock me after all.

Nodding, I reached up and removed my captain's bars. The nano-adhesive struggled to prevent the act, but they came off at last with a tearing sound.

"You're right," I said. "I'm nothing if not a man who plays by the rules as they are written. My rank was illegally given to me."

Halsey stared at my bars, which I offered him. He cleared his throat, and took them from my hand.

"Just so. Now, please hold up your right hand, William of House Sparhawk."

Confused, I did as he ordered.

Then, to my surprise, he swore me in and presented the bars to me again. The gathered group clapped at the end. I'd grossly misinterpreted their presence. They were here to witness and properly approve of my promotion.

It felt good to know my captaincy couldn't be stripped from me again—at least, not without good reason.

-54-

It was two weeks later when I caught up to the man I'd been tracking since *Defiant* had returned to Earth. We were in Paris at the time, a city that had swollen since the Cataclysm and now was home to over a hundred million souls.

We found Edvar Janik at the city outskirts near the shores of the English Channel. Unfortunately, Zye was with me when we confronted him in his dingy flat.

He didn't survive the encounter. Zye's left hand squeezed his neck fractionally too hard and there was a snapping sound heard by all. The body slumped, but it didn't die for quite a while.

The man was a Stroj. Therefore, Zye wasn't guilty of murder, only overzealousness.

After we reported Edvar's death, Star Guard lost interest in locating the missing embryos. They helped us only by providing satellite imagery and access to classified databases. It was enough to find a likely spot on Earth's vast globe to search.

Considering the matter closed, CENTCOM denied my request for a tactical squad. As *Defiant's* captain, I considered bringing my marine contingent down from the ship, but technically, marines were only sanctioned to serve in space, never on Earth unless there was a dire need.

Today, there might be a real threat, but I thought it would be a small one. A lightly armed force would serve best.

Flying to the location and landing on crusty ice, I thought I'd made the right choice as to who to bring with me. Zye marched at my side in the relentlessly blowing snow. Her eyes were hard, and her face was grim. Red scars from her recent injuries still stood out on her cheeks.

Her femur was holding up well. She barely limped now.

Behind the two of us, marched nine of House Astra's agents. In my opinion, they were better troops than the agents of House Sparhawk. My father's men were loyal for the most part, but they were more like butlers and spies than they were true, hardened fighters.

Today, I wanted to lead people who would follow me into the unknown. People who knew how to kill, should the need arise. Therefore, I'd asked Chloe if I could borrow some of her agents, and she'd consented as it was for a good cause.

Zye found the cave herself, in the end. We'd known the general coordinates, but knowing that a hidden location was inside a thousand meter radius was one thing. Finding the actual entrance in the ice—that was another.

She found a suspicious fissure with a stub of artificial pipe sticking up. She crashed her boots and fists into the crusty snow.

The agents gathered around, fingering their pistols and shivering in their cloaks. No amount of explaining had made them grasp quite how cold the Antarctic could get.

Zye broke through quickly. That wasn't really a surprise. This wasn't a fortification, it was a hideout.

We entered the ice cave in Zye's wake. The walls were a glossy blue. They reflected every wavering flicker of our shoulder lights. The camera drones that had managed to survive the icy winds followed us, documenting everything as we traveled underground.

When we reached the chamber we'd sought, we found what we were looking for. Thousands of them.

Zye grabbed up an armful of the clattering steel tubes and hugged them to her breast.

I looked on, understanding her emotion, but finding it strange to witness all the same. To her, these tubes were children, infants. The very stuff of Beta life encapsulated.

Zye turned to me, and I thought I saw a touch of wetness at the corners of her eyes—but that might have been due to the stinging cold. She'd refused to wear a mask.

"Thank you, Will," she said. "I knew you wouldn't let them die."

I smiled, and I patted her arm awkwardly.

Together, we ushered the Astra agents into the chamber and put them to work. They bent and filled sacks with tubes.

One of the agents stopped me when he had as many as he could carry. He gave me a baffled look.

"Captain…what are we supposed to do with these things?"

"Keep them frozen," I said brightly, "and don't let Zye see you drop one if you value your existence."

He turned and saw Zye eyeing him fiercely.

After that, the agents worked with more precision. They handled each of the tubes gently after plucking them from the ice with exaggerated care.

* * *

After a few more weeks, I met with Admiral Halsey on Araminta Station. He squinted out a massive viewport down onto the blue-white swirl that was Earth's dayside face.

"Congratulations on your advancement to full Admiral, sir," I said.

"Hmm? Oh yes, thanks. Make yourself comfortable, Sparhawk."

I walked to his desk, eyed the chair in front of it, but rejected the idea of sitting there. He was standing, so I stayed on my feet as well.

Halsey, for his part, continued to gaze out the window down at Earth.

"Do you know why I called you up here today?" he asked.

The truth was I had no idea. But there were guesses in my mind.

"Because you wanted to give me a new mission, sir?"

He finally looked away from the viewport and faced me. "Your father's spies are still the best. My compliments."

"Oh no, sir," I began, but he put a hand up to stop me.

"Don't bother. I'm not offended. In fact, I now see your political connections as an asset to your command status and Star Guard in general."

It grated on me to have him think my shrewd guess was due to spying, but I kept quiet with an effort of will. I'd learned over the course of my career it was very difficult to get an idea out of a superior's mind once it was transfixed there, and that trying to do so might even entrench the thought more deeply.

"I didn't summon you here just to give you something new to do," he continued, turning back to the blazing glory of Earth again. "I also wanted to hear more about your self-assigned mission to Antarctica."

"I made a full report, sir. The camera drones captured every moment, in fact."

"Yes, of course. I saw plenty of snow and steel tubes. That's not what I'm talking about. What I want to know is why you think the Stroj were placing Beta embryos at our poles in the first place?"

"Poles, sir?"

"Yes. Are your father's agents slipping? We found another stash up at the North Pole."

I hadn't known this. Immediately, I began worrying about Zye's reaction. "What's the status of the tubes?"

"Hmm? I don't know...I suppose we've got them in storage somewhere."

"They're safe?"

"Safe? I suppose. They aren't all that dangerous."

He wasn't getting my meaning. I was thinking about Zye, and how she saw them as helpless infants. I could tell they were nothing more than chunks of frozen meat to Admiral Halsey. But I didn't press the matter. I could look into it later.

"Nevertheless," Halsey said, "why do you think they did it?"

"Perhaps they thought they could rebuild their invasion forces out in the rocks."

"Nonsense. Space is plenty cold enough. No need to transport them down to Earth then back out there. No, the only reason the Stroj did this was to provide raw materials—to build more Stroj on Earth."

I immediately saw his point. "Stands to reason," I said.

"Glad you approve. The strange thing is that Betas could hardly be used as infiltrators, so why keep so many here?"

"You're suggesting they were to be converted into troops?"

"Invasion troops, to be exact," he said. "Commandos. The force would be too small to grab and hold territory, of course, but think of what they could do if they hit CENTCOM. A thousand Beta-based Stroj infantry, taking out our command center. Killing all our cadets."

The thought was alarming. "Is there any evidence to suggest—" I began.

"Not directly, but it doesn't really matter what their specific goals were. They obviously intended to create a force on Earth for ground operations. You know what that indicates to me?"

As he asked this, he looked me squarely in the eye.

"What, sir?" I asked.

"That they aren't finished with us yet. They found their way here and mounted a sucker-punch operation, but they failed to take us out on the cheap. Now, we're alerted. We'll build up our defenses. They have to know that, but they'll come back at us anyway. Eventually they'll come out of the dark from somewhere, with greater strength."

I found his thinking to be difficult to refute. Most of Earth's populace was celebrating now, assuming the threat was over. They wanted to go back to their old ways, without looking up at the skies in fear. Those of us in the Guard, however, remained vigilant.

"You're saying we must build up our fleet," I said. "I'm in complete agreement there."

"I'm saying more than that. I'm saying we can't just sit here waiting around for the enemy to hit us. The next time, they might come at us with a hundred cruisers. We just don't know. We have to find them, Sparhawk. We have to know what we're up against."

Finally, I was beginning to understand where he was going with this.

"The only ship we have that could go exploring is *Defiant*," I said.

"That's right."

"But the battle cruiser is also our best defense."

"At the moment, yes."

We eyed one another. I shook my head. "CENTCOM won't send *Defiant* into the blue. That sort of exploration hasn't been approved since the Cataclysm."

He brought up a single finger and waved it at me. "We'll see about that. What I want to know is where you stand. Let's say a year or two goes by, and we've got a dozen new destroyers and a strong set of missile bases ringing Earth. Would you be willing to command *Defiant*? To take her beyond the limits of our star system?"

For some reason, I immediately visualized the moment when my crew found an ER bridge into the unknown and dared to cross it.

Once a vessel started on such a path, there was no turning back. It was like stepping into an abyss—you just hoped that when you hit the bottom, there was something soft there to land upon.

My heart was pounding, and my eyes were shining. I knew the answer in my heart. I think we both did.

"Yes sir," I said firmly. "I'd be willing to undertake such a mission."

"That's what I thought," he said, turning back to the dazzling glow that was Earth. "Dismissed, Captain. We'll talk further when the time is right."

I left him there, and for the next hour I walked around the outer ring of Araminta Station in a daze.

It had been a century and half since Earthlings had left their home system. To do it again—I didn't think that I'd ever wanted anything more.

The End

More Books by B. V. Larson:

UNDYING MERCENARIES
Steel World
Dust World
Tech World
Machine World
Death World

STAR FORCE SERIES
Swarm
Extinction
Rebellion
Conquest
Battle Station
Empire
Annihilation
Storm Assault
The Dead Sun
Outcast
Exile
Gauntlet

OTHER SF BOOKS
Starfire
Element-X

Visit BVLarson.com for more information.

Printed in Great Britain
by Amazon